Motheater

Motheater

Linda H. Codega

EREWHON

an imprint of Kensington Publishing Corp.
erewhonbooks.com

Content notice: *Motheater* contains depictions of abuse, animal death, character death, religious trauma, and violence.

EREWHON BOOKS are published by:
Kensington Publishing Corp.
900 Third Avenue
New York, NY 10022
erewhonbooks.com

ISBN 978-1-64566-179-5 (hardcover)

First Erewhon hardcover printing: February 2025

10 9 8 7 6 5 4 3 2 1

Printed in the United States of America

Library of Congress Control Number: 2024943952

Electronic edition: ISBN 978-1-64566-181-8 (ebook)

Edited by Sarah T. Guan
Interior design by Leah Marsh and Cassandra Farrin
Moth image courtesy of Shutterstock/Serafima Antipova
Appalachian formations image courtesy of Wikimedia Commons

Motheater

1

Bennie – Now

Benethea Mattox was not raised to be a fool. Yet here she was, fishing a skinny, barely breathing white lady out of a river. She hauled the waterlogged woman up the steep banks of the backwater creek, taking her time on the muddy incline under the bridge. It was probably the stupidest thing she had done in the whole four years since she had moved out to Kiron, and that was saying something.

The thing was Kiron lay along the western Virginia border, nestled deep in Appalachia—there was nobody else coming down this road, and Bennie would be damned if she called the cops before trying to help someone herself. Besides, the woman didn't seem to be in danger of dying. Her heartbeat was steady, if slow, and her lips weren't blue, so she heaved the half-drowned woman on her back and slowly, carefully carried her up the bank. The lady was thin as a reed and weighed nearly the same. Bennie had once carried her two little nephews up a mountain when her brother-in-law said Bennie couldn't do it. One limp, non-braid-pulling woman was nothing she couldn't handle.

At the bridge where she had pulled over, Bennie arranged the strange-looking woman as best she could in the bed of her ten-year-old truck. She might be a bleeding heart, but she didn't want to put a stranger next to her in the small front cabin, just in case the lady woke up and immediately freaked. There was still a leftover moving blanket in the truck bed, and she nestled the lady in as best she could.

There was something off-putting about her—beyond the weird dress she wore or her messily cropped coal-black hair or even the fact that Bennie had pulled her out of the goddamn river. She seemed . . . faded. Drained, or something. Her features seemed smudged, as if her cheekbones should be sharp and ended up rounded out. Bennie stared at her, trying to figure if she had seen her around, if she looked like any of the maybe two dozen families that had lived in Kiron for centuries.

Her nose was a little crooked—maybe it broke when she was a kid and healed bad. She was pretty, if you were into thin ex-cult ladies who needed a good shower. Bennie noticed a nick in her ear, like a dog's after it had been caught in a bad bind.

She rubbed at her own nose, pulled her cap over her braids, and jogged around to the front seat. Before Bennie touched her keys, she took a deep breath and leaned forward, putting her forehead on the steering wheel. Her heart was beating fit to burst, loud and insistent.

What in the hell was wrong with her? As soon as she had seen the shape washed up on the rocks, she had been hoping to find a dead body, or a body part, or something *damning*. She had been disappointed when she had scrambled down and found the woman still breathing on the edge of the slough creek, downriver from one of the White Rock Mining Company's boreholes, and looking nothing like a miner.

Because a miner's body could be pinned on White Rock. Or at least garner enough suspicion to get an injunction to stop work in Kire Mountain for a minute. She was desperate enough to go after dead bodies in Appalachian rivers to prove what she knew: White Rock was letting their miners die in the dark.

Instead, she had a real, live, breathing lady in the bed of her truck, dirt all on her boots, and none on the mining company.

Bennie took another deep breath, pushing down her panic. She needed to get the strange lady to a hospital, and that was that. She could wonder about corpses later. She fumbled with her keys, annoyed that her hands were shaking as she put the car key in the ignition. The truck turned over, groaning.

"All right, I know," Bennie murmured, pulling onto the barely paved country road. "Oil change this week."

She glanced at the rearview mirror, adjusting it so that she could see the woman's arm where Bennie had placed it over her chest. As long as she drove slowly, the woman should be fine.

Bennie took a deep breath and looked forward again. It was nearly twenty minutes into town, and she could only hope that urgent care was open. She couldn't even call to check—service in the mountains was spotty even on good days.

As Bennie drove over a bump in the road, she winced, glancing at her mirror. The lady's arm had moved, but that was probably because of the pockmarked drive. The trees lining the road seemed to arch over them, growing denser as she drove.

Bennie swallowed and glanced back at the woman again, her palms sweaty against the steering wheel. There was a regret like cigarette smoke curling through her heart, thick and choking. She had an unconscious woman in her truck. What the fuck had she been thinking?

Honestly, what was she even doing mudlarking in the White Rock Creek, anyway? The river was full polluted after years of being used as a slough by the company, so she was much more likely to get an infection than she was to find anything that might hint at the mining company's negligence. And the odds of her finding anything in that damn waste was next to nothing. But failure had made her fearless. She had been trying to find out what happened in the mines after Kelly-Anne died for near on six months. Beyond that, it had been over a year since she and her best friend had first started to suspect that White Rock was covering something up in the mines. She needed *something*, and at this point, she was willing to do some extremely stupid shit to find it.

But this? This was bad. This was so, so bad. It didn't matter that pulling the woman out of the creek was the right thing to do; there was no way that this was going to end well. The woman didn't even have shoes.

Bennie slowed through a turn, and a flash of movement crossed her mirror. She glanced up and saw the woman rising, standing up on the truck bed. Bennie's eyes widened. She slowed, and as she turned to tell the crazy white lady to sit down, the woman jumped out and ran into the woods.

Bennie cursed, slammed the brakes, left the keys angrily beeping at her, and ran after the woman.

"Hey!"

God, she was fast—hadn't she just been unconscious ten minutes ago? Bennie could barely keep up with her, even though she was tearing through the underbrush in a sturdy boilersuit and work boots, and this woman was in rags and bare feet. Around her, the Appalachian forest was thick grown with massive oaks and hickory, the spring ferns and weeds running bramble on the ground. Bennie turned around, trying to find any hint of the woman. She spotted movement and, decidedly ignoring the fact that this was hungry-bears-outta-sleep season, ran forward.

"I'm trying to help you!" Bennie yelled, darting around a tree and then under a fallen branch. The wind in the low valley picked up, shaking the spring-green branches, knocking the birches together like hollow chimes. Bennie ran around a large rock and saw the woman fall down, tripping over a piece of the mountain that had been thrust up from the earth.

"Hey, hey, hey, wait now," Bennie said, walking up slowly, as if talking to a frightened animal. "It's okay. I'm not going to hurt you. You gotta be real scared, right? All I wanna do is help."

The woman scrambled to get away from Bennie, lips pulled back in a feral sneer. Bennie hesitated. This woman didn't seem like she had been near death ten minutes ago.

"I'm Bennie," she said, crouching down. She held up her hands as the woman backed up against an outcropping of rock, the moss yielding to her shoulders. "I want to take you to the ER."

The woman narrowed her eyes. They were coal dark, nearly black.

"Please, I know we just met, but please trust me."

The woman whispered something that Bennie couldn't hear. Under Bennie's foot, something moved. She jumped, worried for a second that she'd crouched on a covered-up rabbit warren or snake. As she backed up, the loam under her feet slipped under the treads of her boots. She began to sink.

Shocked, Bennie looked up at the woman, who was standing now, her hands spread slightly. She was murmuring, and the leaves that had pulled Bennie down to her calves in the soft dirt were now crawling up her legs. The paper-thin, silvery shreds of winter climbed up her body, dragging her to the ground, compressing her. Bennie was dragged down to her knees, the leaves sliding toward her like a great slouching wave, traveling up her arms, threatening her mouth. She was being eaten by the undergrowth.

Bennie screamed, panicking, pushing the leaves away. She grabbed onto a branch, heaving herself out of the trap. The litter fell to the ground in tatters. She hiccupped, scrambling back away from the pit that had pulled itself down around her. As she kicked at the ground, the leaves broke into cracking flakes under her feet.

The air smelled sharp and flinty, like a stone breaking. It left as soon as it came, and the leaves were clumped around Bennie's hands and legs. They were just leaves: some brown, some silver, all dead.

When Bennie looked up, the woman was gone. Breathing hard, Bennie rubbed the back of her wrist against her mouth, her terror receding as she saw the forest calm around her. What in the hell was that?

As she glanced around, her heart in her throat, she saw an indent in the stone where the woman had pressed her shoulders against the lichen-covered surface. It looked like the stone had molded itself around her, as if she had been made a part of the rock. Bennie crawled over and laid her hands against the smooth, concave shape there. It was warm. She looked over the hole that had almost swallowed her. Oak leaves clung to her chest as she stood up on shaking legs.

"What in the holy fuck," Bennie said, staring at the hollow in the ground. She did not sign up for this.

She covered her eyes for a few seconds before she turned and picked her way back to the road. There was no sign of the madwoman. Fine. Bennie wasn't about to go wandering on strange property just for the sake of being a good person. She had enough to deal with, and getting run off by dogs or the business end of a shotgun wasn't part of her ideal morning routine.

Moving around a large oak, Bennie started as a small chipmunk scampered across the toes of her shoes. Jumpy, she pressed her hand to her chest, but not a second later, the strange woman ran right in front of her, chasing the chipmunk. Bennie clapped both hands over her mouth as the woman dove and grabbed the small rodent, tumbling over the shrubs, her back slamming against a tree with a shuddering force Bennie did not expect.

"Seriously?" Bennie gasped. The woman shifted on her knees, holding onto the chipmunk with both hands. She grinned, opening her mouth wide.

"Whoa!" Bennie scrambled after her, holding her hands up, alarm making the blood in her ears ring. She almost tripped as she went onto one knee in front of the lady. "Don't eat that. Please don't. I have a weak stomach. I really just . . . I've been traumatized enough today. Don't eat that baby chipmunk in front of me, please."

The woman, hands still clutching the skittering rodent, looked skeptical, but at least she had shut her mouth. The noise the critter was making was enough to drive Bennie off the edge.

"I'll get you food, okay? A meal?" Bennie pleaded. She mimed eating, in case the crazy lady was part of some strange sex cult and had only just escaped the bunker. "Food?"

The woman tilted her head slightly. She considered the chipmunk and then Bennie, as if judging whether or not the promise of food was better than the creature she had in her hands. Finally, she nodded and let the chipmunk go.

"Oh, thank God." Bennie shook her head, stood up, and thought better of offering the woman a hand. "C'mon, there's a burger joint down the road."

The woman blinked at her. Then, slowly, as if she hadn't spoken in a long time, as if her throat had calcified, as if her teeth held spiderwebs she was afraid to dislodge, the strange woman spoke.

"What's a burger?"

7

Sitting in the truck in the parking lot of Happy's Burgers, Bennie couldn't stop staring at the odd woman. She seemed blurry, the paleness of her skin running into the gray of her clothing, her features not completely in focus. She had spread the wax paper across her lap and had proceeded to carefully pick apart her burger, examining each individual piece, taking a small bite of everything, and then carefully arranging it back together. Despite the fact that she, not fifteen minutes ago, had been ready to literally eat a chipmunk alive, she seemed reluctant to bite into one of Happy's famous hamburgers.

Famous for Kiron, anyway. It weren't like this part of the world got famous for anything other than coal mining, oxy, and rockslides.

"Dig in," Bennie said, done waiting for the woman to get the bravery to eat. She peeled back the greasy wrapper and tucked into her own meal. That seemed to convince the woman, who shifted in the front seat, made a face, and then followed Bennie's lead.

It took two bites for the hesitation to disappear. The woman made quick work of the burger and then dug into the fries, putting a whole handful into her mouth. Bennie winced, grateful they stayed in the truck. She hadn't wanted to sit inside the restaurant with the woman wearing a dress that could generously be called a rag, still waterlogged and slightly gross besides. Sitting the damp lady in her truck was not ideal either, but Bennie could clean her car seats.

"Where you from?" Bennie asked cautiously. Bennie hadn't managed to get any kind of conversation out of her yet, but maybe food would change that.

"Not sure," the woman said in between bites. "Here, I suppose. Here, a long time ago."

8

Her voice was just as strange as the rest of her. It was hick as any other voice in Kiron, but slower even, a dark, melting beeswax that dripped off her words. A rougher, lower cadence.

"What's your name?"

"They called me Motheater," she said, making a motion that looked like she was trying to push back bangs that were no longer there. Bennie took a longer look at her.

Her dress was a dark blue, or a gray, with some kind of embroidery on the half sleeves. There was a suggestion of lace at the ends and around the collar, but it looked like it had been torn away. It wasn't quite modest enough to be Amish, but it wasn't fancy enough to be something that the Ren Faire nerds would conjure up.

"Motheater," Bennie repeated, frowning. She looked up at the young woman, but she had already returned to her fries, eating them one by one, savoring them now that she was near the end of her meal. "Why they call you that?"

"Well, I were a witch and refused to marry. And 'fore that, my father was called a preacher by nigh on the town and a snake charmer by the louts moving in."

"You're a witch?" Bennie asked quietly.

Motheater nodded, looking back to her fries. "How else you think I got dead leaves to listen to me, five seasons robbed?"

"I thought that was just the wind? A sinkhole?" Bennie said mildly, trying to offer the woman an out. There was no way in God's green earth that this half-drowned lady calling herself Motheater was actually a witch.

"Surely you heard of witches?" Motheater chuckled, finishing the last crusty fry. "The world cannot have changed so much."

"Of course I've heard of witches," Bennie hissed. "But they're not real. There's nobody really hovering over a cauldron trying to make a love potion—"

9

Motheater snorted, smiling down at the greasy paper on her lap.

"Oh, excuse me?" Bennie asked, eyebrows up. "Have I offended you?"

"I half dragged you down into your first grave, and you doubt what I am?" Motheater said, teasing. Bennie saw something in her mouth, a flash, a shine, and it both terrified her and drew her in. "Fine. Take me to a Neighbor, and I'll prove it."

"Nope." Bennie wiped her hands on a napkin, stuffing it into the empty bag. She didn't know what Motheater meant by "Neighbor," but it probably wasn't someone she'd find in the ER. "I'm taking you to the hospital."

"I don't need a doctor," Motheater said, voice rising. "I need a Neighbor."

"Too damn bad," Bennie muttered. She turned over the truck, and the engine made a rattle that she did *not* like.

"Please." Motheater clutched at Bennie's arm. Bennie shifted toward her and found it hard to look away from Motheater's onyx eyes. Her face was an odd mix of plaintive and demanding. "I need help no doctor knows how to deliver."

Bennie stayed quiet, staring at her. Motheater's hand clutched at her jacket a little harder.

"Take me to a Neighbor, and I will work a miracle," Motheater said, her voice dark and low. "One made just for you."

"Why are you so desperate for this, huh?" Bennie asked, her palms starting to sweat. "I don't even know what a Neighbor is, and I dunno why I should take you to one, even if I knew what you're after."

For a second, Motheater looked stricken. "I don't remember any part of who I am. I only know what I was. I need someone like me, someone who knows how to use magic, who can divine what happened to me. If I am made whole, mind and magic, I can move the whole earth."

Bennie chewed on the inside of her cheek. Motheater was staring at her, unblinking, her eyes so wide that it was hard not to feel bad for her. She didn't know if she believed Motheater, but . . . it wouldn't hurt to play along for a bit. "What kind of miracle?"

"Name it," Motheater said quickly. "I can feel my power; I know it's there. I just have to be able to tap into it."

Nervous, Bennie suddenly felt claustrophobic in her truck. She couldn't look away from Motheater, from the frayed hem of her dress, her pale skin, her hair sticking up at odd angles. "I want White Rock Mining outta Kiron." Bennie's voice seemed to stick to the sides of her throat. "They're killing people. Have been for years. I want them stopped."

Motheater nodded, leaning in, assured in a way that was unnatural. The woman might not have known what White Rock was—Bennie wasn't even sure Motheater knew what year it was—but Motheater seemed to understand the gist of what Bennie wanted. "Get me to a witch, and I will turn them over."

God. Bennie *believed* her. Motheater's conviction was a real thing, nestling in like a seed in her chest. Her heart wouldn't stop beating fast, and she couldn't look away from Motheater. She swallowed her hesitation, mouth dry with it.

"There's a palm reader down the road." Some of the Baptist women liked going to get a thrill when their husbands were watching football. Bennie pulled out of the parking lot, and Motheater's hand fell off her arm. "I dunno about a witch, but she's the best we got."

Next to her, Motheater curled in her seat. Bennie took a deep breath, her hands tight around the wheel. Miss Delancey would have to be good enough.

II

2

Bennie

Two seconds after walking up to Miss Delancey's Tarot and Palm Reading, Bennie knew that she was going to regret this.

Next to her, wearing her threadbare dress and refusing to put on shoes, Motheater peered at the neon light in the window suspiciously. Her disastrously held together outfit wasn't a good look anywhere, but especially not in Kiron. Especially not for Bennie, a Black woman who had already been accused of suspicious behavior. Bennie had thought about getting her a change of clothes but decided the less time spent in Motheater's company, the better. Besides, Kiron had its fair share of strange characters, right? Bennie held onto delusion tightly as she took a deep breath in front of the palm reader's.

"I can't help you if I ain't all of myself," Motheater said, her voice tinged slightly petulant. "But I don't think no decent Neighbor would tart her work like this."

"Vikki Delancey is the closest thing Kiron's got to a witch," Bennie said, resolutely ringing the doorbell. "I don't know anything about Neighbors, and right now, this is the best I can do."

That seemed to placate her, and Motheater moved to stand next to Bennie. She examined the doorbell and then pressed it herself.

"Stop that," Bennie muttered, batting Motheater's hand away. "You'll annoy her."

"It's like a piano key," Motheater justified herself. "It's not magic."

"No, a doorbell isn't magic—"

"It doesn't even sound like a bell."

The door swung open, and the two young women were face-to-face with Delancey. She was a tall, thin white woman with blonde hair wrapped up in a scarf, and she pursed her mouth as she looked at them through bifocals, quickly undoing the magnet at the bridge and dropping the pieces, letting them hang like leaves on a vine.

Bennie could feel Motheater's hackles rise. Some shift in her shoulders betrayed her, gave her a stance like a wounded creature. Delancey might have noticed the expression on Motheater's face, because she turned quickly to Bennie. Her mouth softened.

"Ah, Miss Mattox." She smiled, and Bennie wanted to throw herself into the gutter. Her last desperate attempt at using "magic" had led her here, and she hadn't come away with anything other than a lighter wallet. "Something I can do for you, dear?"

"I'm here with . . ." Bennie paused, watching Motheater warily out of the corner of her eye. "A friend. She'd like a reading if you have the time."

Motheater, thankfully, did as she had been coached and nodded. "I'd like to see my future if you can offer it."

There was something about the way she said it, Bennie thought, earnest and disbelieving at the same time. Like she

13

knew prophecy could happen but was sure it couldn't happen here.

"Of course, dears, come in." Delancey gestured them inside, then led them through to the back parlor. The promise of money was enough to smooth over any judgments that Delancey might have had when she first saw the mismatched pair of them. "Did you find your last reading helpful, hon?"

"Yeah, super insightful." Bennie plastered a fake look of gratitude on her face, widening her eyes. "Thank you."

The real answer was no, but she had come a few months after Kelly-Anne's death, on the verge of breaking up with Zach, lost and looking for . . . well, anything. It was the same reason that she had been driving along the creek that morning. One more vain attempt to find a hint, a clue, something to help her figure out what the fuck White Rock was doing in that goddamn mountain.

They never recovered Kelly-Anne's body. There was no trace of her at all. How could a woman just *disappear* in a modern mining operation?

Delancey smiled as they walked into the parlor, and Bennie was relieved that she seemed satisfied with the half-assed praise. The room smelled of stale incense, and while it stung Bennie's nose and almost made her cough, Motheater didn't seem to notice, looking around the room with a critical eye, measuring the worth of the woman by the cheesy decor and gem collection.

Motheater sat, and Delancey swept around the small table.

"Your accent is unusual," Delancey said, sitting and arranging her skirts. She pet the velvet table cover delicately, her chipped manicure a sickly shade of violet that matched her sour smile. "Where are you from?"

"Here," Motheater said, staring at the woman. Bennie, annoyed that she was relegated to the vinyl-covered furniture, sat on the arm of the couch, angled toward Motheater. Over Delancey's shoulder, Bennie could see a kettle beginning to boil over, the cap left off. She almost wanted to mention it, but the irony of a forgetful psychic might push Motheater over the edge entirely.

"From the mountains?" Delancey asked, picking up her tarot deck and shuffling it.

From her vantage point, Bennie saw Motheater smile. She looked like a predator.

"Yes. My family lived there."

"Well, not many of your folk left anymore," Delancey muttered, still looking at the cards.

"Not many at all."

"Been there a long time?"

"A very long time." Motheater grinned, wider than she had before, showing all her teeth. Were her teeth *filed into points*? Bennie was grateful that Delancey had kept her glasses off, as she couldn't imagine that Motheater's sharp little teeth wouldn't have freaked her out.

Delancey didn't seem to notice the wolf in front of her. Bennie assumed that her prescription must be exceptionally strong if she was missing Motheater practically licking her chops. This was a horrible idea. Maybe she should have just dropped Motheater at the ER and washed her hands of it. Bennie shifted in her seat, the vinyl squeaking.

Delancey looked up sharply. Bennie mouthed an apology, and the woman settled again, looking at Motheater. "I'll give a basic reading, and if you have more questions, we can go further. The first spread is usually paid upfront."

Motheater looked at Bennie. Bennie sighed, dug into her Carhartt jacket, and pulled out her wallet. She put a twenty on the table—the same price as last month's reading—and watched it swiftly disappear into Delancey's sleeve. It was half an oil change, but Bennie was in too deep now. She had committed to this terrible plan, and she was going to see it through. Bennie couldn't forget the feeling of the leaves sliding in between her boots and pants, the crunch of dead leaves that had slipped under her clothing falling apart in the soft spots behind her knees. Wind didn't do that. If that was what Motheater could do now, . . . what would she be capable of when she was made whole?

Bennie had to resist a shiver.

Motheater narrowed her eyes at the bill and looked back to Delancey. Bennie couldn't read her expression as it curdled strangely in the corners of Motheater's mouth. Bennie was fascinated by her every expression, trying to decode the omens written on her face.

"An expensive reading," Motheater said archly.

"Worth every penny, dear." Delancey shuffled the cards, then cut them into three piles. "Pick one."

Motheater concentrated hard on the deck. She tapped the pile on the far left. The other two were swept underneath, and Delancey nodded, as if pleased.

"The first card represents your past," Delancey said, laying a card down. "The Moon, reversed."

Bennie leaned closer. It was the same deck that Delancey had used when she had gotten her reading. This card showed a dog and a wolf howling up at the large, full moon. From her angle, the twin towers in the background were jagged, broken against the background. Bennie didn't know much about the cards beyond what her big sister had recited from a manual back in high school and what her own furious internet searching had turned up after she had asked Delancey for help four months ago.

Motheater leaned forward, frowning, as the second card was placed.

"Your present, the Four of Cups."

A young man against a tree, refusing the fourth cup.

"Your future," Delancey said, in what she was probably hoping was an impressive voice. "The Emperor. Reversed."

Delancey sat back, nodding as if all this made perfect sense.

None of these cards seemed bad to Bennie. No devils or towers or the Ten of Swords that had shown up in her own reading. She hoped that Motheater was at least paying attention, if not intrigued.

"Hm." Motheater frowned. "Explain this."

"Of course," Delancey said, as if being asked was all she had ever wanted. "The Moon in any position indicates fear, darkness, and mystery. Your past was probably full of confusion, living as you . . . living apart from modern civilization."

No response. Delancey continued. "The Four of Cups shows you're entering into a time of rest and contemplation, a spiritual awakening. This is probably because of your decision to shun your family's ways, coming down from your family's homestead in the mountains."

Bennie's eyebrows went up. Sure, Delancey made a living on this sort of thing, but *still*. It seemed a little presumptive to just come out with shit like that. Worse, what if it were true? If Motheater really were escaping some kind of conservative cult in the Blue Ridge, this whole thing would probably just confirm that people in towns were godless.

Bennie felt, very keenly, that she might have made a mistake. She sat up straighter, not looking away from Motheater.

"And last, The Emperor . . ." Delancey hesitated. Bennie saw her eyes flick to Motheater's hands, which she had on the table, held like a prayer. "Your father, or an uncle, a domineering male force. Someone who has kept you under his thumb. Beware his influence; he seeks to drag you back into a life of servitude."

Motheater's brow was folded up like the drying banks of a creek in autumn. She looked over each of the cards carefully, taking in their symbols, the backgrounds. Her eyes hesitated on The Emperor. Bennie didn't see any kind of satisfaction in her pursed mouth, her narrowed, dark eyes.

"I understand," she said finally, sitting back. She glanced at Bennie, and before Bennie had a chance to say anything, to reassure Motheater or tell her they could leave, she gestured at the cards again. "Another."

"What?" Bennie couldn't keep the surprise out of her voice. "Really?"

"Yes. Another. I understand now." Motheater sat up straight, her gaze fiercely direct. The psychic seemed pleased with herself.

"Of course." Delancey looked over at Bennie, who sighed and gave her the last twenty from her billfold. "A reading for direction, perhaps? To help guide your way?"

Delancey had already swept the spread back into her hands, shuffling them into the deck. Motheater hadn't looked away from the cards. Her shoulders straightened, and Bennie could tell there was something changed in her. She fiercely wanted to know what it was. "It doesn't matter."

The parlor went silent. The kettle boiling behind Delancey hissed as water hit the hot steel burner, and Delancey started in her chair. She put her deck down and quickly twisted her specs back together to peer at Motheater intently.

"Would you like to ask a question instead?"

"No. Do it again."

The boiling water sounded like rain against a river. Bennie found herself staring at Motheater's profile, barely breathing. The steam seemed to encompass the room, a horrible moist heat. Or was it just her? Delancey didn't seem bothered by the change to the temperature, her gaze fixed on the self-proclaimed witch.

Delancey sighed and then split the deck three ways again. Motheater gestured vaguely, and Bennie could see that

Delancey was getting annoyed, despite the forty dollars she had been paid for ten minutes of mumbo jumbo.

Delancey drew the first card quickly, putting it down without looking. "The past."

Motheater sat back with a satisfied smile. Immediately, Bennie didn't like that look—it made her teeth tighten like she had sucked a lemon. There was a squeak of protest from the vinyl as she stood up to get a better look.

The card was blank. All that was on the table was a piece of thick, coated paper, with no image on its face. Delancey hesitated. "A printer's proof, my apologies."

She swept the card across the table and laid down a second on the purple-trimmed velvet. It was as blank as the first, but this one had a small stain on the front. The steam was making Bennie sweat, and there was a bit of perspiration on Delancey's eyebrow, threatening to drop on her low glasses, but she had gone very still. Her hands began to shake.

Motheater stood, mouth twisted up sharp and beautiful, like a hawk.

"You are no Neighbor," Motheater said, soft and cold, "and you are not known in any good book."

Delancey flipped over a third card, then a fourth. Nothing. Sweat dripped onto her hands. She spread the deck in front of her, seventy-eight cards, all blank. She stared at them. Behind her, the kettle was rattling furiously, the last bit of its water spitting against the heat, a heaving flood through a small creek.

The heat left, like every window in the room had been thrown open. Bennie shivered, excited, nervous, thrilled. She watched Motheater as if the woman were true north. Bennie had been desperate, hadn't she? Maybe she'd just been waiting for this moment. Maybe all she needed was real magic.

Motheater turned and didn't look back as she left the parlor, leaving the front door open as she walked outside.

Bennie stepped forward and touched one of the cards on the table and was surprised that it was hot, almost burning. She pulled her hand back fast, eyes wide as the laminate started to bubble on the table. The cards were *boiling*. This was incredible. This was happening, real, right in front of her. Fuck.

Delancey's hand stuttered toward hers, and Bennie jumped back. "So sorry," Bennie muttered, almost tripping over her feet as she backed out of the parlor. "Thank you, I—"

"Get out." Delancey's voice became harsh, losing its mystical breathlessness. "Get out!"

"Oh, sure thing." Bennie waved, skipping out of the small home and running to the truck, Motheater already seated inside. This was thrilling. The most exciting thing to happen to her in years, something that she couldn't explain or reason away. She was so excited she was shaking.

"What the fuck was that?" Bennie asked, turning the truck over as soon as she got into the seat. She didn't want to be anywhere near here if Delancey decided to call the cops.

"A small cunning," Motheater murmured, arranging her dress. "More a grammar. It took little from me."

"You knew she was a liar from the start," Bennie said, pulling out of the parking lot, breath catching in her throat. A witch. Real magic. The possibilities began taking shape. Motheater really could help Bennie find the bodies that White Rock buried in Kire Mountain.

"You had brought me here," Motheater explained, voice far softer than when she had been proclaiming Delancey a fraud. "Figured I should at least respect your estimate. Whether or not it was a fair opinion is not your fault when faced against thieves."

"And that second reading? You really needed to give her more money just to embarrass her?"

"Beloved, believe not every spirit, but try the spirits whether they are of God: because many false prophets are gone out into the world."

"I don't appreciate being preached to." Bennie didn't care; she was still grinning. "You spent my last twenty to prove a gospel. Put your damn seat belt on."

Motheater held her hand out, two bills folded in between her thumb and forefingers. Bennie blinked. When the hell had she swiped those back?

"Ain't got time to pay liars," she said, smiling a little as Bennie took her money.

"Was that magic, too?" Bennie stuffed the forty bucks into her pocket. Motheater seemed to have figured out the seat belt. Bennie doubted that even a witch could survive a crash on Kiron's one-lane roads.

"No," it came out *naw*, something low and mountain. "I've met pickaxes who've taken fewer hits than Delancey. 'Course she didn't notice a little slip on the way out."

Bennie laughed. The strange, skinny woman smiled back, her eyes crinkled at the edges, her strange black hair stuck up at odd angles. God, she was *incredible*.

"You need new clothes," Bennie declared. "There ain't no way you can keep running around in a half-falling-apart dress."

"Fine," Motheater muttered.

Bennie took a turn that would get her to the Baptist church. They had a donation closet in the basement. "But you're on a budget."

Motheater smiled at her and then turned to the window, pressing her forehead against the glass. Bennie tried to focus on the road, on the potholes and hidden drives, but she couldn't help glancing at Motheater a few times every minute.

A witch with magic. *Real magic.* Wasn't this Appalachia? Weren't witches as a part of this place as the wild ginseng and hidden swimming holes? Didn't they belong here, same as her?

Bennie clenched her hands around the steering wheel as they passed neat little double-wides. Bennie had tried everything else to bring White Rock to heel, get justice for her friends, protect those she loved who still worked under the mountain. There wasn't a single family in Kiron that didn't have blood or friend in Kire Mountain, working to extract coal for White Rock.

Now, if she helped Motheater find herself—whatever that took, whether it was her memories, magic, whatever—Bennie might be able to save Kiron from the threat that loomed over the whole town. At the very least, she had to try.

3

Bennie

Bennie pulled up to a worn-down apartment building that still looked like the hotel it had been fifty years ago. She glanced at Motheater, who was clutching the plastic bag that contained the thrifted clothes they were able to find in the closet.

"It's small. So we'll have to work around each other," Bennie said, walking out of the truck and up to the second level. Motheater followed, back straight, looking around curiously.

Bennie opened the door to her efficiency apartment and let her in. She turned on the lights, illuminating the half-unpacked corner studio, a dozen novels stacked by a mattress that was meticulously made, despite the chaos around it. She had been here less than a month. A little mess was fine.

"Make yourself at home," Bennie said cautiously as Motheater inspected the stack of books. Taking a deep breath, Bennie glanced behind her.

There, on the small table that folded down from the wall, were a dozen folders, carefully labeled, color coded, and assigned a date. Tacked to the wall above that was a map with red pins in it, looking like something out of a cop serial. Bennie chewed on her bottom lip nervously.

This was it. All the deaths, all the lives, all the people she never knew or had only heard of. Her eyes caught on the most recent pin, labeled with a neat "KAE." Guilt tasted like a sour apple in her mouth. If she was going to move forward with this insane plan—get Motheater's magic back, save the miners—she needed to commit.

"I want you to see this," Bennie said, taking a step back and gesturing Motheater over. Her heart was pounding. She felt like she was standing on the edge of a steep face, trusting someone with all this, barely knowing them, barely knowing anything at all about them.

Motheater seemed to float over. She had been able to change into the oversized sweatshirt and long skirt at the church and looked less like someone you'd expect to see on *Sister Wives*. With her baggy clothes and choppy hair, she looked almost fashionable.

"About two years ago, my friend and I realized people were disappearing in Kire Mountain," she explained. "Me and Kelly-Anne began to track all these deaths. We found accounts of miners disappearing for the past two decades."

"Y'all mining?" Motheater asked, leaning in. "Folks die mining."

"Not like this," Bennie insisted, pulling out clippings from one of the folders. "Not disappearing in ones and twos like this. Mining disasters are huge, Motheater. They take out . . . thirty, fifty, even two hundred people at a time."

Motheater was tense, frowning deeply. Bennie could see her fingers digging into her sweatshirt, almost tearing the thin material. Bennie swallowed.

"White Rock keeps going deeper into Kire Mountain."

Motheater visibly flinched, almost like she'd been struck.

"Six months ago, Kelly-Anne . . . my best friend died," Bennie said quietly. "She and I were working on this together. And then she went into Kire and never came out."

Motheater began to breathe harder. Whatever horrible gut-churning guilt Bennie felt didn't abate. She wasn't doing this just for herself anymore. This was for Kelly-Anne. This was for everyone that had died. This was for everyone that was going to be killed because White Rock's greed kept fucking spreading. She had to do this.

"I need to stop White Rock from mining in Kire."

To her surprise, Motheater nodded immediately. "I reckon you do."

"I've tried everything." Bennie *knew* she shouldn't be telling a stranger all this, especially a stranger as fucking strange as Motheater, but she had nowhere else to turn. "Kelly-Anne was the one everyone in town trusted. The union has filed grievances, but the company's got too many lawyers. The police can't do anything. Local activist orgs got they hands tied."

Motheater's face was dark, every part of her tense. Bennie knew she was rambling, but she needed this witch to believe her. She needed someone to believe her. She had lost her best friend, her job, and then the relationship that had brought her out to Kiron in the first place. Thinking about Zach still hurt—it had been less than a month since she moved out—but she couldn't leave Kiron. Not like this. Not when more people would die if she did.

"You think the company killed 'em?" Motheater took a step forward, tilting her head.

"What?" Bennie glanced from the map to Motheater. "The company's responsible for the miners in the mines. They're dying in the mines, Motheater, of course it's White Rock's fault."

Motheater hummed. "You know what lives in that mountain?"

The temperature dropped in the efficiency. Bennie shivered.

"Nothing lives in Kire Mountain."

"Nothing you seen," Motheater murmured.

Bennie swallowed. White Rock was killing people. The company was killing people.

But magic was real. She had seen it, she had felt it creeping up her hands like broken leather and dark intention. Magic was real, and she had a witch in her apartment, and the temperature was making her breath frost in front of her face.

What if there was something else killing miners in the dark?

Bennie tried to find the words to ask Motheater something, to say anything at all, but a buzz from her pocket distracted her. With a shaky hand, she pulled out her phone.

Fuck. It was Zach. He wanted to come over. She ignored him, instead sending messages to her mother about visiting next month and then a quick text check-in with her coworker at the hardware store. All very normal things, because this was a very normal day, and she was totally, completely normal and not looking to talk about how she had hauled a magic lady out of a stream. She glanced over and noticed Motheater staring at her, no longer observing the map of just over two dozen dead miners.

"You okay?" Bennie asked, eyebrows up.

"What's that?" Motheater pointed at Bennie's phone.

"My phone?" Bennie smiled a little. "Come on, you know what a cell phone looks like."

Motheater shook her head, holding her hand out. "No."

Bennie passed the phone over, almost automatically, not questioning why she was trusting this woman with her personal device. It didn't seem like Motheater was about to do anything weird, but she was acting like she had never seen a touchscreen before. She pressed her finger against it hard, making colors flash over the display.

"Easy," Bennie muttered. "It's glass."

"Oh." Motheater managed to open a mapping application, turning the phone around. "It knows where we are?"

"Yeah, it's got a little GPS."

"A what?"

Bennie took a deep breath, finding patience. "Global Positioning System?"

Motheater blinked at her. Nothing registered; the words seemed to be little more than a foreign language Bennie was speaking.

"All right, come on," Bennie groaned, rubbing her eyes. Magic was one thing—it felt reasonable to accept magic, as bizarre as that sounded. But not knowing about GPS felt like a stretch. "What's going on?"

"I'm trying to put reason to it," Motheater muttered, turning the phone over in her hands, the dirt under her nails putting a strange grammar against the screen. "I must have been kept somewhere before you pulled me from the river. I have a well in me, but I feel . . . old. In two places at once."

Bennie steeled herself. What was one more mystery? As if her life hadn't been consumed by a mysterious death rate for the past two years, as if she hadn't been in a pained, misunderstood grief for months. She reached out to touch Motheater's arm. Motheater flinched before taking a deep breath. She seemed much younger like this, dark eyes wide and lost. It was a far cry from the righteousness she wore when she was denouncing Delancey.

Bennie's stomach leaped into her throat. Damn her bleeding heart. She shifted and moved to hug Motheater, rubbing her back gently. "I need to know my name," Motheater murmured. "I don't know myself."

"We'll get you back," Bennie murmured. She realized that she was becoming a little obsessed. Motheater was endlessly fascinating, and Bennie had a bad habit of collecting the most broken, fascinating things, although they were not typically people. She thought about the cracked snail shells she collected from the edge of her grandmother's porch as a kid, the blue eggshells with little bits of yellow stuck inside, and wondered if Motheater would fit in with those things, chipped-off teeth and all.

As Bennie rubbed her shoulder, Motheater shifted, laying her head against Bennie's shoulder, sliding one hand up to hold onto her waist. It was the smallest acceptance of comfort. Bennie slowly ran her hand through Motheater's short black hair, petting her. Motheater was going to help her bring down White Rock. Or stop the killings. Both, if Bennie had her way.

"I promise, all right? We'll figure you out," Bennie said softly. Her assurance came out easy. It was something, Bennie thought with the taste of a crab apple souring her mouth, that Kelly-Anne would have said.

It might have been exactly what she said.

When Bennie first moved to Kiron with Zach, they had bounced around apartments, trailer homes, and even basements for nearly four months. But Bennie had sworn that she owed it to herself to try with Zach. She loved him. That love was worth fighting for. Zach's Uncle Trip had offered them a basement apartment, but she had only managed to stay under that roof for a few weeks before Bennie couldn't take it anymore.

Living with Zach was fine; living with his white uncle, who was a few years shy of Zach's age and asked stupid questions about her education and complimented her vocabulary, was becoming untenable. She was going to snap Trip's neck. The irony of a man with an eighth-grade reading level thinking that she was smart, but not as smart as him, was not fucking lost on her.

Bennie had only been working at White Rock for a few months when she complained to Kelly-Anne during lunch. The two Black women had spotted each other in the cafeteria and immediately sat next to each other, becoming fast friends in a company that was mostly white and run by the men.

"There's just nowhere to live that doesn't have a leaky roof or a creepy landlord," Bennie said, scanning Craigslist for the hundredth time. "How do y'all find anything around here?"

"Well, you're looking online instead of in the local paper," Kelly-Anne pointed out, smiling a little. "Why isn't Zach helping?"

"Oh, he is," Bennie insisted, still scrolling. "He's just got low standards. If we're sticking around here, I want a real home, not a basement."

Kelly-Anne laughed, got up, and went to pick up a biweekly *Kiron Gazetteer* that someone had abandoned after completing the crossword.

"Here," Kelly-Anne said, sitting next to Bennie. "Property."

Bennie whistled, eyebrows up. Next to the houses and apartments were ads for massive swaths of land, some listed as "Mineral Rights Contingent." "Well, shit."

"This one is in my neighborhood." Kelly-Anne pointed to an ad for a "cozy ranch, forest-side." "I'll take you after work."

"I dunno if we're in the market to buy a house . . ." Bennie said, hesitating.

"That's fine, we'll figure it out." Kelly-Anne smiled, then whipped out a pen, writing her number and address under the ad. Bennie was touched by her openness, how she was so fucking earnest about this. Bennie wasn't an imposition to

Kelly-Anne—she was someone worth taking care of. "Here. Holler anytime. I'll help as much as I can."

Bennie's phone vibrated loudly on the table, startling her. She pulled back from Motheater and checked the text, frowning.

Confused, Motheater glanced over. "What's it doing?"

"Oh, fuck," Bennie muttered. "My ex is here."

"Yer what?" Motheater frowned as Bennie walked over to the door.

She took a deep breath to steady herself. There was no way she would be able to explain Motheater to him. And worse, knowing Zach, he might want to offer advice, or get involved somehow, or just try to help. Which he'd do selflessly, of course, and then she'd be the asshole.

"Don't say nothing," Bennie muttered as Motheater leaned against the counter next to the totality of her investigation. She decided there was nothing she could do about the map. She had left Zach a month ago over this murder mountain shit; he should know that she hadn't given up.

Honestly, the breakup might have been worse if she *didn't* have her conspiracy set up in her bedroom.

There was a knock on the door. Bennie glanced at Motheater. The witch just tilted her head, and Bennie took a deep breath before she opened the door. Taking up her doorstep was Zach Gresham, a young man with cornflower-blue eyes, pale skin, and shoulders that Bennie used to swoon over.

"You can't just come over whenever you want to," Bennie said, tightly.

"I wanted to drop some of your things off," Zach offered, holding out a large canvas bag. He shifted on his feet, trying to look around Bennie into the small studio apartment. She knew he was curious about where she had ended up after she had left their house three weeks ago. Well, it was his house now. Fuck. She pushed that feeling of resentment down fast.

Bennie was grateful that the door prevented Zach from peeking in to see Motheater and the map on the other side.

"Thanks." Bennie took the bag and placed it just inside the door. It was a bunch of knickknacks and souvenirs that Bennie definitely didn't have room for now that she and Zach weren't sharing a two-and-a-half-bedroom.

God, this was horrible. She was still hurting over losing Zach so completely. It didn't matter that as soon as Kelly-Anne had died last fall, she knew it was over between her and Zach, but she had thought that maybe having to go to one of their friends' funerals would convince him. It hadn't.

She wanted to slam the door in his face and lock herself in the bathroom.

But Zach wasn't moving from her doorstep. To his credit, he seemed to have showered after work before coming over. He was out of the White Rock uniform, which was a relief, as he absolutely knew how much Bennie resented the company, but Bennie wasn't about to let a little bit of going tidy sway her. His dark blond hair was still a holy mess, sticking up in the back.

"I wanted to talk—"

"No." Bennie eased the door closed a little more, not totally shutting it in his face, but getting close. She didn't want to argue; she had other things on her mind. Magic, murder, dead best friends. She couldn't deal with her ex, too. "Not now, all right."

"Bennie—"

"Nope."

Bennie took a step back, about to shut the door.

Zach spoke up quick. "I don't want to talk about us."

There was something in Zach's voice that made her stop. He wasn't trying to keep the door open, wasn't pressing into her space, either. Zach had never been pushy, not when they had met at Tech years ago, and not now. Bennie had always felt an assurance of safety around him.

She took a look at him. His hands were worrying the brim of his trucker hat that she hated that he loved. There was something desperately charming about him still, and Bennie felt their years dragging her back. He was a good man, even if things hadn't worked out between them.

"I have company."

"Won't take a sec," Zach said, eyebrows up. "Please, Bennie."

Bennie took a deep breath. Guilt echoed in her chest. She shifted on her feet, glanced at Motheater—still half-hidden by the door—and then gestured Zach inside, resigned.

"Thanks." Zach stepped in and spotted Motheater, dressed in some acid-wash sweatshirt two sizes too big, her arms crossed, dark eyes narrowed. He froze, unsure. Zach might have been prepared for an old friend, but not a new face, especially considering the three-digit population of Kiron.

"Who's this?" he asked, confused. Motheater seemed to uncurl like a snake, her expression strange.

"That's a shitty way to introduce yourself," Bennie snapped.

Zach pressed his mouth. He gave Bennie a sidelong look before stepping forward and offering Motheater his hand. "Sorry, long shift. I'm Zach."

Motheater didn't move, and Zach was left there with his hand out, waiting.

Bennie sighed. "She's having a rough day."

"Right." Zach moved back and looked around, realizing for the first time that he wouldn't have any privacy. The three of them stood awkwardly around, frustratingly still and silent.

Bennie gestured. "You have the floor, Zach."

Zach hesitated, looking between the two of them. Bennie could tell there was something wrong here. This wasn't like

Zach. He was direct; he didn't stumble over what he wanted to say.

"Sorry, I—" Zach paused and then stared directly at Motheater. She narrowed her eyes at him, a twitch around her mouth, like she wanted to tear at his throat. "You're her."

Bennie's eyebrows snapped down. Her heart jumped. How did Zach know Motheater? "Excuse me?"

Zach had gone from nervous to rigid, his eyes fixed on Motheater.

"We pulled a body out of the mine today," Zach said. "We pulled her"—he pointed at Motheater—"out of a coal vein, half in the bedrock of Kire."

Bennie's stomach swooped like she had taken a hair-pin turn on a four-wheeler, just barely off-balance. She had pulled Motheater out of a stream that White Rock used for slough . . . Hadn't she been looking for bodies? Hadn't she hoped to find a body at the bottom of that creek? Her breath came faster, and she turned slowly to stare at the witch in her bedroom.

Motheater's arms dropped, her fingers twitching. Bennie felt the temperature in the room plummet.

It was the same gesture that had dragged Bennie into the loam.

"Whoa, hey—" Bennie immediately stepped in front of Zach, in between him and Motheater. Bennie pressed down her fear and turned to the witch.

"You stand down," she said, pointing at Motheater. Something in her voice must have startled the woman, be-cause she blinked and her hands dropped. "You." She looked at Zach. "What in the hell are you talking about?"

Zach took a step back, near the chair and mattress, slid-ing away from the conspiracy corner. He hadn't looked away from Motheater. "Today, at work, during excavation, we un-earthed a body from inside the mountain."

Bennie glared at Zach. She believed him, she couldn't believe him. She steadied her voice. "*In* the mountain?"

"In the mountain," Zach repeated, still staring at Motheater, who was clenching her hands at her sides, looking murderous. He was pale, his breath coming fast, color along his hands and the back of his neck. He gestured at Motheater. "The body. That woman came out of the mountain, half dead, barely breathing."

"I weren't dead," Motheater hissed. "I was waiting."

Bennie could only stare, the accusations falling like a rockslide down a mountain, picking up more and more debris as it went.

Motheater was a strange creature, not quite human, leaning forward, leering at Zach, sharp teeth on display.

"You were in the mountain?" Bennie asked her, whispering.

"And he was biting into it," Motheater snarled. "I remember the cold stone, I remember the tracks of coal that shackled me. I know little else, but I know now that I was buried for a reason, and *you took me out*."

Zach stepped back, openly shocked and scared. The apartment was as cold as a mine shaft. Bennie couldn't feel ashamed as he glanced over Motheater's shoulder and went red as he recognized what she stood in front of.

He had just admitted he found a body in that damn mountain. He had just admitted that he had gotten rid of a body he had found in the mountain. Any sympathy Bennie had for him melted away. They were done. She was right to leave. For a few seconds, it felt like a bird's wings beat inside of her chest instead of a heart. She took a deep breath, calming down.

Motheater tilted her head up, voice husky and soft. "I don't know what I was doing, life limned in the heart of old Kire, but you were right when you spoke out 'gainst your foreman. You didn't have no right to move me. Now I'm a lost witch with no memory, and you're one of them that woke me up."

The efficiency seemed to close in on the three of them. Motheater took another step forward, raising her hand, but Bennie grabbed her wrist, standing in front of her, getting in between Motheater and Zach again. Panic had made her stupid. Zach's admission had made her resolute. She turned her hand to grasp Motheater's tightly, leaning close.

"Calm down," Bennie said, in the tone that she would take with her older sister whenever she began to start shit with their mom. "Not in my house."

The vibration in the room shifted and Motheater hesitated.

Bennie's grip was firm, trapping Motheater's fingers. She held that tension with the witch a few more seconds, noting Motheater's short lashes, her cheekbones like chopped crystal, stunning like a mountain ridge. Bennie knew her heart was beating fast, not just because she was scared. She turned to Zach.

"Go outside," Bennie said, voice measured. "I'll come out in a few minutes to talk."

"Ben—"

"No, Zach."

Zach, jaw tight, nodded. He looked over at Motheater again, but the witch was deliberately staring at the scuffed-up sneakers that she and Bennie had dragged out of the bargain closet.

"Fine," he said. "I don't know what . . . ." His voice trailed off. He shook his head and left.

Bennie took a deep breath, closed her eyes, centering herself. Motheater tugged at their hands, not trying to pull away, but testing it.

"I'm remembering some."

Bennie looked at Motheater. She seemed small, chastised, like she was used to being driven out in order to make others more comfortable. The oversized sweatshirt certainly made the woman look more like a child.

"The more I'm here, the more people I meet . . . It's coming back to me. Who I was."

Bennie squeezed Motheater's hand again and then let go, walking into the bathroom. She splashed cold water on her face and pulled her braids back, keeping them away from her face with an elastic.

"Just stay in here, all right?" Bennie said as she went to the door. Motheater was still standing where Bennie had let go of her, like a lost puppy. "I'll only be a minute."

Motheater nodded, and Bennie slipped out of the efficiency, closing the door behind her. Zach was pacing back and forth on the porch. Bennie's hurt was too fresh to let her feel anything but ache when she looked at him, hair tousled like wheatgrass, big hands unsure where to go.

He was about to speak, but Bennie held both hands up.

"I don't want to talk about Motheater."

"About *what*?"

Bennie groaned, putting her hands over her face. Why the fuck didn't Motheater have a normal name? Any name, any fucking goddamn name.

"Okay, well," Zach said, his tone going from disbelieving to worried, which was exactly what Bennie didn't want. "Okay. I won't ask, all right. I'll just . . . I just needed you to know that I thought I pulled a dead body out of the stone today, and then it breathed. And then, I thought I had killed someone when my crew threw that same breathing body in the slough. You were right, there's something rotten in White Rock, and I just—"

"I am absolutely not ready to be your friend right now," she said sternly. "I can't do it yet." Especially not when all he could talk about was what White Rock was doing without apologizing. If this is what they did when they found living bodies, what would they do if they found someone dead? She felt her rage building, the hurt and horror and indignation. Where were the rest of the miners who had disappeared in Kire? Where did the bodies go? Where was Kelly-Anne Elliot? Did she need to walk all along that creek where she had found Motheater, poking at drowned critters until she unearthed something human?

He had just confirmed what she and Kelly-Anne had suspected about White Rock's work in Kire. What she had ruined her reputation over, what had got her fired, what drove her to break up with him. This is what had killed her best friend, and he had just admitted that if it wasn't an accident, at the very least he had just told her that White Rock had no compunction about covering up killings.

"I didn't know, Bennie, I swear I didn't," Zach said plaintively. "This ain't normal, and maybe it ain't ever been normal."

"Zach, stop, please." Bennie's voice nearly cracked. Had he come here to confess or get comfort? He thought he had killed somebody, and this was his reaction? She seethed. Bennie hated that mining had made him like this, that Zach had returned home and decided to stay in line to keep White Rock happy. He thought that he had a hand in killing a woman, and his reaction was to ask Bennie to take care of him? Not fucking likely.

"Yeah, all right." Zach's voice was soft, and Bennie knew he was hurting. "Still, I . . . I'm glad I came over. At least now I know I didn't . . ."

Bennie let herself feel some amount of pity for him. He still hadn't apologized, but she was choosing to ignore that. "Yeah, she's fine. Fuck if I know how."

"Right."

"Right." Bennie shivered and took a step back. There was a cold wind coming down from the mountains that surrounded Kiron. "I'm going inside. I'll reach out in a few days, okay?"

Zach didn't respond, big hands still worrying at his hat. The breakup hadn't been easy on either of them; it had been drawn out and extended, and then finally shattered when Bennie realized that his lukewarm acceptance of her conspiracy theorizing would never materialize into actual support, even after Kelly-Anne's death.

"Okay?" Bennie tried again.

She wasn't convinced Zach knew how deeply he had hurt her when his steadiness turned to passivity. Did he really understand the depth of his betrayal when he had simply agreed not to stand in her way? How could they be together when he couldn't separate love from loneliness?

Zach finally nodded. "Okay," he repeated, looking up at her.

The silence, taut as a birch bending under winter, did nothing to convince Bennie that Zach had heard her. She nodded stiffly and went back into the efficiency, closing the door on him.

4

Motheater

Inside Bennie's apartment, Motheater tried to focus. Memories began to drag themselves out of her well. She closed her eyes, sitting down on the chair heavily, pressing her hands into her eyes. Around her there was a humming like the strum of a guitar.

As she lifted her head up, a moth landed on her knee. It must have come in when Bennie and Zach had been arguing at the door. It wasn't terribly pretty, mostly brown, green at the edges. She frowned and picked it up, leaning in.

If she wanted to know herself, she had to listen to the souls sent to her.

In her hands the moth turned around, as if settling, and then began to dissipate, the whole of it turning to motes in the air. The dust from the moth dispersed, and Motheater took a deep breath, shivering.

In the moth's passing, Motheater began to feel out her first few moments in the cold mountain, the hardscrabble seconds as she was driven down into the stone by some force she couldn't quite understand. It felt like she was being sewn together, a hundred needles stitching together in time, mending the fabric of her.

She remembered when she finally stopped breathing and let the coal and granite petrify her lungs, the mountain shifting to accommodate her soft body, her fragility, taking care to cradle her heart. The rock had turned her jaw so that she would be comfortable, so that she would be able to endure an eternity bound by the chains of whatever magic it took to force her so deep into Kire. It was like pressing on a bruise, the hurt spreading, her memory coming back in spits and starts.

There were parts of her returning; she was a cunning Appalachian Neighbor, the feared Witch of the Ridge, the empty space between the Valley of the Shadow of Death and the Lord whom you implored to guide you. She was no ordinary death broker.

Motheater leaned forward, pressing the heels of her hands into her eyes again. Behind her hands, she saw a church. It was an off-white chapel held up against the mountainside, the far end of it against Kire itself, and part of the mountain was the altar.

This was her father's church. She saw him preach with snakes in his hands, talking in tongues as the scales slid over his wrists.

"Behold!" he cried out, two copperheads wrapped around his arms. This was how he performed for the masses. He'd quote gospel for the congregation, declare himself a true voice, and preach that this work was the good work. He'd say, with snakes nuzzling at his veins, that he had been given the Word, that he knew what the Lord's work was.

He was careful, Motheater remembered. Not with snakes—he knew snakes. He always called himself a servant, a part of a whole, a hand of God. Never prophet, never messiah. He was more aspirational than that.

"I give unto you power to tread on serpents and scorpions," the preacher called over the stomps of the crowd, the claps and clamor. It was hot, steaming, the morning burning the dew off the loam outside, and the church smelled like mud and cinders. "I give to you all the power of thine enemy, and nothing shall by any means hurt you. Not nothing by fang and not nothing by poison."

Motheater, a child, dressed in a mockery of a petticoat with her dark hair tied back with a string and not a ribbon, sat in the front row. Her tiny, coal-blackened hands tapped a tambourine, beating a plaintive tempo as her father walked down the aisle, Pentecostal as all hell, bringing the power of God into the congregation.

He might not have been happy with the response, displeased that the teenagers were gossiping in back. Maybe he took quarrel with the old folks taking leave of his preaching, on account of the fire and brimstone he favored. He was too much at the best of times, and Luke and fang were not enough today. He walked up to the front of the church and locked eyes with Motheater.

"Come here, child."

Motheater stood, all of seven, and walked to him. He traded her tambourine for a copperhead that length-to-length could have been held between both her hands and still have enough snake left over to rear up and bite her. There was no strength in her arms but that given from fear.

The copperhead, held in her arms like a puppy, uncurled around her shoulder. It pulled itself behind her head and wrapped itself around her like a noose. Motheater stood stone-still. A hush fell through the congregation as the child stood with her arms supporting an adder as dangerous as any low cave, as mutable as the weather, strong and thick-bodied and dangerous. Slowly, the snake's neck pulled back in a sharp curve, a warning. She closed her eyes and repeated the gospel that her father had urged upon her a hundred times. No serpents, nor masters, would hurt her. No serpents, nor fathers.

Her hands were soft, laden with a serpent that lent its ear toward her supplication.

As her father's preaching reverberated through the eaves of the church, the copperhead lifted itself up, just enough to get its head level with her ear. Its curves became weak, losing their tautness, its cool scales no longer the hushed promise of a grave. The thick, arched head leaned against hers, and it came to her with the reassuring steadiness of Kire itself.

It hissed, its tongue flicking against her skin, and it spoke to her, the first cleverness she ever learned, and under her own tongue she felt two small jewels, gifts from the snake. Weren't snakes the first creatures who listened to God and decided to seek their own power? They slid on the dirt, and they spoke to the oldest stone in the world, the things that rose up on fire and spire.

Seven-year-old Motheater, holding snake, turned her ear from her father and listened to the old voice of the mountain. The next day, she ran into the woods.

"Motheater?"

She looked up, all of twenty-eight, and saw Bennie standing in front of her. Motheater blinked a few times and ran her hands through her short hair.

"I'm all right." Motheater rubbed the back of her neck. "Just remembering."

"It looked like it hurt," Bennie said over her shoulder, a mug in hand as she opened a cabinet full of boxes and colorful papers that Motheater couldn't recognize or read.

Motheater set her feet on the ground, letting the movement remind her where she was. The strangeness of the rubber under the shoes, the way the floor didn't touch the ground, was just a ceiling for some other home. It felt vaguely wrong.

She could still feel the snake's weight heavy on her; a mantle passed down, past to present. "Memories are often painful."

Bennie watched her steadily, waiting by some kind of pitcher that had a cable going through the wall. Motheater didn't know what Bennie wanted to say, but she could see that something weighed on the other woman. Motheater suspected that it had more to do with the man who had stopped by than it had to do with her. Still she waited, hoping to know her, hoping to know something real right now.

Finally, Bennie broke the silence. "You were really in the mountain?"

"Yes," Motheater murmured.

"How did you even survive that?"

Motheater blinked. How did she? Kire Mountain wasn't a kind place, wasn't keen on visitors. She struggled to remember. It felt like she was being pulled in different directions, like the mountain was trying to drag her back into the past. "Kire wanted me alive," Motheater murmured, feeling it out, the places in her heart her words didn't reach. There was a bargain made—Kire would keep her, she would keep it.

"So, you survived in the mountain for . . . fifty years? Sixty?" she asked as the pitcher made a sharp noise. A kettle. A heating kettle.

Motheater pushed her hand through her hair again. It felt odd shorn like this. She must have had long hair before. The miners probably cut it off when they were pulling the whole of her out of the stone. "Do you know the Brothers' War? I went in after the conflict, but how long after, I don' quite recall."

"The Civil War?" Bennie sounded shocked. "You were alive during the Civil War?"

"No, no," Motheater hummed. It was less clear, but she knew she had grown up hearing stories. "When the men

43

came home . . . I was born a few years after the fighting died down. I don't know the dates."

She had been born between war and the modern century. The war had sharpened the gap in between the Appalachians, divided families along lines not drawn by any one kin they had. "Civil a far kinder name for it than we had."

"Goddamn," Bennie muttered. "So you've been in Kire Mountain for . . . over a hundred and fifty years."

A century and a half. It was difficult to comprehend, impossible to assume what had happened between now and then. It seemed incomprehensible, but here she was, surrounded by electric lights and stacks of bound books and strange clothing.

"Reckon so." She needed someone to believe her. She hardly believed in herself. She was exhausted, horribly lost, and had no idea why she had been preserved inside Kire. "I wondered where the horses went."

Bennie laughed, and Motheater smiled just a little, finally pulling off her rubber shoes and crawling onto the mattress that lay on the ground. It was so soft, and the edges all tucked in. No straw or weed poked out of the seams.

"Tomorrow, we're going to the library," Bennie said, watching Motheater crawl under the covers. "If you're from here . . . from the mountain . . . Maybe they'll have some old papers or something we can check out."

History. She was history to Bennie. Motheater curled up, pressing herself against the wall. She glanced over her shoulder as Bennie abandoned her second mug of tea, grabbing a set of clothes and disappearing into the second room. She blinked sleepily.

On the far wall, the red dots were scattered over the map of Kire like a constellation. A herald. A warning. They became blurry as she drifted asleep, pulled under ungently, caught in the black maw of a wolf.

5
Esther – Then

The Richmond businessman who came to Kiron in a red riding jacket called himself Julian DeWitt and touted his credentials to anyone in town willing to listen. This was much to the chagrin of the entire population that didn't have no time to entertain city folk looking for opportunity. He said that he didn't plan to spend much time in town, which was a small relief, but then asked where he might see the Neighbor.

"He might as well call us clay-eating trash," Dinah muttered, explaining the situation to Esther as they hung wash. Dinah's child had come home with a fever, and when he had turned an ashen white, she called down Esther to take a look at him. He had eaten some bad sorrel, and Esther had given him goat milk and a white river stone to suck on. Dinah had been so grateful that she had wrangled Esther into helping with chores.

"Hm," was all Esther said, wondering how she had allowed herself to be convinced to help Dinah after already healing her bain. "And where he gone now?"

"Down Hatfield way. Said he'd be back."

Esther huffed. "Men."

"He's handsome," Dinah teased, picking up her empty basket. "See if you find him comely next time he wanders through."

Esther sighed but didn't protest. Even now, nearly thirty years after the war, women of all ages were in abundance and men scarce. Of course Dinah's thoughts would turn to marriage, even as she disparaged DeWitt's attendance. Esther hung up the last of the laundry and retreated into the wood.

The next day, Esther went into town and hid herself in the morning fog, an easy draw from her well, considering her bargains laid cross by lean along the stones. She was less than a rustle of leaves, more than the light of a storm covering the dawn. Just as Dinah had said, the man came into town, comely as he was rumored, and as desperate as only a handsome man denied could be.

"Please—" DeWitt approached Hera Benneke, who had two children hanging onto her dress. He stepped in front of her, blocking her way. Esther nearly cursed him, but held back, whispering Elijah's prayer under her breath. "I'm not here to cause harm or even seek out dangerous conversation. I seek only a moment of the Neighbor's time."

Hera's mouth puckered as she rearranged her children, her arms laden with the smaller of the two and a sack of ground-up sorghum.

"She in the wood." She stared flatly at the man. "You want to find her? She must be keen to find you first."

"How do I make that happen?" he asked, and he looked so clean and sweet that Hera must have felt sorry for him. Neighbors were typically in town. Esther felt a little bad for Hera. It wasn't his fault that Esther had chosen to eschew tradition for her own pride. Hera sighed, annoyed, and gestured with her chin toward the winding road that led to the miner's camp, and farther up, the church.

"No way to do so but to go to the wood and wander."

DeWitt looked confused, and, as if confirming his age, his naïveté, asked, "What if I get lost?"

"Then she might cast her eye 'pon you," Hera said shortly, pulling her child away. "Bring a blanket."

He stared at the road and then turned to look at the woods that surrounded them. This was Appalachia, full of oak and hemlock, a lost land that no pioneer had ever truly claimed. Esther knew well the fear he must have felt at the thought of wandering into the vast mountain land.

Esther was grateful he had run into the womenfolk and not the men. The women all spoke to her. The only man she conversed with regular was Jasper Calhoun, and he would have loved to personally introduce this fool to Kiron's Neighbor.

She left in an orchestra of crickets, going to her cabin in the woods. She would see what this DeWitt was made of.

Hours later, while she was out foraging mushrooms, she found him, his city-shoes scuffed and shoulders hunched, curled up against an old oak tree at the edge of dusk.

"Ach, wanderer," she said, kicking his ankle and causing him to start, "you're near enough to trespassing to cause offense."

"Are you the Neighbor?" DeWitt asked, leaning against the oak to stand, his skin so white it was near blue, like ice on the edge of a well's bucket. Esther near felt sorry for him, sad little idiot.

"I am," she said, smiling a little. She was dressed simply and cleanly, her dark green bodice mismatched to her black skirt, but all the cloth was pinned neatly, and she had sewn it all with some skill. She knew that she seemed a child, and could tell that DeWitt was already trying to figure out whether she could be the far-spoken-of Neighbor

47

of Kiron—all of twenty-eight and younger looking for her height and frame, affected by lean years when she was young.

She smiled, nearly flirtatious. DeWitt blinked, clearly confused.

"I'm afraid I'm quite out of sorts, Miss Neighbor." His eyes were huge, blue as a jay's wing.

Did he suspect her a Nimüe, meant to lure him into some dark cave? This cunning was mostly for her own estimation, to get the measure of a man who came from the capital and would dare to walk right into her hold, unarmed, practically crawling. What a fool.

"You should follow me," she muttered, "and consider yourself lucky I'm yearning to know what you're doing in these woods." She turned away from him, walking along a path that would only reveal itself once she began to travel it. "So far from home and hearth."

"You are the Neighbor," he repeated with a note of wonder.

"I do not lie," she called over her shoulder, the path closing behind her. "Best keep up, Master Wanderer."

⁓

DeWitt followed obediently. *Well,* Esther thought, *that was something for him, at least.* He stayed silent until they arrived at the two-room cabin that Esther had made her home.

"What's your name?" he asked, sitting awkwardly on the bench near the hearth.

"Kiron calls me daughter," she said, stoking up the fire. "My name is Esther."

"My name is Julian DeWitt," he offered.

She knew this, but he was being polite, so she just smiled and continued to tend the fire. Esther had been out gathering herbs when she had heard him sighing against the old basswood, the message delivered on a sparrow-kite's wings. She had given up on the fool, almost hoping that he had turned back to wherever he had come from.

There wasn't much in the forest that could surprise her, and, although unexpected, the city-bred DeWitt was no exception; he was simply more clean-shaven and handsome than the last city-bred fool.

She heard him shuffle behind her, could practically hear the questions bubbling up. She kept her laughter down and glanced over her shoulder. "Speak your piece, DeWitt. We both know you weren't taking a constitutional."

"I need a dowser," he said, watching her with those watery blue eyes. He pulled his blanket tighter around his shoulders, sitting a fair bit away from her fire, despite the August chill. "The best."

"Aye, well that's the least of my services." She stepped away from her counter and looked over the man. "But you aren't from here, and neither are you looking to lay up a home."

"I'm here as part of Halberd—"

"Then you'll be leaving soon," she interrupted. "I ain't helping Halberd Ore."

DeWitt was silent then. She stayed quiet, too, standing on the edge of her kitchen, her hands under her apron, dug into her sewn-on bags that served as pockets. The fire crackled as it caught the birchwood spark. The smell of sorghum drippings popping in the hearth wafted through the air, and DeWitt swallowed.

"I have money," he offered.

"I have no need for money," Esther said. "I live here, and here my word is coin enough."

"Everyone needs money," DeWitt insisted, smiling a little as if talking down to her, as if condescending to the poor backwater mountain girl that didn't consider money and a paved floor important. "How do you buy clothes or tools? Your knife? I know you can't make that yourself, no matter how skilled you are."

Esther eyed him carefully, measuring him up. On second blush, he wasn't appearing to put on airs around her. He was either sincere or very stupid.

"I trade for it, a more honest way than Richmond deals in livelihood." Her voice was even, but even she knew the iron would ring out. "And you, DeWitt, don't have nothin' I'm keen to own."

"What about this land?" He was persistent, but it wasn't comely. "We can make a deal for some surface property rights."

"I don't need that, either," Esther said slowly. She paused, then turned away from her fire to stare at DeWitt. "Halberd has acquired mineral rights to the range."

As she spoke, she felt the truth of it echo in her cabin. It was an accusation, and such oaths hold power. The wind paused; the flames stopped eating at the wood. In her bones, she felt it, the industry to the north, starting their proud march south and eating the poorest parts of the east coast. There weren't no stopping it, nothing could deter that continental shift. Some folks, Esther knew, deserved worse than this.

Outside, a stag knocked its tines against a tree, ripping the velvet from its antlers. DeWitt started and tried to turn to look out the window. Esther didn't offer a word of comfort. Bargains made, unmade.

"It's getting late, Master DeWitt." Esther turned away. She held a conjure bone in her hand. It didn't look like anything but a rabbit's leg, tied up with birch paper and painted with charcoal to make it black. "You best be heading back to Kiron."

"Miss Esther, please." DeWitt's eyes became wide again, and Esther wondered if he practiced this doe-eyed simper or if it just came natural to lowland folk. "I don't know the way and can't possibly hope to find it. I came here to secure a good stead for the company town, to help improve Kiron! To bring wealth to the people here! To recover after the war."

He believed what he was saying, but he didn't know what he was promising. She looked at him and knew that his wealth had only happened in the past fifty years, with the rise of industry in Massachusetts, with the evil of factory work, with the pressing of young women into machinery, with the blood of the poor coating his hands and staining his jacket. She hated what he wanted. She hated what was coming, what his star made herald.

The mountain Kire was older and stronger than industry. There would be no hesitation when a Halberd bit caught at one of Kire's nerves. The mountain bore the hands of Kiron's miners; it would not suffer the machines of Northern men.

"Are you a faithful man?" Esther asked. She walked to DeWitt, opening the door and gesturing for him to leave. He seemed to recover some of his wits, at least enough to stand and walk out onto the porch. "Do you know the Psalms?"

Outside, Esther stood next to him, shutting the door behind her, not caring to hear his answer. Surrounding her small cabin were three bucks, each of them at least six points each, all of them shedding bloody velvet, strips of skin hanging from their crowns. Blood ran down their faces; one was even chewing on a scrap of skin hanging off its crowning bones.

DeWitt went still next to her. City folk never knew what to make of the world.

"Don't worry none," she said. "I'll shorten it for you, so you can keep it in your head. I'm sure that'll be tough seein' as there's so much learning in there."

"What are you doing?" He turned to her, wide-eyed, shoulders shaking. "What witchcraft?"

Esther began. *"Hear this, all ye people; Both low and high, rich and poor, together. I will open my dark saying upon the harp."*

The stags stepped back and lowered their bloody heads. Esther walked around DeWitt and put a hand in between his shoulders, and he walked forward, compelled. His mouth wouldn't be sewn shut, but he would be silent during his contemplative walk back to Kiron. She pushed down anger and became righteous.

"Wherefore should I fear in the days of evil, when the iniquity of my heels shall compass me about? They that trust in their wealth, and boast themselves in the multitude of their riches," Esther incanted. With the declamation, the ancient words echoed around her, and they remembered. The stags turned and began to escort the silent, shuddering DeWitt down the mountain; one ahead, two on either side. She walked behind him, reciting the psalm dutifully.

Around her, the mountain watched. The wind ceased and out of the grove, moths began to follow her, a wedding train out of silken, silent wings. The night had well fallen, and the chill came up fast. She could see DeWitt's breath misting under the moonlight.

"Like sheep they are laid in the grave; death shall feed on them. Yea, the upright shall have dominion over them in the dawn-light."

One of the stags shifted and left a strip of bloody velvet over DeWitt's shoulder as they marched. Esther stopped at the edge of the birch. He looked back, and she knew what he would see: a strange witch of the unmade stone, surrounded by moths and blue jays in a winding upward tornado around her. A woman with two snakes at her feet and great stags at her beckon.

"Please!" He fought through the conjure, turning back to her, eyes wide. "We want to help you! Halberd plans to build Kiron up into a grand city! A gateway through the Appalachians—"

Esther held out the hand that clutched the bone. Around the charcoal-covered bone grew flesh and tendon, until she held a black hare in her hand, its eyes as glowing embers, flickering like a soul. She would make sure Appalachia shut out Northern men. There would be no gate, no hinge, nothing but tor and holler.

"*Be not thou afraid when one is made rich,*" she recited. Her power writhed in her palm, and the stags lowered their heads, trapping DeWitt between their sharp tines, in a boned and bloody cage. He deserved this unkindness for darkening her doorstep. "*For when he dieth, he shall carry nothing away. He shall go to the generation of his fathers; and they shall never see light.*"

She put the night-hare on the ground, and it ran toward DeWitt. It jumped and entered his chest, a dark stain like smoke across his heart. It happened too fast for him to flinch, much less run. He pressed his hand to his body, looking up at Esther, panic flickering over his expression. Esther smiled.

The moths around her fluttered *selah*.

And then she disappeared from his sight and went back to her cabin, snakes trailing at her feet.

DeWitt would make it back down the mountain, at least as long as he followed the stags nicely and didn't try to run. Halberd would be coming to Kiron, but they wouldn't be coming to a hillbilly town that would invite them in with open arms at a promise of coin and fancy dresses. Halberd would be facing down a mad witch and her mountain, and there weren't no industry that could prepare their operatives for her.

She held her hand out. A few moths landed, and she brought them to her mouth, whispering passage, before they, too, disappeared, sending a warning to their long-dead kin.

6
Bennie

By the time Bennie had finished her bathroom routine, Motheater was fast asleep. Bennie stared at her for a full minute, watching the rise and fall of Motheater's shoulders. She had curled up in the fetal position and turned over so her forehead was nearly against the wall, hands cupped by her mouth like a prayer. Bennie sighed, twisting the last of her braids into a lattice that would easily fit under her bonnet.

She had the next few days off—her retail weekend—and she just prayed that she wouldn't be called into the store. Her manager had seemed to enjoy the drama of Bennie's life: breaking up with Zach after four years, moving out, her mother coming in from Norfolk . . . The production of her upheaval had been the only subject of conversation for the last month. Her manager, gossip that he was, would probably have a conniption if he saw Bennie tucked into bed with a strange girl barely four weeks after her official split with Zach.

But Bennie had bigger things to worry about than gossip. She made herself a mug of herbal tea and held it in both hands for a few seconds. A habit, something to calm her nerves.

She tried not to look at the map, at the cave-ins marked in green, the man-made earthquake epicenters dotted in blue, at the missing dead each red dot represented, at the notes that Kelly-Anne had made in the corners. Hurt echoed through her. Working on this alone had felt like keeping a wound open.

Bennie carefully stepped over her last mug of tea and knelt down. She slid under the covers, sipping the nearly cold tea again before putting it next to the mattress and getting comfortable next to the stranger in her bed.

It hit her, suddenly, how ridiculous this was. How dangerous it could be for her if Motheater was lying about any of this. But there was something about Motheater, a charisma, an intensity. Something about her led Bennie to do foolish things. The witch had a kind of power that Bennie envied.

She watched the slow rise and fall of Motheater's shoulders, much more obvious up close. Bennie inhaled deeply, ash and a rich wooden scent, something earthen in her mouth. Motheater brought a smell like the trail before a storm, the mud on jeans, the mine shaft during inspection, as if it were on its best behavior, trying on a perfume. Bennie sighed and drifted off to sleep, cradled by the dark fragrance of Appalachia in early spring.

༄

Bennie woke up in the middle of the night, blinking slowly. She was still facing Motheater's back, her mouth full of the smell of sweet dirt, but as she slid into waking, she noticed something strange by Motheater's ear. She propped herself up on an elbow and wearily reached out to grab at the strange white cottontail.

She stared at her hand.

A moth.

The bug was delicate and white, something common that Bennie had seen a dozen times before, with brown spots and a shadow of yellow along the edge of its wings. Bennie pushed the comforter to her knees. Easy enough to release the insect outside.

Instead, as the comforter slid down, there was a soft and encompassing rustle. The duvet seemed to lift up, all at once, a living shroud. Moths swarmed around Bennie, and she screamed, ducking under the covers.

Next to her, Motheater shot up, clutching at Bennie's shoulder.

"It's all right," Motheater said, her voice muffled, rustling like the wings that surrounded her. Her accent was gentle, dropping the *t*'s, creating a river instead of a reassurance. Bennie shifted closer to Motheater, wrapping an arm around her back. Motheater's hand spread along Bennie's shoulder blade gently. "I promise, they're just here to talk."

"What is going on?" Bennie's voice was reedy as she squeezed Motheater's leg. She looked up, peeking around the comforter as Motheater sat up straighter. The moths were a Milky Way above them, soft silverine stars dotting the ceiling.

Bennie didn't know any of their names—fuzzy black ones, moths with big brown bodies and white wings. There was one that was yellow, another that looked like it was made of pink pipe cleaners. Many looked like little bits of gray bark, a whole tree stripped and given wings in her apartment. They were calm, a rising cloud at sunset.

Motheater lifted a hand, and one came down and settled in her palm, fluttering against her pale skin.

"Motheater?" Bennie was pressed up against Motheater's side, not at all calm. Motheater smiled and lifted her hands up, cupping them around the moth, holding it up to her ear. To Bennie, the sound of the moths fluttering sounded like a familiar voice in the choir, the kind of cadence wherein you could pick out your neighbor's lilt even through the chorused "hallelujah."

"Ah," Motheater murmured as she kept her hands to her ear. "It has been a very long time." She smiled and shook her hands, and the moth melted into a small puff of pollen, the barest impression of a set of wings floating like gauze in the air for barely a second.

Bennie's eyes were huge as Motheater looked down at her. "I'm not eating them."

It was almost reassuring. "Thank God."

"I'm going to absorb its soul and manifest its ancestral memories," Motheater said, as casually as if she had just asked Bennie to pass the table salt. Bennie nearly choked.

Motheater seemed unbothered as she observed the swarm that fluttered above them, a mnemonic storm cloud of wings. "They have waited a long time to speak to me."

"What does that even mean?" Bennie asked, voice breaking as she stared up at the hundreds of moths above them. This was terrifying.

"These are our family, in a way," Motheater said softly, staring at her hands, where a few more perched, a waiting congregation. Bennie stopped trying to count the bugs in her apartment, fixating on the little creatures that shuffled along Motheater's fingers. "Each moth carries a soul. When I lived . . . When I walked the long path, they came to me for confession, a final hearing before the glory. They whisper their stories, the bright, shining moments of their world. Some make demands or give warning."

Bennie's eyes went wide. Ghosts. Motheater was speaking to ghosts. If there was a way for her to talk to the dead, that was all the more reason to get Motheater on her side. Maybe Motheater could talk to her dead. She swallowed her fear, letting the bugs surround her. "You can talk to dead folks?"

Motheater paused, eyes still trained upward. "I'm only listening. I ain't no appropriator."

That didn't help, did it? Bennie took another deep, calming breath as Motheater shifted onto her knees, Bennie's arm dropping down from around her waist. In the dim light, Motheater tilted her head up and raised her hands, holding them just in front of her face.

As if they were invited to confess, the moths came down into her palms, fluttering in front of her mouth before fluttering past her ear, disappearing into her hair. They came down slowly and then in a rush, enveloping Motheater in a tempest.

Bennie slipped away from the witch, covering her eyes and trying her best not to freak out about the swarm that had found its way into her apartment. She wondered where they all came from, what seams were loose in between the walls, if they had found a rip in the window screens. Maybe they manifested like dew.

Careful not to touch any more of the moths than she needed, Bennie curled up on her chair, arms wrapped around her knees, watching Motheater with wide eyes.

Bennie could see the changes in the witch as she turned her head to each soul that lit on her hands, as she let them hold congress around her. They disappeared into a miasma, a strange shine around her head like a halo of moonlight. Bennie could just barely hear a rustle, but it was like listening in on a crowded theater, the hushed, low rumble of all the voices at intermission.

When Motheater finally opened her eyes again, Bennie could see that they weren't as black as they used to be, but had turned some kind of hazel, a kinder brown that no longer made her pupils look like coal. Her features were still smudged, but at least Motheater looked a little less gray. There were even some freckles and scars visible on her hands, along the outside of her forearms. Motheater hummed a tune

Bennie didn't recognize over the last of the moths and drew her hands through her hair.

As she moved her hands, the dusty memories floated above her, forming a crown and then a veil. Motheater smiled, gently tilting her head from side to side, swaying with the tune of her psalm. Her hair grew out like a waterfall under her hands, long and silver white, some brassy green tones coloring the ends like Spanish moss.

"Jesus." Bennie barely breathed. She was struck with wonder, with something like awe, something like want. There was a horrible ache in the pit of her stomach as she witnessed something unexplainable. A sinkhole, the tarot cards, it might have been explained away, but this? No, Bennie thought to herself, holding her knees closer, this was magic. Capital-M magic. It was a terrifying way for faith to make way for knowing.

Motheater looked down at her hands, the last of the moths' lives disappearing from her fingers. Bennie got the sense of an ending as the last of the shades reflecting moonlight disappeared from her room.

"Is that going to happen every night?" Bennie asked, tripping over the words. "Because I don't know if I can handle waking up to a million moths in my bed at two a.m."

Motheater smiled, shaking her head. "It might happen a few more times," she said, pulling her long silver hair over her shoulder and inspecting it. "I've been gone a while."

Her voice had changed. It was less highland, a little more modern. Taking on all those souls must have shifted Motheater's understanding. Bennie tried to come to terms with the change, the strangeness of hearing Motheater speak with such a familiar accent.

"A strange thing . . ." Motheater murmured. Her voice drifted, low as stone, round as a river. "These souls were sent along. More than waiting, they were saved."

"Are you like, haunted or something?" Bennie stood on

shaking legs, going to the kitchenette counter, never taking her eyes off Motheater. There was no indication that the moths had swarmed her apartment. No broken wings or left-over bodies. It was as if it had never happened.

"Not quite." Motheater shifted to lie down on the mattress, turning toward Bennie. "Those were the folks that died on the mountains."

Bennie stood up a little straighter, staring at Motheater.

"On Kire?" She tried to keep the hope out of her voice, but it still came out breathless and needy.

Motheater turned away from her, eyes on the window. She looked faraway. "Not just Kire." Motheater hesitated as Bennie poured herself a glass of water. "All along the ridge-line. A few down in the holler. Some from my old Kiron that found a moth and never let go. The angry ones. Old ones, further away. Buried alongside me. Kept for me."

Bennie stayed against the counter, sorting all this out, trying to reason with herself in the small hours. She licked her lips. She had to be careful.

"And they talk to you, right?"

Motheater was lying on her back, hands working the duvet like a cat. "Some do."

The silence between them was tense, and Bennie felt like she had stumbled into a very dark place. Potential hung in the air like a forgotten dream, delicate and full of hope.

"I need to find somebody."

Immediately, Motheater said, "I can't do that."

"Why not?" It came out quicker than Bennie expected. She didn't mean to snap, but eagerness pushed her on. Motheater wasn't moving, staring at the ceiling, her hair spread out like quicksilver on the bed.

"I ain't no fox, I ain't . . . I'm just . . ." She struggled to find the words, her hands fisted in the duvet. "I only listen to the moths. I can't call none up to hold court. I don't . . ."

Motheater, suddenly, looked very small to Bennie, floundering in the new epoch.

Bennie spoke quietly. "If I told you who I was looking for, could you . . ." She hesitated, trying to measure out exactly what she wanted. "Could you listen for them?"

In the dark room, lit only by the light that leaked in from the lamp outside, Bennie felt something breathe. She shivered, trying to feel the tips of her toes, her fingertips, all parts of herself she usually forgot about. She was here, she was whole.

Motheater turned to face the wall. "I can pay attention," she said quietly, almost defeated. "But to call up a spirit that's already passed on, that's a deep bargain I can't make no deal for."

"Can't" out of Motheater came out as something half-brogue, a "cannot" turned to a sweeter, lower sound, a valley river, a pronunciation like *kennae*. Bennie didn't want to push Motheater too far, didn't want to ask too much too soon. The witch wasn't saying that she couldn't talk to the dead, just that she couldn't control what they said. There was time. She could still get Motheater on her side. Bennie looked over at her map, at all the missing bodies, at all the lives that White Rock had taken, had ignored.

Maybe they were as angry as she was.

"All right," Bennie said, letting her anger simmer, letting her fear and rage mix together. Kelly-Anne deserved to be set right. All those people still working for White Rock deserved to be made safe. "All right, we'll talk more about it tomorrow."

Bennie felt some kind of guilt in her as Motheater stayed quiet. The poor woman had just been pulled out of the fucking mountain.

It struck Bennie, just then, that maybe, years ago, someone wanted to look for Motheater, too. What if she had been someone else's red dot? What if they were all alive, buried under there, waiting to be found? She curled over herself in the armchair, trying to stay calm.

What if Kelly-Anne was waiting for a rescue, hidden deep in the rock? She could be alive or dead—how was Bennie to know?

Motheater was silent, frowning at the wall. Bennie sighed, trying to figure out what to say, how to convince Motheater to help her. It would have to be tomorrow. Today, she had pushed too hard, asked too much. Bennie put her cup down on the counter and crouched down on the bed, next to the witch.

Motheater didn't move. Her hair was catching the reflection of the lamplight outside, almost glowing. Bennie must have been more exhausted than she realized, because she reached over and touched Motheater's hair, which had spread out like mercury on the pillow. It really was beautiful.

She was about to say something when an alarm sounded outside.

Motheater shot up, eyes wide, and Bennie quickly put a hand on her arm to reassure her.

"It's all right," Bennie said, looking out the window. "That's the mountain alarm."

"What does it mean?" Motheater frowned deeply as the siren faded in and out, louder and softer on loop.

"There's been a rockslide." Bennie licked her lips. It had been years. The last time there had been a slide . . . She didn't want to think about that, about what it might mean for her map. "We'll have to be careful on the roads tomorrow."

The klaxon could take an hour to go quiet. She pressed her hands over her eyes, groaning. "Fuck."

"Do we need to run off?" Motheater asked quietly, still sitting upright, looking out of the window toward the mountain's line, although it was too dark for her to see anything.

"We ain't near any faces, we'll be fine," Bennie said, the siren ringing in her ears.

A second later, a tremor ran through the building, a shudder that made Bennie squeak and grab at Motheater's wrist. The other woman was cold, but as soon as the shake happened, it ended.

"It's fine," Bennie said, markedly less composed. "Earthquakes happen near mine sites." She repeated this to herself, knowing that it was true, but that didn't make the jolt any less startling.

"Ain't the whole earth," Motheater muttered, turning to lie on her side, covering Bennie's hand with her own cool fingers. "Just the mountain trying to shake off the flesh perched on it."

Bennie took a deep breath, getting her breathing normal again. Earthquakes were rarer than rockslides, but the two could go together. "We can stay here," Bennie said, not quite convincing herself. "We're not on a fault."

A few minutes later, Motheater murmured, "How you know?"

"Saw the maps." Bennie turned a little to look at Motheater, taking in her hazel eyes, the green around the edges of her lips, the paleness of her eyebrows. She looked like a different woman than the half-drowned creature she had heaved up the banks of the creek. "Nothing here-on but bedrock and lime. We're safe."

"That's just what you saw. The mountain has deep roots. Deeper veins. It ain't pay a mind for bedrock," Motheater said. She shifted and turned away from Bennie, curling up like she couldn't stand to let any part of herself get away. "Always more out there to see."

Bennie stared at the map on the wall, at the stack of files, reports, and newspaper clippings she and Kelly-Anne had been collecting for over a year. Motheater was right. Bennie just had to figure out where to look.

Esther

After DeWitt left, Esther knew she didn't have much time. If Halberd was already sending young men to solicit her, hoping to woo her away from Kire with promises of fortune, their machines weren't far behind. Iron and steel wouldn't be convinced to turn around with some forest grammar.

Esther knew her strengths. She was a witch of the land, her power culled from offal and worship. She could not make demands of machines, nor pistons, nor rails, no matter how many picks the Kiron miners slammed into Kire and its siblings.

She would have to convene a hedge of witches, and she had no practice with conclave. She was the Neighbor of Kiron, but even among Neighbors, she was an oddity. With a neglectful father, no mother, and only the snakes to teach her magic during a childhood spent running wild in the forest, her cunning was wild, unchecked, soul-bound in a way few dared to approach. But farther north, near White Sulphur Springs, there was a famed elder Neighbor, learned and sure, and more than that, *respected*.

She didn't think twice about it; she needed help. If a conference could agree to turn back Halberd from Kiron, then the corporation wouldn't last two days in Kire's shadow.

It was a long walk north, and Esther had to make sure that all was prepared before she left.

In Kiron, there were many who called her Neighbor and few who called her friend. But there was Jasper. As she was getting ready for the day-and-a-half journey to the Spring, she found her steadfast companion chopping wood behind his cabin.

"Seen your uncle recently?" she asked, coming out of the woods like a shadow. "I like that man."

"Ah, go'n find him yourself." Jasper stood up straight. He was tall, with dark hair and dark eyes, and warm skin that came from his Iroquois father. His accent, lilting like a song, was from his Scottish mother, rest her soul. "He's gone west. Heading for Oklahoma."

"Only a matter of time. He never cared much for Kiron."

"He never cared for the people who settled here," Jasper said, setting up another log. "He didn't mind the mountains."

"Mm." Esther leaned against a tree, observing Jasper. He was a solid sort, the kind of boy she practiced holding hands with before she realized she couldn't share a bed with both magic and a man. Too many bargains made her a poor bedfellow. "I'm off north for a moment," she said, and that caught enough of his attention to get him to stop swinging that ax. He frowned as she continued. "I need to meet with a Neighbor in Sulphur Springs."

"Something happening?" Jasper set the head of his ax against the stump, his dark eyes meeting Esther's.

"Halberd's finally gotten their hands on some deeds," Esther said. She pressed her lips together tightly, biting back the words that would stick to her tongue like a burr. Jasper wasn't unfriendly with Halberd even in the worst of times. He might have even known they'd finalized mineral rights, signed on some paper made from pulp hauled out of another holler in another ridge. The hurt coated her throat like syrup. "The great machines have finally come to Kiron."

"Only a matter of time." Jasper pushed loose strands of his long hair back. "This won't be Kiron in a few years. It'll be Halberd Town. Or . . . what's the name of the headman? Maybe we'll be Keithsville."

"Kiron will stand as long as I do," Esther spat out fiercely. "But if Halberd has its machines primed, ready to plunder Kire bare, ain't long before they march all down the Allegheny and starve Appalachians of the only thing that keeps us safe and barely ahead of modernity."

"You think keeping our hands black keeps us from being eaten?" Jasper snorted. "Connecticut munitions won the war for Virginia's mountains, not men. Modernity is five hundred miles north and a century ahead of us."

Esther's face was hot. He was right, and she hated it. "Thought about this a lot, have you?" Esther's voice was quiet as he walked around to arrange the split wood in the drying rack.

"I read the papers," he muttered, sheepish.

That bashfulness was enough to remind her that he was still her friend and her strongest connection to the people of Kiron. He helped direct her gaze. Her head was in the sky, on blue jay wings. "Where you even get papers?" Esther teased.

As he hefted his ax on his shoulder, he shot Esther a look that was almost fond, but near enough to annoyed to persuade her not to laugh. They looked out for each other, folks both inside and out of favor, with few to share company with. Esther would never want to make Jasper angry, not truly. She smiled a little. "Just watch out for the town while I'm gone.

Them Halberd men ain't leaving fast. You have that bag I made you?"

A calling bag. It was small, made of squirrel leather with a black walnut inside. If the husk broke, Esther would know it.

He nodded. "You'll know if'n I need you."

Esther hummed as he set another cord up on the drying rack. "Halberd already sent one of their more witless errand boys up the mountain. We can't have the company's machines sent up, too."

"What's so wrong with Halberd coming in?" Jasper turned back to his work, setting another log on its end. "Bigger operation, bigger paychecks."

"Aye, and more blood spilled in the mountain, more danger," Esther said sharply. "More families in Kiron means we need to preserve more food every fall, and we're just barely keeping bellies full as is. And after that, authorities move in on top of more sharp picks biting into Kire, into South Peak, into Potts."

"And so what?" Jasper sighed, and Esther felt his resignation echoing through the clearing. They'd had this conversation before.

"I have made sharp bargains," Esther said, voice tight. "Kire will not suffer for the sake of Kiron."

"The mountain is fine," Jasper said, splitting another cord. As always, her dark implication fell on deaf ears. She set her jaw, resisting the urge to stamp her foot, to demand his attention. Jasper held a part of her heart, as sure as Kire did.

"And what of me?" She tried to keep the petulance out of her voice and hoped she came across as contrite instead. Jasper knew the bargains she made; what would happen when they were broken by Halberd?

Jasper split the log in two. He shrugged. "You've proven yourself resourceful."

"During harsh winters, in the face of unknown disease. I can sing up water, I can call on the earth to yield a good harvest and full traps." Esther paused, feeling the weight of it, the extent of her traded powers. She had so many boundaries, even soul-bound as she was. "I cannot turn back an industry."

"Looks like you'll be tested, then." Jasper leaned against the shaft of the ax and smiled at her in a way that made her both furious and cleaved her breath clean from her lungs.

"Weather the town for me," she chirped, pushing down her anger. These days, Jasper dismissed her so easily. The distance between them was growing, and Esther didn't want to risk dividing them further with a cross word. "Read your papers, note any movements, and—" Esther hesitated, pausing at the edge of Jasper's copse. "Keep an eye on my father."

"He hates Halberd as much as you do." Jasper raised his voice, as if Esther couldn't hear him miles away. "You'd do well to speak with him."

Esther rested her hand on one of the trees. There were small holes where bugs had burrowed in—a sprig where a branch would be in a few years. She didn't want to talk to her father, or talk to Jasper about him. "I don't mind change, honest. I just don't want Halberd near Kire."

Kire was a dark place, deep and hungry. Already, she bargained in blood and worship to support the trickle of town miners picking away at its veins. A century was nothing to a mountain, but with the Halberd machines, the drawing of coal would be so full insistent that even Kire would notice it was being bled out. A death by a thousand needles was still a death.

For now, Kire bore the hewing for the sake of the same brutal bargains ancients made to gods on petrified altars. But Esther was one supplicant. The mountain would not suffer miners forever.

Jasper's pained look didn't tell Esther everything, but it reassured her slightly. He knew Kire, too. "I won't be gone a week," she said, turning into the woods. "Hail if you have need."

"Good luck, witch," Jasper called to her retreating back. "Bring me back a new jacket."

༄

The first night of the two-day hike to White Sulphur Springs, Esther camped out against a large oak, wrapped in blankets of leaves and moss. The way to the town was a near line north, with a heading touching west through some lower Allegheny valleys. As she slept, stones gathered at her feet like lost kittens. She sorted through them when she woke, choosing a couple chipped pieces of quartz and sliding them into her pocket.

She shook off the leaves and saw a few moths had found her in the night. She didn't have time to properly attend to them, so she whispered directions to find her cabin and invited them to rest on the fireboard there until she returned.

One of the moths refused to go, and she tucked it in her dark hair, against her ear, so it could speak to her as she traveled. The soul had a lot to say, speaking to the witch about his learning, the books he had read, the classes he took, one more question, always. Esther let the soul confess as she trekked down into the valley next to Sulphur Springs. It was rather peculiar; the newly renamed Methodist university a few counties over didn't have the kind of lessons that this soul related: plays on campus, a banking school, even classes on law.

This was a student from much farther north than her usual chthonic visitors. He was far from yard and dorm; what led him here? What was a soul from Charlottesville doing seeking out the Kiron witch?

She paused as she reached the top of Khates Mountain, looking down on Sulphur Springs. She had been a young child the last time she had been here—not yet a witch but learning to speak between snake and gospel—and the town looked vastly different now. It was almost a city. From her vantage point, she could see paved roads laid straight by buildings. Even the Greenbrier in the distance, a fancy resort for men of means, had been given a new coat of paint. It shone like a waterfall against the august, persimmon-colored trees.

With the sun at her back, Esther reached out to the land. She could feel the hum of the stone, the wold leading to the valley, the trees with roots cracking rock all around her, but there was a sour taste. Bitter, like an oversteeped herb. There was a loss here that was unlike the ridge she walked in her minding; Kire down southwest, Huckleberry, Sarton, White Rock Mountain.

Out here? Khates, Dameron Mountain northward, Roaring Peak just after. It felt wandering, spread out, like there wasn't enough of it to piece together on a map. Where had the worship gone? Where did the witch of Sulphur Springs keep her powers?

The Charlottesville soul would have to wait. Esther's hands tightened along her walking staff, taking in the sight of this modern town, so different from Kiron. She felt a little lost, despite seeing the land laid out clear. A train rumbled in the distance as she walked down. How was the Dandelion Witch keeping the old ways in a place like this, so enmeshed in coin and the upkeep of a tamed countryside? The moth was silent, Esther's thoughts louder than his soul.

Esther resolved herself and continued down Khates Mountain, the sounds of a Chesapeake train running through the mountain.

꿍

Esther found the Dandelion Witch in a townhouse near the center of town, her sign of five flowers entwined like a crown engraved above her door, painted in delicate egg-yolk yellow and eggshell white. It was a beautiful home, made of brick, with small, fussy-looking shrubberies out front that Ester didn't recognize from any hillside. Who imported plants while surrounded by nature? The Dandelion Witch must be getting rich and stupid on lowland money. Esther schooled her expression, drew her paisley shawl tighter around her shoulders, and knocked on the door with the knob of her walking stick.

It was not Permila who answered the door but a young man, dressed like a servant. He looked Esther up and down slowly, and Esther narrowed her eyes, having no desire to attempt to impress this hired hand. She knew she had leaves at her hem, a moth in her hair. This was what a wild Appalachian witch looked like. This is how a highland Neighbor appeared.

Her self-righteousness could have flooded the whole valley.

"Who calls?" he asked, and it was only his age that saved him from being turned out into the street and eaten by the cobbles.

"Esther of the Church of the Rock," she said, not dampening the accent that made her hick, her "rock" sounding like a cut of meat. She didn't offer anything else, and the boy was clearly expecting an explanation, a malady or woe or sob to accompany the introduction. She kept her gaze steady, and he, apparently unused to so hard an individual, bowed quickly and retreated.

Two minutes later, Permila herself ushered Esther in, sending the boy scurrying into the kitchen to prepare tea.

"Take a seat, Esther," Permila said, graciously offering her a seat on a chintzy lounge chair that probably came from Boston. Esther felt like her skin was peeling off her bones. She knew that she was a different kind of Neighbor, bargaining with Kire itself rather than plant and poultice, but she could rare remember a time she felt so wrong.

"I'll stand," she said, voice tight. "It seems clear I won't be staying long."

Permila's shift was plain, but tight-laced in a way that Esther knew required another set of hands. The scarf that covered her shoulders was silk, with tassels that were likely woven by some infernal machine. The threat of industry became loud in Esther's ears, the sudden shudder of the promise of comfort. What luxuries would her town have? What silks would come to Kiron?

"Now, what makes you say that, Esther?" Permila asked, settling on a chaise and pouring them both tea when the young man came in with a tray. "We have much to catch up on. Your letters are quite plain."

Esther glared at the servant as he left and then took a deep breath, steadying herself. Permila was an older Neighbor, someone proper, respected. She should have answers to Esther's problems. Then, like being stung by an insect, Esther felt wronged. Permila should have more than just answers for her. She should have help ready. She should be *prepared*.

There was no time for subtlety. Esther quashed her nerves. Wasn't she the Witch of the Ridge? Didn't she stand level with any Neighbor now? "I wish to summon a conclave."

"A conclave?" Permila frowned as she sipped her tea. "What need have you—"

"There is a great need," Esther snapped, her frustration rushing from her mouth. "Another war looms on the horizon, one that threatens our mountain folk. The machines are moving in, and the whole of Appalachia must turn on them."

Permila sipped her tea, taking her time. "You cast aspersions where many have cast their lots," she said firmly.

"What dark fuels that train, Permila?" Esther hissed, flushing red. "Dreams of a United States that touches two oceans? Continentalism? The Republicans would have you believe that all progress is good progress, but it comes at the cost of our souls, our culture."

"Shining and picking is culture now?" Permila asked archly, her voice tight. "Kiron doesn't have a single paved road to its name, and you're worried about progress?" She lowered her slim, swanlike neck to her china cup, and Esther gripped her roughstaff tighter. Embarrassed and furious, she struggled for words, and Permila took advantage. "You, Esther Ring-Neck, little moth-eater, are afraid of losing your influence. You fear the promise of change. It will doom you. Your reputation as a mad magician in the forest will not serve a Kiron with machine money flowing through it."

"That is not true, and that is not why I'm here." Esther could hear how childish she sounded, how flat her voice rang out. Permila wasn't wrong, but she wasn't right, either. And the insults. Ring-neck, moth-eater. Permila meant to tie her to snake and bug, sin and annoyance.

"When electricity lights the streets, who will they ask to interpret the shadows? When maladies strike your flock, they will go to the learned doctor, and not their Neighbor." Permila shrugged. "What will you do when Kiron's worry is for itself and not its mountain? You have made a poor pact, and now you want the whole Appalachia to align for you? You have no bearing."

Esther allowed Permila space to level her. Her discomfort was shed like dry skin, replaced by a deep-seated resentment. Even among people who would be her peers, Esther wasn't an equal. She was nothing more than a wildling mountain witch, young and feckless.

"Y'all have ingratiated into the auspices of a sorry people," Esther said, still trying to find venom and holding only vinegar. "Beholden to ill folk."

"Ill folk that pay me with money enough to afford comfort. Industry is not a thing you can turn back at the pass; it is an inevitability. Like the rest of us, you must adapt or perish, Esther." Permila snorted, looking up sharply. "Something you might be more kind on if you weren't so tied to upkeeping your mystery, living in cove and hollow."

There was some truth there, too. But Esther would be damned twice before letting Permila, wrapped in silk and nibbling soft scones, belittle her for wanting a bit of story attached to her name. Esther was kept safe by the stories people told about her.

"When was the last time you went up Dameron?" Esther spoke quietly, her hands tight around the walking stick, hard knuckles pale. "Nor Khates, nor Roaring Peak? Have you left the ramp and sang all wild?"

"Don't you lecture me." Permila stood up.

"Nay, neither you vilipend what I hold dear," Esther hissed.

The fire in the drawing room had gone out. The two witches stood across from each other, their magic filling the air. Esther had laid out hard accusations. Now she understood the emptiness she felt on Khates; Permila had sold her soul and soil to the machines. So be it.

If the Dandelion Witch would shirk her duties, Kire's witch would collect.

Permila crooked her fingers and whispered a low hex. Esther felt the rough edges of her staff dig into her palm.

"For respect, I will give you one chance to leave me," Permila uttered slowly, the room echoing with her power.

The Dandelion Witch was on her home territory, and Esther knew that she would be hard-pressed to fight another Neighbor when she was a guest, barely invited.

But what made a guest? Had she been invited by Permila or drawn here along a coal vein? What had pushed her to the place, this land of plenty, this lily in the valley? She was the one who had breathed in loam and log. She ushered the souls of Khates across. She was the witch. She opened the door of herself and let the mountains in.

Like dusk, Esther felt it, dark and open, a maw beneath her. In her hands, access to the power that Permila had neglected. Was this Permila's territory, or was it the mountain's land, and they two merely overseers? Perhaps the old rumors were passed along just to keep Esther bound to a small place. The two women stared at each other, and Esther bowed her head slightly. Permila relaxed, smiling, and took a step back.

"Andre will see you out."

Esther's eyes shot up to meet Permila's, and the Dandelion Witch flinched. Esther tapped the vein of Khates and felt its derision flow through her, so familiar that she knew its shape against her. Permila was no longer a soul-bound witch. But Esther was. She would barter soul and skin for power.

Hurt and hope mixed in Esther's wrists, pulsed into her hands, and Esther dragged her palms down the walking staff, tearing her skin open. She spread her bloody hands, and the walking stick shattered into a thousand slivers of the forest, imbued with betrayal.

Permila stumbled backward, loosing her hex and shattering the chaise, cotton and down covering her dress. As Esther's splinters pierced the beams and balance of the house, they struck like a finch's beak into soft wood, carrying Esther's truth to the core of her work. Permila's eyes were wide as Esther dripped blood and power onto the carpet.

"I leave you here, carrying your own work, unfinished, on my back," Esther cursed. This was never Permila's land. It was never hers, either. She was a conduit, a river, a vein. "I traveled your land, Permila Tschida, and found loss. I claim these souls as mountain angary, and remove you from your post."

"You have no right," Permila gasped. "I am the Dandelion Witch, I am—"

"You have turned into a simpering cur, dark-mouthed and lapping at the politician's ring, begging. *As a dog returneth to his vomit, so a fool returneth to his folly.*" As she spoke, Esther's words carried, and a dark stain appeared around Permila's lips, as if she had bit on blackberries. Esther felt Kire, even here. She called on Khates to aid her, the shards of quartz she collected in the dawn light digging into her palms, floating out of her pockets to embed themselves as loci in her hands.

"Leave!" Permila cried, and her words still held power. Esther was forced back to the foyer, losing her footing, slamming into the wall. She bared her teeth at Permila and spun, driving one of the chips of Khates's quartz into the door with her bare hand, shattering the crystal and sending the shards into her palm. The door flew off its hinges, far faster than Esther intended, and she tumbled into the street, hair out of her ribbon, dress hem in tatters. She stood up slowly and took a few steps away from the witch's house, into the cobblestone street. A carriage veered out of her way, and Esther shot the horse a look so wolfish that it reared up behind her, despite the jockeys' taming.

Esther dripped blood from her fingertips as she strode from Sulphur Springs, back toward the mountains. She had more pride than to waste her time further, even as Permila ran after her. Esther was the mountain's, and Permila was just another Neighbor.

"You have taken nothing from me, Esther Moth-Eater! Adder-tongue! Esther, queen of dead leaves!" Permila yelled from her doorway, her formality lost, even as she drew an audience. She wasn't completely wrong; she still had hedge, and that was enough to keep her body in fine clothes and her hand reaching for dessert trays. "Industry will come to your decrepit coal town! You cannot fight the future!"

"I will not fight it," Esther called out, her back arrogantly toward Permila as she stalked away, annoyed and frustrated. Her words echoed around her like pollen released from a flower, thick and cloying. "I will destroy it!"

8

Bennie

Bennie woke up and, in some kind of early-morning haze, reached for last night's cold tea and took a sip. The regret was immediate.

"Oh," she muttered. "Fuck. Gross."

She looked over at Motheater and saw that she was sitting up, back against the wall, her feet tucked under the covers. In the morning light, Motheater's hair shone a dull silver and soft mint, a gray that resembled stones with lichen. She was staring at the map across the room.

"Morning," Bennie muttered, sliding out from under the covers. "Nice hair."

"Morning," Motheater murmured as Bennie disappeared into the bathroom.

When she came out, Motheater was braiding her Spanish moss-colored hair, a slow twist in a six-strand plait pattern that Bennie was sure she couldn't replicate. She poured her tea out and put the kettle back on for coffee.

"There's a library in town," Bennie said. "If you're from Kiron back in the day, that's the place that'll have history."

"Library how you found all those?" Motheater asked, pointing at the map pinned on the wall, at the many red dots, more than two dozen now. Bennie hadn't been sure earlier, but Motheater's accent was definitely more modern now. Something had changed.

"Most of them," Bennie said tightly. "And I was part of health and safety procedures at White Rock. Had access to a lot of records before I left."

The position was a bastardized twist on her social services degree, and she had been let go before she could get all the details she needed to nail White Rock for any legit safety breach. "Let go" was a nice way to say "fired under suspicion of breaching company confidentiality contracts," but who was checking?

The fact that she had been a part of the safety team was something that haunted her. She knew that White Rock was killing folks, and she still wasn't able to prevent people from dying. Could she have saved even one of these miners? She lingered over Kelly-Anne's dot, responsibility fixing her gaze.

"Well, Black folk have always been miners," Motheater said. Bennie's eyebrows went way up. "And if White Rock is employing the whole town, I suppose they'd hire anyone."

"What's that got to do with anything?"

"Nothing," Motheater said nonchalantly, as if she hadn't just bordered on insult. "When . . . hm." She paused, frowning.

Bennie waited. She would still turn out a racist witch, even if Motheater was the only new avenue toward taking down White Rock she'd found in months.

"There have been other mining companies in Kiron," Motheater said, her brow wrinkled. "Some didn't hire freemen, or women. I think . . . I was worried about that, when I was . . ."

79

Bennie's heart raced. Motheater was remembering. Maybe it was the moths from last night, maybe it was something else, but it was a good thing.

"When you were what?" Bennie asked, sipping her instant coffee and making a face. It was never that good. Her mother never taught her the secret to making it taste mild and sweet. Honey? Sugar? Tea leaves stirred in at the end? Bennie resigned herself to shitty, cheap coffee.

"I was gonna say 'alive,'" Motheater said, almost rueful.

Bennie made a noise that Kelly-Anne would have described as "unladylike" before she repeated it herself, louder and lewder.

The pause lingered in the air, heavy and damp. Bennie put aside her coffee. "Last night you said that the moths spoke to you."

Motheater nodded. She looked small, a grown woman stripped down to bones and sinew. Bennie gripped the counter behind her, keeping her hands from shaking.

"They tell you what happened in that mountain?"

Motheater shrugged. "I had miners from all along the ridge last night. Hundreds of folks have mountains for gravestones."

"So is it White Rock killing them or something else?"

"That ain't how they talk," Motheater said, frowning.

"One of my friends died in Kire because White Rock ignored the accidents," Bennie said, mouth souring. Was this how she spoke about her best friend? The one who showed her how to strip sassafras, how to cuss in Appalachian, how to word cookout invites so everyone knew they were supposed to bring food to share?

Bennie's voice turned hard and bitter, caught in her throat like a burr. "They couldn't even admit that they were at all responsible. Her parents worked for White Rock, too, but the company let them go after Kelly-Anne died."

She saw something shift in Motheater's face. The lines hardened suddenly, and the blurriness around her fell away. She came into focus, sharpened by a hatred that Bennie could feel.

Here it was. Here was how she got a witch of old Appalachia on her side.

"If we can find the body of someone killed in the mines, we can nail White Rock with any number of lawsuits and injunctions. We can stop the work on Kire. We can prevent anyone else from dying." Bennie knew her voice was cracking. Zach was in that damn mountain. Her friends were in that damn mountain.

Motheater nodded slowly. "I dunno about finding a body. The mountain don't give up the dead. But you're right. We need to get people out of Kire."

"You said the moths speak to you," Bennie insisted. "Surely they can tell you where their bodies are."

"No," Motheater said, her eyes fixed.

She held her mug tighter, something eager and aching in her. If Motheater was truly communicating with the Appalachian dead, with people like Kelly-Anne, that was something. It wasn't just a time and a place, it was memory. It was detail.

If Motheater had the right soul, it could spell damnation for White Rock, once and for all, before anybody else had to die in Kire's labyrinth. Bennie pressed hope down like mash in a sill.

"When they come to me, they're all changed up. There's new names, new things. I can't sort much of it," Motheater said. "Sometimes they call out hope or leftover fear. They share moments that mattered, sometimes fixations . . ." She paused.

"What do they say to you?" Bennie's voice was hard.

Motheater frowned, looking up at Bennie. She made a dismissive gesture, and Bennie was overcome by a need to know more, to dive into what the souls delivered into Motheater's hands. "Please," Bennie pleaded, breath hitching, "I need to know."

"They say goodbye, Bennie," Motheater admitted. "Most do just that and pass."

"You have to be able to get more than that!" Bennie snapped. "Motheater, if you can talk to the dead, you can find a way to connect their deaths to White Rock! We can . . . we can figure out where they are in the mountain, request an OSHA team, pause mining ops, give the union real proof to shutter the damn place—"

"The dead don't want to talk about death," Motheater said quietly, and Bennie almost missed her talking, her voice was so low. Bennie pushed down her anger, seeing the look on Motheater's face, soft and mournful. "It ain't no blessing. It's a haunting, Bennie. I made my body a graveyard. They know they can't stay. They know, and . . . then I know . . ."

Motheater looked confused again, pained and hurt, but kept talking. "Did you know that two kids were murdered behind the public school?" she asked, glaring at Bennie. "That y'all built your post office over the last of the Iroquois longhouses? How many men died with dust in their lungs, coughing away their last breaths, curled in pain, blood on the pillow? You know that three miners spent nearly four days dying because of an equipment failure—that's what they said, 'equipment failure'—their bones still caught in the teeth of the mountain, even now?"

Bennie's eyes went wide.

"There's more, Bennie," Motheater said, and now Bennie knew she was just being cruel, that she was a vicious and wild thing, a starving coyote in the mountains. "People here dying 'cause of bad medicine. Little devils in their veins. Using needles to prick into their arms and toes and giving themselves too much leeway with plant and herb."

"There are programs—"

"Programs let people die, foaming at the mouth, forgetting how to breathe. And I'm trapped in the last hours of their lives, and all I feel is scared and confused, and Bennie, reliving death is hard enough, I don't want to speak on it, too!" Her voice cracked.

Bennie's hope gave way to a broken, overwhelming sadness. What would it be like to listen to all of Appalachia in their last moments?

Bennie let her coffee mug slip from her hands, the ceramic shattering on the floor. "Shit," she murmured, trying not to cry. "God, sorry."

This was so much. She felt her shoulders hunching up, something big and empty rising inside her, and was about to excuse herself to the bathroom when she felt Motheater's hands on hers.

"You're gonna cut yourself," Bennie murmured, hurt and aching, as if the weight of the mountain had passed from Motheater's shoulders to hers. She just wanted to go back to sleep; she wanted to close the windows and pretend like she was in some faraway hotel room, in some distant city, where nobody could even pronounce Appalachia without stuttering over its lows and rises.

"I'm sorry I raised my voice. Ain't a kind thing," Motheater murmured. "And you helpin' me out and all."

Bennie squeezed Motheater's hands. She took a deep breath, in control, not going to cry now. This struggle against White Rock had cost Bennie her job, her home, her relationship. She didn't have anything else to give.

"You said . . ." Bennie focused on Motheater's hazel eyes. She still held Motheater's hands in hers, and she didn't want to let go, her heart stuttering, as the witch rubbed her thumbs over Bennie's hand. "You said that the mining companies were in . . . your time, whenever that was."

"Aye, just coming into Kiron. Dates are fuzzy, but that's near enough to the year I disappeared from the mountain."

"And you wanted to stop them."

Motheater nodded.

Bennie squeezed her hands. "Help me stop them now."

Motheater paused for a second, as if measuring what Bennie wanted against her own memory. Finally, the witch nodded. Bennie felt hope rising in her again. Motheater wanted to stop industry, Bennie wanted people to be safe. It was easy to align herself with the strange witch for now.

Motheater turned to look over her shoulder, out the small window, toward Kire. Bennie followed her line of sight. The view was partially blocked by a fraternal order's meetinghouse, but there it was, taking up most of the sky, huge, looming, an ever-present threat over the town of Kiron.

"We best move quick," Motheater said, darkly. "With Kire untended, we might not have much time."

9

Esther

"Is there a reason you've taken up in my cabin?" Esther asked Jasper, glaring at him as she took off her traveling shawl. It had gathered more memories than dust and would need a proper wash before it was presentable.

Jasper, for his part, did his best to look contrite as he stood and went over to her, giving her a fierce hug.

"It's been near on two weeks," he said, pulling back. She pursed her mouth and brushed at her jacket.

"Problems rose up." And she had to secure deals on Permila's wayward mountains. Had to keep her grace and gravity if she planned to stand alone.

"Aye, and not only on your walkabout."

Esther looked up sharply. "What happened?"

"Halberd set up a campsite west of the Kiron holler, near Hatfield," Jasper explained. His father was a part of the town council, and Jasper heard Kiron's news far sooner than Esther ever did. "Already got three operatives there, and they're scouting more land. Starting to tap into Huckleberry and Sarton."

Esther tried not to panic. It was happening too fast. Neither Huckleberry Hill nor the Sarton Ridge had a town established near, and it was obvious Halberd was going to use Kiron as a base of operations for a massive industrial push. If they got a tent town set up already, it wasn't going to be long before someone else came to the miner's collective and offered to buy them out. Small picks replaced by drills, by machines of industry as deadly as the war. They learned their trade from bloodletting and wouldn't pause to keep Kiron's vein open to tap Kire's.

And she didn't have a conclave. There were no mountain Neighbors to aid her. Industry felt too big to turn back now.

"Nobody can help," Esther muttered, venomous. "The spring-witch has turned to simpering at Greenbrier's hand."

"There are others of you," Jasper said quietly, holding onto her shoulders.

"None who would help me," she said bitterly. She had only been to two other towns, but none of the Neighbors she sought out had the range of Permila, and they had their own problems to deal with. "They're neighborly. Kind to all. A witch that ain't got a deep calling ain't gonna fight this." She stepped back, but his hands stayed on her shoulders. "Witches were chased off during the war, or moved north, or were killed, or died without passing on their cunning."

Jasper frowned, his hands tightened. She saw the disbelief in his eyes. "What does that mean?"

"I went to the Spring and found the witch wanting. I went up Dameron and found no kindness there. I sought the nightjar and blue jay and came across only empty nests."

"Do they have to be witches?" Jasper asked.

She pushed his hands away, going to the fire and feeding it a few more logs. "Don't ask that."

"Why not?" Jasper followed her. "I hold no love for Halberd—"

"Nor this town, nor your father, nor kith nor kin, nor nobody but me, and that's only when the shine strikes." Esther spoke bitterly, and regretted it just as soon as the words fell out. Jasper's face hardened, and she groaned, shame filling her up.

"I'm sorry," she muttered, crouching down, breathing in the smoke. "I haven't slept. I'm unkind and mean company."

"You're mean company even after you've slept." Jasper crossed his arms, voice tight.

"Aye, and that," Esther admitted. "I can't ask you to make a deal."

"Well you haven't asked, and I've offered."

"You don't want to suffer Kire." Esther shifted to kneel down. She stared at the fire as it burned through the dark logs. "You don't want to be made like me."

Jasper sighed, walking to crouch down next to her. He touched her shoulder gently. "We can still control this."

Esther groaned, putting her face in her hands again, feeling herself get too close to the fire, her hands burning, the hair along her arms singeing in the heat. She could smell the must off the logs, the sharp sweat-and-sulfur tang of Jasper, the dark, chemical odor of coal on his boots.

The warmth turned to burning.

"*A friend loveth at all times, and a brother is born for adversity.*"

"That's the spirit," Jasper said. "A good proverb for a needy moment."

"You're patronizing me," Esther said, dropping her hands. She saw the fire turn in on itself, creating a ball of white heat in the hearth.

"You do love scripture." Jasper sighed.

"I am the witch of Endor," Esther murmured. "Whose wise counsel both fools and learned men seek."

"Prophesy all you want, it's clearly comforting." He went to the door, found his own jacket hung up, and slid it over his shoulders. Esther knew that he wouldn't want to be here to see this, but he couldn't leave without a final word of warning. "Scripture alone won't stop Halberd. And it won't bring you the aid you sought out when you went to Sulphur Springs."

Esther was still kneeling, glaring at the white flames. She reached her hand into the hearth and took the fire out, cradling it in her hands like water threatening to spill from in between fingers. Jasper paused at the door.

"If you're so worried about Kire, shouldn't you save your spells?"

"It's a different sort of thing," Esther muttered, focusing on the fire spread along her fingers. It burned her, blisters bubbling to the surface of her skin. She blew on the white heat, and in her breath, dark fire-adders came to life, sliding down her hands and pooling on the ground, black and glowing at the eyes and in between their scales. She passed a hand over the three snakes, giving them a purpose, and then, grimacing, clenched her hands, bursting the blisters and dripping fluid onto the adders.

Behind her, Jasper made a noise that might have been worry or disgust, but she was too focused to parse through what it meant. He rarely stayed for her magic. Let him bear witness now.

"*There shall be no reward given unto the evil men.*" Her voice carried over the snakes, and they writhed, scurrying into the hearth again and disappearing into the ashes. "*The candle of the wicked shall be put out.*"

The fire went out along with the snakes, the logs crumbling under the weight of her spell. She clutched her hands to her chest, the pain washing over her in waves, pulsing from the points along her hands. She looked around for water and saw Jasper was already near, holding the bowl out to her.

"You're a fool to fight like this, Esther."

Esther blinked rapidly, tears falling. "I'm a witch. What can I do but this?"

She dipped her hands into the water, steam rising from her skin. She gasped and turned her face into her shoulder, trying to push the tears off her face. Jasper sighed, set the bowl down, and wiped her tears away. They stared at each other for a few seconds, until Esther hiccupped and ducked her head. This wasn't the lowest Jasper had seen her. She had done worse before him.

"Go talk to your father," Jasper said, pulling out his hand-kerchief and passing it over her face one more time before going to the door.

"He'd rather I were dead."

"Aye, but you can't fight Halberd alone, and I won't be trading favors for your fancy if you're gonna be stubborn about it."

She didn't respond, and Jasper slipped out of her cabin. As he walked away, Esther set her jaw and closed her eyes, feeling for her flame-bred serpents, sent to watch and wait, her heart traveling along the coal veins toward Hatfield.

10

Bennie

Motheater's cryptic warning rattled in Bennie's head all the way to the library. She had asked what the witch had meant—not much time for what?—but hadn't gotten much of an answer. Motheater seemed to be having a hard time with the hundreds of lives she had shepherded in the night, staying quiet for most of the drive into Kiron except when she suddenly asked Bennie about the number of states in the union and whether or not planes were real.

"Thank God," Bennie murmured as they pulled up to the library, all too happy to stop fielding questions from Motheater about television, which was, for the record, not going great. There were only a few cars in the lot, typical for a Thursday.

"So when you said that we didn't have much time," Bennie said, opening the door for Motheater, "can you be a little more specific?"

Motheater followed her up the steps, pausing to read over the bulletin board on the inside foyer. "Kire won't suffer miners much longer."

"Is that like a promise, or . . ."

"Kire's an Appalachian mountain," Motheater muttered, eyes huge as she looked around the library. "A mountain with a witch. As sure as I'm breathing, Kire is, too."

"You're talking about it like it's alive," Bennie joked, heading back to the local history section. She had been to enough meetings about the EPA and enough protests against the pipelines that she wasn't surprised that some of the more flowery rhetoric had dripped into Motheater's memories. People had been fighting for land rights as long as there was land to hurt.

"It *is* alive," Motheater said, frowning slightly, walking next to Bennie, focused on her with an intensity that was bordering on burning.

Bennie pursed her mouth. "What do you mean, alive? It's a mountain?"

"I mean it's got a heart and blood and a body," Motheater insisted, as Bennie led her through the library. "I mean it's a god, with its own mind. Kire is a titan."

Bennie tasted sour apples as they passed dusty stacks, heading to the back corner. There was a large bay window nestled back here, the glass so old that it warped the view outside. Past the playground, Kire rose in the distance, obscuring most of the sky, a massive thing. Already there were scars on the mountain where shears had been driven down, bare scrapes that indicated the company roads.

"That's impossible," Bennie said firmly, looking over the books and not at Motheater at all. "We've got tools to measure all sorts of stuff. Like vibrations, and stone makeup, and even where the cleavages are. White Rock basically has an X-ray of that mountain, peak to pound. Ain't nothing living about stone and coal."

"Y'all missed me," Motheater said, voice sharp like a shrike. "You going to say you know everything about this world?"

Bennie took a deep breath, frustrated. What was the use in arguing with Motheater? It was like talking to a wall. But hadn't Motheater come out of the mountain itself? Hadn't she done incredible, unexplainable things? Panic, fear, even a gnawing horror came up. She was willing to accept that Motheater was a witch, an Appalachian Neighbor (she had done a quick internet search this morning) who could do some parlor tricks and command bugs—but saying that the mountain was literally alive? Bennie had to become a skeptic again somewhere down the line.

Motheater stood beside Bennie, looking up at the books.

"Maybe all this learning is what's hurt y'all," she said, touching one of the spines. "Ain't thinking outside."

"That's . . ." Bennie trailed off. It was a ridiculous thing to say. But maybe there was something to it.

"You were taken out of the mountain," she said slowly. "So maybe to get the rest of you back, we have to go back to the mountain."

Motheater's eyes widened.

"Aye."

"Where did you live on Kire?" Bennie asked, going to the bay window and looking up at it. "Do you remember?"

"I don't know the mountain like I used to. I need my name, my bargains, my power."

Bennie pulled out her phone. She had a few texts from a couple friends, and one from Zach that just read "not at work today."

Could he help her? Bennie pushed the thought down fast. He didn't want to be a part of her investigation then, so she wouldn't force him into this one now.

"All right, we need a map. An old one." Bennie went to the opposite side of the room, and then around another corner, finding the cabinet. Motheater followed like a puppy as Bennie searched through the table, pulling out maps of the

Appalachians and Allegheny. After a few minutes, Bennie found the atlas she wanted, a reproduction of an old mining company's shafts into Kire, and moved south into the other mountains that were neighboring: Sarton, Butts, Forks, and Huckleberry.

She and Kelly-Anne had spent hours—days, even—poring over these maps during the year and a half that they had spent obsessively researching the underground pathways that snaked, labyrinthine, through these mountains. They had compared the incident reports that Bennie had managed to take photos of with the tunnels they knew. Bennie even had a whole notebook full of conversations she'd had with miners who had been next to their colleagues when they had, quite literally, disappeared.

Kelly-Anne didn't think much of this detail when Bennie related it to her. The mines had dark places, and the claustrophobia made shapes appear in the shadows. Folks said that fear made them see things. That it was memory playing tricks. Bennie had put it aside, recording the testimony as impression rather than fact. *But . . . what if it were true?*

Bennie's mouth went dry. The memory of the dead leaves trying to pull her into the loam came back fresh, acrid and sharp like sour incense. She didn't look at Motheater as she gathered the maps in her arms.

"Here—" Bennie brought the maps to the table, spreading them out. She could figure out Motheater and work to get the miners out of Kire. "This is one of the earliest prospecting maps. Done by a company back in the early 1900s." The small label at the bottom read "Ackerman O&M." The rights to the mountain had changed hands five times since Ackerman, passed down through different holding companies and mining collectives until White Rock took over in the nineties. That was when people started dying.

Motheater leaned over it, spreading her hands on the map. She pointed at the southern side of Kire.

"Ain't nothing here."

"Yeah . . ." Bennie frowned a little, tilting her head. "Maybe the ore isn't as clear on that side of the mountain."

"So they weren't digging there?"

"No." Bennie paused and shuffled through the maps. She laid out one from the forties (courtesy of Hatfield Collective Mining Industries) and then another drawn up in the seventies from Virginia Coal. She spread them out on the table. "Look, none of these older companies ever dug into the southern side. Or any of Kire, really."

"That's why the miners didn't disappear," Motheater muttered. "Kire couldn't reach into Huckleberry."

Bennie chose to ignore that. "White Rock has only been working the northern face of Kire," she said, looking at Motheater, who was frowning so deep her face might split in two. "The south face was too close to Kiron. They told us it was a safety risk. I always assumed it had already been bore out . . . but it was never tapped at all."

"Where you pick me out of the river?" Motheater said, voice hard.

Bennie found the most recent map—not up-to-date, but accurate enough to have White Rock Creek clearly labeled. "Here."

Motheater's finger traced the creek up, curling around the side of Kire that faced the town, and then moving north, around Kire.

"The exploratory veins," Bennie breathed, eyes widening. That's what Zach had been working on. "White Rock is digging into the southern ore from the bores they already made on the north. They won't have to dig any on the southern side at all. We got tech that will just let us go right through."

"That's why all this is happening now, why they found me now!" Motheater cried out. Bennie made a shushing noise,

94

but nobody was nearby. "Someone was trying to hide me. All those old companies . . . they ain't taking leave from mining the southern side 'cause it wasn't safe, it was because I was down there." Motheater hissed, baring her teeth. "Someone knew to stay away."

A spark of fear nestled in Bennie's chest. Bennie had almost been sucked into the stone herself, hadn't she? What if Motheater had been the thing in the mountain, stealing away miners? Again, the sense of unease bubbled. What was she truly doing, tying herself to this woman?

But she was desperate. She needed to try.

Bennie shifted the maps around to look at Ackerman's old map again. This one had the old Kiron homesteads outlined in red along the southern side of the mountain. "Look here." She shoved the map in front of Motheater again. "What's familiar here?"

"I ain't look at maps of Kire," she muttered. "It's not . . . I never needed map nor compass."

"Great, and now we do." Bennie's voice was tight, raised higher than she realized.

"Bennie?"

Bennie looked up. Cal Yeardly hovered nearby, a venerable white librarian that might have been as old as Ackerman's map. He was a kind sort, stooped and walking with a cane, and he only looked concerned as he walked over slowly.

"Hey, Mister Yeardly," Bennie said, smiling a little, her voice going much softer. "Were we being too loud?"

"Oh, a touch." Yeardly smiled a little. "Nobody here but you two anyway. I figured I'd come over and ask if y'all needed help."

Motheater shut her mouth, her hands worrying at the hem of the sweatshirt again.

Yeardly had helped Kelly-Anne dig out these maps in the first place. He had been a part of protests back in the seventies, chaining himself to bulldozers alongside his sisters. It was admirable, but Bennie had to choose her battles. All she wanted was for people to stop dying. "I'm looking for a record of Kiron from about the Civil War. I think if we can find enough historical value in the old settlements, we might be able to put a stop to White Rock's movements."

Yeardly hummed. "Not a bad thought, Miss Mattox. Ain't much in the way of narratives from Kiron locals, but Zeigler and Grosscup traveled through the area in the 1880s. We got their account."

"Let's see it!" Bennie said, smiling. "We're trying to figure out what the town was like. Names, places, notable people, stuff like that."

"Not many notable men in Kiron," Yeardley said, walking back through the historical section. Motheater glared at him, standing next to Bennie, where only she heard the witch mumble about notable women. Bennie shushed her as Yeardley pulled out the old journal.

"Their North Carolina adventures are more known, but . . . here we are." He flipped to the chapter titled "A Mountain-Side Chapel," passing it over. "See if that helps you some."

"Thanks, Mister Yeardly." Bennie laid the book out on the table. She hovered over it as Yeardly left, and Motheater crouched next to her, hands on the edge of the table, chin resting on the maps. "Can't imagine you can read it from down there."

"You read faster'n me," Motheater muttered. "I memorized lines to avoid reading."

Bennie made a noise, flipping the page. "Well I don't know what we're looking for."

"You don't know how television works, either." Motheater pouted, trying to read over Bennie's shoulder.

"I will get you a book on television and then you can teach me," Bennie muttered, skimming over the account of Kiron, but the authors were more interested in moonshine and the movements of the first industrial company in town than anything else. The two lawyer-authors considered themselves anthropologists of the Alleghenies, and it seemed that every movement of Kiron fascinated them. This book was a long shot across a dark holler. She turned the page.

On the next side was a charcoal print of a building that seemed to be right against a cliff. Motheater snatched the book away, her hands trembling.

"I remember this."

"Easy." Bennie took it out of her shaking hands. She quickly found the caption: "Kiron's notable chapel: the Church of the Rock."

Next to her, Motheater wasn't breathing.

"Oh shit," Bennie said, eyes going up. "This was a snake-handling church."

"Aye." Motheater's eyes were fixed. "My father's."

"Your *father*?"

"I do have kin." Motheater's voice was scathing. "I remember he gave me serpents to carry when I was small. When I could barely hold them up."

Bennie read forward. All that it said about the location of the church was that it was up the mountain. High up on Kire, the book said.

"Oh, fuck." Bennie fumbled for her phone, texting Zach. If he felt as guilty as he had said he did, he would help her. And if she knew anything about him, she knew that he had every part of yesterday memorized. "The church was *on* Kire. I'd be willing to bet . . ."

She got her answer seconds later. Zach had sent her a set of coordinates. As she tried to locate where he had taken

Motheater out of the vein, Motheater took back the book, reading through it.

"Halberd," she muttered darkly. "They must have had a hand in getting me out of the way."

"They moved in under the auspices of the church and the collected Kiron council," Bennie recited as she found the Ackerman map again, the one with homesteads marked in red. "All right here, these were all the surface establishments that the mineral rights didn't cover, before the town moved into the valley."

Motheater snorted. "They had mineral rights in my time, too. Most of the range was divided up before the war, even."

God, that was bleak. But Bennie had to focus. Looking between the text messages from Zach (who seemed more than willing to give her company secrets), the old explorer's book, and the map, Bennie pointed at a faded red square on Kire's southern side. It stood apart from the other homesteads and didn't seem to have much in the way of farmland, or even neighbors.

"I'd be willing to bet this is the Church of the Rock."

"Then it's there I need to go." Motheater's voice shook. "The church will know me. I was protecting something. The rockslide last night, the earthquake. That's Kire waking up."

Bennie braced herself. There were plenty of strange things about Motheater, plenty of magic Bennie didn't understand, but a living mountain? One that Motheater said would "wake up"? It sounded like a threat.

Halting White Rock had seemed so easy this morning: find evidence of negligence, stop the work. But now she had a living body, not a dead one, and apparently a living mountain as well.

"Do you think that the mountain could cause equipment failure?" Bennie asked, barely believing that she was asking this.

"Yes." Motheater didn't hesitate.

Bennie stared down at the map. She had been making progress continuing Kelly-Anne's and her own investigation, and the union lawyer she'd been talking to was sure that with just a shred of solid evidence of negligence, they'd be able to pin White Rock to the ground. It seemed ridiculous to her that all she wanted was to make it safe to work in the mountain—not even pushing for better environmental regulations or better pay, just basic safety—and she couldn't get anywhere.

If White Rock was turned out, if Motheater performed her miracle, it would only be a matter of time before another company came through, and there was no guarantee they would be any safer, just a possibility. And if White Rock wasn't the problem, and it was Kire all along, none of Bennie's work would matter. Equipment would keep failing, safety measures wouldn't work, and people would keep dying.

Bennie looked over at Motheater. Her rough-hewn face, crooked nose, thin lips; her hard-set brown eyes had flecks like a moth's wing, that changed color with every soul she passed on. Every part of her was pressed in, shaped by a hardship that Bennie didn't know.

"White Rock won't go back into Kire for a few days because of the earthquake," Bennie said slowly. She didn't believe this, but . . . what if she went along with it? "But when they go back, if Kire is really waking up, and could cause equipment failure, then we need to keep people from dying."

"I might be able to put the mountain to rest. It doesn't have an alive-thing buried inside no more. Maybe that'll be enough to convince it to sleep."

Motheater made it sound like putting down a dog, but Bennie was out of options. Maybe Motheater knew something she didn't. "We'll have to figure out a way onto the trail. It's company land."

Motheater smiled, wicked teeth and bright eyes. "I am no stranger to trespass."

Bennie felt her stomach flip and fought a blush. Damn her. She could absolutely not be trusted around a woman like this. Someone who believed her, someone who wanted to help her. Someone with the power to follow through.

"Can you prove it?" Bennie asked, finding her voice.

"Prove what?"

"That the mountain is alive. That all these deaths aren't just White Rock being foolish? That some of this is out of their control?" Bennie felt desperation clawing at her chest. If Motheater was right, her investigation would be for nothing. It would mean that the miners were going to die no matter what. The mountain was killing them. It wasn't White Rock at fault at all.

But it would also mean that Bennie wouldn't be the one responsible, that her checks had been thorough, that she hadn't missed anything when going over fasteners and fittings. Instead, it was never going to be safe. People would have always died for no reason. Grief came like bile, like sour apples, and Bennie wished, desperately, that she could have saved Kelly-Anne, that she could have saved anyone. It didn't matter if it was White Rock or Kire—she had to try to save them now.

In the library, across the table of maps, the tension rose like a flood. Eventually, the witch nodded. "Have some faith in me," she said, voice low, a susurration. "We'll find the truth together."

Bennie hesitated. That would have to be good enough, wouldn't it? How much of her life did she lose by holding too tight to her own convictions? Maybe it was the time for faith.

She took a couple pictures of the old maps before sliding them back into the architect's table, while Motheater stared at the charcoal drawing of the church. Part of this felt like letting go of her pride. She had been looking in all the wrong places for six months, had lost everything for nothing. If Motheater was telling the truth, she might have been fighting a losing battle for nothing. If the mountain was alive and causing equipment to go bad. Those were big ifs.

Still, as Bennie tucked the last rendering of Kire away, she tried not to think of the map in her apartment, the possibility that she and Kelly-Anne might never have been able to do anything at all.

꩜

"I need to get onto Kire Mountain," Bennie said into her phone as she drove through Kiron. Motheater was bent over in the front seat, occupied with the book on the history of the Alleghenies Bennie had managed to check out.

"Okay?" Zach's tinny response rattled against her neck.

"Can you disable the security on the south side of the mountain?" Security mostly consisted of motion sensors and fences. Bennie could take care of the fences. She turned down a street, heading to the hardware store.

"Jesus, Bennie."

"You can blame shit going dark on the tremor last night," Bennie pleaded, slowing down at a small roundabout and wincing when her truck grumbled.

On the other side of the line, Zach sighed. "I'll see what I can do."

"My hero," Bennie said sarcastically.

"Look, ever since you got caught rooting around in the records, there's not much I can do about getting in there, 'specially after hours," Zach explained. "I said I'll try."

Bennie pressed her mouth into a sharp line. She glanced over at Motheater, who was watching her silently, almond eyes narrow and face hard. If Bennie couldn't rely on Zach, maybe the witch would have a solution.

"All right." Bennie's voice was quieter. "Let me know."

"Right."

There was an awkward pause as Bennie shifted the phone against her shoulder, pulling into the hardware store.

"Be careful, Bennie," Zach finally said, and even across their shaky connection, Bennie could tell that he sounded sad.

Bennie set her jaw. She wouldn't be sweet-talked into caring more for Zach than she already did. Her heart was in her stomach, solid as a knife. "Talk soon," she muttered, ending the call and taking a deep breath, staring at the hardware store.

"What we here for?" Motheater asked curiously, leaning forward.

"Wire cutters, for the fence."

Motheater blinked, her hazel eyes going wide.

"I got hands, don't I?"

Bennie groaned, leaning her head against the steering wheel. Of course Motheater could take care of a fence.

"Right." Bennie took a deep breath. "But just in case, let's grab something."

Motheater chuckled, sliding out of the truck. Bennie turned off the truck and walked up to the hardware store, the bell chiming. Miles, the owner, looked up at her, smiling and slightly confused.

"You ain't on the schedule, Bennie."

"Just need a few things," Bennie said, smiling and walking past the entrance. "Get that employee discount ready."

Miles rolled his eyes but opened up his paper, busying himself with the news. He hadn't spared a glance at Motheater, who seemed to have collected a couple moths in just the space between the truck and the entrance. She cupped them in her hands, staring at the community board intently.

"What's this?" Motheater asked, frowning at the papers on the board. Bennie read over her shoulder.

"A petition," Bennie explained. "Or, you can follow this . . . address—" There was no way Bennie would be able to properly tell this one-hundred-and-fifty-year-old woman what a QR code was—"And you can read the petition to stop the Mountain Valley Pipeline, and sign it. And then it gets sent to lawmakers."

"A pipeline." Motheater was frowning deeply. She looked down at the moths in her hands and ducked her head. Bennie glanced at Miles, nervous, but he was fully involved in his paper.

"Motheater?"

"I remember the pipelines—they came out of Pennsylvania," Motheater murmured, cold and mournful. "They still git through wood and hollow?"

Bennie touched Motheater's shoulder, pulled her into the aisles. "Yeah, but . . . a lot of people are protesting," she explained, going down to grab wire cutters and, on second thought, grabbing a pair of gloves for Motheater. "It's been delayed for years."

Motheater swallowed, and something shifted. She seemed a little less wounded. Bennie would have loved to know what she was thinking, but instead led her to the front of the shop. Miles didn't even raise an eyebrow at her purchases.

"All good, Bennie?" He rang her up, and she traded her credit card over.

"Someone dumped chicken wire by the road." Bennie offered an explanation anyway. "Wanna get some for a garden."

"Good luck," Miles said, examining the crossword. "Got an eight-letter word for dust? Sediment doesn't work."

"Detritus," Bennie responded immediately, ushering Motheater outside. "Read a book, Miles."

"This is why I keep you around," Miles muttered, diligently writing the word into the boxes.

Outside, Motheater was staring up at Kire Mountain. The mountain loomed over everything in Kiron, a presence that was never out of sight. Bennie swallowed, tucking some braids behind her ears. She glanced at her phone. Zach would need at least a few hours to see if he could sneak into White Rock. It would probably be tomorrow before she could head up Kire Mountain to try to find the Church of the Rock with Motheater.

"There's one close by, actually," Bennie said. "A pipeline."

"One of White Rock's?" Motheater asked, still staring up at the mountain, her fingers twitching.

"No, no. White Rock keeps their operation small compared to other corporations. Helps them keep control of the towns where they set up shop."

White Rock was powerful in Kiron, but it was still bite-sized when measured against the massive faceless corporate entities that were eating up Appalachia.

"What happened to the other mountains?" the witch asked, clearly picking her words carefully. "The ones southerly?"

"Stripped," Bennie said. "Old-country mining. Took the tops off them."

"What?" Motheater stared at Bennie with naked horror. When was the first strip mine operation? Far after Motheater's time . . . the 1970s, maybe?

"Mountain-top removal," Bennie explained. "Destructive, no coal left, turn over your child's grave, kind of mining."

Something about Motheater's expression spoke to Bennie's jaded sense of justice deferred. Working for White Rock had left an emptiness inside of Bennie that she couldn't reconcile, and there'd been more than a few nights where Zach and Bennie slept in different rooms after a fight over the way that White Rock operated in Kiron. Zach couldn't see any other way but through, but he was a miner's son, and none of the Greshams had ever left Kiron.

"I warned against this," Motheater said, voice breaking. "I knew that only destruction would come in the wake of industry."

"Welcome to Appalachia," Bennie said dryly. "Get in the truck."

"I have to see the dead mountain." Motheater scrambled up. "I have to see it."

Bennie was getting used to Motheater's sudden turns from mild to intense. Motheater slammed the door of the truck, piling in like a cat with her hackles raised.

"Why?"

Motheater was breathing hard, eyes wild, her fingers pulling holes in the hem of her sweatshirt. She looked feral, sharp teeth open and bright against her mouth. "If the dead mountain's heart remains, I can take it easy."

Bennie went cold. "And do what?"

"Regain myself," Motheater said. "I was tied to this place. I know it. It knows me. I could find more of my power if I can tap into the heart. If any of it still beats."

Bennie wasn't going to argue about the viability of mountain hearts. If she was going to believe that the mountains were alive, this was the test. Indulge Motheater now . . . or go sit at home and wait for Zach to tell her he couldn't do it.

She turned over the truck. She wasn't going to wait.

"There's an off-roading trail near Sarton that'll give you an overlook of Huckleberry," Bennie said. She remembered the trail clearly, especially after last year's mudding party racing up the peak. "Kind of a bum lookout."

"I ain't after a Kodak moment," Motheater said, and then looked exceptionally confused, almost angry. "What's a Kodak?"

"A photography company," Bennie said, as baffled as Motheater was. "How did you know that?"

"Old memories, old lives, sorting themselves out," Motheater muttered. "There's always something left when the moths come. They're a part and parcel."

It was working. Something was working. Motheater was *remembering*. Bennie felt hope, hot and painful, in her chest. She swallowed it down, trying not to lose focus on the road. "Buckle up, Moth," she muttered, heading out of town, going south to Sarton Ridge. "Most roads ain't paved out here."

11

Esther

Two days after Esther sent the fire-adders to encircle the Halberd campsite, she went to the Church of the Rock. It was early Sunday, before the parishioners had even thought to start their pilgrim's trek up Kire. She dressed modestly, with a shawl tucked around her hair and face, and soft gloves that were more to keep her hands protected than to give her father any kind of comfort. The blisters were still raw, open and burned. They wouldn't improve until the adders returned from watching over the site, and Esther needed to keep them at heel until then.

The Church of the Rock was big and wide, without much in the way of niche or cranny. The walls were freshly plastered and whitewashed, and the paving stones led straight and clean to the front door, with glass that was clear and slightly wavy, enough to see through with only small distortions.

Esther clasped her hands together in front of her. This was still a holy place. It still had a purpose. It would not do to desecrate it before she had attempted to placate its preacher. Although how much good she could do would be up for debate; her father had never been able to control her and had threatened her with an early grave more times than she could remember.

Still, an entrance had to be made. This was a serious matter. It wouldn't hurt to remind her father the power his daughter held in her hands, the command she had over words he had beat into her, verse and rod entwined.

She was being petty. She gloried in it.

"*Enter into the rock, and hide thee in the dust*," she said quietly, whispering Isaiah under her breath. A favorite of her father's, a book full of man continually brought low to cower before the knowledge of the old Gods who still haunted the new world.

As she walked, the scripture hung in the air around her, giving her a lightness and a shadow, a ghost, a haunted thing. Her hands burned; she should not be performing like this, but she was an angry woman, and scorned besides. The doors blew open in a gust of wind, not violent, but to make way for the mistress of the mountain, who entered a building on her demesne.

"*For fear of the Lord, and for the glory of his majesty*," she said aloud, and from the front of the church, the part of the building that was built against the rock of Kire Mountain, the places where rough-hewn stone were given to lichen and moss, where old candles were placed on the coves and crannies of the ridgeline, her father looked up at her. He was a tall man, whip thin and hollowed out under his eyes and cheekbones. His hair was cropped and pushed back with a kind of pomade that Esther was sure she could still smell when she was falling asleep. A haunting, rotten odor.

As she spoke, the candles all lit, and the dust and collected detritus fled out of the church. She came in peace. Mostly.

"*The lofty looks of man shall be humbled, and the haughtiness of men shall be bowed down, and the Lord alone shall be exalted in this day,*" Esther recited as the last of the leaves and old vines tumbled out of the church, and the doors closed gently. It was a small cunning, it took almost nothing from her soul-well. "Peace, father, upon you and your church."

It was lucky that he still held some kind of holy regard for his parish, or he would have spat at her. Still, Silas's look was enough to make her grateful that she held power, too, that she would not be beholden to his whim nor want. She bit back a smile. No use pouring salt on open flesh.

"I thought you enjoyed the Fifth Gospel." She tried again to goad him into speaking, stepping forward, past the first pew. "Have your tastes changed so much?"

"Out of this holy place, witch."

"I am no happier to be here than you are to see me, but I must speak to you." She stood straighter, commanding the aisle as if she were Gospel brought into the congregation. Silas turned from her and arranged the communion table on the altar. It wasn't truly a table, but a slab of stone that jutted out of the mountain, large and ancient. He had carved on the front of it a round of scripture. Any tidewater church would have called it pagan. Silas called it God-given.

"Whatever you wish to say, suffer it," he growled, taking out the church's old King James edition. Esther eyed the bound copy, knowing it had all the words of Christ printed in red, remembering that she had once burned them out under a waning moon. Just one insult of many she perpetrated against his church. She had returned the text later in the month, but she had needed words for a spell. He glowered at her across his preparations. "I'll not have your poison in my well."

Esther knew this was no time to be coy. "Halberd Ore and Mineral has come to the valley. They aim to make Kiron a company town and are buying up rights long the ridge."

Silas paused at that, standing up straight and frowning. "Kiron's a chartered town."

"Won't be." Esther raised her chin. "Not with Halberd. And this church is placed 'top some rich, thick coal streaks. They've already got their sights on Kire."

"I own this property," Silas sneered.

"You don't own the mountain," Esther said, voice low. "You don't own the mineral in it. You ain't got claim on the money that would come out of Kire, but you can be sure Halberd's bare months away from getting their claws in this mountain come springtime."

He seemed to get harder. His joints locked in place above the altar. Esther envied his hubris. "They won't, 'long as I'm alive."

"The law don't honor spitefulness, preacher."

"What are you suggesting, then?" Silas asked.

"Halberd cannot bring their infernal devices into Kiron without men agreeing to run them. If you keep spilling sermons against greed and advise any questioning souls against avarice and the like, I'll make sure the shine is strong, the harvest yields, and our winter is kind."

After a few minutes of silence, Silas humphed. "Mighty opinion of yourself."

"Through the Lord," Esther intoned, more for her father than out of any sense of humility. Her own hubris only extended so far. She communed with mountains. Ain't no better solver for pride than knowing just how small you were.

Silas was looking down at the Gospel, his brow furrowed the same way bark on an old oak folded over itself. He was a man of tight lines, stretched against a dark grain.

Behind the altar was all mountain, and she knew Kire like she knew her own blistered hands. It had rested for eons, but too many hands working it would make it thirsty, would cause it to turn over. She could feel Kire now, when its magic echoed through the church, the slow blinking of a titan waking after its abiding sleep. It wanted to rest, and could only bear so many heavy hands.

She resisted any impulse to conjure or sweet talk; it wouldn't help her father's decision, and she needed the souls of Kiron aligned through congregation. There were unions in Massachusetts, in Richmond, even, but there would be no union representative in Kiron knocking on the doors of folk as liable to shoot a stranger as to offer a wayward traveler a full meal. The miner's collective didn't hold the hearts of the people like church.

"Halberd would bring money to Kiron," he said, weighing his words out. "Hard for men to resist that."

"Halberd would bring authority to Kiron, too." Esther raised her voice. "Hard for highland men to bear that."

"I'll pray on it."

That was the end of it. Unless Esther wanted to call down some kind of storm, there was no more speaking with her father on this. The dawn had full broke, making the room warm, raising the heady smell of leaves and moss. She clenched her hands, the red pain securing her firmly in her body, giving her no room for plangent conjure.

"Will I be welcome for service, father?" she asked, keeping her words precise and sharp, lest the mountain hear a stray utterance and find command there.

Finally, her father looked surprised. It wasn't entrance nor magic, but the request to join his flock at church. He looked over Esther carefully. "The house of the Lord is open to all."

Esther was hoping to be rebuffed; denial would allow her to simmer in the easy meanness of a father's love withheld. After Esther's mother died, Silas could never be persuaded to love his daughter. He had found her too much trouble to raise and had allowed her to run wild in the woods, likely hoping she would meet with some kind of accident.

Magnanimity was frustratingly more complicated. But she had asked, and she needed as much goodwill as she could get. So she bowed her head, just a little, and turned to sit in a nearby pew, neither at the front nor the back, as if she were just another parishioner. She arranged her skirts around her legs and sat up straight, her hands in her lap.

Her father stared at her for a few more seconds and then seemed to decide that ignoring her was the wisest action, and continued to prepare the church for a service that did not send prayers to the protector on high. It seemed impossible to Esther that he didn't know that it wasn't Jacob's God listening in on snakes and taking tithe from the shale altar.

Maybe he did know what kind of titan he preached over. Maybe he did know the danger he took on whenever he made his way up from his cabin to his chantry. Esther believed in scripture, the faith of it, the holy mystery of it. But she used the Word as conduit for a power that didn't need faith. It was her first story.

Esther picked at the lace on her sleeves, staring at her father as he picked out psalms and arranged the letters on the old washboard they had beat into a calling. Perhaps he was too obsessed with his God to know the difference between faith and power.

༄

With her father aligned, with Kiron's snow-hid traps yielding cottontail, with winter roots bearing fruit late into the season and spring weeds poking out early, Esther was satisfied that her bounty was enough to keep Kiron from seeking out comfort in Halberd Ore and Mineral.

It didn't hurt that her fire-adders had set more than a few of their wood cabins ablaze. Most men in the company town were reduced to sleeping in tents in a deep winter, which wasn't really an inviting prospect compared to Kiron's warm cabins.

But Halberd still had the legal rights to the mineral under Kire, and there wasn't any way for her to fight against a piece of paper. But, Esther wondered, if there were no men for the machines, no conscripts for the company, then what did rights matter? Contracts and law might not be within her reach, but men? Esther could turn her work to men.

It was frustrating when the townsfolk of Kiron were fascinated with Halberd. They were so damned curious about the machines, of the promises Halberd was making. More coal, more money, progress, progress, progress.

And what could she do? Her warnings fell on deaf ears.

She hiked up to the peak of Kire, a bald that let her see the world around her. There was a depression in the stone, a shallow well that often collected water like a still pool. It was iced over now, one of the last remnants of the harsh winter that had tested her ability to cull a living for Kiron from the mountain. It was restless now, more every moment that Esther asked it for help, more now than ever before. But it would be fine as long as Esther could mitigate, as long as Esther held her faith and worship constant.

Sitting down, feet tucked to her side, Esther put a hand on the ice. The cold chilled her, creeping through her deerskin glove and penetrating into her tendons and bones. She wanted to close her hand, pull it to her chest, whistle warmth back into it, but resisted. With her other hand, she laid out a thatch of herbs, all braided around a small, delicate squirrel's ribcage, little leaves and sprigs poking out in between the bones. It lay next to her hand, fragile and dry.

She breathed out, her hot breath misting in front of her. As she pulled her glove off, she recited Ezekiel.

"Then said he unto me; Daughter, dig now in the well. And when I had dug in the well, I beheld a door. And he said unto me; Go in, and witness the wicked abominations that they do here."

She raised her hand and slammed it down onto the thin rodent bones. The fascination shattered, some of the shards driving into Esther's unhealed, blistered hand. The cold coalesced around her, small snow flurries drifting down onto her shoulders, a wintering of power on Kire's peak. Esther was breathing hard, a handful of blood and pus dripping onto the iced ballaun.

Kire accepted the pain. It gave her power.

She felt the lightness of the snow on her cheek, cold as a blade, biting. It sharpened its edge against her bones, hard as a bit in stone. This was the hardest part of fire-adders. Bringing them back required cold. Otherwise, their hearts wouldn't quench after their duty had been relayed, and they would stalk the coal veins of Kire, catching fire to the titanous mountain. She could have done this in a bucket of water, but she needed power, and there was no place like Kire.

"So I went in, and I saw."

One of the fire snakes appeared in the depths of the icy mirror, sliding out of the mountain, having traveled through the Hatfield Valley and coal vein to reach its master. It circled in the ice, an ouroboros of fire and scale, sending up clouds of fog, soft cracks echoing in the cold. The clear ice turned dark and stormy, like tarnished silver, and in the reflection, Esther could see the memories of the second snake, still nestled in the pitfire in Hatfield.

Machines. Dozens of them being assembled and carted in. A man she didn't recognize in the center of it all, and DeWitt, that coward, walking around and giving orders. All told the camp had close to forty tents, and there was already a half-risen outpost for the owner. They were moving fast. Spring was coming soon, and they'd start rerouting the water of the Dismal Branch to help cart off the earth and slough they pulled out of the mountain.

Huckleberry was living, like Kire. Older, gone to seed, but still aware. It would bear the indignity of being carved apart. Esther knew, even as she woke up Kire to heed her call, that Huckleberry was not that kind of mountain to rise.

Already Halberd's infernal devices were being lined up against Huckleberry's ridge, likely to test their bite before they moved them to Kire. Esther knew she needed more information if she were going to dismantle Halberd. Her anger and horror would not wait. She sifted through the cold coals of the adder's memory, pressing her hand against the ice, her blood mingling with the dry herbs on Kire's peak. On instinct, guided by Kire's heart, she found a dark coal. Leaning over the smoking ouroboros, she breathed, and the heat of her breath appeared in the adder nestled in Hatfield, igniting its heart.

DeWitt appeared in the iced mirror, talking with the foreman. A third man was there, too; this one also Esther didn't recognize. She couldn't hear them, but he looked angry, gesturing at the machines, pacing. The third man's suit was made of fine fabric, even compared to DeWitt, who had yet to abandon his red walking coat, even in winter.

There might be a reason for that, Esther smirked, remembering the little rabbit that burrowed in his chest, made a warren of his lungs, his heart a new-pillowed coney-garth. Did he have little kittens in his blood?

Still, the third man intrigued her. His shoes were shined, his hair dark and slicked back, a little older than her own father, but he looked fuller, healthier. He looked polished. Refined. The owner? Who was he?

Esther sighed.

"*Daughter of Kiron,*" Esther muttered, "*hast thou seen what the ancients of the house do in the dark?*"

She leaned over the ice, putting both hands on the mirror, her bare skin sticking to the cold surface. She needed to find a weakness. Could she destroy supply lines, like they had done in the Brothers' War? Could she turn machines to rust?

The fire-adder under the surface writhed as Esther gave it her heat, as she pressed her hands into the ice, melting it under her anger to submerge her blistered and bloody fingers in the meltwater.

The third man came to the surface again, gesturing and upset. He had a secretary behind him, a fey young thing with dark hair and a quick pen. The man in the fine suit stepped forward and grasped the foreman's lapels and was about to strike him when DeWitt stepped in. He calmed them down, and they all moved on, the secretary's skirts disturbing the ground behind the third man, covering his tracks as she followed him into some other temple.

Now DeWitt and the foreman were talking, heads together, worried. This was three-headed snake that had come to her valley and would drain it dry? She knew that Kire wouldn't differentiate between highlander and city folk, that if these men took too much, bit deep enough with metal and machine, they would find the mountain had teeth of its own.

And Esther knew that it wouldn't be these city folk digging in the mines.

"They have filled the land with violence," she said, pulling her hands out of the ballaun, letting the adders turn cold under snowdrift and melt. *"Therefore will I also deal in fury: mine eye shall not spare, neither will I have pity: and though they cry in mine ears with a loud voice, yet will I not hear them."*

She pressed her cold hands to her face, pulling at her hair, pushing her bonnet off her head. She would turn the soft land against them. She would haunt them. She would make life difficult for Halberd, in a way that no Kiron resident could be blamed for. They would find Appalachia a crucible unlike any other.

The grammar took hold of her as she intoned, and she writhed on top of the mountain, as the snow came down in a skift around her. The pines and poplar seemed to exhale weather, creating a fog on the peak of the mountain, as if they heard her finish the chapter, and all whispered power: *Selah*.

12

Bennie

The drive out to the Sarton Ridge jeep trail was uneventful, if a little bumpy. It was southwest of Kiron
and just past a nice open meadow that had some kind
of historic marker attached to it, but there was little else in
between Bennie's apartment and the park. The only things
out here were hiking trails and old, broken-down equipment
deserted on the side of the road.

Bennie had stopped by her apartment to grab a snack.
She had given Motheater an apple and a thermos of hot tea
to share between them, and while the witch had managed to
eat the entire apple, core and all, the thermos was proving a
little more difficult.

"I thought you got some memories in you," Bennie teased,
loosening up the lid and passing it back to Motheater as they
slowed around a turn. "Can't recall a thermos?"

"Must not have been too important to people," Motheater
muttered, annoyed. "Nobody dead by thermos this past
century."

"Century and a half," Bennie corrected, smiling. She

glanced over at Motheater and saw her glaring as she sipped from the thermos. There was something about her that reminded Bennie of a large cat. Big eyes narrowed over a thermos, hair escaping the meticulous plait.

"You're very fresh," Motheater said, petulant. "It's not fair. I'm not nearly as clever."

"You're plenty clever, don't be a dick." Bennie rolled her eyes. "You talk to ghosts."

"Souls."

"Whatever."

Bennie turned off the main road onto a low dirt path that turned at the last ridged corner of Sarton Mountain and led north to Dismal Branch.

"Let's see what this baby can do," Bennie said, patting the dash of the truck.

"What's wrong?"

"It's spring," Bennie explained. She pulled up to the creek called Dismal Branch, along where stones were typically placed to facilitate a crossing. "Snowmelt makes this path . . ."

"Ah." Motheater looked up, understanding what Bennie meant now. The Branch had clear washed over the road. Bennie was delighted.

"Love this shit," she muttered, tucking a few braids behind her ear. The Branch wasn't all that high; this was great. "Gonna get rocky. Close your thermos."

Motheater did as she was told as the truck powered through Dismal Branch, mud splashing up onto its sides. Bennie was grinning, feeling the pull of the truck under her, the way the wheels slid on river stones. She whistled as she gave the engine more gas, and the truck shot forward before continuing to struggle up the scenic route along Pine Swamp Ridge.

"It's hard to know where you are," Motheater muttered. "Not having the mountain under you."

"Why's that?" Bennie was only half asking, concentrating on keeping on the road, carefully going around slim turns that were particularly treacherous just after the springtime shift, where branch and bracken were slid down the mountain from melting snow and soft mud. It didn't bother her, and it certainly didn't bother her baby.

"Can't listen to what it has to say," Motheater said. She was being somewhat cryptic, if Bennie was being honest, but that wasn't really high on her priorities right now. Instead, she took a turn and gripped her steering wheel tight, heading up to the peak of Pine Swamp Ridge.

"I didn't take mountains to be talkative."

"Not much in the way of conversation," Motheater admitted, smiling. "But they offer knowledge freely."

Bennie smiled a little. She liked the way Motheater talked about the mountains. She spoke about the range like she could take it to dinner.

Bennie took another turn, and they arrived at the scenic pull-off. The truck hummed under her. Bennie leaned forward in her seat and pointed at the mountain in front of them. "That's Huckleberry."

Motheater didn't respond, her eyes wide. She dropped the thermos and scrambled with the door, fighting with it for a few seconds before unlocking it and stumbling outside. Motheater looked like she was in pain.

Bennie turned off the truck and walked out, watching Motheater go to the guardrail and then, like an absolute idiot, stand on top of the frail metal. Bennie's eyes widened. She had seen rails buckle when a bicycle hit them, much less having a full-grown woman riding on one.

"Motheater—"

"What happened?" Motheater asked, her voice wrecked. "Huckleberry's *gone*."

Bennie didn't get closer, standing on the other side of the truck. She tore her eyes away from Motheater to look at Huckleberry. It was definitely more like a tall hill than a mountain. Most of Huckleberry had been scraped away, little by little, and then put back afterward.

"I told you, Moth," Bennie muttered. "It got mined." Her voice was soft, like she was guilty of doing it herself.

"It was kilt," Motheater said, hands outstretched. "I don't feel anything."

Bennie looked out to Huckleberry, seeing the strange low hill there, the smaller knob, the Forks behind it. In the distance, Kire. But barely. A group of birds flew up and then over the next mountain.

It wasn't dead, it was just smaller. There was growth, but the trees were shorter, and there were big, bare patches, dark and brown against the verdant spring green around it. It was still beautiful, in its own way. What was Motheater seeing that she didn't?

The wind picked up. The flock of birds, half a valley over, flew up again, murmurating across the mountain, above Bennie's head. More and more birds swarmed, orioles and starlings and small blackbirds. Motheater's arms were still stretched out. Bennie froze, heart leaping into her throat, hand clenched on her truck.

"I was the wolf at your door!" Motheater screamed, and wind coming down off Sarton shook the railing. As if she called the coyote, as if she could bring the Appalachian wolf back from the dead, Bennie heard yips in the distance. "I was the bear at your back!"

Across the valley, Huckleberry *shuddered*.

Bennie pressed her hand to her mouth. Along the stepped mountainside, the mud shifted, loose from the rain and meltwater. The roots were soft, the grass was young. This was normal. A mudslide. They happened. But did they happen on command?

"I broke your chest! I ate your heart!" Motheater's voice tore from her throat like an eagle at a hare. More of Huckleberry began to slide down, trees bent back, more birds shot upward. The wind was a living gale at Bennie's back. Would Motheater bring the whole mountain down?

"Motheater!" Bennie went for the witch. What had she gotten herself into? "Stop!"

In the distance, past Huckleberry, a puff of smoke went up. The pipeline. Bennie grabbed Motheater around her waist, pulling her off the railing. Motheater breathed raggedly across Bennie's face, and before she could scream again, an explosion, loud enough to rattle Bennie's fillings, echoed across the mountain range.

Bennie pulled Motheater against the truck, bracing. There were stopgaps all along the pipeline, and it would be contained, but that was only if the equipment was working, and only if the calibration hadn't been shaken off by a mad witch.

Motheater wrapped her arms around Bennie's shoulders as the stink of oil and mud and chemicals rose around them, brought to Sarton fast on the storm Motheater had called up. Fuck, Bennie didn't want it to end like this. She heard cracks and shakes along the ridge, and boulders began to tear themselves loose from their cradles.

"Make it stop!" Bennie yelled into Motheater's ear.

Motheater gasped, dug her nails into Bennie's neck, leaving small, bloodless crescent moons against her skin.

"*Mountain, rebuke me not in thy wrath.*" Motheater's breath was hot against Bennie's cheek, the power echoing over her skin. "*For thine arrows stick fast in me. There is no rest in my bones because of my sin.*"

The wind fell, the crashing boulders stopped, settling on the mountain. Animals were still calling out to the witch.

Bennie held tighter to Motheater, kneeling with her in the mud. The popping from the pipeline in West Virginia continued, a hard reminder of the tenuous ways that industry pressed against the boundaries of the mountains.

Just as Bennie was about to speak, Motheater finished quoting. "*For mine iniquities are gone over mine head: as a heavy burden. They are too heavy for me.*"

The last of the howls and bays died down, and even the sun seemed a little brighter, hot against the back of Bennie's neck. Bennie pulled back, achingly slow.

The witch was crying.

She had curled up, tears streaking down her dirty cheeks. Bennie's heart was still beating too fast; her hands shook. That was real power, something big, and unexplainable, brought on by one woman's rage. It made her want to leave Motheater to the animals; it made her want to run. This was way too much. She shouldn't trust this mad lady; she shouldn't be dealing with magic and dead birds.

Instead, Bennie turned to the dead mountain, the trees all down, the dark smoke of a chemical fire in the distance. What did Huckleberry look like a hundred and fifty years ago? Was it as tall as Sarton? As Kire? She needed Motheater. The witch was terrifying, but better a terrifying witch than a toothless one. Bennie took a deep breath, rubbing Motheater's back gently.

"I remember reading about the machines they made for the Secession," Motheater hiccupped, pushing her tears away fiercely and saving Bennie the trouble of pushing down the instinct to do it herself. "Monstrous things. Ships of metal. Guns that could shoot off two hundred rounds a minute. A single gun. Two hundred bullets."

Bennie stayed quiet. Motheater shuddered.

"They kept making machines of war." Her voice cracked as she turned to look at Huckleberry. "Ain't no man could ever hope to defeat."

Bennie didn't have the heart to tell her about the later wars, the other machines men had made. Maybe there were things the witch shouldn't know. Instead, she rubbed her face and stood up, offering her hands to Motheater. She would use the witch for as long as she could. She needed to find the truth.

"Come on," she muttered, missing the closeness of the witch. "The pipeline might be thirty miles out, but it'll cause a stir in Kiron."

"That's what it is?" Motheater took Bennie's hands and stood. She didn't let go. Her hands were shaking.

"Yeah, it runs down to Florida."

"Crossin' light the whole land."

Bennie stayed quiet. How was she supposed to explain the full bearing of industry devastation to Motheater, who had seemed offended at the scale of White Rock's small operation?

After staring at the black cloud for a while, Bennie sighed.

"Let's get dinner," she said, squeezing Motheater's hands. "Figure out what we can do."

Motheater nodded. As Bennie was about to pull away from her, Motheater reached up and gripped her jacket. Bennie paused, wary.

"I took what I could from Huckleberry. Little better than your White Rock. Ain't much, but it's something," Motheater muttered. "The bargains I made don't hold no more. All I got is the leftover power of me."

"Is that going to be enough?" Bennie didn't let herself hope too much, pushing down her eagerness. They were so close.

Motheater shrugged, unsure. "I'll keep pulling my strings."

"We'll go up Kire tomorrow." Bennie took Motheater's hand, squeezing it tightly, not looking away from her dark, potent gaze. Her heart was still beating with the shock of it, and even now, the animals on Sarton refused to settle. Kire, in the distance, seemed to loom larger in the corner of Bennie's gaze.

"We better. Kire would have felt that," she muttered, squeezing Bennie's hand. "It's waking faster now."

Bennie's hands went cold.

"Come on," Bennie said, voice shaking as she opened the door for Motheater, feeling protective. She needed to get down the mountain fast. She needed cell service.

If Kire was waking up, it would cause more rockslides, more earthquakes, more equipment failures. And Zach was on the mountain, trying to disable a fence that her witch might have been able to tear down herself.

⚬⁓

It seemed that Motheater, like most of the population of the world, was happier with chicken and waffles in front of her. The local diner did a savory waffle and hot chicken that Bennie adored, and Motheater dug in a hell of a lot faster than she had with a burger.

The pipeline explosion was small enough that there was only a brief mention of it on the radio as they drove into town, and Bennie was too relieved to be scared of the fact that Motheater had caused a minor environmental disaster just by throwing a temper tantrum. Instead, she only felt excited. She could use this woman.

It was probably for the best not to think too hard about the way Motheater looked when she was holding onto Bennie, the way her body curled into Bennie's, all angles and elbows. Desperate and needy and unguarded. Nope. Didn't think about that at all. Bennie busied herself with her chicken.

Motheater was asking nonstop questions about mountain-top removal. A lot of the details Bennie didn't know, despite having been a part of White Rock for near on five years. She had gone from an assistant job to a health and safety position, but it didn't mean she knew much about the actual mining. She made schedules, inspected equipment, ordered supplies, crunched data, and alerted crews when EPA or OSHA showed up. And, on occasion, she investigated missing money and snooped around old archives to find the records of accidents that went underreported. That might not have been in the job description.

More on, none of her administrative skills helped Motheater understand how men moved mountains with machines, but Bennie found some articles on her phone and swiped through the pictures. Motheater's face got darker and darker, and her mood was clearly soured in a way that not even sugar-covered diner waffles were solving. It seemed a different sourness than the vitriol she had spewed on top of Sarton.

Motheater took another bite of waffle and sat back. "What I don't understand is how Huckleberry bore it."

"What?" Bennie looked up from her milkshake.

"Why didn't it fight back?" Motheater asked.

"It's . . . a mountain."

Motheater stilled, fork held above her waffle. "Aye. An Appalachian mountain."

Bennie and Motheater stared at each other.

Without much warning, the fight left the witch. A dullness returned to her face. Bennie felt her heartbeat pounding in her ears. She couldn't lose faith now.

"Appalachian mountains can fight back." Motheater swallowed. "Mountains are made up of more than stone, trees, and loam—they have their ways of living. Of fighting. I remember . . ." She trailed off, and Bennie waited patiently as Motheater sorted through whatever memories she could reach.

Motheater shifted and put her head in her hands. She mumbled something Bennie couldn't hear. As Bennie leaned in closer, the door opened, and the sound of multiple voices carried over the sound of early evening diners.

Bennie glanced over her shoulder and saw four White Rock miners coming in, people she recognized from the office, a few of them in uniform.

Bad enough that Bennie would be recognized, but Motheater? The woman they pulled out of Kire, breathing? At least Motheater had long hair and was wearing a nineties sweatshirt, but how many folks would forget a face after literally carving it out of stone?

"Moth," she hissed. "Hey, Motheater. It's time to go. Wrap that thigh up in a napkin."

Motheater didn't move. Bennie made a noise and tried to kick her under the table and missed. The witch was lost in memory or thought or something that Bennie did *not* have time for right now. "Motheater!"

"Hey, Ben!"

Bennie winced. Fuck. That was Helen DeWitt, Zach's foreman. Bennie looked up and smiled a little.

"Hiya, Helen," she said, putting on her best "let's get this the hell over with" face. It was almost kind, but Helen would know better. "Good to see you."

The three miners who had come in with her had gotten a table. One of them called out a very jovial "Hi, Bennie!" from the booth, smiling. Bennie waved back.

"You heard that pipe burst?" Helen asked, eyebrows up, clearly excited to share destruction. She was the kind of petty white lady that Bennie had learned to avoid in high school. "Put tremors all through Kire, would have given you a heart attack."

Bennie didn't smile. "Everyone out?"

"They shut everything down to do an inspection, but we'll be back tomorrow." Helen shrugged, and Bennie felt her chest constrict. If Zach was trying to get into the office, now was the perfect time. The skeleton crew in White Rock wouldn't care about the security booth when everyone was busy checking fittings and braces.

"Even with the rockslide last night?" Bennie's voice was tight.

"Yeah, tech teams worked through the night. No big deal," Helen said, hands in her pockets, nonchalant. Like this wasn't anything, like people weren't dying underground. "You'd think I'd run into you more."

"Town's larger than you think." Bennie forced a small, pasted-on smile as she entertained her former boss. "We always forget."

"Heard you and Gresham broke up."

Bennie's shoulders stiffened. The audacity was unbelievable, but then again, folks in Kiron just said whatever they wanted. And she couldn't just tell Helen to fuck off. She was old Kiron, owned swaths of land, and Zach's supervisor besides. She swallowed her pride, feeling it burn the whole way down.

"Yeah, mutual split," Bennie said tightly. "Just got a new place."

"Oh, good for you," Helen said in a way that definitely didn't make Bennie think she was congratulating her. "I'd have figured, your family being in the tidewater, you would have moved out."

"Well, I like it here," Bennie said. It was true. When she had first moved to Kiron with Zach, she had been deeply suspicious. But there was a nice Baptist church she dragged Zach to, the mountains were beautiful, and the cost of living was dirt cheap. She could run her truck through big creeks and spend evenings watching the sun get eaten up by high peaks. Sure, she couldn't get her favorite Irish butter at the store, and packages took an extra few days, but Bennie didn't care. There was something about the mountains that loved her back.

"Sure enough. And your friend here?" Helen had a look on her face that made Bennie want to scream. Bennie looked over at Motheater, who shifted to stare up at Helen.

As she did, all color drained from Helen's face. Her pale eyes went wide.

"This is an old college friend," Bennie lied. "Liz. Her family lives nearby, and she decided to visit."

Motheater glared at Helen, her eyes narrowing darkly. Anger flickered across her face, like a blade across a whetstone. Her eyes were fixed on Helen's name tag: DeWitt, in big block letters.

"Old college friend?" Helen repeated.

"Aye. Learned," Motheater spat, and any common affectations she had picked up by the hundred souls she had taken in last night had dropped completely. She was as hillbilly as Bennie had ever heard.

"Liz, I . . ." Helen blinked. She took a step back, and Motheater slid out of the booth, following her.

"Oh, shit," Bennie muttered, scrambling for her wallet as Motheater spread her hands, and the temperature in the entire restaurant dropped.

"I recognize your voice. I knew your kin," Motheater whispered. Somehow it carried throughout the restaurant, a cat's tail across your neck. She took a step toward Helen, but one of the miners had noticed the commotion and stood up, walking over to them. Motheater clenched her hands, and the tension snapped out of the restaurant. "Ain't nobody going to believe you."

Helen looked horrified. Bennie dropped a pair of bills on the table and swiftly grabbed Motheater's hand, turning the predator away from her meal. "Good to see you, Helen," she said, pulling Motheater to the exit. "Y'all have a nice dinner."

Outside, Motheater pulled away from Bennie and went over to the edge of the parking lot that bordered an empty patch of land. Bennie felt the sharp wind against her shoulders, anger in her own hands. What the fuck was Motheater thinking? What the fuck was she implying?

"What are you doing?" Bennie jogged after her. "We're leaving, we don't have time to dig up weeds."

"Ain't weeds." Motheater pulled out a young plant that seemed tall for springtime. "This is hedge."

"Call it whatever you fucking want, Motheater, we need to leave now."

"Not until I complete the curse."

"The *what*!?"

Motheater shredded the leaves of the plant in her hands, wincing slightly. They released a tart smell that Bennie could only liken to sour asparagus. Bennie didn't see Helen or any of the others coming out, so at least they weren't being followed. Yet.

"She were there with your Zach." Motheater's accent blurred the vowels easily, and Bennie felt a heat on her own hands as Motheater continued to tear at the weed. "She knew me in the mountain. She threw me out of it. Gave the order."

"Motheater—"

"She would have me kilt, Bennie," Motheater growled, her hands full of green.

"We need to go," Bennie pleaded.

"*Said the bracken to the cedar . . .*" Motheater started, confused. "Be our king?"

"Motheater." Bennie crouched down and put a hand on the witch's slim shoulder. Motheater was staring at her hands, which were no longer pale but a bright, angry red. Bennie put a hand under Motheater's elbow, pulling her up. Curse or not, this was no place to be kneeling in the dirt.

"Come on," she muttered. "Let's go home."

"There's something wrong. I can barely make plant magic work for me."

"Yeah, what else is new."

"No, Bennie, I mean *wrong*. My soul ain't whole. I got honey in the rock."

There was a twist to her mouth that was strange, a gash against her face, a far-off look. Bennie had seen it before after cave-ins, after slides, after ODs. Near-death had a way of haunting you. Motheater had her fair share of ghosts simmering under her skin.

"Let's talk at home, all right?" she said, walking Motheater to the truck. "And no cursing DeWitt, hear me?"

Motheater frowned and nodded. She let the leaves fall from her raw hands. Bennie was grateful that something seemed to have shaken her enough to stop. Helen was a hard-ass, and a little oblivious, but didn't deserve whatever retribution Motheater could intone with a bit of weed that was somehow burning Bennie's own hands.

They got into the truck, and Motheater flexed her fingers as Bennie pulled out of the lot, heading home.

"We in real danger, Bennie," Motheater said. "My hold on Kire done loose, I feel it slipping. Y'all have gone too far into the rock, and I have left it cold."

Bennie gripped the steering wheel tighter.

The look that Motheater gave her was haunted. Behind her eyes, Bennie saw something shift, something old. Her mouth went sour.

"We'll set it right," Bennie said resolutely. "You'll find what you need in the church. We'll settle the mountain." *And no more people will have to die*, she thought, her hands tight on the truck wheel.

"We better," Motheater muttered as they headed back to the efficiency. "Kire's mad enough to spit nails, and it ain't going to be soothed by kind words. I need to find my name. I need my full bargained power back. If I stay helpless, we ain't gonna survive Kire."

"And going up Kire will do that?" As they drove, the mountain loomed, casting a shadow in the evening, an ever-present threat in the distance.

"It'll be a start. There's a memory of me in Kire; I just need to find it."

Bennie felt a chill just before the rockslide klaxon began to blare again, as if warning her away, as if reminding her that she was fighting against a force of nature that was greater and older than she could even comprehend.

Well, fuck that, Bennie thought. She wouldn't let Kire take anyone else. If Kelly-Anne could die, if Huckleberry could die, so could Kire. If that's what it took. Bennie glanced at Motheater, who was staring out the window, eyes narrow and dark.

All right. She had a witch, a do-it-yourself attitude, and a pair of wire cutters. She could handle a mountain. Even a live one.

13
Esther

When Esther came down from the mountain, she was grateful to have a distraction. Lent was over, and while the congregation didn't think much of giving up comfort when so little entered their lives, there was always a good excuse at the end of the season to have a party. Holy Saturday was fine as any, on top of being a powerful day for storytelling.

Besides, hadn't she been the one coaxing sleepy stags to the hunter's trails? Hadn't she made the squirrel's dreys fall open underfoot? Hadn't she been the one to whisper for birch bark to stay soft, to give the pine needles a sweet scent under the burdock root and chickweed patch? Didn't she encourage the hopniss and pinweed? Saturday was for her, for her bloodletting. She looked at her hand, barely healed from her call on the adders, and swallowed. She had foresworn plenty.

The spring season was long in the mountains, and Esther had made it easy to survive Lent without resorting to cold dandelion and hawthorn. Her own cabin had a copse of mountain ash nearby, and she had prepared a tart out of acorn meal and rowanberry to share.

When she arrived at the celebration, she knew that she was late. There were four rows of houses in Kiron proper, about fifty homes and sets of cabins total, spread out along a grouping of three main roads, each with a small plot for near farming. Down the valley, in between Kiron and Hatfield, there were a set of land easily plowed that made for good raising, but staples were kept close.

In the town, there was a communal stable, a ramshackle post office that was only manned once a month, and a meeting hall. A few other places were set aside for the community, but not much more than that. The fact that the main road through town that lead down to Blacksburg was made of cobbled river stone for the mile through the center of Kiron was a source of pride.

The party was held in an open space off the river stone road, where they had laid down planks to keep it from turning to mud under the snow. There were a series of makeshift tables set up along stumps, and a gathering of folks on a nearby porch already picking a new ballad handed out at Ashville's last state hanging.

The food on the tables were mostly gone, but she still laid her tart there. Nobody wanted to be the first to eat her food, and until someone who wasn't her tried the offering, it would stay untouched.

Esther knew this. She tried not to take it personally as she took a slice of acorn-and-birch mast bread and buttered it. The shine was distributed from a still outside of Lon Yeardly's porch. She didn't go over.

All around her, Kiron pulled away. Mothers held their children's hands tighter, men averted their gaze. Even women whom she had helped out of childbirth, or through it, didn't do more than nod in her direction. That was fine.

Appearances. She found a stump near the fire and sat, trying not to feel the weight of the stares, trying to ignore the way people's fingers skipped over easy melodies as she stayed in the light. She was a Neighbor, but she wasn't a friend.

"I'll admit, I didn't expect you down." Jasper sat next to her, grinning broadly, passing her a cup of shine. "Nice to see you out of your cave."

"I don't live in a cave," Esther said, keeping the petulant edge out of her voice long enough to take the whiskey.

"'Course not." Jasper was smiling, clearly in a good mood. Esther resisted the urge to point out that he had watched after her house before, and instead took a sip of the whiskey.

"Go'in eat some of that tart, Jas," she muttered. "Ain't fixing to cart it home nor do I want to eat it all myself."

"Your rowan tart? That yours?" Jasper looked over at the table, judging the grouping around it. "Not a problem, darlin'," he said, standing up and going over to the potluck.

Esther smiled a little, watching him. He moved so easy between people. Everyone smiled at Jasper, everyone spoke kind to him. A hard worker, kept to himself, never so much as flirted with anyone's taken woman. Esther felt a pang of jealousy, watching him.

Kiron loved Jasper. Loved him like they treasured all their sons and daughters. She took a deep breath, sipped her whiskey, and nodded at Garret Vance and Mate Wayne across the fire, and then stared at her hands. The loneliness didn't eat at her much, just at times like this, when it was clear she wasn't quite fit for Kiron.

There were about two hundred people in the town, another hundred in the surrounding hills. Most Kiron were here tonight, even the Black families that had their own encampment a few miles away. Folks gathered in groups by porches, around other fires, in front of Lon's house, breaking out their own instruments, spoons, a fiddle, a concertina that looked like it had been taken off a privateer's ship.

All this life, all these people—many of whom had crowded into her father's congregation, who had seen her balance rattlers on her shoulders at seven—and none would speak to her. She wasn't God-touched for holding snakes; she was just poison.

"I have to say I'm always surprised when you manage a sight of cooking this good," Jasper said, sitting back down next to her. "I always expect magic to taste like dirt."

"I don't use magic to cook," Esther muttered, finishing her whiskey. She looked up, and he was grinning at her. She sighed. "Enjoy it, you rogue. None else will touch it."

"Ach, don't look so glum." Jasper leaned in conspiratorially. "I have news for you."

Esther sighed. Her hands were just starting to heal, and the cool cup against her palm was soothing. "Out with it then; you're too excited by far."

"Halberd Ore ain't got enough cash."

Esther's head snapped up. Her eyes went wide as she watched Jasper's face in the shifting fire. "What you say?"

"Halberd's only got investment to last through summer. Maybe a little on, but that's it."

Esther's mind raced. That's who she had seen in the fire: the investor. Whoever was backing Halberd. A gentleman from some city who saw potential in Virginia coal now that the taxes off'n the Brothers' War had softened the highland people and made them desperate. She swallowed.

"Who's got their eyes on Kire?" Esther asked, burying her hands in her pockets.

"Some new-elected statesman, I heard. Wanted to invest in the earth. This one rode down from Washington. Now we got time, we need to prove to Kiron that Halberd's got nothing we can't do ourselves."

Esther frowned. She took a deep breath, trying to sort out this new information. The winter hadn't quite broke; there were still a few places on Kire that were nestled in a snowdrift. This had turned from a war of the earth into a war of attrition, and Esther was sure that if she could turn it right, she'd be the mule that led Kiron out from the summer unscathed.

"How you 'pon this, Jas?"

Jasper's wicked smile made Esther's stomach flip.

"Jasper."

"Oh, don't look so sour, one day you'll fix yourself like that," Jasper said, rolling his eyes and taking another bite of her rowanberry tart. "I might have made myself amenable to one of their men."

Esther's mouth was a thin, disapproving line. She didn't care who Jasper took to bed; Lord knew he wasn't the first man she had known to favor the company of their own sex, but a Halberd man was trouble, no matter what kind of compromise he had made. She shook her head.

"You're a fool, Jasper Calhoun."

"Oh, full names now?"

"I need another shot." Esther stood, brushing off her dress. "*A fool lies with fools.*"

"Aye, preach some more, preacher's daughter," Jasper said around another bite of tart. "Come back when you'd like to know more, aye?"

Esther sniffed, annoyed that he was right about her return, and went over to Lon's porch. The crowd, while not comfortable, had at least accepted her presence. They parted but did not scatter as she took her cup to the still.

"Fine night," she spoke softly, taking a small portion. Lon stared at her, and she stared right back. Slowly, she took a drink of the whiskey, a sip that burned like it was trying to throw fire out of her heart and chest.

Lon smiled, just a little, just enough, and the crowd moved around her again, surrounding her in a way that was near to family. Esther ducked her head. Something about sharing wine and food brought a mass together, called a congregation to order, no matter how strange the folks in the pews. She turned and immediately Dinah Spencer and her bain were there, asking about a rash on the wee lad's arm.

Esther crouched, smiling, and took the boy's arm, and that's when she noticed that the same stillness that had occurred when she had entered the holler came about again. Esther shifted, still on her knees in the dirt, and looked over toward the hush.

DeWitt's red jacket stood out immediately.

"All this for sharing?" he asked, grinning at the food that was laid out. "An excellent spread you people have managed, for sure!"

The man next to DeWitt was tall, balding, and pale. He looked like he had never worked a hard day nor struggled in any winter. He pursed his lips, looking over the communal meal, and even from twenty paces, Esther could see he found it wanting. He had been next to DeWitt in her visions—the foreman. He was the man who knew mining, who was an industrial sort.

Esther let go of the child's arm quickly, not wanting to pull out more hives in response to her temper.

"Eat up," Jasper called out. It came out "et," like the Latin in church, and everyone suddenly stared at him. "Ain't gonna last through the contra."

Esther stood up slowly, glaring as Jasper broke the friction around the two men. While most people stuck to their own, a few of the more curious denizens of Kiron went over to talk to the two men. Esther sipped her whiskey, told Dinah to keep her boy dry after running outside, and walked along the edge of the planked platz.

She already had a few moths in her hair, and she knew that she needed to see to the dead. It was warm in Kire's shadow, in the great titan's lap, but elsewhere in the Appalachians, the night was a cold, unwelcome thing, and it would not be so kind. Besides, she didn't want to be around the Halberd men. She was as likely to hex them as pass them by, and murder was never her first instinct. It wouldn't do, after all, to have Kiron more afraid of her. She was no hedge witch; she was an Appalachian Neighbor, and her power was as great as the mountains.

As she was about to slip away, Jasper grabbed her arm and turned her around—none other would be so bold—smiling at her.

"Dance with me, witch."

Esther pushed down her calling, ignored the moths that settled in the folds of her dress, in her long heavy shawl, and nodded. She was weak, she supposed, to want a friend. Esther swallowed, allowing Jasper to pull her into the stepping line, holding his hand tightly.

꧁

The music started, fast and wild, and the caller had no trouble keeping pace with the clawhammer banjo. Jasper barely had time to pull Esther into the line before they turned and went around in a quartet, passing partners hand over hand. In a contra dance, with two lines of dancers, there wasn't room for hesitation. She grabbed Will Gresham's arm and pulled him close, and he grinned at her.

"Miss Endor," he said brightly, inclining his head. "Off your wilderness."

"Not for long, Will." Esther smiled a little. They were near on the same age—he was one of Jasper's friends. That made him friendly with her, but not much closer. "Ain't got much time to spare tonight."

"Ah, well, the night lasts long this time of year," he said, turning her around, an arm across her lower back, the other holding hand at chest level, a promenade as he turned her around. "Good to see you breathing outside of church."

"Could stand to see you breathing in it." Esther squeezed his hand. The Greshams were secular folk, didn't hold with snake handling. Sat with their own Bible in their own rooms.

Will just grinned, stepped away and bowed. He followed the caller, passing Esther to the next man.

In the contra, Kiron softened to her. She tripped over her skirts and got caught by waiting hands, she laughed when the caller said something raunchy, she got sweaty, and her hair came out of the ties she had put it under. Her shawl was tied up around her waist, and her dress was the same dark blue that half the women in Kiron wore. For tonight, perhaps she could be both witch and woman.

And then, near the end of the reel and with Jasper still two partners ahead of her, her hand was clumsily taken by Julian DeWitt.

He spun her under, brought her around, took both hands. She glared at him, pressed to his chest, and then moved away.

"Wouldn't have assumed you a stepping man."

"Wouldn't have assumed it of you, either, Miss Esther."

She could feel the moths rustling under her bonnet. It had already fallen around her neck, and the little things had found a secure place to rest amid her moving skirts and shawl. As she danced, she saw one resting on the sleeve of her dress, another peeking out from the buttons up her front.

DeWitt stumbled as she turned around him, and she wouldn't have denied it was because she moved a little faster than needed, knocked his shoulder with her own as they got the call to do-si-do. She was being cruel on purpose, and there was a part of her that loved it. The black coney flickered in his chest, and something tugged at her, a knowledge that she didn't want to see.

"Watch your step," Esther said, baring her teeth, sharp and canid. "Ground's soft when it wants to be."

He stared at her, confused, but she had taken his hands— soft, long-fingered, with no work roughed up on them. Fey hands, fair hands. If Esther hadn't known him, she would have called him Oberon, with his fair hair, blue eyes, bright smile.

If DeWitt was Oberon, Jasper was Puck, flitting around, smirking, making trouble. It struck her suddenly that this was likely the man whom Jasper had taken up with. Anger ate at her throat, making her mean. She wanted to call the coney out of his chest, she wanted to bring the stags down to run him through, she wanted to tear out his heart for want of any other feeling.

Her hands gripped his tighter, and she saw a snap of fear cross his face. Good. Let him be afraid of her. Halberd could stand to be wary of Kiron's Neighbor. With tight hands, she led him around, reversed their positions in the line so that she was the lead, and when the call came to switch partners, she pulled him through another pair entirely and deposited him in front of Jasper.

"I have work to do," she said, almost sneering. "Enjoy the night."

She turned on her heel, stalking away. Behind her, she heard laughter, Jasper's loud voice full and bright. The whiskey sharpened her vision, made of her a hot knife through snow. The drift melted under her feet, and moths came out as she left the warmth and light, following her as she disappeared into the darkness.

The moths were all around her, and as she walked up to her cabin, high on Kire, close to her heart, she listened to the souls that came for passage. This one, a young child who had caught a cough and never recovered his breath. This, a man who had gone out for food and broken a leg while tracking a deer. Another soul came to her, holding the last breath of a Blacksburg man who had taken a walk and gotten turned around, ending up in a part of town that wasn't kindly for strangers.

The witch held another soul close for a long time, listening as the young girl talked about the mines that had eaten her father, that had left her without warmth or food, a mine far south, in a Smoky Mountain ridge. Esther looked up and saw her cabin, surrounded by birch and hawthorn, a swatch of dark ground leading up to her abode.

She swallowed and went onto the porch, sitting on the rough bench there. All the way up from Carolina. All the way down from Blair Mountain. Where were the ridge witches? Where was her salt-and-sire? Who looked after the dead?

Moths surrounded her, each one begging for attention. She looked up at the encompassing cyclone of wings and last breaths and sighed, closing her eyes. Had she called them with her anger, with her own pettiness? Or were there simply no other witches waiting on the dead? She could not be the last one. Between the war, between the industry, between the call of the city and the luxuries it afforded even small-time hedge witches who could pass their wares as spectacle and occultism to those who thought themselves enlightened, who was left?

How long would Kire suffer its witch to draw herself thin? To draw from the dark well of the mountain itself? She felt the lives of the mountains around her, and she knew that she would not be able to serve so many masters—God and Kire and Kiron, the teeth of the world, the arching back of the highlanders of Appalachia. It weighed on her, but she took on the souls and let them confess and pass. She had to focus. Kire, Kiron, witch, woods. Around her, knockers came, flashes of light like sparks against the sky, bumping against trees and shadow, giving off dark, hollow sounds.

It was morning before she stood from her bench. She stepped off the porch, among the skift that came falling gently down. Under her, she felt Kire breathing, a dark thing, a tusk of a titan, the shell of an old creature. It opened its jaws under her, taking on the anger of her heart, breathing in the darkness she carved out for Halberd.

She took a deep breath, tilted her head up, and let the sun fall on her face.

Esther gripped her spells. Snakes and the coneys in the warren. Wrapped up in Jasper's arms, Julian DeWitt turned into a black rabbit. Just for a second.

14

Bennie

The rockslide klaxon kept Bennie up most of the night, and she woke up constantly, dreaming of her home shifting, of falling, of getting sucked down into stone. Motheater had seemed resigned when she pulled herself into the boilersuit she had gotten from the church—an old uniform of some kind, maybe from the company that had been in Kiron before White Rock.

"The shifts took out the power in the offices," Bennie said, reading over the text messages from Zach. There were even notices on the employee site (she had known Zach's login for years), listing out the dozen or so people expected to be at work. A skeleton crew, at best. "Only the emergency services will be kept on with the backup generator."

"I almost know what that means," Motheater said as they climbed into the truck. She clutched a map they had picked up from Hubbard's Gas and Grits on the way back from the diner. It was marked up with the most likely place for the Church of the Rock, as well as some old hiking trails that

Bennie had traced out from an old map of the mountain that had Kire Klimb in bubbly sixties font.

That old map had been a gift from Kelly-Anne's family when her husband started clearing out her things. The Elliot family was extended, but only a few were still in Kiron; the rest had moved to Norfolk, Raleigh, Atlanta. Places with larger Black populations and more opportunities for their ambitious teenagers.

Carlo, Kelly-Anne's husband, had handed her a box full of maps, notes, books on mining, union pamphlets, even her prized VHS copy of *Matewan* with James Earl Jones's cramped signature across the top. "You probably want this stuff," he had said at the end of a long day of packing. He was leaving, too.

"You sure?" Bennie asked, pulling out the film. "You could sell this for something, if you wanted."

"Not enough to make it worth selling." Carlo picked up another box, walking past her to the moving truck. "Just take it, Bennie."

In the foyer, Bennie took a long, deep breath. Chased out, driven away, denied the chance to thrive. They had deserved better than this. She clutched the box tighter, feeling the tight hot tears getting ready to drip down her cheeks again. She wouldn't let herself be ran out of town. She'd find a way to stop White Rock. Whose home would she be clearing out next if she didn't?

"This was an old deer track." Motheater pulled Bennie out of her memory, drawing in colored pencil on the map. She was frowning deeply, a couple of moths making a nest in her hair. "But here . . ." She stopped at a small stream. "This used to be called the Whiskey Reed. There was a . . ."

Her voice trailed off as her hand moved. She paused over an area of the map that looked, to Bennie, like any other. Green. Some elevation changes.

Motheater's hands crinkled the edges of the map. "Damn it."

"What's wrong?"

"I don't remember." The witch frowned, glaring at the map. "It's waiting on my tongue like a hound at the hunt."

Bennie pressed her mouth, anger, fear, a bit of helplessness fighting in her chest. They seemed close to finding real answers. She took a deep breath, pulling into a public parking lot that led to a local preserve. The blazed trail was one that led south, toward Huckleberry, and into a kind of swampy part of the lowlands. They would be going the opposite way, up Kire.

Bennie grabbed her small backpack, water bottle and wire cutters nestled in, and got out of the truck, slamming the door shut, causing Motheater to startle inside and then glare at her.

"Come on then," Bennie called out, zipping up her jacket. "Memory ain't going to come to you sitting there."

"It could have!" Motheater sighed petulantly, sliding out of the front seat, holding out the map and arranging it to line up with where they were. "Now we'll never know."

Bennie smiled a little, and Motheater took a minute to let the souls pass through before they started down the blazed trail. Motheater followed behind Bennie, and when she glanced back, the witch was staring up at Kire, through the trees, to the summit.

Bennie was starting to get nervous. Rockslides, trespassing, a killer mountain. It was a lot. She took a deep breath, and as they approached the turn that the blazes insisted would lead to the swamp, she hesitated.

But the weight on her back was greater than the wire cutters. Would she let more of her friends die in the mountain? Would she let Zach die, too?

She felt Motheater's hand sneak into her elbow, squeezing gently.

"I ain't gonna let a thing happen to you," Motheater muttered, her eyes intense, ferocious. "We ain't losing each other today."

Bennie let out a breath. She had a witch. She had a map. There was magic in the mountain. She nodded, feeling gratitude, relief, and something else that made her stomach swoop. She did not want to dwell on that.

"Lead the way." Bennie stepped to the side.

Motheater flexed her hands and nodded. She took a step into the bramble and it parted for her.

"*Her bitter end shall be as wormwood,*" Motheater muttered, the hush of the mountain sending her words out. "*Her feet go down to death; her steps take hold on hell. Lest thou shouldest ponder the path of life, her ways are moveable, that thou canst not know them.*"

More of the mountain cleared for them. Bennie didn't recognize the quote, but didn't ask, her mouth dry as she was surrounded by magic.

As they hiked, she remembered how much she loved this: the crisp scent of stone and trees, the way spring made everything bright, that soft, almost rotten scent of ferns and flowers. It was wonderful, and she couldn't help smiling as she walked.

"How does it feel?" Bennie asked.

Motheater glanced behind her. Bennie thought she saw something like confusion or doubt, but then Motheater's face hardened, and she looked ahead again. "I feel like I'm underwater. It's familiar; I know what water feels like, but I'm still not made to breathe it."

Bennie nodded. She watched Motheater as they walked, noting that she constantly looked around her, at the trees, the canopy, the animals in the brush. Despite the rocky, uphill climb, Motheater didn't look at the ground once. Bennie wanted to touch her. Wanted some of that confidence to rub off on her, wanted some of that bravery back.

Bennie watched her feet as they continued up the trail. Kire, alive. The mountain, breathing, deathly, under her feet. She imagined she tread on bodies, on skeletons, on the pulsing heart Motheater had described with coal flowing through like blood.

Bennie swallowed.

"Motheater?"

"Aye?"

"You remembering anything?"

Motheater paused. She tilted her head like she were a puppy listening to its owner.

"The trees that grow on are the same that grew when I lived here." She reached out to touch a maple tree, its leaves a dark ochre, almost red. "Or near kin. All roots and rackam kept these trees steady for generations. The stuff here, on the mountain, I mean . . . I know it. Moving it aside isn't taking from me like I thought it might."

Bennie smiled, and this time she did reach out to touch Motheater's arm. She was warm, more than she should be without breaking a sweat. There was something magnetic about Motheater, something that drove Bennie to do stupid things, like trespass on company property. They hadn't reached the fence yet, but it would be coming up soon.

"Don't get dehydrated," she said, offering Motheater a drink from her water bottle. "We got a while to go yet."

They walked in silence for a half hour before Motheater looked over at Bennie. "Why isn't Zach with us?"

"He didn't ask to come," Bennie said, her voice tight, although Bennie tried to tell herself it was because of the steep hike and not the subject. "I dunno."

Motheater looked away. "He loves you."

"Yeah, I know that," Bennie snapped, glancing over at Motheater. Her backpack felt hot against her shoulders, pressing in, forcing her to look up again. Fuck, this was the worst.

"And you . . ." Motheater pressed.

"Don't want to talk about it." Bennie was so close to bitterness it felt like a cousin. She couldn't think on Zach, or she'd just get mad.

They came to the fence that cut off Kire as private property suddenly, without any real warning. It wasn't any different to any part of the mountain, the fence weaving in between trees, a perfunctory effort.

"Step aside," Bennie said, her heart in her throat as she pulled out the wire cutters.

"I can—"

"No." She wanted to do it. This was her fight, another way to spit in White Rock's face. And Motheater needed to save her magic for the stuff that mattered. She began clipping up the fence, surprised by how easy the wires gave. It felt good to break something. She kicked at the broken fence, fumbling her way through the gap.

Motheater followed, looking up at the mountain, and then behind them.

"The deer track is near." She turned, heading toward a large outcropping of rocks that would definitely be a bit of a scramble. "We'll follow that."

It took a while, and Bennie had to stare hard to figure out the difference between that patch of bare mountain and this bit of weed, but something changed in the way she saw the brush around her. A new pattern appeared. There was no magic, just an old animal path that held onto memory and knew not to grow underfoot. There was only moss, soft as carpet, laid out like a river.

Another hour and they arrived at Whiskey Reed. Motheater looked up and down the banks, considering. Bennie came up next to her and put her hands on her hips, judging the passage. The stream was wide for a meltwater source, almost two meters, and the water didn't run clear.

"Has it been rainy?" Motheater asked, studying the map.

"Uh, yeah, a bit," Bennie said, grateful for the chance to pull her bag around and take a sip of water.

The witch took a deep breath and spread her arms. Slowly, she brought them together, the sound of the wind picking up as it shook the trees.

Bennie's eyes widened as she quickly took a step back from the banks of the Reed. As she did, the boulders and stones along the sides rolled in front of Motheater, forming a step-along bridge that wouldn't dam the water and gave them a dry path to cross. Bennie whistled.

"Must be nice." Bennie thought about what she would do if she had magic like that. Probably start with an apartment that would never need dusting.

Motheater flexed her fingers, rubbing them out slowly, looking over at Bennie. She picked her way across the stones. "Ain't the worst."

Bennie followed, wishing that she had a walking stick for a little extra balance. Suddenly, the rock under Bennie's feet shifted, unsettled in the Reed. She reeled back and overcompensated, leaning too far to the side to keep her balance.

"Bennie!"

Motheater's hand was out, and Bennie twisted, not of her own momentum, and she was pulled into the witch's arms. Motheater caught her, pulling her up the bank of the Reed, and the stones that had composed their makeshift bridge dispersed into the river.

Motheater had her arms around Bennie's waist, holding her, half kneeling on the side of the bank. Bennie was breathing hard, the adrenaline making her fingers tingle. She laughed, eyes wide, not missing the irony of Motheater saving *her* from a river. Grinning, she looked over at Motheater and saw a rise of color on her cheeks before the witch took a step back.

"Thanks," Bennie said, getting her feet under her. She squeezed Motheater's shoulders as the last few stones they had used as a bridge slipped under the Reed's near-frozen water.

"You all right?" Motheater asked, her hands clasped behind her back.

"Yeah, peachy," Bennie muttered, reaching up to adjust her cap. Bennie tried not to think about Motheater's hands on her back, the way that the other woman was so white her blush made her complexion go pink and splotchy all over. Bennie was already half in awe of the woman—it was frustrating for her to realize that she was also thinking about Motheater's mouth, the exact shade of color that spotted high on her cheeks.

Meanwhile, as Bennie was fussing with her clothes, Motheater had already turned away, making her way resolutely up the mountain. Bennie stared after her, annoyed at herself. This was the wrong time to start liking a weirdo. *Bad idea, Benethea. Super bad, no-good idea.*

Bennie took a deep breath and pushed on, trying to ignore the heat in her own belly. Motheater was a centuries-old witch carved out of the mountain. She wasn't exactly available. Best not think about this anymore. Could Motheater read minds? Nope, Bennie pushed that down, too. Couldn't think about that, either.

"Hey!" Bennie called out, straying off Motheater's footsteps to pick up a walking stick, a piece of ash that seemed to have snapped in the cold winter. "Your magic. How does it work?"

"Have you been sitting on this a while?" Motheater teased. "Sounds like you got questions same as money burnin' in your hand."

"Maybe," Bennie admitted, breaking off the small twigs on the stave, trying to find a good spot for a hold. "You going to share?"

"My magic comes from a bond." She glanced back at Bennie and shrugged. "When I feel . . . angry, scared, happy, righteous, I can bargain with that power and make of it my will. *Keep your heart with all vigilance, for from it flows the springs of life.*"

"Feel something, make something," Bennie said, trekking just behind Motheater. "Sounds straightforward enough."

Bramble and twigs snapped under their feet. Motheater didn't respond. By the set of her shoulders, Bennie thought that she might have insulted her. Bennie waited a few more minutes before trying again.

"Could you teach me?"

Motheater halted, and Bennie was more than happy to lean against her new walking stick and take a breather. The mountain had turned up, and they were walking along a ridgeline. Bennie didn't want to look too far left, or she'd see a massive drop-off. Motheater turned, a funny look on her face. Bennie pulled out her water again.

"Or not, whatever," she muttered.

"You a faithful woman, Bennie?" Motheater asked, frowning slightly. "Do you believe without proof, walk without sight? Have you made your faith a shipwreck or a mountain?"

"I went to church on Sundays," Bennie said, taken aback. She knew that Motheater was all tied up in the church, but this felt angrier. Clearly, Bennie had found a chink in Motheater's armor. "Is this about God, because—"

"Ain't about God." Motheater's voice was sharp as sin on a conscience. "This about you. You got your own faith? Your own certainty? The love under you?"

Motheater took a step closer to Bennie, frowning a little. Pieces of her long silver hair had come out of the braid, and Bennie could see the green streaks running through it, the pink of moth's wings that made Motheater seem like she had smeared the bugs' guts all through her hair. She seemed feral as she closed in on Bennie, dark eyes wide. "Do you know that your anger can move mountains? That your compassion can heal the sick, restore sight to the blind, that your fear can lead your people out of the caved-in mine shaft?"

"Is that it?" Bennie asked, not looking away, not backing down. She wouldn't be intimidated by Motheater; she refused. Bennie wouldn't deny that she was scared; there was something wild about Motheater's eyes, something strange in her posture. But she was Benethea Mattox, and she wasn't backing down just because a hot girl with mystery hanging off her shoulders got sharp with her. "Just *knowing* you can do things?"

"Faith is only part of it. There's more fire in me than blood. You pull on my red string, it's liable to lead you to Old Scratch himself. You want to be a witch?" Motheater hissed, eyes wide. "For magic, you have to tie yourself to something greater, to a baptism. You bind yourself to a power, an old creature, an ancient thing: the Witch-Father, the Devil's Wife, the Moon Raker, the Drunken Child, the Last Bride. The old witches, the nightly powers. Then you give, and they give back."

Motheater's voice didn't rise, but as she spoke, she became more intense—a dip in cadence, the mountain tone echoing in her words. Bennie understood, deeply, that this was what Motheater believed. If there was any true faith Motheater held, it was this, and not in the scripture she quoted. It was scary and exciting.

"So who are you tied to?" Bennie asked, quietly.

Motheater blinked, pressed her hand against her chest, took a step back. She took a deep breath and shook her head. "I don't remember the name of them. And it feels like an arm's been cut off. Like I'm only seeing three feet in front of me, like my spirit ain't close to whole. The shape of them is in me, I know it, but . . ."

Bennie could see the pain on Motheater's face, the way she drowned in the loss. "That's why we're going to the church."

Motheater nodded, looking up at Bennie. "That's why we're going to the church."

જ∽

As they continued to weave through the forest, the ground became rockier. The forest seemed to close in, the broad-leafed trees at the base of the mountain giving way to sturdier, gnarled pines and evergreens. The new growth on them was bright and soft; the needles had not yet grown stiff.

"We're getting close."

"You sure about that?" Bennie asked, leaning against her walking stick. "How can you tell?"

"It's in the air, hung like smoke. I ain't one to call capital down on my father's old church, but the weight of his religion dug into Kire like a thorn. But you can't feel that, can you?" She smiled over at Bennie and then pointed at the ground "See for yourself," she said. "The mountain does not keep secrets."

Bennie looked down. On the ground, the pine needles were arranged the same way. She swallowed and looked around, seeing the needlepoints of a million compasses drawn, inexplicably, to a true thing. She took a deep breath, the hair on her arms turning to gooseflesh.

"Shit."

Motheater smirked, turning back to face the unseen pull. Bennie gripped the stave tight to keep her hands from shaking. The witch called over her shoulder. "We won't be able to miss it."

Bennie was a little too shocked to move forward. This was a magic that had lain dormant for years, that had moved over this ground and pulled it forward, season on season. As Bennie gaped at Motheater, the witch barely took two more steps before something caused her to stumble back and double over. She gasped and fell to the ground, clutching at her stomach.

"Motheater!" Bennie ran forward but wasn't fast enough to catch her. To Bennie, it looked like Motheater had just run into a fence waist high. She crouched down and helped Motheater off the ground, sitting the witch upright. "What the hell just happened?"

Motheater licked her lips. She shook her head, and Bennie saw something flash out of the corner of her vision, something bright and early. "They knew I'd be back."

"Who?"

"Whoever shoved me into the mountain." Motheater grimaced, shifting onto her knees, looking up at the foliage. Bennie's hands stayed firm on her shoulders. "Now I know it must have been Kiron that left me in the stone."

Motheater took a deep breath and closed her eyes. She clenched her hands into fists on her lap. Bennie spread her hand along her back, pressing her mouth. Motheater looked small, confused and brittle.

Bennie took another deep breath, letting Motheater lean into her.

"I'll need your help," Motheater finally said, looking up at Bennie.

"Tell me what to do," Bennie said immediately. No way in hell were they turning back now. The wind picked up around them.

Motheater pointed down the path.

"See that?" Motheater asked, pointing at the glinting through the trees. Bennie stood and nodded.

"There's hanging a witch ball. A curse. I can't get through as long as it's there."

Bennie narrowed her eyes. Ahead of her, she could see something like a chime stuck in a tree, silver, half-hidden by the pine needles that held onto the branches, dark green and stubborn.

Bennie glanced down at Motheater. "It won't hurt me, will it?"

"No," Motheater said quickly, shaking her head. "It's held against witchcraft. It won't touch you."

Bennie nodded, hefting her walking stick on her shoulder like a bat. She didn't play three years of college softball just to look like an idiot now. Either she was feeling particularly stupid or brave; she really couldn't tell the difference right now.

"I got this," she said, walking forward. She hoped she sounded a lot braver than she felt. But Motheater needed to get to the church, and if some old tree ornament was in the way, then she was going to bust some balls.

Taking a few steps toward the glass bauble, she looked back at Motheater. The witch had her hands pressed on the moss, kneeling down. She looked like a painting, eyes wide, shoulders hunched, the way a man might think a lost woman in the woods would seem if she had stumbled and lost her way. The difference was her mouth. It was twisted into something like pride, something like admiration, and Bennie quickly turned away before Motheater could see her blush.

In the tree, the blown-glass witch ball was unnaturally still, dangling down without wavering at all, tied to the branch by a slim chain that had been grown over by the thick branch. She steeled herself and poked the orb. It was foggy, almost clear, but with some sort of strange smoke burned up inside. Maybe it was moving, or maybe it was the shadows. There was a silver sheen over parts of it, like a worn patina, that obscured it.

Bennie took a step back, put her staff over her shoulder, set her stance, elbows up. She narrowed her eyes at the witch ball, and something in it moved.

"Not today," Bennie muttered, taking a swing at the glass.

It shattered under the stave, and a burst of warmth emitted from the shards as they fell. Bennie shielded her eyes and glanced down. A tiny wisp of fog rose into the air. In a second, it had twisted and formed into a snake, rearing back, mouth open.

Bennie stumbled back and was about to call for Motheater when something blue dropped from the tree. The snake turned, and as it did, a screaming blue jay dove through its body. The head of the snake fell, and the entire thing dissipated before the head hit the pine needles. The jay circled the tree and then lit on a nearby branch, letting out a loud screech that seemed far too big for its body.

"Jesus Christ," Bennie gasped, bending over, pressing a hand to her heart. She closed her eyes and shook it off, counting down from ten as the bird screamed again. Why the fuck was that bird *screaming*? Didn't it know how to whistle? Or sing?

Glancing back, Bennie was about to gesture for Motheater to come close, but the witch was already walking up to her, moving carefully. It was a different kind of careful—considered. Like she was afraid of another magic fence digging into her stomach.

"Exciting," Motheater muttered, immediately kneeling near the broken glass and frowning.

"You got a twisted sense of humor," Bennie gasped, eyes tracking the blue jay. "I didn't realize they sounded like a dying cat."

"Noisy bastards," Motheater agreed, standing up. "But they're good folk." She was smiling a little, watching Bennie. "You may have found yourself a guide."

"A guide where?" Bennie asked, still cautiously eyeing the bird. The jay screamed again.

Motheater gestured. "You packed food? Fruit and nuts? Give him a little."

"You want me to give the dirty bird my organic granola?" Bennie might have sounded annoyed, but she passed her stick to Motheater and took out a baggie from her pack. She pulled out a few raisins and some oats and offered it to the blue jay. The bird didn't hesitate, but it didn't fly fast down to her hand. It clearly telegraphed its movements, flapping its wings, spreading its tail, and then jumping closer before fluttering down to rest on Bennie's thumb, eyeing her with a curious tilt of his head before picking at the food.

"Holy shit," Bennie said, her brown eyes wide. "I feel like Snow White."

"I don't know what that means," Motheater said, but in a way that was more amused than annoyed.

"Jays are trickster birds." Motheater nudged the glass shards with her boot, frowning again. She couldn't be happy for more than two seconds, it seemed. "Loud and brash. I knew a witch from the north that could travel in a flock of blue jays."

"Like a vampire?"

This time Motheater actually groaned, and Bennie laughed. "I don't know what a vampire is, either."

"Oh, we have some very bad movies to watch tonight," Bennie said, grinning as the jay took off from Bennie's hand after it finished the fruit she had laid out for it. She put another few pieces of granola in her palm and like a dart, the jay returned, pecking at it. This was *incredible*. She had never been much of an animal person, but this was pretty cool. Hesitantly, Bennie reached out and drew a finger down the jay's back. It ruffled its feathers but didn't fly away. She let out a shuddering breath.

Motheater gestured. "There's more curses up ahead. I can't see 'em, but . . . I feel it."

"Can you tell how many more are hung up here?" Bennie asked as the blue jay finished and flew away.

"Four? Five?" Motheater shook her head. Bennie watched her, frowning. "They must have spent years crafting them. They'll be in a pattern . . ." She pulled out her map before sinking to her knees on the ground.

"The glass—" Bennie protested, but Motheater had already set the map on the path, folding it to the section where they were standing. Bennie watched with only a small amount of disgust as Motheater picked up a shard of the murky witch ball and pricked her finger. She bit her tongue as Motheater drew blood from each of her fingers, curling her hands in to keep the blood from spilling onto the map.

"*Your word is a lamp to my feet and a light to my path. I have sworn an oath and confirmed it, to keep your righteous rules.*"

This time, Bennie felt it: Motheater's magic. Like the world stood still, like it shivered. The pause before a quake, the last full breath you took before being dragged under the water.

Motheater clenched her hand, causing the blood to well at the seams of her palm. Slowly, she passed her hand over the map. Five drops fell, and after a few seconds, Motheater stood, holding her hand away from the paper.

"Six dark wards," she muttered, standing up. "A strong binding." Bennie tried to find something different about her, something changed, like the moths against her hair, like anything, but she was still just a scrawny woman with bones that stuck out and eyes that Bennie could never really memorize.

"They really didn't want you coming back here, huh?" Bennie looked around, as if she could see the ghosts that haunted this place. All she saw were pines and birch, rustling in the up-mountain breeze.

"Here," Motheater said, offering the map to Bennie. She pointed easterly. "You'll find three of them in that direction. Go slow, look up."

Bennie took it, frowning, turning toward the west, intending to break the nearer ones first. A shrill scream came from nearby, and Motheater smiled a little. "He'll help."

She caught sight of something strange on Motheater's arm. Her sleeve had been pushed up when she held the map out, and around her wrist, Bennie saw something dark, like a bruise.

"What's that?" she asked, rearranging her stick and reaching for Motheater's arm. She saw Motheater freeze and moved quick, snatching her hand and pushing her sleeve up. Around Motheater's wrist was a slim tattoo—a snake. At least, it looked like a tattoo, dark ink pressed against her pale skin, but it was strange, something a little off.

"A ring-neck." Motheater swallowed. "It started burnin' like a bit of grease when you took out the curse."

Bennie's eyes were huge. It didn't look like a tattoo now that she had it right in front of her. It was smooth, no jagged lines, no mistakes at all. A perfect little creature overlaid on Motheater's pale skin. There was life to it, in the dark eyes, in the curve of its back. Bennie blinked and looked away quickly. There must have been some kind of optical illusion in the scales to make them look as if the little snake's body were breathing against Motheater's arm.

"That's creepy as hell," Bennie muttered, dropping Motheater's hand. If Motheater was getting branded, imprinted with the pain of whatever was trapped in the witch balls, where would the rest of the magic contained in the spell-glasses go? Was it like a scar? Would it fade? "You still want me to take care of the rest of the little Christmas ornaments?"

Motheater nodded, still staring at her new tattoo.

Relieved, Bennie nodded back. She didn't know what she would do if Motheater had asked to give up now, to turn back. Nervous, she walked toward the next curse.

Bennie noticed the jay out of the corner of her eye, darting from branch to branch next to her, following along. Bennie gripped the walking stick tighter as she approached the tree in the approximate area where Motheater's blood had landed on the map.

She saw it easier this time: a little shine up in the tree. It was just over her head, and she reached up with her walking stick and poked it. The branch it had been tied to slouched around the fastener and part of the bauble itself.

"Just like last time." She took a step back, checking to make sure she had room to jump backward after she had let the little curse loose. She narrowed her eyes, took a deep breath, and swung.

The glass shattered, and the smokey snake hidden in the trinket wrapped around the end of the stick. Bennie jumped back, eyes huge. She beat the end of the stick against the ground, but the snake didn't dissipate.

"A little help, bird!"

Like a dart, the jay came down. In a flash of blue and silver, the snake was pinned to the ground, its head torn off. Bennie put her hand over her heart. The blue jay hopped over to her and pecked at her leg, causing her to scramble back again.

"Don't do that," Bennie muttered, getting her fear under control. It was just a little bit of smoke. Mist in a jar. She watched the bird jump around the glass for a few more seconds. Four more to go.

She destroyed the next one without hesitation. This time, the jay came in quickly, dispatching the ghostly serpent fast. Bennie looked at the map, at the three on the other side of Motheater. She walked back to where she had left the witch and found her on the ground again, this time lying down.

"Motheater!"

Bennie ran over, dropping the stick, helping Motheater sit up. She was paler than normal even, her face ashy white without even a trace of pink. There was a smudge of dirt over her eyebrow, and when Motheater blinked at Bennie, she felt an overwhelming sense of relief.

"Had me worried."

"They're all here," Motheater muttered, holding her wrists up. Like shackles, the ring-neck snakes encircled her arms, mouths open. "I don't know why."

Bennie swallowed. "Do they hurt?"

"Only the flash of 'em." Motheater took a deep breath, shifting away from Bennie. "I ain't had these before, I know that."

"Yeah, they're pretty smooth for the nineteenth century," Bennie joked, trying to lighten the mood.

"They could have been mine," Motheater muttered. "The familiar animals. Bound for centuries to preserve me under the mountain."

"You think they kept you safe?"

Motheater shook her head. "I think they just held me fast."

"We've got three more before we can get close to the church, right?" Bennie asked, standing up. She stretched out her arm, looking through the brush, trying to spot the telltale silverine flash among the pines. "Nothing to it. Me and bird have this totally handled."

From the ground, Motheater smiled at her. "I'll be here."

If Motheater was lying about the pain, about whether or not she actually would be fine, she hid it well. Bennie grimly turned back along the eastern edge of the ridge, following the map pocked with witch's blood.

She glanced back at Motheater and saw her with her hands against her temples, as if fighting back a headache.

Bennie resisted the urge to go over, to be motherly, to be *caring*. She resisted the feeling inside of her to be kind. It was actually painful, but Motheater could handle herself. Whatever was happening in between her hands wasn't something Bennie could fix, and she was done fawning over folks that had told her they could handle their own shit.

She pushed through the bramble to the fourth curse, hanging against a tree, half-grown-in like a wart through the bark. She swung her stick, and the curse broke, some glass embedding in the end of the ash. This time she didn't even watch as the bird swooped down and beheaded the snake. She was too focused to be afraid.

Resisting the urge to head back to Motheater, to see if there was another tattoo, she pushed on to the fifth ball and dispatched it, and then went searching for the final mirror.

"Where the fuck is it?"

Made sense it was hidden. Didn't want curious onlookers to try to pull them down and release the witch too soon. Maybe that's why there were six of them.

She paused at the last curse. What if this was a mistake? What did she know about Motheater, really? She was dangerous, and old, and the mountain answered her call. But what was she capable of? What did she want? She swallowed. *What if it had been Motheater all along, murdering miners in the mountain?*

Fuck it. She had no other options. Motheater was a desperate gamble, but she had no other choice. She would deal with the consequences later. Right now, she had to have faith. She had to trust Motheater. Maybe she were a liar. Maybe not. But Bennie was going to take that risk. She couldn't abandon Kiron now. She suspected Motheater couldn't, either.

Bennie swung; the curse shattered. The snake fell from the tree, but this time it was thicker—a stout, dark thing, grown noxious in its prison. Bennie took a step back, eyes wide. The jay swooped down, and even the weight of all the lore on its trickster wings wasn't enough of a club for this serpent.

"Oh shit."

Bennie stepped back, swung again, and this time she saw whips and scales clinging to the shards of glass in the staff. The snake tilted back, rearing like it was about to strike, and Bennie slammed the staff down, heart pounding in her ears, terror rising like a flooded creek.

The snake re-formed under the walking stick, infected, broken, but not shattered. The jay attacked it again, going for the eyes, and damn, if that little bird was going to be brave, what excuse did Bennie have?

"Get back!" She swung the stick again, and this time she must have caught on something vital, because the snake finally laid down and melted into the pine needles like fog in the sun. Bennie swallowed and stepped back. The bird flew around, pecked at the ground, and then flew to Bennie's shoulder.

"You're pretty great," Bennie muttered, turning away from the shattered bauble in the ground. "Gonna have to name you if you figure on sticking around. I can get you a nice birdhouse from the hardware store if you like that sort of thing."

The bird tugged on one of Bennie's braids, and she grumbled, putting her hand in her pockets and finding some more granola.

"Dirty-ass bird," she muttered, smiling, as the jay went to her hand and started picking at the oats.

At the old path, Motheater was still on her knees. Her hands were braced against the ground, and Bennie's mouth went dry. If one dusty old snake had given her a weird tattoo, what had six done? She jogged over and crouched down.

"Moth?" she asked, tilting her head, trying to see her face. "You all right?"

Motheater nodded.

"What's going on?"

"I'm listening," she murmured, her voice slurred, soft and light. "Give me your hand."

Bennie shifted and held out her hand. Motheater took it and pressed it to the ground, still leaning over, still on her hands and knees. Her hand covered Bennie's, and she could see the inky little ring-neck snake poking out from Motheater's sleeve, harsh and coal black against Motheater's pale skin.

And then, under her hand, Bennie felt Kire breathe.

15
Esther

Near Christmas, Jasper showed up at Esther's door, knocking with loud, sure raps.

"I need to find some ginseng," he said when Esther had opened the door and glared at him, up to her elbows in a spell to stave off the worst of winter's chill.

"It's past season." Esther made to close the door.

"I have news."

Esther paused. She sighed and opened the door again, ignoring the wry smile on Jasper's face as she stepped back to let him in. "I'll clean and come down."

A few minutes later, they walked side by side, heading past White Rock creek and northerly, toward Forks. There were hidden places nearby that held copses of wild ginseng, and although most of the telltale red berries would have fallen off their stems by now, there were still a few visible.

She waited until Jasper had picked up a few of the roots before fixing him with a keen stare.

"What news, then?"

"I've been elected to the council," Jasper said as he

crouched down to brush aside some leaves. "In charge of resources and apportioning."

"Weren't that Collum's position?" Esther frowned. There was some communal work involved in keeping Kiron running, and apportioning happened a few times a month depending on the need. Esther made sure to lure more animals into traps that week, giving some of the families incentive to offer more to the group yield.

Jasper made a noise, finding a root and twisting it up. "His eyes are bad. Can't take the numbers right."

His eyes had always been bad. He got one half blown out in a mining accident years ago. Even Esther couldn't save it entire, but she had managed to stitch the parts back together, giving him one white man's blue eye. At least he still had his head.

Esther resisted the urge to tell Jasper that this wasn't the kind of news she cared about. Instead, she led them farther into the woods, trying to find patience. "Congratulations. A fine position."

And one that indicated, once again, Kiron's love for Jasper was something she would never know.

"We need to open up a new mine shaft."

Esther stopped walking. She turned back to Jasper. He was still crouching, looking up at her, his hand in the dirt. She shook her head. Not too far away was Kire's slowly shifting mass. She knew how much mining hurt it, how much it wanted to rest, that between its witch and her wards, it could not sleep. "No."

"Esther—"

"No, Jasper, don't ask this." Esther clenched her hands. "If we open up another cut, it will only make Kiron more enticing to Halberd."

"We have more people in Kiron than ever before, and the original mine is no longer viable. We only have one now, and that's not nearly enough."

"The old mine is good," Esther insisted, clenching her hands. She couldn't tell him how hurt the mountain was. He didn't know.

"It's got nothing there."

"I'll inspect the old shaft." Esther was trying to be reasonable, but even she heard the petulance in her voice. She turned sharply to leave.

"Esther!" Jasper cursed, jogging up to her. "The only way we keep Kiron men clear of Halberd is to give them what Halberd's offering. If Kiron can get the coal it needs, get the money out of the mountain, then they won't go looking for some industry to take their paycheck."

"It's dangerous," Esther muttered, pulling herself free, disappointed. Didn't he trust her? Didn't *anyone* trust her? Her hurt turned sour. "If you open a new shaft, you will have blood on your hands," Esther warned. "Kire will not suffer you."

The frost in the air fell, sheets of ice appearing over trees and on the ground as Esther drew her power close. Jasper had to make constant bargains with land and plant to tap his magic, just like any hedge witch. But Esther was a soul-bound Neighbor, and she only ever bargained with the mountain. It held her soul and in exchange, she held a deep well of its power.

"Will Kire be the one to kill me, or will you?" Jasper found his voice, pitching it high to get over the wind that came from behind Esther.

"I am protecting you!" Esther screamed, and her voice was carried on owls' wings as they swooped down in between her and Jasper. "We fight the industry; we do not fight each other!"

"Industry won't have none to fight it if Kiron can't get coal out of that mountain without Halberd's machines! What do you expect us to do, witch? We can't survive like this!"

He was right. God, it hurt, but he was right. But maybe there was another vein, a different streak of coal away from a bloodthirsty mountain they could tap. She had forced Kire to wake up to its pain, and now the mountain would come to bear down on Kiron.

"I just need time," Esther pleaded, and already she heard her desperation echo along the empty trees. She could find more coal, she could find some way for industry to be satisfied away from this holler, she could soothe Kire . . . surely, she could.

"Stop acting like a child, and start looking after Kiron proper! What good are you if you ask us to starve?" Jasper took a step back, shielding his face. Esther wanted to rip him apart. She wanted all the things that Jasper had: conviction, decisions, the love of Kiron. Why wouldn't they love her, too? Why didn't they understand?

"Nothing you take from Kire is free!" Esther screamed at him, snow melting around her. "I pay in blood and soul, and you bargain in small worship!"

"We will not worship at your feet to sate the unknown demands of a mountain," Jasper spat. "Halberd will cut Kire a thousand times, or Kiron will cut it ten times. These people will not become derelict for your pride."

Under her feet, there was a hum, an echo, a crack that could have split the heavens, and a megalith on the west end of Kire began to shift down the mountain. Esther could feel from Kire her own anger reflected back, the love she desired held there, if only she gave into it. She would attempt to bargain with Halberd, despite her poor reputation in that camp. She would ease Kire's next cut; she would find a way. She would. She would. She would.

The owls surrounded her, and in a winged rush, she left Jasper alone in the copse, all the ginseng withered for a mile.

16

Bennie

What the fuck is happening?" Bennie's eyes were huge as she held her breath. She could feel something under her hand, something that shifted, like a snake shedding its skin, like a dog with too much scruff under a fist. It held a wild violence, and she wanted to pull her hand away. She knew it was an untamable force.

"Listen," Motheater murmured, and Bennie thought she sounded like someone in rapture, a girl whispering to her lover in bed. The milky scent of pine needles, damp and warm, rose up around them, and Bennie felt the power here, the strength of an unyielding faith.

"Listen," Motheater said again. Bennie looked up at her, at the ecstasy there, like some Gentileschi painting in black and light. Motheater closed her eyes and leaned forward, resting her head against Bennie's shoulder, and Bennie flushed at the closeness. She was about to say something to the witch, and then, as if she were being dragged in an undertow, Bennie slipped down, into the stone.

It was dark and cold, but there was movement, more

than she would have expected from a ridgeline that had settled millions of years ago. She almost felt trapped, but she
could still feel her knees against the ground and Motheater's
mouth near her neck. She wasn't trapped; she was in the
mountain.

Motheater drove them down, and Bennie felt the roots of
the trees brushing against her back, breaking over the surface
of the ground, their systems driving deeper into the stone.
Stretching out, prying deeper. She could feel their momentum, curious and cautious, growing slow enough to split shale
and granite, keeping themselves attached to the mountain
and tearing it apart.

"What is this?"

"This is the mountain."

Motheater shifted them away from the noisy trees who
never stopped talking to each other like creaking doors. She
moved them farther along the mountain's range, sliding down
the hills and valleys of the stacked bedrock, leaning into the
heat and fury, finding those small fissures.

There was something else here, a steadiness that was
different from the rest of the mountain. Motheater paused,
curious. Even Bennie could feel it was different-not-different.
Another lodestone driven into the land.

Then they came upon Kire. Bennie held her breath, and
the mountain was still. She let it out, and there was a shift.
Motheater had buried them so deep that there was no difference between the three of them, held under the stone,
breathing together. Imagine thinking that simply because
it wasn't visible meant it wasn't constantly shifting, in the
smallest, most incremental of movements. Bennie leaned into
Motheater.

Again, and this time Bennie could recognize it for what
it was, Kire breathed under their hands. Not with flesh and
lungs, and not with air, but with the steadiness of a creature

at rest, the nonzero movement of all things. It was the ebb of a tide, the wane of the moon, the revolution of the world, ready to break apart if Motheater just gave it the smallest nudge in the right direction. The witch had been right all along.

Bennie could distantly feel the cores and shafts that White Rock had opened up in the side of the mountain. No . . . not just White Rock. All the companies going back to Halberd Ore and Mineral. Kire was helpless under the machines that dug into it. A *learned* helpless. It only seemed fragile now because it had been waiting, bearing its hurt over three hundred years. Had Motheater kept it down? Had she subdued the slouching beast?

Bennie wanted to look deeper, wanted to find the heat of the mountain, the coal catamount that curled here, that old, dark thing. But Motheater's hand gripped hers tighter, and they retreated slowly out of the mountain, the witch leading her away from the great stone.

When they came up, the taste of mineral and moss still on Bennie's tongue, the air around them had settled, and the trees leaned into them, drawn to the power.

Motheater shifted and sat back, her eyes closed.

Bennie stared at Motheater, still holding her hand. Bennie was furious, suddenly, angry and hurt. The pain that radiated out of Kire was immense, a history of violence written on its body in a way that Bennie understood. A generational pain it had borne over the past three hundred years.

The witch leaning on her seemed tired, shoulders slumped, strange, not-bruises around her neck and wrists. How many snakes were imprinted on her now? One for each curse? Would Motheater let Bennie see them? Bennie licked her lips and tried not to think about why she wanted that.

"All right," Bennie muttered, heart racing. "I'm willing to admit the mountain might be alive."

Motheater grinned at her, squeezing her hand. She stood up slowly, like she was in pain. "Been a long time since I did that. Connected."

"You love it," Bennie said. "The mountain, here, this place. You love it."

Motheater nodded. "I was supposed to protect it."

The mountain or Kiron? Bennie kept herself from getting angry, from asking why Motheater couldn't protect the miners, too. Was only the mountain worthy of being loved? Was taking the only kind of love Motheater recognized?

The witch pulled her hand away from Bennie's to rub at her face. Bennie felt that, too—the bone-tired ache of being near something so old. As Motheater had led them through the world, they hadn't missed the shafts like wounds, the mountains like Huckleberry that were missing tops, the strip-mined range to the south. An empty drum against the mountains' cacophony of life.

"We been mining this mountain for years," Motheater said, with a clarity that changed her tone. She was less modern again, something a little more highland. "This whole damned area."

"You remembering now?" Bennie asked.

"Slow, like a sill," Motheater murmured. "I remember the smell of sulfur and zinc in the morning during spring and summer; the heat from the rock blew it across the mountain."

Bennie took her hand again and squeezed. The witch looked up at her. She smiled a little, and Motheater's eyes turned from something somber to something a little softer, kinder. The creases around her mouth smoothed. She was still all angles, but she didn't seem so sharp.

"There used to be pressure holes we drilled," Motheater said, turning slightly, pointing over to the eastern part of the mountain. "They dripped muddy sludge, dark like blood out of a beast."

Bennie looked at her and wondered if she was still in the mountain that trapped her memories like dead roots. She set her stick against the ground and stood up, pulling Motheater up along with her, holding her hand tightly.

"They're digging too close to Kire's heart." Motheater let go of Bennie's hand, and Bennie immediately wanted to grab it again. She wanted to feel Motheater's fingers as she spoke. Motheater paused, and then spoke with the surety of a Cassandra. "I ain't with it. Kire's waking up."

"You were in its heart."

"Aye," Motheater muttered, frowning. Her words were venom. "Trapped, intent."

Bennie knew that anger, that horror. She felt it, too, surrounding her—something of Motheater's cunning still clinging on like an empty cicada shell. The mountain was waking up. It was real now, it was as familiar as Motheater's hand in hers, it was looming, a presence in the back of her head that she couldn't shake off. Bennie glanced at her feet, unsure of where to plant her next steps. Her mind raced. If it was waking up, what the fuck did it want?

Motheater broke her spiraling thoughts. "We're close," Motheater said, heading along the memory of a trail. "I want what my father tried to hide from me."

Bennie watched her go, then looked down at her feet again. She remembered that feeling of breathing, the bigness of it, the impossibility. What would a creature like Kire do, awake, aware, and understanding?

Bennie set her jaw, fixed her cap, and gripped her walking stick, following Motheater. Under her feet, she felt the mountain shift again, the only sign of disturbance the shaking of branches, a soft crack like a sigh in the distance.

17

Esther

Only a few weeks later, warmth broke out of the
Appalachian winter like a weed. One day it was
cold; the next it was warm, and then it stayed that
way. On the third warm day, when the last of the mountain
ice was melting, Esther felt a stirring. The miners of Kiron
were restless, and despite the kind winter at Esther's hands,
they wanted to make their living.

Kire shuddered as she spoke soothing words to the titan
under the rock, reminding it that this was the price of worship—that you cut off parts of yourself to keep your adherents
happy, to give them something to remain faithful for. It didn't
seem to hear her, its claws in the bedrock.

And then, it was enough. Kire shifted under her sweet
talk, bracing for the coming bloodletting, settling deeper into
the earth. Another hibernation.

Esther visited last year's mine shaft early in the morning
after she spoke to Kire. As suspected, the miners had brought
up logs and beams they had milled over the winter, and already one of the women on the drill team was laying them

out, shifting them over one by one, aligning each with beams that matched their breadth and width. She had hewn pegs with her and was measuring them out, taking them over to the sawhorse set up nearby to get them trimmed to task.

"It's a clear shaft?" Esther asked, announcing her presence as she walked out of the woods after the woman had put down her saw.

The woman looked over at her, eyebrows up, and Esther recognized Maisie O'Connell, a Black widow who had moved to the freeman's town without her husband four years ago, chased out of a Kentucky holler for some reason nobody had ever figured out nor asked too many questions on. But mines didn't care about color or sex. When you came out covered in coal dust, everyone looked the same. Maisie nodded, turning back to her work, having no fear of anyone, witchcraft or no.

"Aye, a couple slouching pieces, but nothing that'll impede the work. We got a clear line for about thirty feet."

Esther flinched. Thirty feet of picks and pikes driving into Kire. That was a good ten feet longer than she had expected. But Jasper was right. Kiron was growing, and more and more miners needed to earn a living off the coal they could pick out of the mountain.

"That's good news," Esther said quietly. She pushed the storm of fear down fast. "Seems that'll be enough to keep the town busy for a good while."

Maisie shrugged, glanced at Esther. "Another shaft scouted, too."

Esther's face remained neutral. "Oh?"

"Had Jasper dowse up a bit of a vein," Maisie said. "Twin the two, we'll have enough to stay out of Halberd's trouble."

Esther nodded, her fury returning. Was her allegiance to Kiron or Kire? Should she warn against taking too large a bite out of the titan, or did she return to the leviathan, hands spread, pleading for her people? What master held her leash?

She traded with Kire for power, but what good was she if she kept her work selfish? And Halberd was knocking with more and more fury. At least Maisie seemed to understand the dire nature here.

And Jasper, he had done exactly what she had asked him not to do. Hadn't she killed the moon to keep him away from Kire? She was the place of places. The witch unmade herself to make herself for everyone else.

It had to be Kiron. Otherwise, she was just a well.

"That's good," Esther said quietly. She stepped forward, closer to the mine. "No ice inside, neither."

"None," Maisie said, crouching to push a beam aside. "The winter was kind."

If Esther heard a thanks there, she ignored it.

"I want to go in."

"Ain't held up." Maisie turned toward Esther as she passed, heading into the mine shaft. "Some of them beams are rot out."

Esther didn't bother. She walked into the mountain, letting the black swallow her.

The mine shaft was a raw wound in Kire's side, and despite his size and strength, she knew he felt it. He was titanous, cavernous, a leviathan, but he was also a living creature, and when he was cut into, he knew. She walked along the open tunnel, her hand trailing along the mine. The shaft quickly became small, and she stopped when the ceiling got so low that she would need to go to her hands and knees to keep on.

The slit went farther into the mountain, cutting into the shear of it. Esther shifted close to the dark coal, the inch of it, the layer that was pressed hard between unforgiving shale, the muscle striations of the great mountain hunched over, flayed for his adherents, open and wanting.

She put her hand on the dark coal, took a deep breath, and listened to Kire.

❦

Esther came onto Jasper's land surrounded by a swarm, her anger and fury unrestrained as she marched down the mountain and through the outskirts of Kiron. As the spring was breaking open like an old jarfly clinger, so even the shells had come to a rustling life and followed her through the trees, a torrent of sound beating the air.

At Jasper's plot, she stopped short, unable to move closer to his home. She could see his cabin directly in front of her, but she couldn't move past the tree line. It wasn't painful, but there was a pressure at her temples like her head was being slowly squeezed.

He had put up a *warding*, buried something to keep her from approaching. But Jasper's deals with bones and leftover loam wouldn't stop the swarm, and the noise rose as the cicadas came to her, drawn like bees to a blooming bush. The hollowness of the mass, the dead husks, were able to pass through his barrier, and they went up to his windows, dashing themselves against the leather covers. A few managed to scurry in between the tacks and the wood, and Esther bared her teeth as more and more dead carapaces edged into Jasper's home.

"Witch!"

The door slammed open, and Jasper stalked out half-dressed, his shoes untied.

"You put up a fence," Esther said tightly.

"Aye, to prevent your magic from entering, to prevent this exact moment, right here, from occurring!"

"I can't exactly knock on your door with them stakes up, can I?"

Jasper looked surprised. He glanced from side to side, noting the place where he had placed his magical wards. Esther frowned, and while the jarfly swarm continued to mass around her like a murmuration, shapes and wings all a flutter, merging and condensing behind her, the clingers stopped trying to attack Jasper's windows.

"It was only meant to stop your spells," he explained, hesitating slightly.

"I am a spell!" Esther yelled. "And I need to talk to you!"

"See this, though? Look at all this!" Jasper gestured, exasperated. A grouping of carapaces landed on his arm, and he shook them off, annoyed. "This is why I made that boundary! See what you brought in here?"

Esther stamped her foot, petulant. "That ain't fair!"

"Look at the state of you, witch! Is this how you come to a friend's home?" He swatted at the dead shells.

"I ain't call them!" Esther was getting desperate. The jarfly swarm around her buzzed louder, an ever-present plague, the threat of a storm about to break on a ridge. She had opened her body like a gorge to receive power, and Kire could not be fully controlled. "These things just happen, Jasper!"

"And I'm tired of them happening to me!" Jasper snapped. "Say your piece and go."

"You dug into the stone! You have overwritten my careful dealings with the titan!" Esther cried. "And now we've got three open wounds in Kire's side!"

"You think that one vein you slit two years ago is going to comfort Kiron now? With Halberd breathing down our neck?!" At the very least, Esther noticed, he had the decency to look a little embarrassed about taking over her job. He knew that he was breaking pacts she had forged in blood and worship. "I did you a *favor*."

"You have no idea what you did," Esther said, voice like a whip, cracking through the air. Her words were caught in jarfly wings, and they tossed it around the wood, each syllable an echo, shattering the air. Jasper jerked back, flinching, and his hair finally came loose of its tie, falling around his face. "You have tramped over my bargains with Kire."

"I ain't sign nothing."

"I cannot hold the leviathan back, Jasper! If you infringe on what I have bargained for, Kire will never know peace!" Esther's panic was trapped in the empty carapaces. Her words revolved over themselves, tumbling like a rock in a stream. "I cannot hold him down forever!"

"Then you've got a decision to make!" Jasper yelled back, his hair floating behind him, caught in a river of Esther's power. "Kire or Kiron!"

Esther bared her teeth and flung her hands out. He did not know the breadth of Kire, he did not know the titan she held back. He spoke with disdain. The trees around them bent back, revealing the darkening sky, the clear stars, the moon, high and light, pressed against the heavens, soft as a kiss.

"Turn out your company man," Esther hissed. "Take him to the ore you've found and let him down into the shaft first. Let him be the first to sacrifice his life for Kiron's progress."

"I ain't going to do that neither," Jasper said quietly, standing tall, staring down the witch. "You are tasked to protect our town, witch."

"You've damned us all," Esther spat. Kire would take from Kiron that which she could not provide.

"We've been damned before," Jasper said.

Esther clenched her fist, and the trees surrounding Jasper's plot snapped, cracking like gunshots across the valley. Jasper ducked and covered his head with his arms. Esther slipped back into the weald, the cicadas disappearing into the darkness, the clingers on Jasper's shirt and in his home turned to dust.

18

Bennie

"You got a funny look on your face," Bennie muttered after another ten minutes of walking past the string of broken curses that had kept Motheater out. Above them, the jaybird flitted around, alighting on branches near them.

"I feel like I got flowers blooming under my skin," Motheater muttered, her voice dry and cracked. "Ain't this the whole age of my life? Ain't I old enough to ache?"

"Depends on how you measure it." Bennie smiled a little. "If you're talking about since, like, your date of actual birth, for sure."

Motheater walked ahead, and Bennie felt like she had ruined their moment. Under Motheater's footsteps, the pine needles that still pointed toward some kind of true north rustled behind her, floating in small bursts of orange-and-copper clouds. Motheater were just such a part of this place that even the dead leaves on the ground couldn't leave her alone.

"There's another thing here—we felt it," Motheater muttered. Bennie made a noise—the lodestone in the hollers. "More than just the mountain keeps me."

"What's that mean?"

"Ain't all of me in one place."

"So not just in the church?" Suddenly the trees thinned, and it appeared without warning, the moss-covered sides of the church camouflaged it among the branches of Kire Mountain. Bennie paused, eyes huge as she looked over the dilapidated building, noting the broken-off cross, the parts of the whitewash that were as gray as the heaving ridge that it stood near, a cliff that ran up fifteen feet before continuing its slope upward. Bennie swallowed, pausing to look over the building that was most definitely fucking haunted. This was not final girl behavior.

Motheater stopped at the doors, and Bennie jogged a few paces to catch up with her.

"Damn," Bennie murmured, leaning against the stave as she stood next to the witch. "I didn't realize it'd be standing." She had expected a foundation, maybe a wall. There were old ruins all over the mountain, some marked on the map and others, like Motheater's place of worship, left forgotten.

"It rests on spite," Motheater said bitterly.

The church was modest in size, the sides intact, but the roof was slightly buckled. As Bennie stepped closer, she saw the far end of the church wasn't just close to the mountain, but built against it; the gaps in between the ridge and the wooden planks of the sides allowed moss and stray vines into the church.

"What do you remember about this place?" Bennie went to the doors and touched one with her stick. It didn't budge. That was fine; she wasn't going into that old, rickety building anyway.

"Not much," Motheater admitted. Bennie stood in front of the entrance as the witch paced around the sides of the church before returning to the doors. "My father was the preacher. We took copperheads and cottonmouths in our hands to prove our faith. We sang, and the mountain listened."

"Sounds like a blast." Bennie took a step back from the doors. She wondered in what universe did she imagine herself hanging out with a nineteenth-century snake-handling Pentecostal preacher's daughter witch, and immediately decided that was a die she was going to roll another day. "You going in?"

Motheater swallowed, glanced at Bennie, and then nodded.

"I have to, I think."

"Well it'd be a fucking shame if we turned back now after all the effort it took to get up here," Bennie huffed. She took a few steps back as Motheater moved to stand in front of the doors. She noticed Motheater's hands clenching and unclenching. A few moths had appeared during Motheater's inspection of the church, floating around her head.

Bennie gestured to the insects with the end of her stick. "You got some friends."

Motheater blinked and turned her head slightly. She reached up, spreading her hand, and the moths settled gently into her palm. They were small, mostly brown with yellow underwings and blue spots. Motheater closed her eyes and leaned over them.

Motheater turned a little, almost as if she were giving Bennie a chance to watch. Her jaw moved as she whispered something to the little wings that peeked out in between her fingers. The moths fluttered and then faded, some kind of dust taking their place, coating the witch's hands before she lifted her hand and twisted a dark buckwheat-colored strand into her white hair, one of her eyes turning blue around just one corner.

Motheater swallowed and took another deep breath, hands in fists by her side.

"Who were they?" Bennie asked quietly, staring at Motheater's bluish eye.

"The elder faithful," Motheater muttered. "We're not alone."

Bennie tightened her grip on the stick. Above her, the jaybird screamed, swooping in to rest on the mossy roof of the church. It struck Bennie that Motheater was scared to go in. Bennie looked down at the pine needles on the ground, which formed a dark, rust-colored halo around the church, floating up to the rocky side of the mountain.

"No," Bennie said, stepping up and taking Motheater's hand, feeling rather bold, and squeezing it gently. She felt a little bit of heat rise in her cheeks, but she wasn't about to let this weirdo witch know that she was embarrassed to be this blatant. "We aren't."

Motheater's eyes went wide. Bennie looked down at her and smiled as Motheater held Bennie's hand like it was a lifeline. Under them, the mountain seemed smaller. The wind seemed a soft breeze and not the ever-present rush of warm wind being forced upward along the cold stone.

"Come on, stop staring at me." Bennie turned, glaring at the door. She didn't want to think about the way that Motheater's eyes flicked over every part of her face. "You got a door to bust down."

Motheater looked at their hands.

"I was raised in this church."

"That's right."

"This is my mountain," Motheater said, a little firmer, and glared at the doors, with their grimy paint, their broken, rusted hinge, the leaves poking through the bottom of the door. She took a deep breath and squeezed Bennie's hand. Bennie tried, very hard, not to get embarrassed, or warm, but she couldn't help it, and affection came fast and hard.

"I think all the Psalms are about love," Motheater said, and Bennie knew that her face was full hot now. "And not about God at all."

Bennie swallowed, her eyes wide. Her heart was beating faster, heart caught in between the wings of a blue jay and the ground.

"*Because she is at my right hand, I shall not be moved*," Motheater quoted. She let go of Bennie's hand and stepped forward, and the pine needles around the church suddenly turned, a ripple out from the church as the true north of Kire Mountain shifted toward Motheater.

Bennie took a step back and gripped her walking stick as the witch took a deep breath, steeling herself, making herself a tower. Motheater raised her hands to press against the doors of the old Church of the Rock and shoved them open. They moved stiffly, and Motheater grit her teeth and slammed her shoulder against the door, pushing it open a few more feet before the doors slid in, and one of them dropped off the hinges entirely. Bennie didn't help. This wasn't her past.

Inside, Bennie could see that what pews were left were in disarray, pushed up against the sides of the church or broken. At the far end of the church was the steep rock face, lichen growing over it. The patchy ceiling let in plenty of light to see directly back to where the building abutted the mountain.

The aisle leading to the altar was covered in moss, a sage-green carpet that had crept in from the edges of the building where it abutted the mountain. Ahead of Motheater, carved out of Kire itself, was the altar, crosses and scripture engraved into the stone. It was ancient looking, a brutal part of the church, and Bennie knew that whatever god they had worshipped here, it was not the same as the Spirit that came into her church on Sundays.

She wanted to leave, wanted to run in and pull Motheater out of this wreckage of a memory, but she didn't say anything. She stood in the doorframe, unsure of whether she should go in. Above her, the jay screamed again and swooped to land on the top of Bennie's walking stick.

Motheater glanced back at her, and Bennie could see the moment that panic spasmed across her face.

"Get back!" Motheater yelled, throwing her hand up, pushing Bennie backward, out of the church. Bennie stumbled but kept her balance as a large black snake fell from the rafter above the frame, its thick body landing where Bennie had been standing.

"Oh, fuck no." Bennie quickly lifted her walking stick and batted the large snake to the side, swinging the branch like a golf club. The jay swooped down, spreading its wings, attacking the head of the snake. It had been struck to the edge of the clearing, and Bennie turned to look quickly into the church.

Around Motheater, snakes appeared out of the shadows, every dark corner alive and writhing. The witch turned slowly around, eyes huge, as a swarm of reptiles formed out of darkness. Bennie was frozen, whether by fear or an old curse, and could not enter the church. Behind her the jay screamed, and whatever reptile had snuck out of hell to try to fight her would have their hands full with the blue bird.

Bennie struggled to break free, panic rising as Motheater backed up until she was flush against the ancient altar, and then scrambled on top of it, surrounded. The snakes were focused on her, and Motheater glanced to Bennie. She saw terror there, and concern, and Bennie found life in her legs. Just fear, then. Just fear as Motheater looked at her and saved her spells for those who really needed it.

"Get 'em, Motheater!" Bennie screamed out, safe from the snakes coiled in the church.

"*Behold!*" Motheater yelled, raising her hands up. Around her, shades formed, becoming clearer and clearer. These were those who died on the mountain. A few still had on White Rock uniforms. It was hard to make out much else—their features were smudged, their skin all coal-dirt-blackened. Bennie clutched her stick and did not look them in their eyes, keeping her gaze down, toward whatever serpents might come to her. She might not be the most constant churchgoer, but she knew enough not to stare the dead in their faces.

The ghosts in the church became a chorus, a revenant echo that repeated Motheater's words back at the smoky rat snake. *"I give unto you power to tread on serpents and scorpions, and over all the power of the enemy: and nothing shall by any means hurt you!"*

The ghosts of the stone stepped forward onto the cottonmouths and timber rattlers. Bennie forgot to breathe as the snakes writhed, burning up where the dead stood on them. They crowded around the altar stone, pushing their way up the carvings. One reared back, preparing to strike at Motheater, but the witch crouched and grabbed it, faster than any adder, her thumb digging behind its head, the other holding its body so that it couldn't flail around. Her hands were sure and practiced as she brought it up to her chest.

"Who sent you, adder, into my home?" Motheater whispered. The ghosts that marched through the church spoke it, too, and Bennie heard every word clearly as Motheater knelt down on the altar. She looked around, but there was nothing for her to do but witness the witch.

With one snake held fast, Motheater kept sway over the rest of the brood. Her ghosts had swept through the church, and as the last serpent melted back into the corners of the mountain, Motheater kept her hands tight along the body of the cottonmouth that had tried to bite her.

One of the ghosts stopped in front of Bennie, and her heart stopped. The shade had dark smears on her face, and Bennie couldn't tell if Kelly-Anne Elliot had coal or blood under her eyes. She was still wearing her uniform, her hard hat, and her hair, natural, curly and wild, poked out from underneath.

That was a safety violation, Bennie thought to herself, lost in grief.

Motheater and Kelly-Anne spoke with the same voice, the witch to the cottonmouth, the miner to Bennie. "Were we not friends once?"

"We still are," Bennie said, eyes huge. Kelly-Anne's face was impassive. She wasn't here. She wasn't in the mountain; Bennie would have felt her when Motheater drove Bennie into the stone like a pick. Kelly-Anne was just an echo. One of the last miners killed in Kire, the shallowest grave. Bennie's heart broke again, like biting into a sour apple. It wasn't Kelly-Anne in the shadows of the magic, it was just a shade.

The ghosts melted back into mothdust, and Bennie held tight onto her staff to keep herself from crumbling. Inside, Motheater was alone on the altar with the serpent. It hissed, the sounds of leaves against the ground, and its body wrapped around her arm, the tail of the long creature sliding around her neck.

Suddenly, the cottonmouth went soft in her hands. Motheater sagged and, like an old video being remastered, the desuetude chapel became the unholy Church of the Rock. Bennie gasped as she saw it change: full whitewashed sides and polished windows, plaster arches, the smallest of gold leaf details under the curves, small colored panes along the top of the doorframe. The pews were dark, a stained sycamore that grew in the valley, flowers hanging off the ends. This must have been as it was when Motheater was alive; this must have been what she saw when she entered the church.

The glory of the old worship rang in Bennie's ears. She couldn't see exactly what was happening between the pews with clippings of mountain laurel fastened at the ends, but like mist rising in sunlight, Bennie saw the shapes of men taking form.

They were ghostly, faded and translucent, with patches opening up across their shoulders and chest as the dust settled around them, making them an incomplete memory. Bennie looked at Motheater, who was staring, eyes wide, as the men formed around her. She must have recognized them, these ghosts and half men, but Bennie had no idea what to make of them.

But this was Motheater's resurrected memory. She had spent one hundred and fifty years in the grave, and on this day, the stone was rolled away.

Bennie swallowed and stepped back. One of the men paced along the side of the church, watching Motheater, who was still kneeling on the altar, her hands still wrapped around a soft cottonmouth.

A bell rung out like a whoop through the night, and Bennie startled, eyeing the forest warily. There was no great movement, but at about knee level, soft blue balls of light started to pulse. Bennie's mouth went dry. They clicked, like a knock against the ground.

"Moth . . ."

She turned back, and saw Zach Gresham walk into the church.

Her mouth dropped. But he was different, ghostly, pale, missing parts as he walked into the church, wearing suspenders and a hat that looked like it was made of reeds. It wasn't Zach; he was shorter than this man, but the echo had his build, his hair, his face.

She walked toward him as he walked into the church, her eyes wide. For some reason, this boy was sharp-edged, outlined in a way the other shades weren't. Bennie saw Motheater track him into the church, a sneer on her face.

The last ghost to appear, the last memory to rise from whatever magic Motheather had called up, was herself. Bennie stepped aside as a quicksilver witch formed: a woman with moonstone eyes and hair braided in an intricate pattern at the nape of her neck.

The ghost witch followed not-Zach into the church, and Bennie trailed close behind, but as soon as the memory-Motheater stepped across the threshold, the doors slammed shut, right in Bennie's face. The church, returned to its old state, even if just for a moment, was shut to Bennie, and with shimmering, frosted-glass doors preventing her from entering, she couldn't see what was going on.

"Motheater!"

The misted shapes became indistinguishable, even the silverine witch a formless creature behind ghost doors. Bennie was loath to touch the doors, but she got close, and while the ghosts were blurry in the depths of the church, she could see the real Motheater, the flesh-and-blood Appalachian witch struggling on the altar.

Bennie took a deep breath, heart racing, terrified. What was she against this? Against magic and spells and knockers at her legs. The pulsing, vibrant, milkweed stars had come closer, bouncing, almost playful as they circled the church, revolving around Bennie.

She swallowed and put her hand on the foggy doors, but they felt solid, cold as stone. Lifting her stick, she struck the door, but it didn't budge. Around her legs, the pine needles were floating up, some strange power causing them to turn and twist in midair.

Whatever the fuck was happening in that church, it wasn't good.

The jay screamed above her, and Bennie took a step back, hefting her walking stick.

"I ain't afraid of no ghosts," she muttered. With a grunt, she swung the staff at the church doors. This time, the shards of glass from the witch balls embedded in her staff dragged at the shimmering grammar there. The doors became ragged, like ghostly rags tattering against the glass shards.

Bennie smirked, set her feet again, and swung. She beat at the door until she could see what was happening: a mass of shades huddled at the back of the altar, and Motheater bent back, nearly in half, like she was recreating a scene from a bad horror film, her mouth open, the snake thrashing violently in her hands.

Whatever was happening at the back of the church, whatever memory Motheater was reliving, it was killing her. The knockers pressed against the side of the church, and Bennie grit her teeth, swinging frantically at the doors, no longer trying to pretend the staff was a bat. Even the jay dropped down to peck at the door, wearing it out strand by strand, like pulling apart a tapestry.

Motheater dropped the snake. Her hands went to her throat, clutching at something there. Bennie saw the mass of shoulders and backs against the stone ridge of Kire; she saw the cottonmouth dragging itself up from being stunned.

This was hell.

She drove her stick against the door, her arms shaking with the effort as she pried just enough of an opening for the blue jay to fly in and attack the snake before it reared up against Motheater.

Bennie needed to get in, she needed to help, she couldn't let the witch die here, she couldn't let the old magic take her. She was supposed to save people.

Motheater slumped on the altar, a hand at her neck, head hanging over the side of the stone.

"Motheater! Get up!" Bennie cried, stepping back to kick at the door. Fury mingled with the panic now, fear and anger and righteousness. This would *not* be how it ended. "Get up! Get up! Get up!"

In the church, Motheater screamed.

Bennie was pushed back from the door as if a gale had come through the church. She heard a crack and immediately thought of a cave-in, the sound of stone breaking, of cleavage sliding alone a plane, and her heart stopped. What if the ridge was breaking? What if the mountain had moved to swallow Motheater whole, right here in this temple?

Bennie shielded her eyes, dust and cracks echoing across the copse. The mountain must have sunk; this was the sound of the chapel collapsing into the ground, this was the end of the Church of the Rock. She turned back to the church and her mouth dropped.

Motheater stood on the rubble of the altar, and around her, the walls had broken from their foundations, and as glass shards and mossy thatch split apart in the air, the Church of the Rock was lifted up.

Bennie took a few steps back, her eyes huge, her breath coming in small quickening gasps. This was the witch on her mountain. This was what the fire could do to you. This is what you could do with power. Bennie's heart pounded in her ears, behind her eyes, and she scrambled back, eyes huge, pine needles catching in her hair.

"You failed to kill me!" Motheater screamed, and above her, the chapel continued to split and break apart in midair, rotating like a gyre. The ghosts were gone, torn to shreds. "You merely slowed me down!"

Bennie flinched, and the blue-light knockers that had been surrounding the church played at Motheater's feet, rising up with the chapel, burning the wood wherever they touched. It was a smolder, cracking embers along a plank. Motheater's hands were in fists at her sides, her hair loose in the controlled cyclone, her eyes upward at the remains of worship.

Bennie couldn't look away. Motheater drew her in, like the witch drew everything to her. Here was the promise of power, the whisper of it. If anything looked like prophecy to Benethea Mattox it was this: written in shards of the Church of the Rock that revolved in a slow orbit above Motheater, dowsing sticks crossing and uncrossing along Motheater's fault lines. She stared up at the debris that circled in the air, a church unmade.

Motheater moved, raising up one hand. If she spoke scripture, Bennie couldn't tell, but the half-burned remnants floated outward, far past Bennie and the area around the church. Motheater sank to her knees, driving her hand into the rubble of the altar, and the shards of the church pummeled themselves against the mountain, the mythic rolling thunder along the ridge.

Bennie clapped her hands over her ears as the Church of the Rock was destroyed. The thunder faded, and eventually Bennie calmed down enough to pull her hands away from her ears, to open her eyes and look over at Motheater. The witch was on her hands and knees on the broken altar, covered in dust. The snake was nowhere to be seen. Bennie dropped the staff and jogged over, slowing as she got near.

"Are you all right?" Bennie asked. She couldn't keep the fear out of her voice. Motheater had done something incredible, and now she looked like she was half dead. Was that the price of magic? "Motheater?"

Motheater swallowed and looked up at Bennie, shifting to sit up. Bennie quickly leaned in, helping her slide down the altar, sitting on the flat ground. She held an arm around Motheater's slim shoulders, keeping her upright. The witch was pale; her hands were shaking in her lap. Bennie wondered if the first aid course White Rock had forced them to go through a few times a year would be any help. Maybe Motheater was in shock?

And then she glanced down at the collar of Motheater's shirt. "Jesus Christ, Motheater, your *neck*."

Motheater put a hand to her collar and winced.

"It'll go away soon," she whispered.

Draped across Motheater's neck were a pair of hand-prints. Dark, ugly bruises that almost looked like mud smeared on Motheater's pale skin. She swallowed, rubbing her mouth. "What happened?"

"Nothing that matters now," Motheater muttered. "I got put into the mountain."

"That sounds like it matters some," Bennie said, her arm still around Motheater's shoulders. Motheater sighed and leaned into Bennie, her head resting against Bennie's collarbone.

"My father was a cruel man at the best of times," she said quietly. "He was only ever looking for an excuse to kill me. Seems he found it."

"Well he didn't kill you," Bennie said, getting comfortable on the ground. "You're still breathing, aren't you?"

The pause stretched out, the silence of the woods becoming obvious. No birds, no squirrels, just Motheater and Bennie and the ruins of the old church.

"Depends who you ask," Motheater murmured.

Bennie could feel Kire now, could feel it breathing and waiting. It was a living terror, the land itself resentful of the feet that tread upon it. It made Bennie want to run.

Bennie's heartbeat was pounding in her ears, and Motheater was nuzzling into her jacket, the smell of something burning hanging in the air. She could feel her face getting heated.

"It's getting dark," Bennie said stiffly. She pulled away from Motheater slowly and then stood, brushing dirt off her pants. Motheater just blinked, staring at her. "I hope you can stand up," Bennie joked, offering Motheater a hand. "I don't think I can carry you down."

"I ain't so far gone," Motheater whispered. Bennie pressed her mouth, knowing the bruises around Motheater's neck would make talking, eating, and even turning her neck too far uncomfortable. There wasn't no way to ignore getting choked out. Motheater winced as she stood, taking Bennie's hand, her whole body jerking and moving stiffly, like her strings had been cut. Bennie shifted to slide her arm around Motheater's waist, supporting her as they walked out of the wreckage.

Above them, the blue jay screamed again, and Motheater flinched, startled.

"Damn bird," Bennie muttered, leaving Motheater wavering as she ran over to get the staff that the bird had landed on. She picked it up and hesitated, watching the jay. It circled them slowly and then went to a tree, clearly waiting for Bennie to go back to Motheater and help the shaking woman down the mountain.

She had a thousand questions. What did Motheater remember; what magic did she hold now; was Kelly-Anne gone forever? Bennie swallowed a few gulps of water from her bottle before offering it to Motheater. Would they destroy White Rock now or later? Could they rip the offices from their bases like the church? Bennie pushed it all down—the eagerness, the anticipation, the longing.

"I'm starving," Bennie said instead of interrogating the witch. She put an arm back around Motheater, her other hand grasping the walking stick. "We should go get some pizza."

Motheater sighed. "What's pizza?"

Bennie laughed, and Motheater smiled, looking up at her. The White Rock offices were closed. Nobody was in the mountain. Kire breathed slowly. She could wait to ask questions. But . . . maybe not too much longer.

"Motheater, you are going to love pizza."

19

Esther

Esther found the shaft that Jasper had culled. It was farther west, away from her cabin on the northeastern side of the mountain, and a good set away from her father's church on the south. Now there were three deep cuts into Kire: the old shaft, the new one Esther had made two years ago, and this one. The area around Jasper's tunnel was cleared out, and there were already the makings of a path into town.

That meant they found coal. They wouldn't build the road if they had only run into stone. Whatever deal had traded hands between Jasper and Kire, it had given him a true thing, and gospel was always expensive. Esther was more than willing to sell her soul for power, but she had done it for Kiron. There was a reason that the women in town didn't make deals, entreating Esther instead. Being a Neighbor was dangerous work.

She clenched her hands. A petty, small part of her wanted to tear up the road, to prevent them from ever being able to profit off this scar. She was a demanding force, made of stone and spells.

But this was not where her magic was needed. Punishing Kiron for keeping up with demand, for trying to outpace Halberd when the industry was breathing down their neck, sleeping with their sons? No, destroying any part of this would only drive Kiron into the arms of Halberd again, into the promises of machines and ease.

She focused on Kire. The tunnel in front of her opened like a wolf's maw in the dead winter. It glinted, the lichen around its entrance like a blanket of jewels leading Esther inside the two-foot wide cave. When she put her hand on the stone, it was warm, not iced or freezing like deadened stone ought to be. It wasn't numbed or sutured, it hadn't been cut off from the titan—Jasper's dealings had only done so much. They were digging directly into Kire's flesh.

Anger made her hands warm. Fury made the stone darken. The shaft opened wider, inviting her in. Was Kire angrier, or was she? Her words had been discarded, her warnings ignored, and here was Kire, titan in the rock, gnashing its teeth.

The stone creaked farther down, a rush of hot air breezing across her face, melting the snow and causing the water to drip into the cave. Esther eased herself deeper into the tunnel.

"What are you doing here?"

Esther whipped around as Jasper came up the road, pushing a wheelbarrow ahead of him. He was followed by Maisie, who had her own pack of lathes and measures.

"Should know better than to sneak up on me," she said, turning her nose up and looking back at the seam.

"You're being mighty secretive," Jasper complained, pushing the wheelbarrow up to the landing. "Even for you."

What was she supposed to say? That when they cut through to the quick of any Appalachian mountain, they flirted with titans beyond their ken? It wasn't like every range had a leviathan like Kire, but there were enough of them alive that running into one was a tidy risk.

She swallowed her pride, *again*. "I am inspecting the new mining shaft."

"Aye, and to what purpose?" Jasper asked, unloading the gear, setting a lantern on a nearby stump. "You are no miner and have said so many times."

"I can still look," Esther snapped. "Leave me be."

"Jasper," Maisie whispered, almost an admonition. "Let her work."

Jasper huffed, rolling his eyes. "Women."

Esther narrowed her eyes. "Say that again, and you'll see what women's work can do."

It was a half threat, but Jasper didn't respond, turning back to his barrow. Esther was annoyed he was ignoring her, but apparently he wasn't interested in fighting with her right now. She had gotten her way, but now she stood in front of the gash, glaring at it, frustrated and disappointed. Whatever she had felt from Kire fled in Jasper's presence. He was at least able to push Kire back himself, but for how long? She should help him, or at least try to warn him away from this.

She might as well say something by way of explanation.

"This is dangerous."

"Aye," Jasper said tightly. "That's why Maisie is going to set up our stock and beam."

"That ain't going to make it less dangerous." Esther clenched her fists. "You are digging in a bad way. You will need constant deals to keep this shaft open. You ready for that? You gonna take this on?"

"What you know about digging, Esther?" Jasper hissed. This time he did turn to her, and Esther didn't meet his eyes. He was right; she wasn't a miner. But she knew that this was a bit of coal close to Kire's flesh, and it would not suffer picks for long. "We got six miner's kids coming up this year, and three families from out in the Allegheny who've sent letters inquiring about land and means here. We'll have plenty of people eager to work."

And more potential hands to sign for Halberd, Esther realized. She needed to speak to Kire, but there was a rabid beast at her door. "And what of the industry?"

"As long as we can keep our profit, we'll be fine," Jasper said, and this time his voice sounded softer, more reassuring. It did not help.

Instead of arguing, Esther turned away from the shaft, stalking into the woods. She didn't do what she had intended when she felt the warm rock: to suture the wound, to turn Kire away from its fury, to hold back her own anger . . . but if Jasper had hubris enough to dowse out his own vein, he could very well suffer the consequences.

It was a bitter, petty thought, but it kept Esther warm as she walked south, heading toward the Reed and Sarton Ridge in the distance. He was infringing on her dealings, but they had not been completely broken.

❧

Esther spent three days and two nights on the Sarton Mountains. The trio of peaks lay just east of Hatfield Valley, overlooking the camp where Halberd had set up their machines and rebuilt cabins. They were built out now: mud-and-log creations that wouldn't have felt out of place in Kiron. Esther didn't like that; it meant they were putting down roots.

She spent her time counting men and horses, noting where they were building their roads and drying them out for the late spring thaw, when the mud would be impossible to escape until May.

Esther hadn't sold all of her soul to Kire—the temptation to go down into the valley and commit a biblical slaughter was not over strong. She didn't want to kill them; she just wanted them gone.

Maybe she only had to kill one man, she thought, perched on a rock on the ridge, glaring down at the camp. Her arms were wrapped around her knees, holding onto all of the heat of her body. She had some resistance to the chill, but it was still cold, and the wind went through her clothing like it wasn't there.

Around her, dormice and possum had come up, huddling around her back and thighs for warmth as well. She didn't mind—they weren't bold enough to put holes into her clothing, and the small chattering noises were a small comfort.

Maybe she could make a deal with Halberd. There were dead titans down south, old mountains whose hearts still held coal, sinking slowly deeper into the ground. Maybe if she offered to dowse a vein or two, they might be willing to leave Kire alone.

It was a slim thing and required biting back more than a little pride, but if it kept Halberd from offering their machines to the miners of Kiron, it would be worth it.

She stood, scooping up a little joey that had forgotten to cling to its mama as it trundled away. She'd find another jill-possum to take it later, but right now, she slipped it into her pocket and stepped off the cliff, whispering power under her boots. She strode along the treetops, floating into the valley.

As she got closer to the camp, she let herself jump from branch to branch before alighting on the ground a good distance away. She walked in carefully, stepping over the half-built fence and approaching one of the buildings that had a crowd in front of it. It was noon, and they had set up their cooking pot in a communal area, the delegated cook spooning out whatever they had managed to scrounge from the nearby forests.

Esther was low, but she wasn't so petty as to make this valley barren. Kiron would suffer, too.

Their voices halted as she approached, her hands in her pockets, her dark hair loose around her shoulders, full of twigs and a few moths.

"Afternoon, gentlemen," she said, stopping a few yards away from the nearest member of their little band. "I'd like to talk to DeWitt."

The group of five eyed her warily, confused and suspicious. One even had the gall to leer at her. If she were in a fighting mood, she'd turn his eyes away with force.

"And who's calling?" one of the men said, an engineer by the looks of the grease on his pants and cuts along his hands.

"A Neighbor," she said, tilting her head up. "I'll wait here."

The engineer gave her a long look, and Esther matched his gaze, unflinching. He shrugged and turned away, going to one of the larger accommodations. After a few minutes, Julian DeWitt came out, jogging over to a second cabin and bringing along with him the same sallow-faced, white businessman who had come to their sharing a few weeks ago. The well-dressed investor she saw in the fire was absent.

As they approached, Esther became aware that other men had come out of the cabins. Miners, engineers, businessmen. The company Halberd made. She saw guns. The engineer had disappeared, maybe spreading orders through the camp. Esther was not afraid. As long as she was close to Kire, even bullets couldn't kill her.

She had scars to prove it.

"Miss Esther," DeWitt said, smiling at her, but not wide enough to convince her that he wasn't nervous. "I don't think I've introduced you to Mister Ochiltree. He's heading up the mining portion of this operation."

Esther had to put her hands in front of herself, holding them tight, to keep from hexing Ochiltree into oblivion. There were a lot of guns.

"We've not met," Esther said as Ochiltree nodded slightly, at least pretending respect. "I 'port you were one of them that told DeWitt to find a local dowser."

"As much as I am loath to trust in hill-folk mumbo jumbo, yes," Ochiltree said tightly. "Locals tend to have a sense about these things, we've found. Easier to pay a few mountain dowsers than spend real money on coring."

Esther's vision went black. Was that what he thought of her? Was that what all the lowland folks thought of the mountaineers? Her pale hands, clasped tight in front of her, turned pink. DeWitt must have sensed the tension (Maybe he had that rabbit heart in his chest still, maybe his eyes were too large for his head, maybe he knew, maybe he felt it) and stepped in, putting a hand on Ochiltree's arm for a second.

"No disrespect meant, of course," DeWitt said gently, but he was trying to smooth down the fur along a puma's spine.

"I have reconsidered my first refusal." Esther decided to ignore Ochiltree's insult, speaking to DeWitt instead. She would answer Ochiltree in kind later. "I am prepared to find coal in the southern mountains." She pointed toward Butts Mountain and Kimbalton. "There are rich mountains a step down that way."

"We're not interested in heading south," Ochiltree said. "We're interested in Kire, and the border mountains at Potts and Forks."

"If you go closer to Kimbalton, you will be nearer New River and Pearisburg," Esther explained. Potts and Forks were Kire's neighbors. If they went in there, Kire—and Kiron—would follow soon after. "It'll be easier to transport the coal on the water, and you'll have more hands available."

Ochiltree paused. Esther couldn't read DeWitt's face, wariness tugging his mouth down. Ochiltree, too, was a blank slate, a businessman who dealt in more money than Esther had likely ever seen, and he was not one to give anything away.

"We're interested in Kire, and the rights in West Virginia." He sounded almost disinterested. "The mountains by New River are more likely to hold lime deposits instead of coal buildup."

That wouldn't be so for the veins Esther found, but she couldn't help the way her eyes widened. He was keen on West Virginia, and Kire provided a pathway into the rest of Appalachia, hidden away from prospectors for so long. She had to turn this man away. Halberd wanted to run up the whole ridge.

"I am willing to reduce my fee," she said quietly. What more could she bargain with? She didn't have Jasper's way with words. "It will be well worth your time."

"I'm sorry to disappoint you, little miss." Ochiltree spoke slow, patronizing. The smirk on his face made Esther's skin crawl like teeth on stone. "We have the deeds already drawn up, and we're not looking to move. I'm sure Mister DeWitt can give you a meal to take home for your trouble. We can pay you to find a wellspring if it's money you're after."

Esther started counting guns. She felt the joey skitter in her pockets, and she reached into her dress to hold it gently in her hand, calming it down.

Maybe Ochiltree was Pharaoh. Maybe she was a plague.

"I would like to entreat—"

Before she could offer either advice or a threat, she felt her tie to Kire yank on her heart. She lost her breath, her eyes going wide, and she turned from DeWitt and the foreman, staring at Kire. Something was happening.

"Now, I'm sure you're upset about this, but—"

"I'm done talking," Esther cut him off, glancing back. She loosed her hand around the little possum. "I need a horse."

Finally, Ochiltree looked off his center. There must be something wild about her. "I'm afraid I can't—"

"Take mine," DeWitt offered, cutting Ochiltree off before he could incite Esther to call a swarm of toads up from the banks of the river. He led her to a brown pony, something sturdy that could take the rocky path to Kiron. It wasn't saddled, but it had reins and a thick blanket across its back, and she accepted his hand and heaved herself up on the beast.

"Is everything all right?" he asked, leading her out of the camp, sounding genuinely concerned.

She looked down at him, sitting sidesaddle on the blankets. She shook her head.

"No, Mister DeWitt," she said, fixing her sight on the titan. She felt her anger echoing back at her, a devastating fury let loose. "Something terrible has happened."

♪

Out of sight of Halberd's camp in Hatfield, Esther turned to sit properly, urging the horse to run with a quote from Job. The pony's hooves echoed like thunder through the valley as she rode into Kiron. As soon as she got to the town, there was a full complement of folks in the center square.

They looked up at her, at their Neighbor, at their witch, and she felt the weight of their accusation like a bit in her own mouth. Wasn't she their helper? Did she not intercede on their behalf?

"What's happening?" Lon called from his porch.

Esther didn't answer. She kicked at the pony's sides, urging it on the makeshift path that led up to the new shaft. At the opening, she saw a crowd of miners, most of them covered in dust and coal. With a sickening lurch in her stomach, she knew exactly what had happened.

Cave-in.

She slid off the horse, running up.

"Who's hurt?" she called out, looking for blood as the crowd of twenty miners, men and women alike, parted to let her through. "I can save limbs if you show me now."

"Esther . . ."

She looked over and saw Jasper sitting at the edge of the shaft, and something in her chest loosened, just a fraction. She let out a breath and went over to him, touching the blood at his temple lightly.

"You're all right," she muttered, looking over him carefully. "But head cuts ain't a thing to take light—"

"Esther," he interrupted her, taking her hand and pulling it away from his head. "Gresham got caught."

Esther's heart stuttered. She looked into the cave, the long dark shaft that got progressively smaller. They had hollowed it out fast, with twenty pairs of hands and Maisie setting up the beam and broadside to keep it all open. The shale must be soft. The flesh is weak.

No, Esther thought. *The maw is open.*

"I can go get the body," she said quietly, squeezing his hand. "Who else here is injured?"

Esther looked over at the five miners who had come forward, one of them already splinting her leg between two pike shafts. None were close to death, and no limbs were near falling off.

But as she tended to them, she felt the tug again, the draw, and this time she knew it was Kire calling to her. It was a demand, an insistence, and the titan was awake under the forest. She put a hand on the stone, and it burned, hot as a sill, angry like a wildfire. Her lips parted, her eyebrows going up slowly.

"What is it?" one of the men asked. Jasper paused, his back to Esther.

"He's alive," she whispered, glancing back at the miners. "Gresham's alive."

"What?" Jasper's eyes went wide. "I saw him fall. The stone went right over him."

A slide like that would kill anyone. But Esther could feel his heartbeat, his breathing, the fluttering of his eyelashes against the stone as Kire dragged him deeper and deeper into the mountain. Playing with him. Hurting him.

"He's alive," Esther repeated. For now. Alive, but not for long. The woods went on around her, the trees knocking against each other, the birds singing—none seemed aware of what was happening under the mountain. The forest didn't care for men. That was a Neighbor's job.

Esther took a few steps into the mine shaft, wrapping her shawl around her mouth and nose. She tongued at Daniel, searched for a proverb that could still her heart and give her courage, but none came. Instead, she held onto her dress as she walked into the mountain, preparing to meet Kire.

20

Bennie

ennie was nervous the whole hike down the mountain, but navigating the wake of Motheater's destruction and the desperate belief that the security on the mountain was shot meant that she was too focused to let it get the better of her. The bird followed, alighting from branch to branch, and Bennie was grateful it kept its beak shut. Motheater was quiet and cold as they walked, not even tending to the moths that had fluttered around her since she had torn the church to shreds. She seemed weaker. She had mentioned she was unable to make bargains with the plants when she tried to curse DeWitt; had wrecking the Church on the Rock taken too much water from her well?

In the truck, Motheater stayed quiet for a few seconds. "I felt an echo in the mountain. I think there's a part of me buried somewhere."

Bennie made a noise, turning the truck over and heading out of the trailhead parking lot. "I heard it, too."

Motheater ran her fingers slowly over the hem of her boilersuit. "I might have sent a part of my soul away from Kire to protect myself. Or I might have given a shard to a friend to keep safe . . ."

"You had friends?" Bennie teased, still stressed, but at least they were off the mountain and heading away from the horrible creature in the stone.

"I'm sure I did," Motheater muttered. Bennie felt an ember of frustration nestle in her gut. All this and for what? For Motheater to send them on another fox hunt through the hollers. "I'll make a candle or something, find a way into the past . . ."

"I need to get people off the mountain," Bennie said sharply. "People are going to get hurt."

"Ain't enough," Motheater muttered. "I got so much, and it's still not enough. I'm bargaining with so little, and all I can do without taking too much magic is move stones around."

Bennie's hands clenched on the wheel. She had just trespassed on a private holler, traipsed all up and down a living, breathing mountain, fought ghost snakes and real ones, and here was Motheater calling for more?

"I need more than that," Bennie said quietly. She ached for Motheater, what she had been through, but this was bigger than either of them. "We ain't done all this for you to say that."

"I know," Motheater said, frowning deeply, cupping a moth in her hand gently. "I know, and I'm sorry for it."

Bennie swallowed. "White Rock is putting people in danger. If you're saying you ain't got enough in you to stop Kire, then we need to buy ourselves some time." Bennie pulled back onto the road. "We get the miners to safety, then we deal with the mountain."

Motheater finished with one moth, had another inside her palms. Bennie glanced at her. The witch seemed all the more fierce for the dark lariat around her neck and new, strange tattoos curling over her arms. Reliving her trauma hadn't dissuaded her.

"Tell me what to do," Motheater murmured, just loud enough to be heard over the truck. "Even if it draws from me. I will be your hands."

Bennie's breath hitched. She looked forward, driving along back roads that curved like a lung. "A rockslide."

"I can do that," Motheater said, her eyes hard.

Fear gripped Bennie's chest, tightening. "We break a road," she said. "We break a road, make it impossible to get to the mining sites and offices."

"I can break anything you like, darlin'," Motheater said, turning back to the insect in her hands. "You just claim what needs upheaval."

Bennie knew she was blushing now. She swallowed and nodded, and at the next fork took the left turn that would lead her around to the White Rock offices. She had to pass Delancey's, but hopefully the woman wouldn't be looking out the window as she did so. (Even so, she held her breath as she drove by, praying Vikki wouldn't see her.)

It was nearly sunset, and with everything going wrong, Bennie hoped that there wasn't anyone at the offices. When she drove to the road leading up the private way to the White Rock offices, the gate was closed—and locked. She felt relieved; this was just the luck she needed. The day's foreman was in charge of setting the box and activating the cameras, and the blinking indicated that everyone was off the mountain. Even the camera didn't bother her. Bennie knew exactly where to stay to keep out of the line of sight.

She gripped the wheel tightly, her nerves through the roof. But she and Kelly-Anne had tested this, marked out on trees with cuts exactly how far they needed to stay back.

"That it?" Motheater asked, fingers silver with magic.

"None other," Bennie said, eyes narrowed. She glanced

over her shoulder, down the road again. It was never guaranteed that someone wouldn't come up, but she wasn't technically doing anything illegal.

Nothing about witchcraft in Virginia law, far as she knew.

Motheater unbuckled herself and reached for the door handle. Bennie grabbed her arm, saw Motheater wince—the snakes must still be hurting her—and slid her hand down to Motheater's.

"Stay on this side of the truck. They've got cameras," Bennie explained. "Disrupt the road far enough that they can't get around by driving through the wood."

Motheater nodded. Her stern face softened slightly, and she squeezed Bennie's hand before slipping out of the truck. Bennie watched her and then hurriedly looked around again. Nobody. Motion sensors were off; the camera wasn't pointed at her. She was going to be fine.

In the middle of the road up to White Rock, still just out of the camera's sight, Motheater crouched in the dirt.

"*I have long time holden my peace; I have been still, and restrained myself.*" Motheater's voice echoed in Bennie's head, and she shivered, gooseflesh pimpling her arms. Something had changed on the mountain, and now Bennie could feel it caving to Motheater, feel it bending to her. Kire seemed to listen to her. "*Now will I cry like a travailing woman; I will destroy and devour at once.*"

Bennie felt it before she heard it. A pressure at her throat and then, a tumble from up the mountain like thunder. Motheater slowly stood up, and mercury threads connected her hand to the ground. Her voice was a hiss. "*I will make waste mountains and hills, and dry up all their herbs–*"

The mountain *shuddered*. Bennie clenched the wheel tighter. Somewhere near, the rockslide klaxon began wailing.

Motheater was standing up, her hand in front of her mouth. Just past the gates, the mountain was cracking open.

A boulder slid up from the gap like a snake poking its head out of a warren. Something crashed, and the echo made Bennie's teeth hurt.

All this, and she couldn't stop staring at Motheater, the witch, the woman she had asked to break the world, who was doing it for her. Bennie was so fucking gone.

"—*And I will turn the roads to wilderness, and I will allow none entry.*" Motheater's voice retreated into the woods. She took a shaky step back, and then another, and before Bennie could get her wits together to help her, Motheater had made her way into the front seat again.

"Fucking hell," Bennie muttered.

"Just wait until you see what the rest of me can do," Motheater said, sitting back in the seat, closing her eyes. She seemed sallow, exhausted, blurry around her edges.

"You're goddamn incredible." Bennie shakily put the truck in gear, driving away from the site.

"I'm one of those things." Motheater chuckled. "I can still ask Kire for favors."

Bennie swallowed, driving through town, heading back to her apartment. She swung by Otto's to grab a pizza to go and quickly foisted it onto Motheater's lap. All the way back to her place she stayed quiet, a buzzing in her fingers never going away. She had questions, dozens—but more than that, she could feel it in her chest where Motheater had ripped the earth open.

There was now something raw in her. A new wound. An open letting. She couldn't shake the feeling that the boulders and stones that Motheater had unearthed had done something to her, too.

At Bennie's apartment building, Motheater carried the pizza up the stairs and waited for Bennie to unlock the front door. The blue jay had hitched a ride in the back of the truck and was now perched on the railing outside, happily enjoying a bird feeder that had been left out by a neighbor. The bird was absolutely not looking at any of the moths surrounding Motheater's head. Bennie assumed they might have had a shine to them, a glow that told the world whom they belonged to.

"I should make a box for him," Bennie mentioned, trying to be casual as she opened the door. "If he sticks around."

"He will," Motheater muttered, walking into the efficiency, at least a dozen moths floating around her head, accumulated just between the truck and the front door. "He's familiar."

"Like, a familiar?" Bennie went over to the high-backed chair and immediately found her charger, plugging in her phone. The battery had been completely drained on Kire. "I thought only witches had familiars?"

"Ach." Motheater dug into Bennie's bag, pulling out the map she had used for notes, spreading it on the fold-down table and comparing it to the murder map. "Familiar beasts do as they please. He may stay for a short time or forever. You'll only find out tomorrow."

Bennie huffed. That was unhelpful. She put down her phone. "I'm going to take a shower. You should eat. Leave me a few slices."

Bennie slipped into the bathroom, starting the shower. She'd have to wash her braids after going up and down a damn mountain all day, and she started braiding sections together.

Maybe she should have warned Motheater that this might take a while. Whatever. As long as the witch left her something, it was fine.

She had just stepped into the shower when she heard a knock on the door.

"Bennie?" Motheater seemed insistent enough that Bennie was almost worried she'd barge in. "Your box-phone is rattling."

"That's fine, Moth!" Bennie called out, selecting her conditioner. "It's just getting my messages!"

She didn't like that pause. If there was something worse than a nineteenth-century witch trying to figure out a piece of technology worth more than most of Bennie's possessions put together, Bennie had yet to know it.

"It's like telegram," Motheater said through the door, and Bennie smiled.

"It's like telegram! I'll take care of it when I'm out of the shower!"

When there was no response, Bennie let out the breath she was holding, working on her braids again. They were about a month or so old, and they'd be fine for another few weeks. It was the most low-maintenance style she could handle, and Zach had liked the way they looked.

Bennie hesitated. She liked the way they looked, too.

After she wrapped her head in a towel and changed into a robe, she saw Motheater curled up in the chair with a novel that was definitely going to either blow the woman's mind or make her think that the past century was a hell of a lot weirder than it really was.

"Phones aren't so strange," Motheater said from her perch. "It's like scrying, but knapped down to something you can hold in your hands."

Bennie snorted. "Yeah, definitely not magic. Just like . . ." Bennie grabbed a slice of pizza. "Like combining all the things that make life easier and storing it into one little thing."

Motheater carefully dog-eared the corner of her page in the novel. Bennie noticed she was moving stiffly and thought that the bruises around her neck were likely only the start of her injuries.

"Like using a gun to kill someone instead of using your hands."

Bennie dropped the pepperoni slice. Motheater looked up at her, smiling a little. Her eyes had more gray in them now, probably from whatever moths had followed her into the apartment. Bennie shuddered and picked the pizza off the floor, immediately tossing it.

"I ... right." She took another piece and bit into it, leaning against the counter. "You should take a shower, too," Bennie said. "There's an extra towel in there, if you want it."

Motheater glanced warily at the bathroom, despite having used it multiple times before. "Running water, and hot, too," Motheater muttered, half in awe. "And everyone has it."

"Most everyone." There were still a few places around here that didn't get it. A few trailer park encampments that were adamant about staying off the grid. Bennie tried to parse out the look that Motheater was giving her. Half wonder, half sad, as if she were putting things together that Bennie didn't understand.

"What's wrong?"

"This is progress," Motheater said sadly, looking down at the cover of the novel she'd been reading. "And it's good."

Bennie frowned. "Ain't all good, Moth. Progress hasn't done so much. And none of this came from White Rock."

"I ain't thinking about the mining companies," Motheater said quietly. Bennie couldn't read her expression.

"Go take a shower," Bennie said. She reached over and squeezed Motheater's shoulder, resisting the urge to flinch when a moth nestled in the strands of her silver hair crawled across Bennie's hand. "We'll figure something out after."

As Motheater headed to the bathroom, Bennie tried to sort out the feelings in her chest. It was an odd mix of protectiveness and utilitarianism, and when Motheater looked over and caught her staring, she got a little red.

"Turn the knobs in the shower," Bennie explained. "Left is hotter, right is colder. You'll never get it perfect, but try not to burn yourself."

"Would you like me to make him disappear?" Motheater asked seriously, pointing at the phone on the table as it buzzed, Zach's name appearing on the screen. "It wouldn't be the first time I chased away a stubborn lover."

"No, he's just worried," Bennie reassured her, scrolling through the messages from Zach. She had told him to disable security for her—of course he'd reach out. Of course he was texting her.

Motheater slipped into the bathroom as she began to sort through her texts, leaving the door slightly open for some reason. Bennie glanced up at the open bathroom door, Zach's texts buzzing in her hands, watching the steam roll. What now?

༄

Bennie got dressed while Motheater was in the shower, carefully patting her braids and undoing them so they wouldn't coil as they dried. She tied them back with a bit of string, cleaned her efficiency and, after a second, poured out some granola in a bowl, walking outside and setting it on the railing. As soon as her hand was off the cheap, chipped ceramic, the blue jay swooped down and began to peck at the oats and raisins.

She couldn't help smiling at the bird. This thing had probably saved her life, and definitely saved Motheater's. Hesitantly, she reached out and touched the bird's head. It didn't seem to mind too much, but it certainly wasn't interested in her. Bennie smiled and gently drew a finger down its back.

"Thanks for today, kid," she muttered. "I hope you stick around. Nice to have someone brave nearby."

The bird didn't even look up from the granola. Bennie smiled a little and left the jay to its meal, walking back into the apartment.

Motheater stood, clutching a towel in front of her chest and dripping water on the floor, her skin a blotchy pink from the hot water. She didn't even have the towel wrapped around her, but that wasn't what shocked Bennie. Five of Motheater's new tattoos were on display, little ring-neck snakes wrapping under her collarbones, across her shoulders, circling her ankles and her wrists.

"Your man a Gresham."

Bennie blinked. That was not what she was expecting. "Excuse me?"

"You got his full name on your phone box. I read it."

Bennie tore her eyes away from Motheater's neck. She could feel heat crawling up her neck, spreading across her face "He's not my man."

"He's Gresham, then? He's got a channel upstream," Motheater said. Which didn't explain anything and wasn't the least bit cryptic, but what the fuck did Bennie expect from the witch? When was she ever speaking straight?

"I don't know what that means."

"Ain't you see his kin on the mountain?" Motheater asked, taking a few steps forward, and Bennie was definitely not expecting to see this much of Motheater's skin right now, and it was bordering on uncomfortable, mostly because Bennie was absolutely useless around pretty girls, and whenever Motheater got super intense like this, it was wickedly attractive.

It took a few seconds longer than she would have liked to put all the pieces together, but that was mostly because Motheater's collarbones were right there and not at all distracting. "Yeah, at the church." Bennie frowned. "I thought it was him at first."

"That was a boy named William Gresham. We grew up together. We were friendly, and . . ." Motheater stopped, looking hurt. "I didn't think he would do that."

"Why are you asking about Zach?" Bennie asked, and as hard as she tried, she really couldn't help but stare at the tattoos curling over Motheater's pale skin, the detail of them, the way they looked ready to move at any second, rounded heads resting on the top of her feet like stigmata.

"I want to know why Will did it. Why he led me to my first death. With Zach in hand, Will's memory makes an easy calling for a Neighbor like me. I'll get more of myself back. I'll know better." Motheater smiled wide, the brilliance of having found a way to be useful. Bennie felt the shift in her. She was confident, assured. Bennie shuddered. Honestly, she would never get used to the fact that Motheater's teeth looked so fucking sharp. What did she even do to make them look like that? "Can you get your Zach here?"

"Fine. But stop calling him 'my' anything," Bennie said, going to her phone. She decided to call Zach—this was probably going to be too weird for texts.

He picked up quickly. "Bennie? I was getting worried. You off the mountain?"

"Yeah, I'm fine," Bennie said, glancing at Motheater, who, apparently, didn't care at all for modesty and had dropped the towel and was changing into a new set of clothes. Bennie sat down on the chair, turning away to try to give the witch some space and to stop herself from getting too heated while on the phone with her ex-boyfriend. "Motheater wants to talk to you."

"What?" He sounded a little hurt. This was clearly not going how he wanted.

"Can you come over tomorrow?"

"That him?" Motheater said, walking over to Bennie, head tilted. It was clear she had no idea what was happening

217

but was very excited. She still had not put proper pants on, wearing just her oversized acid-wash sweatshirt and a pair of underwear, and Bennie could not handle it, staring at Motheater, mouth dry. "This him on the phone?"

"Yes, but—Motheater!" Bennie turned a little as Motheater perched right on the arm of the chair, leaning in. "Yes, it's him, no, Zach, I'm fine, just—"

Motheater was staring at Bennie, who glared back at her. "I just have a very insistent witch in my personal space who wants to talk to you, and if she gets any closer, I might shove her back into a coal mine."

Motheater smiled and leaned over toward the phone. Bennie, wisely, put the call on speakerphone and held it out to her.

"Zach Gresham," she said, almost yelling, concentrating. "Do you have any family heirlooms, Bibles, or portraits?"

"What?" Zach was clearly confused. He had only wanted to talk to Bennie, and now he was dealing with a strange witch interrogating him over family ephemera. Bennie would have laughed if it wasn't so absurd. "I mean, I might have something?"

"Good," Motheater said, sitting back, satisfied. "You should bring those things. I would like to use them."

"Can I talk to Bennie, please?"

"I'm still here." Bennie's eyes strayed over Motheater's tattoos along her ankles and legs. "Do you need something else?"

"I wanted to talk to you—"

"Zach, you can come over for a few minutes tomorrow morning," Bennie said, her voice like iron. "We're moving on." God, this still hurt. It was like an unhealed bruise, an old love, a collection of burst blood that refused to melt away into her skin. Hard to see, but painful anyway.

Motheater put a hand on Bennie's shoulder but seemed to be deliberately looking somewhere else.

"We're not moving on together," Zach said softly. Motheater's hand pressed against Bennie's back.

"That's the point, Zach." Her voice was not soft at all. "I'll see you tomorrow. Text when you're coming over."

"Yeah," Zach muttered. "Bye."

Bennie hung up and very carefully put the phone down. Motheater shifted a little and put her forehead on top of Bennie's head for a few seconds.

"You smell nice," Motheater muttered.

"Thanks," Bennie said, smiling a little. She leaned into Motheater, the witch's arm around her shoulders. Bennie pressed a finger to Motheater's wrist, along a snake's body, and tried not to sort through the feelings building in her stomach. She still felt anxious, but they had stopped White Rock for a little while. Kire was next. "Tell me about the new ink."

Motheater shifted, holding up her arm—pale, thin, and marked by a mess of tangled coils. "These are innocent things. Not rattlers or cottonmouths, but sweeter reptiles," she said, turning her arm over. Bennie didn't know much about snakes, but the shape of the head on these snakes was less angular than she had been warned about.

"These are snakes that couldn't hurt you if they tried. They aren't dangerous . . ."

She trailed off, and Bennie shifted a little to look up at Motheater's face, at the way her mouth pursed in concentration.

"What?"

"I don't know what they are," Motheater admitted. "Were they mine, back when I kept familiar creatures at beck and call? Are they just shadows? Did my father catch them just to shackle me inside the mountain?"

Bennie reached out and took Motheater's wrist gently, pulling it close. Her heartbeat pounded in her ears. God, this woman was unfairly weird and all the more attractive for it, and for the power she commanded.

"You usually have an intuition about these sorts of things," Bennie muttered. "What do you feel when you see them?"

Next to her, *against her*, Motheater took a deep breath.

"I can feel my power rising to the surface. It's coming closer, sharp and aching, and . . ."

Bennie stayed quiet as Motheater thought. Around her, the sounds of the efficiency complex echoed. A mom and two children downstairs, someone cooking next door. A car beeping in the lot. The blue jay screaming on the porch. A conversation between neighbors down the row. A familiar hum of people, present and totally unaware of the kind of person Bennie had in her apartment.

"There's something empty. Like a tunnel, long drawn. A holler in my chest."

"That's where you're tied?" Bennie asked. That was it, Motheater's power. The thing that would stop people dying.

Motheater nodded, and Bennie noted the look on her face wasn't scared or upset, but determined, excited. This was a woman who had power, who knew it. "I got most of my memories back after the church," she said, smiling at Bennie. "But the last few years before I got thrown into the mountain, I only got patches of. I remember the first industry that wanted to come into Kire, I remember . . ."

She drifted off, still smiling, but lost. The sounds of the building closed in on them again. It must be some kind of trauma response. Blacking out the memory that led up to the moment she was thrown into stone by her own father.

"It's fine," Bennie said quietly. "We'll figure it out and keep Kire asleep."

Motheater nodded, frowning deeply. "There are far easier ways to kill a witch. Why did they work a cunning that wouldn't kill me?" She turned her arm to the side but didn't pull away from Bennie's grip. They both looked at the snake, and in the dim light, with the strange, almost otherworldly paleness of Motheater's skin, it looked for a second like the snake shifted around her wrist.

21

Esther

Around her, the darkness threatened to pull Esther in. There were no fires, no lanterns, not even a match. Esther kept a hand on the rocky flesh of Kire, feeling all its pulsing strength and anger, and knew that the farther she walked into the shaft, the more sensitive the mountain would be. It had suffered under the picks of miners for near on a hundred years, since the first settlers had come across the sea and suspected these mountains of having gold.

This world, Esther thought, had been very badly used.

The tunnel narrowed; here was where the sloping space became more of a crack. This was where Esther had knelt down when she first entered the shaft, but now she went on her hands and knees, annoyed that she didn't have time to wrap her limbs nor joints, and crawled through the shaft.

She could feel Will ahead, panicking, barely breathing—echoing in her was the knowledge that Kire was swallowing him up, dragging him through the coal veins to the whole of it, the darkest, deepest part of the mountain, the part that craved blood and pain and retribution for the decades spent chipping away at its coal and crater.

Crawling slowly, she could feel Kire alive around her. She could taste it, like copper and chalk, the taste of an old bone with dried blood on the gristle; it was a dark, deep heat, an anger, a fire. What was she thinking, hoping to liaise with a creature like this? What had she done, tying herself to a power this massive, this present? She should have lashed her heart to the moon.

"*Doth the hawk fly by thy wisdom, and stretch her wings toward the south?*" Esther asked the mountain, and around her, the stone shifted. She could hear a distant rockfall, and she knew that she was rearranging the mountain around her.

And Will Gresham was still trapped inside. It would have been easier if he had passed out—then he wouldn't remember any of this. But he had his senses, and he was struggling, and the fear drove into Esther like a rail spike.

Esther swallowed, turning her head to get air enough to quote, "*Doth the eagle mount up at thy command, and make her nest on high?*"

Was she Job in this moment, in this mountain? Was she God, who commanded all the beasts of the sky? Did it matter at all when around her, driven by her own damned will, the stones shifted to let her through to where a panicked man was reaching out to her?

She saw his fingers, his face still hidden, blood coming out of his glove. If the mountain was crushing him, Esther knew that she didn't have much longer. Kire would suffer its witch for blood and worship, but it would not suffer this man.

Esther took a deep breath, desperately reaching for Will's hand. He immediately held onto her, struggling, still alive, still breathing, still one of her own. She remembered the joey in her pocket, and for the first time since she entered the cave, she closed her eyes.

"*She dwelleth and abideth on the rock, upon the crag of the rock, and the strong place,*" Esther spoke, and around Will the stones just barely shifted. She turned on her side, reaching down with her other hand to hold onto the baby possum in her pocket. It squirmed in her grip. "*From thence she seeketh the prey, and her eyes behold afar off.*"

She tightened her hand. A squeal pierced through the cave-in, viscera coating her palm.

Kire stopped moving. It took what she sacrificed. Esther took a deep breath, letting the blood flow over her fingers, forcing herself to feel the snap of bone, the stopping of a heart, the horrible knowledge that she did not have to kill the creature, but that it was a choice. Every joint in her body ached, but she did not loose her hold.

Will's hand was still in hers, and as she pulled him forward, the stone moved, and his face was revealed. He was covered in dust and coalblack and snot, blood seeping out of a cut on his forehead, a trickle of blood out of his eyes like tears. He stared at her, eyes bloodshot, red, wide. He was trying to talk. Esther didn't want to hear it. Men could not be bargained with like gods.

"*Her young ones also suck up blood,*" Esther said, crawling backward, dragging Will with her, never letting go, never breaking her eye contact with the miner. Whatever he was trying to say was lost in the cavernous creaking and sliding of the mountain around them, the roots above them snapping, the echo of worried voices behind Esther as she bent even Kire to her will. "*And where the slain are, there is she.*"

༄

Slowly, inch by inch, with gore on her hands and Will's life in her charge, Esther dragged them out of Kire. The shaft had collapsed behind her, and she could hear the echoing sound of stone moving, like a waterfall crashing around them, like a mudslide that brought all the houses to level. Kire wasn't letting her through without a fight.

She kept her hand tight around Will's wrist, and they made it to the rubble that blocked the way out. This was less of that press of lungs against a sheet, less like a flea trapped between a body and a mattress. Now it felt like a natural cave-in. This was just stone and air, and Esther could command both with a word.

"Keep with me, Will Gresham," Esther murmured. She took a deep breath, found the last of the heat in the dark blood that was smeared in her pocket, the sad, sorry state of things, the pieces of herself she left dead and buried in the mountain, and the rubble ran away from her, rolling out of the shaft. Light blinded her, but she pulled Will close, scrabbling with her free hand at the wall, heaving the miner up as much as she was able.

"Help!" She couldn't hold him up and keep Kire back. The stone wanted them back. The hungry mountain would not be satisfied with magic and a dead possum. It wanted a man, and Esther would not give her people up like pigs to slaughter. She was Kiron's Neighbor, but she was not Kire.

Jasper pushed through the remaining stones, hauling them out of the way, Maisie and another miner clearing the rubble beside him. He reached past her and heaved Will out of harm's way, passing him back to the waiting hands, and the stone underneath Esther lurched.

Jasper's eyes went wide, and Esther spread her arms, as if she were Atlas himself, her fingers splayed against the stone that wasn't just warm, but burning.

"Go!"

He hesitated, just for a second, and around them the tunnel closed like a fist, all sides moving in.

Esther's heart was in her throat, and the scripture wouldn't come. She felt like a hare being chased, a hare in

225

a trap, a hare tangled in a snare. What was she going to do, caught between her power and her purpose?

Jasper got his wits back and pulled Will out of the cave-in. Esther was trapped, the coal and shale moving to trap her hands, her legs. She was a witch who had gone against her warp and woof, a witch who had defied the power she had made a pact with, and she was not willing to back down.

She couldn't let Kiron die. These people were hers. She made deals for them. She would barter the last scraps of her soul to Kire and keep the coal open to them. She could still save Kiron.

Fear and anger choked her, and then it was stone and dust. The light faded as Kire closed her off from Jasper and the miners, and the last thing Esther saw was her friend staring back at her, his eyes huge and frightened.

Esther took a deep breath and felt her mouth solidify, the stone creeping around her neck and legs, the fury of Kire betrayed. In that second, she was torn from the tunnel, feet fixed, jaw locked, and death took her into the mountain. She was pulled through the stone and shale to the heart of Kire, to the place where, fifteen years ago, she had been born a witch, the womb where she would be unmade, torn from her Witch-Father, and left to crumble under the stone.

22

Bennie

The night passed uneventfully, and Bennie would absolutely not admit that she had ended up curled around Motheater on the mattress. She was struggling to sort out her feelings. She ached, a kind of emptiness that Motheater threatened to fill. She was something strange, something that could never replace Zach or Kelly-Anne, or any other relationship that Bennie had lost in the past six months, but Bennie couldn't help it. The hurt in Bennie was too deep for Motheater, but Bennie was sad, desperate, and burning for the witch.

In the early morning, she untangled herself from Motheater and stepped just outside of the apartment to call the hardware store, asking to move around a couple of her shifts.

Miles gave her a hard time but switched schedules with Bennie himself. It was fine, he had said when Bennie tried to apologize. She managed to extend her break a few more days, and as she hung up on Miles, she hoped it would be enough.

Outside, holding her phone, Bennie looked over Kire. On the southern side, heading west (where the ruins of the

Church of the Rock would be embedded in the stone), the trees had all shifted, slid to fall during the night. They bent over; a whole swath of the forest on Kire lay flat, like the trees on Sarton before Motheater had made the West Virginia pipeline explode. These oak and hemlock seemed as though they were praying, a hundred trunks or more laid prostrate to the mountain, worshiping.

But the ground hadn't gone downhill, Bennie realized, it had moved *up the mountain.* There was a tree Bennie recognized, a giant fir that had at least three dreys in it, and it was farther up the hill, lying along a different ridge. It looked like the dirt had been tugged up like a blanket in the night, protecting the mountain against a chill.

And she hadn't heard anything. No alarms in the night, no cracking rocks, nothing. Just a shifting behemoth under the loam. Bennie dropped her phone. She cursed and picked it up, her hands shaking. This was it, wasn't it? Motheater's warning rang in hear ears, a pounding that wouldn't stop. The mountain wasn't just alive, wasn't just waking up. It was *moving.* Now.

How the fuck were they supposed to stop this?

As she stared at Kire, she felt something pulling at her. A dread, deep in her gut, the kind of horror that was usually reserved for things she saw on the news, for brutality, for something unthinkable. It felt like the world was shrinking, narrowing down to just Bennie and the mountain. Motheater had done something to her when the witch had driven her into Kire on their way up to the church, and she had this sense of Kire now, a wrongness she felt in the back of her throat.

Whatever White Rock was doing couldn't compare to what Kire threatened. White Rock's miners disappeared in ones and twos. If Kire woke up, it could destroy the entire operation. Hundreds of White Rock's miners, killed all at once, lost to an Appalachian appetite.

A screech pierced the air, and the blue jay swooped in. Bennie flinched, but the bird just landed on her shoulder.

"Rude," Bennie muttered, shooing the bird away. It jumped to the railing and looked at Bennie expectantly. Bennie sighed. "I guess you want food, huh?"

The bird just tilted its head. Bennie should get a feeder.

Bennie's phone buzzed in her hand. Zach's text said he'd be over soon. She responded quickly before going back into the efficiency. Motheater had gotten out of bed and slipped into the bathroom. Bennie looked around and tried to judge if it was worth putting away the dead man's map before Zach arrived.

No. Bennie felt a weight lift. She wouldn't put anything away.

In what felt like no time at all, Zach was knocking on the door. Bennie knew it had been at least half an hour, judging by the number of dishes she had gotten through and the fact that Motheater had inhaled two slices of cold pizza, but it still felt as if he appeared on her doorstep too fast.

Motheater had neatened the bed and the stacks of books and clothes in the efficiency. The witch pushed up the sleeves of the oversized shirt that she was wearing and nodded when Bennie glanced at her.

Bennie had her hand on the doorknob and smiled. She wasn't alone. She and Motheater would face whatever Zach had for them together. She stepped over a pile of books to get to the door, letting Zach in.

The man entered, putting down a small plastic bag before pulling his hat off, his dirty blond hair sticking up at odd angles. Motheater crossed her arms. He stared at her, a strange expression on his face. Bennie glanced between them and, satisfied that they weren't going to tear each other's throats out, decided this was not something she'd be able to get between.

More than a few moths had flown in when Zach had

entered, and they clung to Motheater's hair like a crown, delicately spreading their wings around her temples and down her braid. Zach could not look away, even as he spoke to Bennie. "She's not going to really eat them, is she?"

"No," Bennie said.

Motheater walked around Zach, frowning. "What did you bring?"

Being circled by a mean-looking witch seemed to deflate whatever purpose Zach had brought into the apartment. He tried to catch Bennie's eyes, but she just looked determinedly at her phone and not at him. She heard him sigh and saw Zach pull a few items out of the flimsy grocery bag out of the corner of her eyes.

"I found a medal from the Second World War, I think?" Zach said, and Bennie's eyes widened. She was no longer pretending to be interested in her phone, and she watched Motheater, who had her brows drawn down in a furious scrunch that Bennie recognized, as the time-stopped witch made swift calculations in her head.

"A book of Psalms that Dad gave me when I moved out, and . . . an old cross-stitch a great-great-aunt did?" Zach had his hands full of mementos, holding them out to Motheater, but the witch looked directly at Bennie.

"There was a world war?" Motheater asked, incredulous. "Twice?"

Bennie sighed. "I'll get you a history book."

Motheater seemed to realize that she didn't have time to learn about global conflict (probably for the best, Bennie thought—how was she supposed to explain an air raid? An atom bomb?) and turned to look at Zach again. She took the stack of things, turning each piece over in her hand carefully. She flipped through the book of Psalms and paused at the back of the book. Bennie knew that was where Zach had a family tree, written in faded brown ink. Motheater narrowed her eyes, reading over the names, before passing that back to Zach along with the cross-stitch.

The medal stayed in her hand, and she nodded.

"The Greshams kept to yourselves, away from the church. Maybe for the better." She held the medal in her palm. "But ain't no family deserve this pain."

"What are you talking about?" Zach said, confused and annoyed, clearly out of his depth. "Bennie, I been accommodating, but what the hell are you thinking?"

"I have tried everything to get that company to own up to Kelly-Anne's death," Bennie said, voice measured. She didn't think it'd be much use talking to him about Kire being alive. It would be easier to guilt Zach with his part in the mining operation. "We're going to try something different."

Zach stared at her, his face going pale. He was complicit, too. He hadn't ever taken her seriously. Well, that was about to change. He needed to know how much it hurt.

"I need to talk to your father's father, going back to the man I knew," Motheater said. "You got blood flowing back to when I'm from. And I need my memories back. All of them, or I'll never be able to put Kire to sleep."

"Is that what's happening? I'm just . . ." He drifted off, and Bennie knew that Zach was too kind for this. He might be intimidating to anyone from the tidewater, a miner's son, an Appalachian boy with an accent thick as mud in a creek, with coal folded into his crow's foot wrinkles, but he was a good man. And he probably didn't deserve to be fed to a wolf like Motheater.

"I will open your chest like a still. I will find that drip of memory like moonshine and see precise how your false kin betrayed me." Motheater's voice seemed to echo.

Bennie groaned, putting her face in her hands. Jesus Christ, that was not going to reassure Zach at all, was it. How did Motheater know exactly the worst thing to say?

"Now, hold on!" Zach took a step back.

"Ain't gonna hurt," Motheater said, trying to be gentle and failing spectacularly, considering she had just said she wanted to treat his body the same as a cadaver, opening it to find his ancestors in a magical unearthing. "Like falling asleep," Motheater explained, and this time Bennie could hear her contriteness. That was something. "Rocked by a river."

"Rivers also pull men under," Zach said, not looking away from Motheater now. Maybe the Greshams had always known there were Neighbors.

"You pulled me out of the mountain," Motheater said, voice hushed. "You held my hand as you eased me out of the stone under my father's church. You dropped me into the slough, and I survived that river."

Zach flinched. Bennie held her hands together in her lap as the temperature dropped, a rising tide, cold water from a well.

"I won't let you drown." Motheater offered her hand. "We're just going to take a walk, Zach Gresham."

Zach paused. Bennie knew him well enough to see the guilt play out on his face, the way he felt the weight of his actions, the callousness of what he had done, what the mining company had done. The poor boy was a bleeding-heart vegetarian, for God's sake. He had visited a packing plant at age twelve and swore off meat that day. He felt deeply, he cared too much, was too soft for this damn town, and Bennie had loved him for it.

Zach, guilt-struck, tender-hearted, a man who should have been built from a highland mountain and chose to be kind instead, nodded and took Motheater's hand. They held the medal in between them, a locus into the past, and Motheater intoned a single line.

"One generation passeth away, and another generation cometh: but the earth abideth for ever."

To Bennie, it looked like all the color had drained from the both of them. Motheater's hair, once streaked with brown and green mothdust, was almost completely white. The only pink left on her was at the edges of her knuckles, the lightest brush on her mouth. Somehow, she hadn't managed to get the dirt out from under her nails. Zach's blond hair turned brassy, and it was as if they had stepped into an old painting, holding each other's hands, diving into some kind of past that Bennie couldn't understand.

Not for the first time that day, Bennie felt very alone. She pulled her knees up to her chest, helpless as the witch pulled her last lover into the past.

23

Motheater

The medal hadn't been the oldest thing that Zach had brought with him, but it had the most attached. Psalms and hymns were a balm to the faithful, but spilled blood was a stained memory. You passed down stories of soldiers, not choirboys.

The fact that he had brought more than one talisman from his family was touching. It said something about the boy, even if the Greshams of the past were a sorry and sordid lot who would rather see their Neighbor buried than stand up to another man.

Motheater remembered very little of her past, of the *specifics*. She remembered her deep anger, hauling Will out of the mountain during a cave-in, but how did he end up in the Church of the Rock? How did she end up fighting against her father one last time? The bruise was still fresh around her neck, and she wore it like a torque, something honored.

Motheater steadied herself, squeezed Zach's hand, and tugged on the time around the medal. She slipped backward, the rage and bitterness consuming her.

Anger was something she understood.

Zach's hand was an anchor, a steady heartbeat in the present that kept Motheater from disappearing into the last moments of Hal Gresham's life, age seventy-three, a heart attack at home, gone forty years after the Second Great War. She walked past him, trying not to stare at the tanks, ignoring the machine gun fire that felt like an excavation. She tried to forget that they were mining men.

From Hal, she spoke to Uriel Gresham (of Kiron, Virginia) and Bernadette Yaeger (formerly of Allenville, Kentucky), a couple of lovebirds who failed to ever get married and caused a scandal as they raised a family together anyway. In the early twentieth century, with the memory of a war of kindred still fresh on the ground, the nation bearing scars of self-flagellation, their friends didn't blame them for not wanting to graft two things together when there were so many axes waiting.

Motheater took a deep breath, knowing that she was treading on the eidolon of memory, the stories passed hand over fist like a bucket of coal. She went through Zach to Hal to Uriel to William.

Zach bore the weight of history in his bones, the marrow of himself formed from generations of Gresham men, family roots spreading like capillaries through his strong arms. Zach shuddered as Motheater found William, and it was easy to read their past in the calluses of Zach's hands. She tapped into his ancestors like a coal vein. She tried not to bare her teeth, not to clench his hands too tight, but here was William, huddled in a Halberd cabin down in Hatfield, and here was the plan laid out on the table.

No, it wasn't enough; this was the plan, but what was the reason? There had to be a purpose.

William was a miner, and she sifted through his memories, the shadows of them she could pull out of Zach's skin.

She saw Will sitting at a table her fire-adders had snuck into over the winter, and the memory of them burned her hands. She was so close. She almost knew herself again.

William wasn't speaking, but he watched as one of the managers working for Halberd Ore and Mineral laid out a map of the area. Motheater observed over his shoulder. The map was beautiful, and Halberd had obviously taken a lot of care to create an exact map of this area of the Appalachians, noting Kire Mountain and the surrounding various elevations in soft blue lines. The town of Kiron was marked in red, homesteads and public buildings ticked up the mountain in maroon. The two mining excavations were green, and there were a few symbols for prospective slough shafts, dumpsites, refineries, and roads.

Motheater walked around the table, examining the map. She hadn't dragged Zach bodily with her, but she could feel him just behind her temples, an ache, a ghost behind her eyes. He was here, too, seeing what she saw. Maybe he would recognize the sections of the map that were blurry, maybe forgotten, maybe lost. She saw one last symbol, high on the western side of the mountain, a small cross for the church.

As she circled the map, she held tighter onto the medal awarded for a war that hadn't happened yet, and the map came into sharp relief. Halberd had acquired mineral rights for Kire, and judging by this map, they had managed to slink into the forest when she wasn't looking. There were notes that marked where dowsers and corers had identified possible dig sites. One of them was right by the church.

There were other sites scoped out, too, farther along the ridge into West Virginia, places that felt familiar to Motheater, but not for any reason she remembered. It was an itch along her neck, something heavy that weighed on her. Motheater circled the memory, eyes fixed on her small town that threatened to be enveloped by a destruction called progress.

"Preacher won't stand for it," William said, glancing up at the foreman. "That church has been there before Christian folk came 'round the mountain. He believes God created that church alongside the sun and stars. He calls Kiron the Sinai of the Americas."

"Preacher doesn't have to like anything. Not-liking won't stop us from carving that church out from under him and his flock," the foreman said. Even with a century of distance, Motheater could feel the sneer as if it were pressed against her face. "If he won't let us come in the front door, we'll blast that damn church off the mountain. See what he does with rubble."

William glanced down at the table. The men next to him appeared, coalescing out of his memory. Representatives of Kiron and the freetown nearby. That was Nathan Benneke, a freeman who made sure the Black folk got all the news they needed from Kiron, who cried during the Easter stations; here was Jack Spencer, a white man who had seven daughters who called Motheater sister, because she had pulled them out of Dinah Spencer's womb one by one; the fourth was Collum Calhoun, a Native man whose brother led the twenty-second Kanawha infantry during the war. Something about Collum pulled at her, and she stared at the old man, the dark lines of his face that seemed to have dust tattooed into them.

"Ain't you heard of the preacher's daughter?" William asked, leaning forward. "Ain't no love lost between 'em, but she won't let nothing happen to that church."

"I'll inform you just the once that I don't give a shit about what a woman wants," the foreman said, pointing at the church. "We have received information on good authority that there's a thick rib of coal under that building, and if the preacher won't step off a cliff, we'll evict him."

Collum was looking down at his hands. Jack elbowed him. Collum glared and then looked up at the foreman. "I got as much invested in this mountain as any man here. But you ain't from here, Mister Ochiltree, and you ain't seen what that girl can do. She ain't one for edicts."

"What in the bloody fuck does that mean?" Ochiltree snapped. Motheater's hands twitched. She couldn't do magic in here, couldn't tear Ochiltree's throat out with her teeth. She was a catamount in the shadows, only here to watch.

"She a witch," Collum said, calm as a cold still. "My son's one who calls on her kindly. I seen her do things you ain't want to cross, whistle, nor look twice at."

Ochiltree, who wore a suit with hand-stitched lapels and had a linen cravat tucked disastrously into his front pocket, snorted. Motheater walked around the table, narrowing her eyes. All the features of these men were fuzzy with age, but Ochiltree was clearer—he had been at the church. He was wearing a Halberd Co. pin, right at his collarbone, and Motheater had to clutch onto Gresham's dead medal in her hand to keep herself grounded in the past. "A witch. You can't be serious."

Collum looked down the line of Kiron miners and foremen. All of them refused to meet his eye.

"If one of you good folks don't speak up, I'm liable to throw you out and cut you from any deal we may foster here today," Ochiltree growled. "I've seen that girl around—she came into the camp naught three weeks ago, begging us to take her south to dowse away from Kire. Just because none of you are man enough to tame her doesn't make her a *witch*."

Besides Ochiltree and the Kiron men, there were two others from Halberd. A tall man who seemed to loom over the map even sitting down, blue eyes drawn down. The third stood in the corner, wearing a long red jacket that looked new, staring at the ground. Something about him tugged at Motheater.

William shifted and nodded. "Mister Calhoun's right," he said quietly. He still had scrapes on his face, but Motheater struggled to remember why they were familiar. What happened to Will Gresham?

"I saw that girl talk to hare bucks at midnight," Jack added. "She cured some scarlet fever a few years ago. When she was thirteen, she preached bravery into a union regiment heading south, and all of 'em returned in two weeks, medaled up and given a hero's pension. All Kiron knows her and where she stands."

"You cannot believe that you have a witch in your town. I refuse to accept it." None of the men moved. Ochiltree glanced over them, down at the map, and then back to the miners. "Do the rest of the good Christian folk of this town believe this same nonsense?"

"She's a well-known Neighbor, sir." Jack shrugged. "They come to her for balms, potions, medicine of any kind. She made a girl's freckles disappear just last week."

Ochiltree snorted. "The fact that you all believe this bitch has some kind of power is bad enough; the fact she's got the entire town wrapped around her fantasy is a fool's war."

Motheater almost got angry, but she pressed it down. She had to stay focused. She forced herself to watch William's face, gone pale and confused. What was he thinking?

Collum shook his head, a lick of his black hair, held back with an oil pomade, falling across his dead eye. "Ain't no flight of fancy, sir. She's a Neighbor, sure as I'm a miner and you're a businessman."

"I do not have the time to deal in rumors and stupidity," Ochiltree snapped.

"That witch is not a rumor," William said carefully. "Now, I ain't call her friend, but it pays to be on speaking terms with her. Her father's only got love for her when she brings in a tithe to the church. But mark me, you go after her with a gun on a dark night, you're liable to end up with parts of you in three different hollers."

"Ain't no exaggerating, neither. Remember Rare Thomson?" Nathan shifted in his chair. "He took a fancy to her and tried courting her. Poor boy ended up spread across the Appalachians like butter."

Ochiltree's face was red. He was the only man standing at the table, and his fists were clenched tight around a ruler, looking like it might snap. Motheater circled him, glaring, only half paying attention to the memory she was here to witness.

"You mean to tell me that the mere thought of this one woman is enough to turn you all into cowards? To turn away from any progress and fortune the collective could offer to you and your backwater town? You're all content to eat gruel and shine all for the sake of a rumor?"

"Now, Mister Ochiltree." Collum leaned forward in his chair. "You ain't truly met her. She came to you hoping to trick you into thinking she was just another woman, just a dowser looking for trade. You ain't *know* her. I'll forgive what you said about my own fortitude, but just the once." His voice was measured, but there was a tone that came off sharp as stone's cleavage, and Motheater frowned deeply.

His son was Jasper Calhoun. Jasper was her pack. Where was Jasper now? She remembered and felt it slip away. A pain in her chest, a sharpness like a needle. How could she have forgotten her friend? Where was Jasper? She jolted and looked up at the man in the corner.

His name was DeWitt.

As Ochiltree sat down, Motheater went around to DeWitt, trying to parse his memory. DeWitt had come to her . . . and to Jasper.

Her mouth went dry.

"Fine. There's other parts of the ridge. We'll deal with the witch later," Ochiltree said, drawing Motheater's attention back to the map.

Motheater bared her teeth at him. There was a bit of protection around Kire; she remembered turning away their dowsers, hanging squirrel bones to haunt the woods, making circle paths to turn inspectors around on their tail, burying jars of piss to keep them out. But looking down at the map, Halberd's sneaks had still managed to get veins out of Potts and Huckleberry, and even Locust Knob, far closer to Kire than she would have liked.

"We might have to deal with her sooner rather than later," William said, shaking his head. "She lives somewhere along those mountains. She'll turn up, and she's made clear she ain't gonna endure industry mining."

Jack, Nathan, and Collum went still. William's hands were shaking. He wasn't looking up at Ochiltree at all. He was barely keeping it together. What had happened to him? Motheater went and crouched by his side, trying to find answers in a memory. This was a shadow, a shade, and there wasn't much she could do from this distance, from so far away.

"What do you mean, 'she lives somewhere'?" Ochiltree groaned.

Collum gestured over the map. "Her house ain't normal. It's got a path, and a few signs along property she's claimed, but the only people who find her house are them that got her permission to enter. And if you go in protected by another Neighbor, she's got all manner of curses strung up to call you off and get you lost in the dark."

A movement—Motheater stared at DeWitt. He had flinched. Motheater suddenly remembered when the company man came to her forest in the dark. His rabbit heart still

241

beat, even now, even then. She could feel it scrabbling in the blood.

"Jesus Christ, you people." Ochiltree rubbed his temple. "You understand I can't tell anyone in Richmond about this? That there's some—and I hesitate to even use these words, gentlemen, as it seems like it only encourages this delusion— but you are of the opinion that there's some Appalachian witch standing in between you and the coal that will go to rebuild our nation?"

Collum shrugged. "If you can't appease the witch, you ain't going to move nothing out of our town."

"We've invested in Kiron specifically to get into Kire Mountain," Ochiltree said sharply, accusing. "We brought you four in to help us get started, to convince the town to get behind us. We will not be turned away."

Nathan looked over the map. "Preacher's more keen to listen as long as you keep off his church land. Coal has made Kiron a decent place. Tithe is enough to keep his church full of new books and coated in fresh paint."

Motheater felt a stone in her throat.

"You think that this preacher is willing to compromise?" Ochiltree asked.

"I'm saying that maybe he'd be willing to help you get rid of his daughter if you agreed to let his land alone. He might know how to put the witch in the ground, and if you help him get rid of her, you might get a crack at the north half of the mountain, and the rest of the unmanned ridges up here," Nathan continued, drawing his hand up the peaks along the Virginia border. "But this . . ."

"She looks after all that land," William said, finding his voice again. "And right now, we don't know where she is."

"Well then," Ochiltree said, still frowning. "If this is the only way you men are willing to move forward, fine. Get your little town on track, and we'll go talk to the preacher."

Collum's face was blurry. The whole memory was fading. Collum's eyes slid closed, and he pressed his hands tight against his legs. He held his own kind of hatred for her. Was it so bad that Jasper had been like a brother to her? Was it so sickening that she kept his company?

Motheater focused on the map. William, Collum, and the other town leaders finally managed to shake hands with Ochiltree and leave the room. DeWitt stepped forward, through Motheater's body, and the witch was left, a swiftly fading shadow. She felt his heart beat, a stuttering banjo through her chest as he left her to fade. She tried to latch on to the last moments of this memory, analyzing the parts of the mountain before she let herself fall back in time, pulling herself, drop by drop, out of Zach's bloodstream, and into the arms of Bennie Mattox.

24

Bennie

Bennie could see that Motheater and Zach were coming back. Where they had gone was unclear, but they had stood almost totally still, faint expressions echoing across their faces. Pink lit across Zach's cheeks, and Motheater had a soft green flush rise. Bennie stood up, swallowing her fear and panic.

Zach moved first, blinking like he was lost. He took a step back and put a hand out on the counter to steady himself. As he pulled away, Motheater swayed. Bennie put a hand on Motheater's shoulder, and the witch shifted toward her, leaning into Bennie's chest.

"I got you," Bennie muttered, struggling to keep Motheater upright. She was quickly losing her legs, and Bennie carefully lay her down on the mattress, sinking next to her. Her breathing was low, and Zach didn't look much better, leaning against the counter, hands over his eyes.

The medal fell between them, and Bennie stared at it. It looked like a mirror, like something mercurial had been dropped on it, shifting and spreading in the morning light. Bennie tore her eyes away from the trinket on the ground.

Motheater's hair was entirely white again and had a strange texture to it. Fuzzy, like a moth's wing, like she had collected pale souls in the air and the entire strange occupancy had settled into her. Bennie put her arm around Motheater's shoulders, holding her against her chest. Motheater was mumbling, but it was incoherent.

Zach slid down the counter, head tilted back, holding his cap in both hands, clearly trying to focus on his breathing.

"What the fuck happened?" Bennie asked quietly.

Motheater started to shake. Bennie pulled her closer, shifting so that the witch was half in her lap, holding her tightly. The woman hadn't moved at all during the magic, had just stood there, serene, as whatever they were doing happened to them. That was it, really. Motheater had just let it happen. While she had seemed totally calm as she had pulled herself through Zach's bloodline, Bennie suspected that keeping yourself even was key to keeping yourself from drowning. She couldn't imagine that it made Motheater's magic easier to channel.

Zach finally moved, standing up slowly to pour himself a glass of water.

"Zach? What happened?"

Zach downed the glass, then another. He rubbed at his temples, exhausted. He looked like this after a double in the mine. Bennie tightened her grip around Motheater's shoulders.

"We took a walk," he muttered, running his hand through his hair, making it stand up at all kinds of angles.

Just as Bennie was about to respond, there was a terrible grating noise outside, loud as a train crash, and two different alarms blared out in horrible, piercing time. She started and held onto Motheater even more fiercely, but the witch didn't move, still mumbling in a highland accent that Bennie didn't have the energy to parse.

Zach scrambled to the door, going outside. Bennie's heart was in her throat, and after a moment, she carefully laid Motheater on the bed and followed him.

Most of her building's residents were out as well, and Zach pointed east, up the mountain. "The lodge," he said, pointing at the Elks' meeting place at the base of Kire. "It's gone."

Where there would usually be a well-lit building, proudly announcing the brotherhood's claim on the area, there was a half-destroyed wall, looking like it had been split in two. There was nothing left besides a ruin. Bennie tried to pick details, but the lodge was miles away and usually only visible because of its elevation and the spotlight it had on the cheap statue it had erected on the front of the property. Carefully manicured trees around the lodge looked like they had been pushed over.

"That's the cave-in alarm."

"At least nobody's down there. Y'all closed after the pipe-line exploded two days ago . . ." Bennie felt her mouth go dry. The mountain felt even more threatening now, and it felt like it was coming for her, crawling closer and closer every second. Would she even know? How much warning would she have if the old hotel got eaten by a dark, deep hunger?

With Motheater shivering on Bennie's bed, clearly drained from the magic she had just done, there wasn't even the chance that she could have commanded the mountain to move. This was all Kire.

Zach didn't look away from the wreckage, eyes big.

"Maybe the lodge was built on an old mine shaft? We don't know where the first miners dug into the mountain. Could be a warren under it," Zach said quietly. A strange look crossed his face. He pressed the back of his hand to his mouth and turned away from the mountain, looking at Bennie.

"What?"

"I got a memory," he said quietly. "A map, from back then. I know it."

"So is there an old mine shaft under there or not?" Bennie narrowed her eyes. So he had been there with Motheater. He had seen the past.

He shook his head. "No . . . It's too close to the creek, and too likely to flood. They didn't try anything right there, but it's part of the mountain . . . It's bedrock all through."

"What else did you see?" Bennie demanded.

Zach glanced at Motheater, curled up and shaking inside the efficiency.

"We saw the men who wanted to kill her," he said softly. "The people of Kiron seemed like . . . they didn't want her gone, they just wanted to mine the mountain. They wanted to partner with the corporation."

Zach's mouth twisted. Bennie knew that expression. Zach was lining all the information up in his head.

"White Rock's been here since the eighties," Zach said quietly. "Just after clear-off was banned. Before that, Virginia Coal took down Huckleberry, Thompsons . . . My father worked those jobs."

Bennie pressed her mouth. This wasn't new information; she had spent the last year and a half digging into the history of Kiron with Kelly-Anne.

"Folks didn't die during those jobs," Zach said. "Virginia Coal didn't touch Kire. White Rock didn't, either, not until the nineties. That's when they finally got state approval to dig into the big mountain."

The nineties were when people started dying. When White Rock went into Kire. Maybe four months ago it wouldn't have made a difference, but now? It meant that

White Rock was safe before Kire, and dangerous while digging inside of it. It meant that Zach knew that something was going wrong in Kire, really wrong, more than what happened while mining in other mountains.

Bennie stared at Zach. All the time she had been investigating the deaths on Kire Mountain, he had never volunteered this information. It hurt. Bennie began to shiver. She couldn't stop, her hands shaking against the railing. When Zach stepped close and tried to put an arm around her, she jerked back. They stared at each other for a few seconds before Bennie finally spoke.

"It's Kire that's been dangerous. It wasn't just mining—it was mining Kire." Bennie's mind raced; her heart stuttered in her chest. Kire was alive. Kire had always been alive. It didn't matter if the mountain was sleeping or not—Kire was a living titan, and it was killing people. White Rock might have been negligent, trying to shift the blame off itself (and maybe, Bennie thought, they should have given up on the mountain long ago), but at the end of the day . . . It was Kire killing people. It was Kire that killed Kelly-Anne. "The equipment worked before and then it didn't. And you knew?"

"Equipment goes bad, Bennie," Zach muttered, looking back up the mountain. The last bit of the Elks Lodge wobbled, and then, with a shudder that they could feel even through her building, the wall completely collapsed. Bennie started, panic settling in her bones. Zach knew the risks, and he had gone into the mines anyway. He knew, and he had let Bennie work for White Rock, regardless of the toll. Because it was what his family did.

The Greshams were miners. Zach was a miner's son. What else was he supposed to do? What choice did he really have? She wasn't angry at him, just sad for him.

"It ain't White Rock, Zach." Bennie's face was hard. "It's Kire."

Tearing her eyes away from him, she looked back up the mountain. Bennie remembered the unimaginable fury that she had felt when Motheater had driven her into Kire on their way up to the Church of the Rock. Kire had been angry for a long time, had been waiting for the chance to be loosed on those that hurt it.

Maybe Kire was a righteous creature, but it wasn't the miners that hurt Kire; it was the system. It was the industry. White Rock wasn't even owned by Kiron folk. Any money coming out of Kire was going out of the state, into investors' pockets somewhere else. If the folks working in the mountain were just doing the best they could, every Kiron miner was being victimized, too.

Bennie closed her eyes. The people in Kiron didn't have a choice. So many of the miners were just like Zach. What else were they supposed to do out here? It wasn't like they didn't pay for it, coughing coal, retiring too early, but it was a living. It was enough.

But for Kire, it was too much. What nuance could she expect from a creature who was older than coins and currency, a creature who was older than the idea of humankind? It only held what it was given.

The lodge's crash reverberated in the air like a twang. It held the promise of violence. This was the season of Kire, and it was coming fast.

"I'm sorry," Zach said, so quiet Bennie almost missed it. "I should have believed you."

"You should have *helped* me," Bennie said sharply. The hurt came back, and just as quickly, the thorn was pulled away. Instead, she let her grief come over in waves. She was mourning Kelly-Anne, she was mourning the life she knew, the girl she was. Bennie wouldn't let her past hold her down anymore. She would let it go. The sting faded. The hurt remained.

"I know." He touched her hand but didn't hold it, didn't even keep his fingers on hers for longer than a second. He pulled back, and Bennie knew that this was the end of them.

"I want to help now."

A pressure eased in Bennie's chest. He was going to help. Now, they were three people against an industry that didn't give a shit if they died and a mountain that, very likely, wanted them all dead. Somehow, with just one more man of Kiron in their corner, Bennie felt better. She could use another ally. She smiled a little, looking away from him, staring up at the ridgeline. "Good."

"When she wakes up, she's going to want to find the grave of a man named Jasper Calhoun," Zach said, some of his pride coming back. He stood a little straighter, looked a little more confident. "Don't let her go without me."

"Why?" Bennie frowned.

He turned to her. "She aims to raise him out of the earth for a chat."

Bennie's frown deepened. "Weren't your kin enough?"

"The two of them were close. Friendly. I could feel her emotions while I was with her. He's got something of hers."

Bennie turned to stare at Motheater. The witch was curled up on the bed, shaking from the effort of dragging the past out of Zach's blood. She looked even more hollow, brittle as bird bones.

"Her soul, I think," Bennie muttered. "A friend to keep her safe."

"I don't much like the sound of that." Zach ran his hand through his hair and put his cap back on, digging into his pocket for his keys.

"Me neither," Bennie said. Bennie wanted more; wanted answers; wanted conviction. But this was faith, and hadn't Motheater trusted her? She nodded once. "But there's something wrong with Kire Mountain, and White Rock sure as shit ain't going to help. We might as well give the witch a chance to exorcize a demon or two. I don't have anything left to lose."

⌒〭〭

After Zach left, Bennie made herself a cup of tea and curled up in her chair, watching over Motheater as she slept. The sirens made it impossible to relax, and she felt as if Motheater might simply stop breathing, lost in whatever memory she had pulled out of Zach.

Bennie was staring at her map. She had just assumed that she couldn't get access to the death records of the past companies, but now it seemed the truth was much more simple. There simply hadn't been people dying. Not like miners were dying on Kire, a few every year, disappearing in ones and twos into the stone.

But if Bennie had found this sooner, would she have been able to save Kelly-Anne? She had a husband, they were trying for kids, and Kelly-Anne always joked that when she got assigned an office job with Bennie, they wouldn't get anything done. They'd trade books and plan hikes and fishing trips, they'd talk shit about their coworkers and cover each other's backs as they navigated the Kiron social scene together.

She remembered one barbeque at the Elliots' house—an event that didn't need an invitation and saw at least a dozen Kiron families pass through, leaving a dish on the communal table. It was hot, sweltering, really, and the cicadas were already buzzing out of the forest acreage that the Elliots' property bordered.

"You ever get worried?" Bennie asked, her eyes on Zach and Kelly-Anne's husband as they carefully arranged veggies on the grill so they wouldn't touch the meat.

Kelly-Anne shrugged as Carlo wrapped the asparagus up in foil. He was Venezuelan, with a thick accent. He and Kelly-Anne met in a tidewater college, and he moved to Kiron after their graduation.

"Sometimes. But it ain't much I can do." She took another sip of her beer, smiling. Bennie felt her chest tighten. "The mines are more dangerous than Kiron, I think."

"That's putting a lot of faith in Kiron," Bennie said, frowning.

"Maybe." Kelly-Anne smiled at her, and Bennie felt reassured by how kindly she said it, how earnest Kelly-Anne was. She was gentle, she cared. "But I don't know any other way. This is my home. Lots of good people living in the mountains, despite some of the racist shit others pull."

Bennie looked away from her, a little embarrassed that she might have suggested otherwise. Kelly-Anne wasn't wrong; all it took was looking at the spread that people had laid out in the backyard. There were kids running in and out of the woods, and even the fact that Bennie and Kelly-Anne weren't the only Black people at this event (Kelly-Anne's family had shown up) made her feel less impossibly singular. Hadn't she been hugged and greeted by name as families and friends cycled in?

Even Zach, it felt like Kelly-Anne was talking about him, too. Didn't Zach bring Carlo into his circle of friends, treating him like family, too? (He had known Kelly-Anne since they were kids, even.) Their debate about the best way to grill corn was heating, but even from a distance, Bennie could hear it was playful, boisterous like men got around a barbeque.

Bennie smiled a little, looking back at Kelly-Anne. "And what are the mines full of?" she asked, half joking.

Kelly-Anne had just shrugged, looked away. "Good people."

As Bennie stared at the map, she noticed moths finding their way into the apartment. Pushing Kelly-Anne's memory away, she focused instead on the bugs. They came through the windows, the bathroom, one even shimmying between the door and tile to come in. The lost souls of Kiron, wandering without a tender. Most floated above Motheater, held up by some magic updraft, hovering in place like a mobile over her head.

A few hung around Bennie, curious.

How long had Motheater been listening to the dead folk of Kiron? How long had she been burdened with the whispers of the past? Motheater had told her these were the dead that died on the mountain, but maybe the winged graveyard that circled her head had spread out a bit since she had last been around to shepherd the souls across the Appalachians.

Maybe there were so many because the Kiron families spread out, going to Richmond or D.C. or California, and these ghosts had to fly back home to seek peace. Maybe they were just any number of dead hikers or backpackers that held a memory of Kiron in their hearts. Maybe they were the lost souls of every mountain, the disappeared camps and enclaves, the Native people that were killed or evicted from their ancestral land. Bennie imagined that everyone was returning home, seeking out the last witch left to give them a final witness, one more chance to speak a truth into their world.

Bennie sighed, putting her tea away. She couldn't focus. She went outside, staring at the half-empty space on the side of the mountain where the Elks' wreckage was. At least the sirens had stopped.

Maybe White Rock would blame it on erosion or loose foundations. The town would speculate about White Rock getting too close to a weak spot, or they could blame a contractor who should have been in charge of knowing stable from shaky.

Then, like a dog pawing in his sleep, the area surrounding the broken-down lodge *shifted*. It turned, just a little, just enough that Bennie thought she had imagined it. It shivered, and the trees around it swayed without a breeze.

Bennie's eyes went wide and she pressed her hands to her mouth. Kire was waking up. It was waking up *now*, it was moving now. And there were no sirens this time, no movement in the town, nothing. It was an exhale.

She could feel it: anger, fury, wave after wave of indignation. Kire was going to shift and turn all the mine shafts into cleavage, all the bodies buried beneath its hulk into dust. She thought of Kelly-Anne, buried there, and turned away from the mountain.

Going back inside, she saw Motheater sitting up on the bed, eyes wide, moths fluttering all around her, agitated. Bennie gently pushed some away as she set up her kettle for another cup of tea, her hands shaking.

"Moth, take care of these, please?" Bennie asked, voice tight.

"Kire is coming."

"Yeah, I know," Bennie said, finding resolution suddenly. The doom and gloom act was getting old, and if she wanted to listen to someone talk about the end times, she'd go catch up with Mister Anderson at the bingo hall. "But so are we."

Motheater blinked at her. After a few seconds, the witch smiled and then turned her face up, hands reaching out for the moths that fluttered around her. She began her ablutions, spreading the dusty souls of the moths through her hair, which turned a shining, brassy gold, streaks of mossy, faded green at her temples. It was bizarre, but Bennie thought it was charming, a strange, weird look for a strange, weird woman.

Bennie offered her a cup of tea, after it was all done. "Have a nice nap?"

"Mm," Motheater hummed, taking the tea and drinking some of it. There were a few moths waiting for her, taken up in her hair.

Bennie crouched in front of the witch and hesitated.

She looked older. Maybe it was starting to hit her, the scope of what they had to do. They had to stop a mountain. Bennie nervously reached out and pushed some of Motheater's hair back, around her ear. Motheater looked up with wide brown eyes.

"Hey," Bennie muttered, leaning in. She should stop. This was too far, even for her, even for this witch. But she couldn't help it; Motheater had a fire in her that made Bennie want to burn. "You okay?"

Motheater blinked, slowly. The room suddenly felt leaf-warm and sunny, a spring morning by a cool creek. "I'm all right," she said quietly. "I drew up too much talking through Zach."

"Your magic?"

Motheater nodded, blinking again. She rolled her shoulders a little, rubbed her face, as if to reassure herself that these parts of her body still worked, were still here and ready to serve. "I ain't whole. I think . . . I asked a man to look after Kiron before I was put into the mountain. I need to find his kin or where he lies and get back what power I gave over."

"We need to put the mountain to rest, Motheater," Bennie said, still leaning in. "Kiron can't survive a giant rockslide or cave-in—the town is too close to the mountain. Do we really have time to go visiting your old friends? We're barely hanging on, and we don't get help out here."

Without coal, Kiron was just another poor town in a backwoods part of the world most people pretended didn't exist. Without money, Kiron would become just another punchline.

Motheater nodded solemnly, her eyes steady on Bennie's, her stare so intense that it made Bennie shiver. "Before I was trapped in Kire, I gave a friend part of my power. It's calling out to me. I find what I left with Jasper Calhoun, and I can build the church I am."

Bennie shivered. This was the plan. Motheater was the plan. Do what Motheater wanted until she could put the mountain to sleep. Bennie might have felt trapped, but she wanted to see Motheater do it. She wanted to be a part of that power. She wanted it herself. She didn't just want Motheater, she wanted to *be* Motheater.

"Where is he?"

Motheater frowned, shook her head. "Here, close. Buried near. But I did too much with Zach, I don't think . . ." She trailed off, and her face went soft, blurry again. She sighed, and God, didn't she seem older? Sadder?

Before Bennie thought too hard about it, she wrapped an arm around Motheater's shoulders, pulling her into a hug. Motheater reached for her arms, sliding close. In Bennie's embrace, Motheater smelled of pine sap and woodsmoke.

It was nice to hold her, if slightly bony. The woman had slim arms and a figure that was likely thinned out from a century of eating itself. Motheater's hands around Bennie's wrists were calloused and firm, and Bennie shifted to sit next to Motheater, her head level with Motheater's shoulders.

"I used to be able to say a Word and have rock shatter instantly. If I can't do that, I ain't the witch I was." Motheater paused. "And I still don't know my own name."

Bennie rubbed Motheater's back. The witch turned, pressing her face into Bennie's shoulder, and Bennie absolutely did not think about how nicely she fit next to her, how sharply she missed touching another person, how hard it had been to not have that kind of easy affection. She just wanted to be near someone.

"All right," Bennie relented. They needed every tool to be sharp, Motheater most of all. "How do we find your friend?"

"I'm not sure yet. Maybe we go back to y'all library? Maybe I find a rabbit to lead me through the wold?" She yawned, sleepy even though it was barely noon. "He's nearby. I can feel that much."

"And Kire?" She still wasn't sure what Motheater was planning, what she thought she could do about the mountain waking up, about stopping the doom she had prophesied.

Motheater nodded, blinking sleepily. "It needs to go to sleep."

That was something. But even half asleep, Kire had managed to kill near on thirty miners, if not more. What would happen when it woke up? Bennie's hands clenched, and she tried to find the right way to tell Motheater that asleep wasn't enough.

"I can't figure how you got so brave," Motheater muttered, leaning back. "You ain't stupid."

"Thanks," Bennie said, caught off guard. "That's the sweetest thing you've ever said to me."

Motheater paused. "You making fun of me?"

"I'm teasing you, Moth," Bennie muttered, squeezing the witch. Motheater was silent, but she nodded, leaning into her. Motheater pressed the top of her head against Bennie's neck. "But you make me brave, too."

Bennie rubbed Motheater's back as they held each other. Bennie shut her eyes and found comfort in the arms of the strange girl. Motheater had so much power and magic simmering under her skin, but she called Bennie brave? Not that Bennie was about to argue, but . . . still. That felt nice.

Motheater spoke quietly. "You're being so kind and . . . I ain't do nothing but impose."

Bennie only hummed.

This was the closest she had been to a girl like this since college. There had been a few flings, but nothing serious, and then she had met Zach. But now here was Motheater, curled up into her, breathing on her neck, and Bennie felt her heart all the way through her fingertips. Motheater was a bizarre creature, a witch out of time, and she was beautiful and strong, and Bennie hadn't wanted to kiss anyone this bad in years.

Motheater sighed against Bennie's neck, holding her tightly, and Bennie felt something in her resolve shatter, her heart pounding, desire encouraging her to just kiss Motheater. *Just kiss her!* She didn't, staring at a small discolored spot on the wall instead. This was, frankly, the worst.

"Thank you," Motheater said, pulling back, looking up at her. "I wouldn't know what to do without you."

Bennie pulled away from Motheater slowly, aching. Fuck, this was bad. She was so fucking gone. Motheater's eyes were huge, but watery, and it looked like she might fall over at any moment. A few moths had settled on her shoulders. Bennie was flushed, her face heated, and she tried not to let the cute girl see her look so panicked.

"Lie down," Bennie said, standing up and brushing settled dust off her pants. Her palms were sweating. What had she just been about to do? Her heart was pounding in her ears, and she didn't want to admit that she had been staring at Motheater's mouth.

"Where you going?" Motheater asked, looking up at her with wide eyes.

"I'm just going to work on my truck." It was mostly the truth. It did need an oil change, and Bennie suspected that there were a few other tune-ups she could do before they set out on a wild ride to find Jasper Calhoun's grave. More than her truck needed TLC, Bennie needed air. She needed space or she would do something very, very stupid. "I'll just be outside."

Bennie had to resist the urge to kneel down and kiss Motheater, tangle her hands in the witch's brassy hair, and press her into the bed. She tried not to seem nervous, hoping that Motheater wouldn't recognize her awkwardness for what it really was. She shoved her arms through her jacket and turned away, almost stumbling. God, she wanted to kiss that sleepy look off Motheater's face.

"Just rest, okay?" Bennie said, going to the closet and pulling out her toolbag and spare oil that she had shoved behind her sewing kit housed in a cookie tin. Anything to distract herself from the witch in her bed. "And don't do anything weird without me."

Motheater smiled a little, and Bennie's heart flipped over faster than a NASCAR crash. *Yikes.* That was not good. That was so not good. How was Bennie supposed to recover from this? Motheater shifted to grab the novel she had been reading, leaning against the wall. That was, apparently, the end of the conversation.

Bennie really didn't want to think about the way Motheater's mouth moved around the words as she read. She really didn't want to think about the way her hands spread across the pages, the way her eyelashes fluttered half-closed when she was concentrating on a new word. Bennie, who knew very well what the fuck was happening inside her chest, didn't want any of it to happen at all, because she knew what it meant. She was getting attached. More than attached, she was falling for the witch.

Instead of doing any of the stupid things she was thinking about, Bennie went to her truck and opened the hood. She focused intently on the engine in front of her and not the sirens that occasionally went off around her, or the witch in her bedroom, or the jaybird that perched on the side of the hood. Most of all, Bennie didn't think about the strange feeling on the back of her neck, like she was being watched, not watched over.

25

Esther

"Easy on." Jasper's voice was soft and low. Against Esther's mossy mind, it felt like velvet, like rabbit fur. "Breathe."

She did as she was told, taking a deep breath, and then another. She hadn't opened her eyes, and all her limbs felt heavy, like she were loaded with stones.

An arm wrapped around her shoulders, a sag down—she was on a bed. She smelled the pinewood fire, a squirrel-bone broth boiling in a cast iron. She leaned into Jasper.

Where was the mountain? It wasn't with her.

She blinked, forcing her eyes open, and saw the cotton of his shirt as she leaned against his chest, as she was pulled upright, a bowl of broth held against her mouth. Esther didn't question it, drinking, her fingers light on the bowl. Jasper continued to murmur a reassurance, his arm around her.

Esther moved against him after she had finished and tried to speak, but it came out like a croak, as if her throat were coated in sand.

"Rest," Jasper said, bodily moving her so that her shoulders were against the wall of his cabin. He left her side to get more broth, bringing it back. This time he sat next to her, and she could see him clearly. His hair, which should have been shining and coal black, now had a few silver streaks in it.

"Jas . . ." She reached out for his hair, touching it gently. He smiled.

"Don't look worried, it's only been a few weeks."

"You look old," she croaked.

"You like older men."

Esther hit his thigh weakly, and he offered her the bowl again. She took it and drank, closing her eyes. They sat in silence, a comfortable kindness, the fire's warmth penetrating the bones of her. Birds sang outside—there was the rustle of a creature in the creaking, bare-branched trees. Another sound, like an echo, and she tried to ignore that, but it was like a handshake that wouldn't ease.

She looked up and saw, collected on the ceiling, hanging from beams, a swarm of jarfly, not making much noise, but rustling their wings. Esther's heart caught in her ribs. Witch of bugs and possum. Witch of tor and holler.

She closed her eyes.

"What happened to Will?" she finally asked, the bowl resting on her lap.

"He's alive. Hanging onto a jagged limp, left hand in a splint, but he'll recover just fine."

Esther felt Jasper's hesitation in the air, like she felt the jarflies above her, like she felt the stone calling her, like she felt the sun rising on Kire.

"What happened to you?" Jasper gently put a hand on her wrist, leaning in. She could hear the fear in his voice.

"I spoke to Kire," Esther said softly. No, that wasn't right. "Made my last bargain."

Kire was a god who listened. She had traded her whole soul, no more parts or pieces or remedial bloodlettings. All of her was Kire.

Perhaps the Dandelion Witch was right; she held onto the old ways because they provided comfort. What did Kiron truly need from their Neighbor?

She reached out for Kire and found something missing, a maw, a dark valley in her chest. Where was her killing moon? Where was her last bride-made thing? Above her, the jarflies began to move, began to shuffle on cracking carapaces and jeweled wings.

She had left her anger in Kire. She had left her hatred and fury and rage in the mountain. *And Kire was a god who listened.* A cold dread ran through her. How was she here?

"I think the truer question is, what did you do, Jasper Calhoun?"

When Esther turned to look at Jasper, he didn't avert his gaze but stared back at her, dark eyes like loam.

"I brought you back."

Fear struck her. The swarm began to mass, and she tightened her hands on the bowl of broth. The implications hung in the air like fog on a cold morning.

"You made another deal," Esther whispered. Jasper had made a second deal with Kire, for more than just years or worship, the small things that he had traded for the mountain to simply reveal its secrets.

"You were gone for three weeks, Esther," Jasper said, face open and pleading. "And after a week, people thought you dead, and now Halberd's moved in." He rushed forward, words tumbling fast, all the syllables muddied together. "And you were right. Kire near on killed Gresham on spite alone, and when you denied him, Kire dragged you into hell instead."

Esther was breathing hard. Jasper had made a deal. Jasper had tied himself to something greater and stronger. Jasper had made himself a temple.

"I ain't want this."

"None of us wanted this," Jasper said, squeezing her wrist. "But I needed you back. And so does Kiron, whether or not they know it."

The cyclone of cicadas above them wasn't as furious, but it was there, a wait before the water rose. Esther tried again to reach for Kire and felt only a faint shudder. What had really happened in the stone? It was more than being kept, it was more than being watched.

"Open the window," she said, shaking her head. "Let me get the bugs out of your house."

Jasper hesitated and Esther caught it. She huffed, annoyed. "You got him here."

Jasper smiled, a little ruefully, and stood to open the window. Sure enough, as the cicadas started to fly out into the woods, she caught a glimpse of DeWitt's form on the porch. He startled as the jarflies swarmed, and Esther shot Jasper a piercing look.

"None of that." Jasper stood up. "The industrialist has had a change of heart."

Esther wanted to say something biting, but she was in no position to deny help, even if it came from unsavory men. She had dealt with worse before. She finished her second bowl of broth as Jasper went over to let the man into the cabin, and DeWitt at least looked ashamed enough to make Esther feel a little less like cursing him again.

"Good to find you well, Miss Esther," DeWitt said, holding onto his hat with both hands, looking like a chastened child being caught with something he shouldn't have touched. Esther, for her part, tried to be gracious.

263

"You've found an appropriate jacket," she said tightly. She looked down and realized she was wearing one of Jasper's shirts. Three weeks. And Jasper taking care of her in his own home. This was bordering on a disaster. She closed her eyes, and under her, the foundations shivered. "I'd like to know more about this deal, Jasper."

"I'd like to tell you to bother me later, but you're not going nowhere, and I know you won't stop until you get answers." Jasper sighed.

Esther stared at him, and DeWitt awkwardly moved around the cabin, finding a seat on a stool amid the wood shavings from Jasper's last whittling project.

"I spoke with Kire," Jasper said, leaning against the door-frame. "Went into the shaft and talked long enough to pull you out of the mountain's wicked grasp."

"At what cost?"

Jasper held her gaze. "Nothing I wasn't willing to trade."

Esther stared. Did he truly think that Kire would treat him better, would love him more than she did? He had done this for her, so why did she feel left behind?

"You fool. You have broken my treaty with the god," Esther said, voice chipped. She felt her face flush red. "You should have left me there."

"I couldn't do that."

"Why not!"

"Because Halberd has truly come to Kiron," DeWitt spoke up, coming to Jasper's defense, his blue eyes big, pale, wide. "You were missing. Kiron miners don't hold your faith, and after what happened with Gresham, they wanted reassurances. Halberd's technology and resources mean safer mines, and safer mines means more money."

Esther shifted and put her head in her hands. This was all her fault. If only she hadn't opened Kire up when she was a child, if she hadn't destroyed its sleep, hadn't tapped its

264

power. She could have been a fine hedge witch, but she had traded parts of her soul before she was even a woman because nobody was there to tell her to stop. Her power outstripped her ambition. And now, all her bonds were broken, she only had the magic left in her well, and Kiron was in danger because of her. All the technology in the world wouldn't be able to stand up to Kire.

"Kire will come for you, Jas."

"Aye, well, you'll be set on Halberd and Kire like a great big dog of war, so it's a fair exchange," Jasper said, and even looking away from him, Esther could hear his smile. "And you know I ain't got much love for here. If I become a drink of flesh for an old spirit, ain't that gonna be an adventure?"

Esther shifted, trying to move out of bed, but her limbs were still leaden, soaked in silt, a waterlogged beam in a deep current. Her heart ached. Jasper had traded his soul for her body. He didn't know how tenuous her tie to Kire had become. She still had power, she could still reach and find her fire, but Kire had become something twisted, something dark, something more human than any god should be. Her bargains would not hold. And what would a mountain like this demand of Jasper? Would it be satisfied?

"How long till Halberd sets up proper?" Esther asked DeWitt, trying to ignore the way that Jasper stood apart from her, watching her fight to move off his bed. He didn't offer to help, and she didn't know if that was out of pettiness or propriety. She hated it either way.

"Another week or so," DeWitt said. "But . . ."

"But what?"

"If you can convince the miners, we might be able to delay Halberd's work into the mountain." DeWitt's voice became more confident. "We have two months of funds. If we don't start working by June, our investors will pull out and shift focus farther south."

Esther paused. Who knew what the town thought of her now? Who knew what rumors had been turned, what stories told and whispered around a still. Was she a ghost, a witch, or a Neighbor? Was she a daughter of Kiron or Kire? She hesitated. She wanted her snakes, she wanted her flowers, she wanted her herbs, and most of all, she wanted the reassurance of her mountain.

Both men were staring at her. It was hard to read what they wanted in the weight of their eyes, but she knew that they trusted her, that they were willing to choose her over Halberd, her over Kire. They believed in her.

Esther nodded, resolute.

"Aye. We will try. Between us . . ." Esther commanded the mountain; Kiron listened to Jasper; DeWitt could expose Halberd's hand. "We have all the tools we need."

She had to try. If only for the sacrifice Jasper had made to bring her back, she had to try, one last time, to placate the leviathan, to protect Kiron without expectation. It was demanded that she protect her home, destroy an industry, and fight with all her power for the people of the highland.

Wasn't she the Witch of the Ridge, who commanded Dameron to Kimbalton? Wasn't she the moth-eater, adder-eyes, soul-bound? She was Esther of the Rock, and as she shifted to look out of the window, up at the looming Kire Mountain, she felt something open up within her, as big as a spine, as big as Appalachia herself. Wasn't she made for this?

꩜

When Esther stepped into the worshipful Church of the Rock, three weeks after she had pulled Will Gresham from the mountain, the entire congregation stilled like a deer sensing a hunter in the brush. Even the snakes, held in wooden cages at the front of the church, stopped moving, the rattlers frozen in their heel, cottonmouths holding their fangs open, showing off. The notes themselves dropped from the air as Esther, Lazarus of Kiron, appeared, back from the dead.

Silas, leading the psalm, started the verse over again, and Esther did not intervene. She stepped into a back pew and pulled a Bible from the keep, flipping through to the proper page. It was pretense, as she had most of the King James memorized, but it was a good show.

This wasn't an occasion; Silas didn't pull out the snakes and preach. They stayed in their cages, a silent threat, the fear of God made real in the small, enclosed space of the Church of the Rock. He ignored her, the impedance in the back of his church, the adder in the cradle. That was fine, Esther thought, going through the motions of the Sunday words. She had made her statement. Besides, all the other folks in the congregation were sneaking their eyes back toward her, were indulging in moments of curiosity in between reverence, and Esther knew that she had them, that she was the power once again in this town, alive, dead, and then risen again.

There was nothing, she had decided, that could kill an Appalachian witch like her.

The service ended, and the congregation filed out, most of them only glancing sidelong at Esther as they left. The witch didn't mind, standing up and letting their regard pass without remark. She didn't incline her head as the full mass passed through, and within a few minutes, it was just her and her father in the church.

"Should have stayed dead," Silas spat, walking through the pews, picking up after his flock. Esther could hear the disappointment in his voice. He would truly love to see her corpse.

Esther brushed down the front of her dress. "Hell ain't got nothing I haven't seen before."

Silas shot her a look that would have withered an apple on the branch.

"You scared them. First in your manner of going, now in coming back."

Esther frowned. She and Silas were aligned, weren't they? And holding snakes had never been about keeping folks calm. "We can still turn back Halberd—"

"No." Silas cut her off, standing in the center of the aisle, staring at her, holding a pair of hymnals in his hands. He looked like any other preacher. He turned away from her and continued to pick up the discarded pamphlets, tucking books into the pew. It was a dismissal, a disappointment.

Esther's hands clenched. In the back of the church, the rattlers began to shake. Under her feet, centipedes and silver bugs forced their way up through the foundation, a skittering, many-legged battering ram, filing through the cracks and weak joints. This was not her magic. She was a part of Appalachia now.

"Kiron will not be convinced by me. I offer everlasting salvation, and Halberd a different kind of balm," Silas said. "And they will surely not listen to you."

Esther stared at her father. He seemed different—not defeated, but resigned. What had happened in the three weeks she had been kept in the stone? "I am the one who grabbed Will Gresham 'round his collar and tore him from the bone," Esther said, as mice found their way into the church, no wariness of serpents keeping them at bay. "I have come from hell a new witch."

"Aye, and placed yourself as far from a tolerable Neighbor as any I've seen." Silas turned from her, stepping on the bugs without hesitation, a mouse caught under his heel. Esther's breath caught in her throat. What was she now?

"I will not give in so easily to evil men," Esther said, drawing on the last of her righteousness, the last thing she could place against her father's will. "Nor will I suffer them to corrupt my people."

"Are they your people if you are not of them?"

Silas was behind the altar of stone, hands on the slab, staring at Esther. She had stepped out into the aisle, and around her feet was a halo of creatures of all sizes, circling her, spreading outward from her power, from her call. A squirrel ran across the pews; a possum trundled in. There was the sound of a woodpecker in the eaves.

Esther wanted to break the church in half. She wanted to turn Silas into a thing with boils, she wanted to bring a tornado down on the mountain, God in the whirlwind.

Her will alone wouldn't make his words less true.

She turned and stalked out of the church, and the creatures and crawling things ran from her, burrowing back into the woodwork and spire.

The congregation had headed down the mountain toward the meeting place in Kiron. They would be there, even the Greshams, sharing a meal, trading gossip, and Esther knew that hers would be the name out of everyone's lips.

But she needed the town. What good were all her machinations if she left Kiron unsatisfied? Why would any of this matter if Kiron decided that it had had enough of its witch? There was no point protecting Kire if she didn't protect Kiron alongside it. There could be harmony here, she was sure of it.

She tucked her hands into her pockets, walking slowly down the mountain, pausing at the last turn before she descended into Kiron. It was a ridge above the town, and from here she could see the small village laid out. It was slightly haphazard, but passing fair. The roads were near enough to straight, and the meeting hall was well-built. Most of the cabins had two or three rooms, many had little plots out back. She knew every family in this town, she knew who worked, who tended children, she knew who had a talent for finding ramps and sang, who had an ear for birds, who could trap even the quickest game. She knew Kiron.

Why didn't they know her?

As the families went into the meetinghouse, she spotted Jasper and his father holding court as they walked, three or four people following them, heads leaned in to better hear Collum's low voice. The Calhouns were distinctive, with long strides and clothing that seemed to be tailored rather than mended. It was easy to recognize what a man like DeWitt would find pleasing about him.

Then something drew her eye. A slight shimmer, a brume, and to Esther it looked like there was a second man just behind Jasper, a shadow's shadow. It was the haze of dust through light, a creature that was formless and following. The dim thing stuttered as Jasper went in the door and then it disappeared, melting like pollen into the air. Kire's bargain come to collect.

Jasper had paid too high a price to return an unwanted Neighbor to Kiron. It struck her that she would have been better kept in the mountain, where she could hold Kire close forever, allowing Kiron to take what it needed. She had been too selfish and too scared to commit to Kiron before, but a lifetime in the mountain for an age of prosperity in the holler seemed the frustratingly obvious solution now. She should have made this bargain before. Could she make it now, or did Jasper hold Kire closer?

Already, she could feel her well of power dwindling. As long as the shaft was open, her own magic would be more difficult to drag out of the rock.

She made her way down the ridge, walking into Kiron and passing the well on her left. As she did, she whispered encouragement and sweetness, and drew up a new trickle from the old spring, despite the hesitation it took to rise, the toll it had on her. It was always a good idea to be kind to the water.

Pausing in front of the meetinghouse, she stood just to the side of where she had seen Jasper's shade disappear. There was nothing: no extra footsteps, no scent in the air, no shadows or missing parts of the path. It was as if nothing had been there, and if Esther didn't know what Jasper had done, she would have assumed it had been a trick of the afternoon light.

"You coming in?"

Esther turned to see Dinah Spencer and her two babes hanging off her skirts, her arms full of a cast iron cauldron that reminded Esther of how hungry she was. It would do her no good to imagine enemies here. Esther nodded. "Let me help."

She took the cauldron and Dinah shooed the children, no older than six, into the hall. They ran through legs and skirts, searching for their friends inside the smoky room. Esther clutched the food tighter and for a second wished it wasn't wrapped in cloth, wished it would burn her hands and arms, leave a scar, leave something behind.

"Been a while since you came around," Dinah said, walking in with her. "The women were getting worried."

"Naught but rumors of my disappearance," Esther said softly, looking over the meeting hall, laid out with benches and tables, a row of food in the back. She and Dinah headed there, and the miners, mostly men, shot her sidelong glances, giving her a wide berth. She spotted Will Gresham with his thatch of gold flax hair, and the boy immediately tensed, as if he could feel the weight of her gaze on him. "It'll take more than a mountain to get rid of me."

"Well don't go leaving soon," Dinah muttered, attempting to keep track of her wild offspring. "I heard darling Cora has a sight on university. Will need a mighty conjure to help her get in."

Esther set the cauldron down, pushing what smelled like squirrel dumpling stew farther onto the wood. A girl from Kiron going to university. "How'd she even hear about that?"

"Papers are coming in every week now," Dinah explained. "Cora saw an ad at the back, and it struck her fancy. She penned a few letters, saved up for stamps and everything."

Esther didn't know what to think. Was she proud or hurt? She had heard confession from many students, flitting to her on soft wings, but what had they known? What were they doing that was so much better than what there was to do in Kiron?

But she didn't say any of this. Dinah continued, talking about the recruitment booklet, the application process, which seemed to mostly involve an extended correspondence, and the fact that now Cora had two female colleges to choose from, both right nearby. A place called the Roanoke Female Seminary, another called Augusta, bearing the same title. Esther stood and nodded as Dinah went through all of the notes Cora had gotten, the way they wanted to offer her scholarship, how her writing was so strong that it would be a shame to lose her to a mining town like Kiron, where the most she would be writing was preacher's sermons for distribution on Tuesday, and ain't Cora got words of her own?

Dinah was glowing. Cora was near enough to her in age that she saw her as a younger sister of sorts, and it was clear that this was nothing but exciting.

And Esther only felt shame. Was Kiron so bad? Was this place so deep in the backwater that even universities were eager to take pity on them? Learning places coming to snatch their bright young women, industries to take their men, government figuring to take their livelihoods? How long did Kiron have before everyone started looking outward?

Esther was about to excuse herself when Jasper came over and tucked his hand against her elbow.

"You mind if I steal her 'non?" he asked, smiling brilliantly. Dinah shooed them off and smiled conspiratorially at them both. Esther glared at him, but Jasper, for ill or worse, didn't seem to care at all about his mean witch.

"I'm trying to ingratiate myself into the hearts of the people," Esther hissed. She pulled her arm away as they walked off. "Ain't that what we want?"

"I just thought I should warn you before—"

The doors opened, and Esther smelled something awful wafting through, a sourness that cut through woodsmoke and salt pork. It must just be her; nobody else reacted to it. The Halberd miners had come to the meetinghouse, bearing gifts and food. Ochiltree walked behind them, a look on his face that was not unlike that of someone who had stepped in particularly ripe horseshit.

Esther's eyes widened. Jasper's hand on her arm tightened.

"Before what, Jas?" Esther's voice cracked.

Jasper glared at her. "Don't do nothing."

"You ain't got the weight to tell me what to do," Esther hissed.

"I think this time I do." Jasper squeezed her elbow, and something warm shot through her. She looked at him with wide eyes, remembering that he had been the one to sever many of her bargains with Kire's foundation, that he had traded something eternal for her freedom.

She clenched her hands, pressed down the urge to ice out the whole valley, turn spring back to winter, to whither crops and make kairn of rutting stags. The desire to beggar Kiron was deep in her, and she stared at Halberd's men as they walked through the population.

When the Halberd men had come to the winter contra, she ran. When she went to Hatfield to bargain, she ran. When they came into Kiron, offering safety and solutions

273

after Will had been near killed, she wasn't there. Halberd had been behind her back for too long. But now she resolved to claim them like Dameron and Khates.

Esther glared at Jasper, the lines of his handsome face drawn down in warning. They looked like lovers in a quarrel. She yanked her arm away. "I will not touch them here."

"If you wait out in the trees like some vulture—"

"That's an idea," Esther nearly growled. "A painter in the dark."

"Esther." Jasper's tone brokered no argument. Esther rolled her eyes and pushed at his hand. He didn't move away from her, and her eyes flicked over the operation, noting their numbers, comparing them to the Hatfield settlement.

She counted quickly. "Most of 'em are here." Now was the time to strike; now was the opportunity. But Jasper had a faraway look.

Esther frowned. "Jasper?"

He didn't move. She turned to see where he was looking, and on the other side of the birchwood window, lit from the inside with a tallow candle, something large and dark shifted. The birch fluttered, as if a creature were breathing on it. Kire's emissary. Jasper had given himself wholly to the mountain, and it was waiting for him.

"Jas," Esther hissed, turning him around, forcing him to look away from the window.

He turned, as if in a trance, acting strange, and Esther saw more than a few people staring at them. DeWitt, by Ochiltree; Jasper's father, Collum; the eldest Benneke sister, who had always had it sweet for Jasper, but never thought to approach. And Silas, his eyes narrowed at the two of them. The high Halberd men were here to make friends, to make fast their position, and she was a distraction.

Jasper's eyes were far away, and the plan Esther had been fomenting to approach the Hatfield camp like a Moses and liberate Halberd's investment chain by chain. With the great men of Halberd here, she could make a pit of Hatfield holler, but Jasper's palm was already turning cold. She wouldn't sacrifice him to take advantage of Halberd's lowered gates. To attempt it now would destroy her.

Perhaps this was an opportunity lost, and perhaps she was running away again, but Jasper was her friend, and she would not let him be killed by the mountain. If she was resolved to save Kiron and not Kire, she needed to start somewhere.

She had two months to deal with Halberd, to drive them from hut and stead. Surely there would be other chances to cut the head from the adder. She held onto Jasper's hand and dragged him from the meeting room, pushing dark instinct aside. She only had right now to save her friend.

26

Bennie

After Bennie had finished working on her truck, she took Motheater to the grocery store to stock up. Besides more granola, apples, and the usual trail staples, Bennie also ended up spending more than she had budgeted because Motheater kept touching things. The witch seemed entranced by the sheer variety of green things on display, and honestly, the look on her face when Bennie gave her a bag of grapes and told her to go nuts was, frankly, priceless. It also threatened to split Bennie's chest in two, but she had resolved not to think about that.

The rest of the night was spent making crepes and talking about what Motheater had remembered from her journey through Zach's blood. The map had come down, spread across the bed. Around one crepe, stuffed with raspberries and Cool Whip, Motheater pointed at a small patch of Kire and said, "That's where I killed the moon."

Bennie choked on her tea. She was sitting next to Motheater, legs crossed, her knee just barely not touching

Motheater's thigh. Bennie had been deliberately not thinking about this for the past thirty minutes.

"What?"

Motheater stuffed the last bit of crepe in her mouth, cream stuck to her cheek.

"That's where I tied myself to power," she said, smiling a little. "I was fourteen."

"You became a witch at fourteen?"

"I been talking to snakes since I were coming on seven." Motheater sounded proud. "They know things."

"Yeah, what else is new." Bennie took another crepe and smeared chocolate spread on it. "All right, say I want to be a witch. I go chat up a cottonmouth and kill the moon. Easy."

"Well, you got to get to an agreement," Motheater said. "You both have to enter into a deal."

"Is that how it works?" Bennie took a big bite of the crepe.

"There's some details missing, but . . . you start with desire. There's a thermal, like taking someone to bed."

Bennie snorted. She wasn't expecting that.

Motheater was grinning at her. Bennie realized she had almost gotten used to Motheater's pointed teeth, the look on her face like a creature waiting for prey. She still had cream on her cheek. Bennie's face heated up, and she leaned forward to brush the Cool Whip off with her thumb.

Motheater was still smiling, and Bennie didn't mind the predator she saw in front of her. Oh, God help her, she was *infatuated*. Fuck, she was so screwed. She shifted a little, noticing again that her leg was against Motheater's leg, and she was so goddamn done, she didn't want to pull away, the line of her thigh against the witch's sending small little shocks up her spine.

Bennie gestured. "You got—"

"Sure," Motheater said, some greenish-blue color high on her own cheeks, the closest thing the pale woman could come to a blush. Bennie's heart was racing, and before she could do something absurd, she took a big bite of her crepe, turning deliberately away from the witch.

"Tell me about this moon murder," she said, deliberately not looking at Motheater. "It clearly didn't stick." She waved her hand in the general direction of the window. "Moon's still there."

"It's metaphorical."

"Ooh, big word." Bennie grinned, taking another bite and finishing off her crepe. "Talk metaphorically to me, Motheater."

Motheater's face was worth it. Bennie laughed, standing up to make more tea, avoiding the rough tension in between her and Motheater, her absolutely inane desire to rebound with a hundred-and-fifty-year-old witch.

"Tomorrow we're gonna find Jasper's grave, right?" She bustled around the kitchen, starting on the dishes. "And then what?"

Bennie couldn't see Motheater's face as she was turned toward the sink, but the air suddenly became cold and still. Bennie deliberately didn't turn around. This was a test, she knew it, but she had to ask. If Motheater needed closure on an old friend to stop Kire's waking, then so be it.

"Find his grave. Take back my soul. Reclaim my power." Her voice was soft. "I'm betting that he'll be the last piece of my magic that needs finding. Then I can make true bargains instead of licking at the edges of my sill and be the Witch of the Ridge again."

"And then what?" Bennie asked. Who was Jasper Calhoun to Motheater anyway, and why the fuck was Bennie feeling jealous over a dead man?

"We stop the killings."

Bennie didn't move, shoulders tense. What happened after this? After Motheater took her power back? Would she return to the mountains or stay in Kiron? Would she stay with Bennie? Would she even want to? Bennie's stomach was clenched in uncomfortable knots. What else could she do? She had to move forward.

"You got a way to find him?" Bennie was already thinking of ways to get information out of the Kiron library's index about nineteenth-century gravesites. The kettle boiled, and Bennie immediately made another mug of tea.

"Aye." Motheater looked over the map, tracing the invisible lines between the red dots that marked out the dead. "Like to like. Kin to kind. Our selves are twined together, sibling things."

Bennie watched Motheater's hands, her fingers trailing over the topography, the dirt under her nails, the blue tinge near her cuticle white folks got when they were cold.

So why was Bennie always staring at her hands?

"Let's get an early start," Bennie murmured, placing her mug down. She headed to the bathroom, looking for any excuse to be away from Motheater right now, to not remember that they were sharing a bed. "We'll text Zach in the morning."

Motheater didn't respond, and Bennie escaped into the shower. She didn't know whether she was being silly or if she was just a coward. Maybe both. She imagined Motheater's face turned up to hers, those dirty hands around her arms. She imagined adding another bruise to Motheater's collection, kissing down the scales of her neck tattoos.

Bennie, for the record, didn't hate the idea of Motheater biting her with jagged teeth.

"I'm so screwed," Bennie groaned. Under the water hitting her cap and the sound of a new klaxon in the distance, she could only hope that Motheater didn't hear her.

Bennie found herself grateful that she slept through the whole night without waking up to a swarm of moths fighting in through every crack and crevice. It seemed that Motheater's ministrations throughout the day were enough to allow their boatman some rest during the dark hours.

What Bennie didn't love was waking up with Motheater's slim arms around her waist and the witch's face buried against her shoulder blades. Nope. Did not love that at all, didn't wake up breathless and scared, absolutely didn't hate that slightly petrified and turned on seemed to be her near-constant state since she had brought the Appalachian Neighbor into her home.

Bennie's mouth was dry, and her hands were not, and when she put her fingers against Motheater's, she didn't expect to have her hand gripped fast. She screwed her eyes shut and ignored the fact that Motheater was pressing against her back like a big cat, nuzzling into the divot between Bennie's shoulder blades.

Bennie was sure that Motheater could feel her heart. Did Motheater know that she had been seduced so thoroughly? Probably not. Bennie squeezed Motheater's hand.

"Let me up, Moth."

Motheater groaned and, to Bennie's intense mortification, shoved her leg in between Bennie's. It was sleepy, not at all sexy, and Bennie would have liked to know what god was to blame for this overwhelming need to turn over and kiss Motheater until her fool mouth was swollen.

This, Bennie decided, was a very bad idea.

She pulled herself away from Motheater. The witch sighed and flopped forward, cuddling into the empty space where Bennie had been. Motheater sighed. "You're mighty warm, darlin'."

Motheater's voice was so soft that it might have been missed if Bennie wasn't hyperaware of every single thing happening in her apartment right now. Motheater spoke low and misty, voice husky from sleep, and Bennie knew, in that exact moment, that she was monumentally fucked.

"Bathroom," Bennie said, because it was the least sexy thing she could think to say and the best way to escape from this situation.

Even after washing her face, Motheater's words were still haunting her. Bennie pressed her forehead against the mirror. *Great. Super great.* Bennie steadied herself. She could ignore this, right? Didn't they have a job to do?

Bennie stood up straight, looked herself right in the eye and swore that she was not, no way, in any universe, going to make a move on the weird pantherine witch in her apartment. But she had that look on her face that meant Bennie was making a promise she was going to break, and she groaned.

"I'm so fucked."

She slowly eased out of the bathroom and went to gather clothes. Motheater had already changed into jeans and her oversized acid-wash sweatshirt, and Bennie absolutely did not spend time looking over the absolutely devastating shape of her cheekbones, the angle of her neck and shoulders, the way her tattoos shifted as she pushed up her sleeves.

"Watch me work this electric kettle," Motheater said, smiling brilliantly at Bennie as she pulled the kettle off the stand and filled it with water. Bennie was almost overwhelmed by Motheater carefully checking the water level, arranging it on the stand, and then pressing the button to turn on the kettle. The witch turned and grinned at Bennie, eyebrows up, and Bennie had to remind herself that this was a dangerous creature who could tear a church beam from brace without a second thought, and here she was proud that she had managed a basic function of modern life.

Motheater's face fell. "Did I do it wrong?" she asked, looking back at the kettle.

"Oh, no, great." Bennie rushed, immediately turning to grab two mugs and a pair of teabags. "Like a natural."

"I'm getting the hang of this century," Motheater crowed, walking over to pick up Bennie's map, staring at it. "Soon I'll be caught up enough to operate your automobile."

"Not happening," Bennie said, hoping to cut that idea at the root.

"I'm very good with horses," Motheater said, kneeling on the ground, leaning over the map. "I can tame your beast."

"It's . . ." How was Bennie supposed to explain a driver's license? In fairness, half the folks out here were driving around on expired or borrowed licenses anyway. The police had bigger things to deal with than coal men trying to drive to work. The nearest DMV was a full county over. "Maybe."

Motheater grinned up at her, and Bennie wanted to die, her traitorous chest constricting. She had no intention of letting Motheater drive her truck, but fibbing seemed an easy price to pay for that smile. God, she was so, so absolutely fucked.

Luckily, before Bennie could wallow in self-pity any longer, her phone buzzed. Bennie was more than grateful as text messages popped up. Finally, a distraction from Mount Doom rumbling in the background.

"Hey, Motheater?"

Motheater was still tracing the red dots on the map. She glanced up at Bennie.

"Zach's coming over to help find Jasper." Motheater's hands spread like roots against the map. Moths had snuck into the room, fluttering like living jewelry around Motheater's wrist and collarbones.

Motheater nodded, shifting to stretch her arms upward, dislodging the moths on her skin. "I wager I could conjure a way to a grave, or perhaps find one of his descendants, or . . ."

Motheater froze. Her arms dropped, and a look of confusion and horror passed over her. She scrambled up, going to the sink and turning on the water. She found a bowl and placed it under the tap, murmuring. Bennie was startled enough that she dropped her phone.

"Motheater?"

"Oh, God," Motheater said, staring at the bowl of water. She left the tap running as she walked out of the apartment, balancing the bowl in between her hands. "I need a bone—something dead."

"Uh, all right?" Bennie turned off the tap, picked up her phone, and then peeked into her fridge. It was abysmal, but there was half a rotisserie chicken still there. It would have to do. She brought it out, following Motheater onto the porch.

Outside, Motheater faced the rising sun, holding out the bowl of water. The blue jay had flown over, deciding to use her wrist as a perch, and was peering intently into the bowl. She made a face at the picked-over chicken as Bennie offered it to her. "That'll do."

"I don't know what you were expecting," Bennie said, frowning as Motheater balanced the bowl on the railing. She was clearly unimpressed as she looked over the rotisserie chicken.

"People used to keep hares for this sort of thing," Motheater muttered, reaching over and pulling out a few bones from the carcass.

"What sort of thing?" Bennie was trying her best to keep her feelings of mild horror off her face but doubted that it was working.

"Scrying." Motheater held the bowl in one hand and the chicken bones in the other, clutching them over the water. She took a deep breath and let it out slowly, turning to face all four cardinal points, pausing in each direction. Bennie took a step back as Motheater did magic on the veranda. The witch murmured softly, bowing to the east, and Bennie could feel the charge in the air shift. It was a stillness, a calm. No breeze, no sounds; even the cars in the distance faded to an indiscernible hum. And in her own chest, it echoed. She could feel it, she knew it, like she knew Motheater pressed against her back.

Motheater put the bowl back on the railing and held the bones in both hands. The blue jay was circling above her head, the moths collecting on the supports like an audience.

"*Greater love hath no man than this,*" Motheater said, breaking the bones over the bowl of water. The gristle and meat became fiery dust; the bones melted like wax. It coated her fingers, her hands, and the viscous, slick liquid slowly dripped down into the water, hissing. Bennie's breath caught in her throat, fear and jealousy making it hard to breathe. "*That a man lay down his life for his friends.*"

As the tallow writhed in the air, it fell much slower than gravity would want it. The salt-fat formed shapes in the air, opened their mouths like snakes before collapsing down into the water. Steam rose up, and Motheater's hand spread over the bowl as all the water disappeared, dissipated by the Word.

Motheater leaned over, frowning as symbols appeared, solidified in the cooling tallow. A soft magic.

Bennie wanted to ask what was happening, wanted to know what Motheater divined when she leaned over the bowl, wanted to See what Motheater Saw. Instead, she clutched a chicken carcass and let Motheater do her work.

As the last of the steam disappeared, Bennie realized that they were just hanging out on the front porch of her building, and anyone could come out at any time and see whatever the fuck this was. She took a step toward Motheater.

"I hate to interrupt, but we are visible as hell right now, and I don't think that these folks are keen on grown ladies doing science experiments ten feet from their door."

Motheater nodded, grabbing the bowl and heading back into the efficiency. "Call Zach," she said, putting the bowl on the counter and scratching notes on the back of one of Bennie's hastily photocopied reports. "I can find Jasper's grave."

Bennie hated to be bossed around like this, but Motheater was the one with the magic wax. She texted Zach and then went to look over Motheater's shoulder. She had pulled out her map of Kire from the hike and had folded it over to only show a part of the valley near where Old Kiron had been.

"You think he's buried there?" Bennie asked, wiping her hands on a dish towel.

"The lines are blurred," Motheater explained, gesturing to the bowl. The cooled bone-wax was stuck to the sides in patterns Bennie couldn't make head nor tails of. "Some are clear. Some read like prophecy."

Picking up the map, Bennie groaned. "You read anything in those chicken bones about an old manager?"

"What?" Motheater looked up, confused.

Bennie tapped the area of the map that Motheater showed. "That," she said, resigned, "is Helen DeWitt's property."

༄

"You want me to come in with you?"

Bennie was in the diner parking lot, hands gripping the wheel, staring at the door. She glanced over at Zach, who was leaning up from the back seat, one arm over her headrest, the other on the divider between the driver's seat and the pilot's. It had been discovered that Motheater got wickedly carsick in the back seat, so Zach, long limbs and all, had squeezed in the second row of Bennie's truck.

"No," Bennie said, fumbling with the seat belt. "No, I think . . ." She paused to catch her breath. Motheater was staring at her, and she was doing everything she could not to look back at the witch.

"I think I need to talk to her alone."

"I can still curse her," Motheater said absently, looking over toward the abandoned parking lot, probably for another branch of pokeweed. "If'n you wanted."

"No." Bennie took the canvas bag with the map in it and put it in her lap, opening the door. "This is for me."

Motheater stared at her, but didn't say anything. Zach sat back, shifting to put his legs up on the seat. This was it. The confrontation that she had always wanted to have with Helen DeWitt. Bennie gripped the canvas bag tighter and slipped out of the truck, leaving her cap behind and straightening her jacket.

The afternoon was already warming up, but Bennie kept the Carhartt on. It was a piece of armor, a small sign that she been here, that she was still Kiron, all for being new to the area, that she had patched and sewn and fixed up her damn jacket just as much as anyone else. She straightened her collar and went into the diner.

Helen was sitting in a booth near the back, a mug of coffee in her hands and a dreamy look on her face. It was strange, Bennie thought, to see her in the off-hours. She was a different person.

Bennie walked over and sat down, not bothering with a "how's your morning." Helen looked up from her coffee, slow like sap, deliberate, coordinated.

"I was surprised to get your text," Helen said, sitting up straight.

"I was surprised you answered."

"Against the advice of counsel, I'll have you know."

"You got a lawyer?" Bennie couldn't keep the surprise out of her voice.

"I got an advisor," Helen clarified, taking a sip of her coffee. "You and the Elliots are arranging that suit."

Bennie swallowed. The rumor that Kelly-Anne's parents were looking into a wrongful death suit was one of the more vicious to circulate through town. The Elliots wanted nothing to do with Kiron anymore. It was just Bennie hanging on like a fool. Bennie felt an ache. She wanted to fight for her friend, but that wasn't why she was here.

Instead, she reached into the bag and pulled out the red-dotted murder map she and Kelly-Anne had been working on for eighteen months. Bennie spread it out on the table, moving Helen's saucer and pushing the ketchup to the very edge of the table. Seeing it here, outside of her efficiency, in public, made all her anger come back. Here were twenty-eight lives ended on Kire. Here were twenty-eight families hurt, harmed, all because White Rock was ignoring the looming creature it dug into.

"What—"

"This is a map of the folks reported dead on Kire, and where they were disappeared or killed," Bennie cut Helen off. "This only goes back to the nineties, but before that, I didn't find any deadly equipment malfunctions in any other dig sites."

"So what?" Helen sipped her drink, frowning.

Bennie knew that Helen was trying to be hard, but there was something in her voice that cracked. Bennie pressed the advantage.

"You and I both know that this ain't right," she said, lowering her voice. "This many deaths, with no real big accident, disaster, or explosion attached? This ain't the way people die in mining operations."

"Disasters aren't the only way miners die," Helen said.

Bennie thought about the explosion in West Virginia, the bad fuse in Kentucky. Miners died en masse: thirty, sixty, two hundred all at once. Miners dying one by one? This many, with no real consequences in the courts? No. This wasn't how black gold killed its adherents. This was different.

"You and I both know that this ain't it," Bennie hissed, leaning over the map. "And I been poring over everything White Rock's done, and I hate to say it, but everything I've found says the company's been by the book for near on thirty years."

She reached into the bag and pulled out a folder of reports, incidents, newspaper clippings, photos, library scans made with the pennies she had taken out of the give-one, get-one jar at the store. Here it was. All the work she and her dead best friend had compiled. Everything she had given herself into for the past year and a half—the thing that had cost Bennie her job, her home, her boyfriend. And here she was laying it all out in front of the woman who had fired her.

"Now, Ben . . ."

"You call me Bennie or Benethea, Helen. I ain't playing right now," Bennie snapped. "This—" she said, laying her hand on the papers—"is bullshit. And I think it's something you know about."

Across the table, they stared at each other. The waitress steered clear, even as Helen finished her mug and Bennie stayed without any kind of service. The silence between them drew out, tense as a cable in a shaft. Helen swallowed nervously, and Bennie leaned in.

"You seen the ghosts. Are they here now?"

If Helen was sitting still before, she didn't move a single muscle now, her eyes wide, her hands wrapped around her mug. Bennie thanked whatever god Motheater had on her side and shifted closer.

"Little black rabbits, running around?" Bennie asked, not looking away, leaning in. Helen was pale, big blue eyes watering. "You've been haunted your whole life, ain't that right?"

"I don't—"

"Don't lie." Bennie's voice was much calmer than she felt. "I got a way to let you off the curse."

Helen shook her head, and Bennie saw a shadow there, beady red eyes, dark hair, fur across the backs of her hands. She was cursed. Motheater was right. Helen had haunted blood. This whole damn town had bled into the mountain, and Motheater refused to let that sacrifice go to waste. The DeWitts were cursed for coming to Kiron, Motheater had said, drawing up plans hours ago, and now they were cursed to remain. The witch had recognized something from her past and got to work.

Bennie knew that Motheater could have been here, that Zach could have done this, but Motheater was too strange and Zach too kind, and Bennie was fine being mean if it got her what she wanted. There was no reason for Helen to help her without some kind of exchange, and Motheater had not let Bennie go unprepared. Bennie reached into the bag and lifted out a candle, teeth pulled from roadkill pressed into the wax, Motheater's etchings standing out in stark relief against the sides, having been rubbed with bright yellow asafedity flowers found growing up the side of Bennie's apartment.

"I need access to your property." Bennie shifted the map and pointed to the area Motheater had outlined in yellow, a large swath of land in a holler that had been in Helen's family for generations. "This area."

"Oh, I . . ." Helen glanced from the candle to Bennie's face, back down the map. "I . . ."

"You take this candle, light it in a cornmeal cross, and you'll be free." Bennie pushed the candle closer. "It's real Neighbor-made. It's for you."

When Motheater made the candle, she kept a pained look on her face near on the whole time, taking close to three hours and sending Zach out for supplies on four occasions. Motheater had even scavenged the dead squirrel herself, although Bennie had drawn the line at boiling its flesh off in her apartment, and the witch had grumbled all the way down to the creek.

But here it was. A banishment candle for the ghosts that haunted Helen DeWitt.

Helen hesitated, her hand shaking as she reached for the spell.

"Helen."

The foreman looked up at Bennie, scared, hopeful, a lifetime of haints hanging like blue bottles off her whole body. "Take the holler," she whispered. "Cast my ghosts out of Kiron."

Bennie nodded. This didn't feel as satisfying as she had hoped. All she felt was sad.

Helen took the candle carefully, her hands turning a furry black as she touched the wax. Her eyes went wide, and she quickly laid it in her purse, a flush rising across her cheeks, red rimming her eyes.

"There's a handful of service entrances for the valley," Helen muttered, finally turning back to the table, taking the pencil that Bennie offered. She marked a few places on the street. "There's a gate, but it's got nothing but a cross lock on it. Just open the door and go in."

She dropped the pencil. Bennie felt sympathy rise up, a hurt she didn't want as she extorted Helen for access to her property. There was something desperate and sad, a shaking in her hands that belied more than she probably wanted them to. Whatever blood ran through Helen, it had taken hold of her whole soul and tied her to Kiron. Her family doomed to root and rot in one small town that barely loved her back.

Bennie reached out and put a hand over Helen's, squeezing it tightly. She was going to save Kiron. She was going to start with Helen.

"We're going to get rid of what's haunting Kire," Bennie said, and for the first time, she believed she could. She wanted to save Kiron, wanted to save Helen, wanted to save every last ornery bit of Appalachia. Everyone deserved to live. To survive here. "We're going to protect our kin here."

Helen's shoulders sagged. She nodded, squeezing Bennie's hand back. They paused for a few seconds, holding space for the grief, the tension, the harm between them, between all of them. Helen let out a shuddering breath and pulled her hand back. She dug out a pair of bills and laid them on the table for her coffee.

"See to it."

Bennie smiled, and Helen quickly left, clutching her purse. Bennie was relieved, almost ecstatic. She carefully packed her folder back up and arranged her map in her bag. After another minute, she stood and left the diner. Outside, she saw, to her horror, Motheater standing in front of Helen, blocking Helen's route to her car.

"Motheater!" Bennie wanted to tell her that it was fine, that it had worked, that they could go to the valley untested, but Motheater held her hand up, and Bennie shut her mouth. She couldn't make out anything that they were saying. The blue jay swooped down and landed on Bennie's shoulder, distracting her.

"Oh, hey." Bennie smiled, putting up a hand to pet the bird. "I got some more granola for you, man."

The bird didn't say anything but nodded its head, chewed on one of Bennie's microbraids, and then jumped off. When Bennie looked back, Motheater was walking toward her.

"You good?" Bennie asked, almost scared of the answer. Motheater smiled up at her, reached out to take her

291

hand, the same one that she had reached out to Helen, and squeezed.

"We're all right." Motheater's voice was soft and husky again, and Bennie wanted to hold her hand for hours. "It's been kept."

Bennie held Motheater's hand as they went to the truck, trying to remember what it was like to feel this hopeful again.

27

Esther

Jasper's hand in hers was warm and dry, like clay along a hearth. As he followed Esther, frowning slightly, strange emotions flitted across his face. What magic had he invoked to draw on old wounds and ancient understandings?

Her magic faltered before his, even as she searched out patterns in his fingers, tried to pry it open at the seams. His deal with Kire could not be unmade by her means.

"Esther," he muttered, like a curse, and she refused to look at him, dragging him through the woods of Kire, pulling him into her forest.

Was it her forest? Was this her mountain? Was Jasper hers or the land's?

She dug into her fire and found her path, and before her, hawthorn trees appeared, their delicate pink-tinged green leaves barely blooming. Her cabin was ahead, and she pulled him in without hesitation, slamming the door and kicking over the beam that would settle into the cradles on either side, barring the door.

But it was just a beam, and beasts prowled in the dark.

"Esther."

He seemed himself again, confident and stupid and brave. God, she loved him.

"I cannot be kept away from it."

"I will keep you." She snarled, turning around her cabin. Jasper swayed but didn't protest. Esther went to the cabinet and shelves, pulling herbs and dried flowers, trying to remember what she could make, what she could give up, what would channel a magic deeper than her blood, as deep as Kire. Jasper would not be taken so easily.

"I made a choice," Jasper said, his voice remarkably even considering the bargain with Kire that shadowed his breath. "It was the right thing to do."

"You should have left me in the rock!" Esther whirled on him, snarling "At least then, the town might have been safe! At least then, we would have been able to keep the mountain down!"

"What?" Jasper blinked.

"I could have bound it to me," Esther gasped, tearing up. In her hands, she clutched a sewing kit, a hock, and an iron hook usually kept over the fire to hold a cast iron pot. "I could have bound Kire to my will."

"You're a fool to think so."

His voice was gentle, but it cut her to the quick. The wound was made deeper because he was right. The small cabin became smaller, down to just the two feet between her and Jasper. She held tighter to the hook.

"I could have *tried*," she said softly, looking back at Jasper. He was leaning against the barred door, arms over his chest, looking like he hadn't a care, like this was nothing but another one of his friend's temper tantrums. The only thing that gave away his state was the milky glaze over his eyes, already far away. "I want to try now."

"I made a deal with Kire." His voice was even, his gaze just as steady. "I keep my word."

"Let me *try*," Esther pleaded, her voice wavering. In her house, among herbs and glass, a ring-neck snake in the corner, curled around eggs, she knew that nothing else could speak here. In this house, at least, he wouldn't be compelled by the breathing at his door. "Please, Jas, let me intercede—"

"This isn't a game, Esther!" Jasper snapped, stepping forward. "You cannot take a new set of cards because you lost a bet with your first hand. I have done it. It's finished."

"I am not yet done!"

Her voice echoed, and some dust fell from the rafters as she shook the foundations. Crickets halted their orchestra, and the world settled around them. The birds outside stopped their songs, and in the last light of the night, in the dusk hour, Esther's cabin was lit up as if it were on fire, as if it were doused in gold.

Jasper looked up, as if searching for patience.

"I can't let you die for me," Esther said, clutching her supplies to her chest, the hock smearing grease over the front of her dress. "I can't let you get taken away from me. People love you, people want you. You could save this town from disappearing to industry."

In the cabin, the stillness faded, turning to copper. A delicate coo came from outside as a mourning dove found her voice again. Esther's eyes welled up with tears, and she took a step back. Jasper shifted from his post and walked to her, putting his hands on her shoulders.

Whatever he was about to say, whatever placating moment he was going to offer, he didn't get a chance. Esther dropped her supplies and drove a needle held between two fingers into his sternum, hitting his bone with a pinprick of cursed metal.

Jasper's eyes went wide, and Esther met his surprise with her own determination.

"*I will praise you*," she said, and power filled her. Jasper's face twisted, and he tried to grab at her wrist, but True Words were being spoken, and he was in the witch's house. "*When I remember thee upon my bed, and meditate on thee in the night watches.*"

"Esther . . ." Jasper's voice trailed off as he began to fall under her spell, held fast by an invisible thread that began to weave through his chest.

"*Because thou hast been my help, therefore in the shadow of thy wings will I rejoice.*" Esther's voice went into his heart, filled his lungs with her will. He was not Kire's yet, and now he was hers, captured by her words. She swallowed the rest of the psalm as she took a step back, looking at Jasper as he swayed on his feet. She felt herself burning up, a living flame. She could do this.

Quickly, she took a basket and threw supplies into it, wrapping the hock in a waxed cloth, adding herbs and dried flowers, and finally, she gently placed the ring-neck snake on top of the stash. This would be big magic, bigger even than hauling Will out of the mountain's maw.

A knock on her door startled her. She clutched at her chest and looked around for a staff or a knife or something else to use. She picked up a fire poker instead. With Jasper bound to her, she couldn't risk another spell, and who knew what would be at her door.

"Miss Esther?" DeWitt's light city tones came through the braced door. "Is something wrong with Jasper?"

Esther lowered the poker but didn't let her guard down. DeWitt's rabbit must have helped get him here. She pulled at Jasper's arm, and he moved out of the way of the door, held steady by the needle. With the beam still in place, she cracked the door open, and true enough, it was Julian. He looked pale and scared, and she decided to let him in.

Jasper didn't react as he stepped over the foyer, and DeWitt stared at him, eyes wide.

"Has it happened already?" he asked, taking a step toward Jasper. Esther got in between them.

"No, but it'll happen soon."

"Can we stop it?" DeWitt asked, his blue eyes never moving from Jasper's face.

"We can." She grabbed DeWitt's arms. "I need time to prepare a spell to break the curse, but until then, we can keep him safe. I'll need your aid."

"Anything," DeWitt whispered, and Esther saw his hands shaking. "Tell me what to do."

"I'll keep his soul intact," Esther said fiercely. "But you have to *stay here*."

DeWitt's eyes went doe soft. He folded to the floor, gentle as silk. Esther's shoulders heaved with the effort of the second spell, and this time she did feel her well dip. She dropped to her knees, pushing up his sleeve. She cut his wrist along the bone, allowing his blood to coat the steel. A whisper, and it had stitched up again, but his bloodline was now hers to parlay with.

She stood and strode out of her cabin, Jasper trailing after her, bound by needle and spite.

⁊

Blue fireflies surrounded them as they walked down into a low holler, crossing over the White Rock Creek into the valley next to Kire. Locust Knob was in the distance, and she knew, even if she couldn't pick it out, the Hatfield encampment was only a few miles away, woefully unprepared and unmanned and ripe for pruning.

She couldn't think about Halberd right now. She had to focus on Jasper, on keeping him alive, on giving herself more time to find a way to fight all these fronts. Her father, Halberd, the spirits of the Appalachians that followed Motheater like a swarm, Kire itself. All these demands on her, all these insistences that she should just get out of the way.

"My soul followeth hard after thee." Esther's psalm rose through the night. She pressed down her trepidation like apples in a mash as they crossed over a small draft. There was no space in her for doubt. *"Thy right hand upholdeth me."*

In the low holler, by this soft creek, Esther felt it. A low pulse, an empty beat. Kire didn't reach here, but neither did any other mountain. There was no greatness in this place. She let her pack fall from her shoulders, leaning it against a large tree as she looked over at Jasper, who had followed her, dutifully, in a daze.

The fireflies followed her like a wedding train as she took Jasper's hand. The two of them glowed strangely in the firebugs' light, a mythic blue green. One bug's glow pulsed in time with the other, a rhythm of light like a heartbeat. A small creature prowled at the edge of their clearing. Not the ghostly emissary, the strange deer, nor the hare she had placed in DeWitt's chest. This was one albino fox, its bushy tail waving as it walked in a circle around her, prowling.

This was a neutral place. No ghosts, no towers, no mountains. Just a witch and the wood.

She turned to the sycamore, roots nestled in a small draft, and pulled Jasper toward it. He stared at her, something in his eyes like betrayal, but Esther wouldn't allow that to affect her. She shivered and dug into her pack, taking out the ham hock and the snake. She put the reptile around her neck and held the hock in her hands, breaking it apart, her fingers digging in like claws. The fox came closer and the bugs followed, a maelstrom of azure St. Elmo's fire and magic, drawn to the meat, drawn to her. She finished the psalm with her hands on the tree, smearing fat, skin, and bone down the bark.

"*But those that seek my soul, to destroy it, shall go into the lower parts of the earth.*" It was a promise, it was a curse. It bound the tree to her, protecting it, making it safe. "*They shall fall by the sword: they shall be a portion for foxes.*"

Moths alighted across her shoulders like a mantle as she stepped back from the tree. Behind her, Jasper stood as sentinel, cursed and enthralled. Her hands shook as she let the magic settle like silt in a lake.

Jasper's mouth was a hard line, and he stared at her, hands clenched, fighting against the enchantment. He didn't want this, and Esther knew it. She turned back to the tree. The bark and mast of the thing had pulled back, a throat, a mouth, a canoe. She spat on both hands and, ignoring the fox that twined in between her legs, the bugs, the man at her back, the mountain in her mind, drove her greasy hands into the tree, prying it apart with her fingers.

She would not let Jasper go.

28

Bennie

Bennie was wired. When Motheater had told her about the rabbits in DeWitt's blood she hadn't half believed her, but . . . She had seen it, she had felt it, she had fixed it. And now they were going to discover the truth of Motheater's past. The final puzzle piece to restore her memory, her magic, and her ability to take out the leviathan that mining had made from Kire Mountain.

There was an unofficial evacuation happening across Kiron, more cars than usual on the streets and trucks piled up with belongings. The nonstop sirens in the night had spooked even the most hardened residents. Bennie drove slower than usual, often contra most traffic and forced to the side of the road more than once.

Motheater sat in the front seat with the map spread out on her lap, giving directions. In one hand she held the notes she took after the bone-scrying ritual, in the other, she delicately balanced one of the blue jay's bright feathers on the very tip of her finger, making it stand upright, turning slowly. As they drove out of Kiron, headed toward the admittedly large area that was the DeWitt property, Motheater continued to recite scripture, eyes focused on the feather.

"*The fool foldeth his hands together, and eateth his own flesh. Better is an handful with quietness, than both the hands full with travail and vexation of spirit*—Ah!" Motheater sat up. "We need to head west! West!"

"Fuck, okay. Hold on," Bennie said, slowing down as she turned left, onto a road that was barely paved.

"I thought the point of talking to Helen was to figure where we were going," Zach muttered.

"The reason we saw Helen was to make sure that she didn't call the cops and guarantee that nobody was coming out with a shotgun," Bennie explained. She was still annoyed that Zach was here at all, but after his little magic show with Motheater, she figured she owed him a tagalong invite. "There's three gates leading into the rough area Motheater's scrying picked out. The land covers at least thirty acres, going up into the mountains."

Zach stayed quiet, folding his arms in the back seat. He might not be comfortable with this, but he seemed fixed on finding Jasper. Bennie suspected it had to do with the newly forged connection he had made with Motheater when she dragged him into the past.

She drove as slowly as possible, giving Motheater time to use her cunning. The witch was still leaning over the map, whispering Ecclesiastes to the blue jay feather. "*There is one alone, and there is not a second; yea, he hath neither child nor brother.*" She looked up as Bennie turned down a road, passing Happy's Burgers.

Because of the winding nature of rural roads, Bennie had to make a few turns to keep heading west, and they passed by Delancey's shop, *again*. God, this was embarrassing. Bennie peeked over as they drove by and saw Delancey sitting on her porch with a sweet tea and some kind of steamy romance novel in hand. The truck decided to belch at just that point, and Delancey looked up sharply and, seeing Bennie, dropped her novel.

Bennie made a face and turned forward again, just as Motheater gestured for them to head more northerly.

"She freaking hates me, man," Bennie muttered, turning along Fork Road.

"Who?" Zach asked curiously, having arranged himself to look over Motheater's shoulder, watching the feather.

"Delancey. I took Motheater over there like . . . five days ago. It did not go well."

Zach snorted. "Well, Delancey doesn't do real magic."

"Okay, Zach? The fact that you just said 'real magic' with a straight face should tell you that none of this is normal, right?" Bennie groaned. "You could at least . . . pretend like you're shocked or something."

"Well, now we know better," he said, turning to smile at Bennie in the rearview window.

For the first time in weeks, Bennie didn't feel like she wanted to curl up and gasp for air when he turned that charm on her. Instead, she shook her head and sighed, glancing at Motheater when the witch leaned forward.

"We're close," Motheater announced. "Get a little more west."

"That's a harder ask than said," Bennie muttered, driving slowly along the dirt road. She found a thin, grown-over path that looked like it might have been one of the gates DeWitt marked on the property. Bennie hoped Motheater led them to the right place and pulled off the road. She drove over the small runoff ditch and weeds, nudging the truck's bumper against the gate that was absolutely off its hinges. Maintenance gate seemed ironic.

She paused, looking over the map, and then the gate. This certainly could be one of the gates DeWitt marked. It could also be a totally random piece of land that didn't belong to DeWitt at all and was just neighboring close enough to fool Bennie. She hoped her GPS was right about land boundaries.

"What can your magic do for bullets?" Bennie asked Motheater, turning off the truck.

"Before or after they're fired?" Motheater asked, folding up the map. She slid carefully out of the seat, focusing on the feather balanced on her finger. The blue jay swooped down and lit on her shoulder. Bennie struggled to find a response.

"That's encouraging," Zach said, following Motheater as she walked around a broken-down part of the stone fence and began to march onto the property.

"Yeah, maybe," Bennie muttered, reaching into the trunk to grab the ash walking stick she had kept from her first walk up Kire, following the two of them.

The property wasn't marked; the DeWitts likely kept it as part of a family parcel. It didn't look like any upkeep had been done. If Bennie didn't know better, she might have assumed it had been foreclosed on years ago and forgotten about. They walked in single file along the beaten dirt path, following Motheater's feather. Motheater veered left, into the woods, toward the valley in between Kire and the next southern peak.

Bennie paused, watching the witch and Zach just behind her. She took a deep breath, feeling the pressure of the air around her. A storm was coming. It would be night before it broke over Kiron. She shook out her arms. She was here. She was here, and she had to press on.

She jogged to keep up with the pair ahead of her.

Around them the trees shifted, almost immediately going from thick-trunk oaks and maples to slim birch and aspen trees. The change was unmistakable, as if the trees had suddenly decided to lay claim over different parts of the land.

"We're close," Motheater said, sliding in between the shaking trees. Zach, who had grown up a hunter before swearing off meat, followed silently behind her. It was just Bennie who was slightly awkward walking off the trail, looking twice before she placed her feet. The blue jay screamed above her.

Motheater paused, then looked back at them. "Can you feel it?"

Next to Bennie, Zach nodded immediately. Bennie felt a stab of annoyance and jealousy and pushed it down. She didn't feel *anything*. There was just an overwhelming sense of smallness that she had felt for hours. This holler was just another patch of Appalachia to her. But hadn't Motheater dragged Zach through a blood vein into the past of his ancestors? Stands to reason he'd be able to feel something.

Still, Bennie thought, trying not to be petulant. *It kind of sucks to be left out.*

Bennie pushed through the last of the brambles before the three of them arrived in a clearing. The birches had thinned and created a ring. The earth dipped down, small rocks and sheared-off boulders marking the ground inhospitable. There was a small river down in the holler that passed along the back end of the clearing. Bennie suspected this was the Epling Draft marked on the map. It was a small relief to know that they were actually on DeWitt's property.

Next to the Epling was a massive tree, broad and wide, with spreading branches and thick, pale gray bark. Motheater stopped, staring at it, frowning deeply. The map crumpled in her hand, and Bennie skipped forward to pry it from her fingers.

"What's wrong?" Bennie asked, standing next to her.

"This ain't no graveyard," Motheater said, stepping along some of the rocks until she got down to the flat, clear land near the banks of the creek. "Why is Jasper set here?"

"Are we lost?" Bennie asked, looking down at the map. "Did the magic go wrong?"

Bennie glanced at Zach, but he didn't seem to be so knowing anymore. Bennie tried to orient herself, glancing between the map and Kire in the distance.

This seemed a peaceful, calm place. Small, but comforting. Around her the air was still, and she leaned her head back, her eyes fluttering closed. The storm was still hanging around. Weather wasn't a thing that happened; it was a thing that surrounded you.

She felt it on all sides, the slow, steady press of a distant rain. It was a comfort.

It was a few seconds before she opened her eyes and looked around again. It seemed slow here. Bennie shook off her desire to rest and went to stand next to Motheater, who had ended up in front of the sycamore.

With its wide branches, huge trunk, and spread-out roots that crushed rocks and changed the course of the stream, Bennie guessed that it had been planted before even Motheater had been born. Motheater's face was still deeply curdled.

"Something ain't right."

"Like what?" Bennie asked, still looking up at the massive tree.

"Don't pass near, Bennie." Motheater took a step closer, an arm's length from the trunk. Bennie huffed, annoyed.

"What's she doing?" Zach stepped up next to her.

Bennie shrugged. Motheater walked around the tree slowly, her hand on the sycamore. She paused along a deep, dark scar in the tree that had grown out, like a thick piece of rope had been caulked into the bark. Motheater stared, her hand pressed against the seam. Bennie wondered if this was it, the last piece of her past, lying overgrown like a field turned fallow. Maybe she had cut the tree in the 1800s, a memorial to her dead friend.

"*Intreat me not to leave thee, or to return from following after thee.*" Motheater's voice echoed in the holler. "*For whither thou goest, I will go; and where thou lodgest, I will lodge. Thy people shall be my people, and thy God my God.*" Motheater's voice held steady, echoing around them. She stepped back from the tree, and the seam down the sycamore tree cracked, splitting with a creak that echoed across the clearing. Bennie gasped, pulling away from Zach and jogging over to Motheater.

Motheater's fingers were dug into the bark. Bennie looked into the seam Motheater had broken apart and saw, for a second, a man's face nestled inside the mast of the tree.

Motheater stumbled back, knocking against Bennie's shoulder and then tripping over a rock and falling without any grace. Bennie immediately knelt down, putting a hand on Motheater's back gently. The witch seemed to be in shock, her dark eyes wide. Motheater leaned forward, putting her face in her hands, unable to look at the tree. Bennie hesitated as Motheater seemed to curl down, small and lonely.

"I hurt him, Bennie . . ." Motheater murmured through her hands. "Why'd I do a thing like that?"

Bennie put her hand in Motheater's hair, which had been loosened from its plait. She could see, just barely, Jasper's brassy skin showing from inside the pale wood of the tree, a small horror catching in her throat. She swallowed and found her voice. "What'd you do?"

"I must have put him in there," Motheater sighed. She turned to look at the tree, faced with one of her sins. "Why did I do that? Why did I leave him?"

Zach stepped forward.

"Don't—" Bennie called, but Motheater didn't respond, just watched Zach intently. If the witch wasn't going to stop him, Bennie would just shut her mouth.

Zach went to the tree and peeked in the seam. He dug out his penknife and slid it carefully in the seam. She couldn't see the look on his face, but he rubbed his mouth and shook his head, walking back.

306

"He's breathing," he said, crouching down. "Got fog on the steel, same as you in the mountain."

Motheater nodded. "I have to get him out." Her voice was soft, sad.

Bennie made a noise, helping Motheater stand up. "I guess it's foolish to ask if you need an ax."

Motheater shook her head. "Just some time. I have to unwork whatever cunning I laid into that tree. Not quite a bargain, just . . . an unlacing of the magic I already laid."

"Wasn't Jasper your age?" Zach asked as Motheater went back to the sycamore. Bennie's mouth went dry. Motheater had never said, but maybe Zach was remembering the past.

"A year younger, even," Motheater muttered, going to the seam and running her hands along the rough, raised bark. Above her, the sycamore shook, as if it were in a wind, the birch around them still, bearing witness.

"Yeah," Zach said, frowning. "That's definitely not the case anymore."

Motheater took a step backward and then another before kneeling down. The witch placed one hand on a root from the tree and settled.

Bennie's shoulders felt warm, the sun spreading over the back of her neck. Motheater was in the sun, but Bennie was standing in the shadows. Why was she suddenly feeling warm? Why were her legs cold, as if they were against stone? Bennie shuddered. The feeling of being too small suddenly became claustrophobic, and Bennie's mouth went dry. She didn't want to be here to watch Motheater pull an old boyfriend out of the past.

"I'm going to have to convince the tree to let him go," Motheater said, closing her eyes. "Could take a while. Trees don't do nothing fast, and aren't keen on no type of change."

"How long will it take?" Bennie asked carefully, rubbing her hands on her jacket. "Hours or . . . days?"

Motheater grasped the root tightly. Bennie felt it, too—the roughness on her palm, the heat that Motheater drew from her well. She flinched as the witch struck a green nerve in the tree, and she felt—she could truly feel in her fingers—a few roots dry up and shrivel. Seeing magic was hard enough; feeling it by proxy like this was near terrifying.

"All day," Motheater muttered, settling into the work. "If I can even undo it."

Bennie glanced over at Zach. He was staring at the slim line of Jasper's face nestled in the bark.

"I'm going to get us snacks then," she said, the brook's echo pounding in her ears. Anything to get away from whatever was reverberating in her chest, an emptiness, a calling, a connection that she and Motheater were forging in this clearing. It was too much. She wanted Motheater to stop Kire Mountain, but she did not plan to be this drawn into magic. This was too much, overwhelming. It drove too deep a wedge into her chest. Maybe magic should be left to things like Motheater.

Motheater didn't respond, and Bennie wasn't about to wait for permission. She turned to Zach and elbowed him.

"I'll keep an eye on her," he muttered. He glanced at her and smiled, just a little. "Take your time."

Bennie swallowed, eyebrows up. He knew that she was having a hard time here, could sense or feel or see that she was upset. She took a deep breath and nodded, reaching over to squeeze his arm, grateful that he was here.

"Thanks."

Before she left, she pulled out her phone and dropped a pin, taking a screenshot just in case something happened. The man in the tree was creepy as fuck, but Motheater would take care of it, right? Bennie just had to come back soon.

Anxiety crawled along her arms like spiders as she scrambled up the small slide out of the holler. There was something caught in her throat, something weary and fearful that she couldn't name. But the three of them couldn't stay here until sundown without at least a bottle of water, and it was better to make the twenty-minute trip down to the nearest gas station now.

Motheater was still kneeling. Zach had gone to the tree, leaning in to watch. Bennie swallowed, the hollow feeling in her torso getting bigger—if Motheater pulled Jasper out, would Bennie be turned away? Bennie never quite figured out exactly what Jasper was to the witch, and learning he was her lover might hurt her more than she'd want to admit. She needed to leave.

Bennie turned away, stung that even the blue jay didn't follow her back to the truck. As she started up the vehicle, she stared down the dirt road toward the hidden sycamore, worry tugging at her. She pushed her jitters down and pulled onto the road. Wouldn't do no good getting nervous.

As she drove away, the string between her and Motheater became tenuous, but Bennie could still feel part of herself in the holler. Bennie's hand felt rough and tight, and she knew it was because Motheater kept her grip fast on the root.

Bennie shuddered. Was this what magic felt like? Being too small for this world? Motheater had pulled some strange shit out of thin air, but a man in a tree? There was something horrific about seeing someone trapped like that—trapped because of Motheater. She set off down the road, ignoring the anxiety clawing up her throat.

She kept both hands on the wheel as she drove along the country roads. It was a distraction to pay attention to every tree, every pothole, every uneven turn. She knew that she was running away, but right now it was a relief.

At the gas station, Bennie parked slightly haphazardly. Inside, she picked through the small convenience store for sandwiches that didn't seem too soggy, snacks, and water. She knew that when Motheater said all day, she meant it. Bennie paid for the provisions and walked out.

She spotted the patrol car immediately, the low-level anxiety of Jasper forgotten, briars catching in her throat, her heart gearing up fast. There weren't really police in the area—Kiron was too small a town to have a police department—but they contracted with the county sheriff department to send deputies out. They didn't come around often, and seeing a patrolman was never good, and especially not for Bennie.

She went to the truck and put her groceries in the front seat. As she was walking around to the driver's side, she saw movement from the police car. She took a deep breath to steady herself and found her slim wallet, putting it on the hood of her truck. She stepped away from the vehicle and waited, and sure enough, the officer raised his hand, smiling as he walked over to her. Bennie let out her breath, a little relieved. Mark Hall had grown up nearby. He and Zach were friends, and he had been at a few of their barbeques over the years.

It wasn't enough to make her comfortable, but it was enough to slow her twitchiness, at least a little.

"Morning, Miss Mattox," Mark said, walking around the front of the truck and staying right there, a hand on the front light, but a good six feet away from Bennie. He had an easy demeanor about him, but that didn't do nothing to ease Bennie's nerves. He was still a white man in a uniform. "Hope you're doing all right."

"Right enough," Bennie said, keeping her hands on her hips. She smiled, just a little, forcing it on. "Something I can do for you, officer?"

Mark chuckled. "Hey now, take it easy on me, Bennie."

"You came up on me!" Bennie said, smiling, and still not moving her hands. Like hell she was going to take it easy. Mark might be friendly, might even be her friend, might even be a good man, but he had a heavy belt and authority.

"Yeah, okay, on business." He held up his hands, shrugging. "I ain't gonna bother you much, but I gotta relate something strange."

"If this is about that ugly-ass Elks building, I swear it wasn't me," Bennie joked.

"No, no," Mark said, waving his hand. "The Giles office has been fielding calls for near on three days from Vikki Delancey—"

Bennie's eyes went wide. She had been expecting a slap on the wrist for an old forgotten parking ticket, maybe some small talk, if Mark was really feeling lonely. This, an actual *complaint*, was much worse.

"Talking about how you and some Amish girl came into her home and abused her?" Mark said, his tone indicating that he believed this was as absurd as it sounded. "Says you stole some cards that she told us were priceless, browbeat her a bit, and threatened her business. Now I looked up those kinds of playing cards, and they're not worth more than forty bucks, and I suspect that she's just raising Cain to feel high on, but can you help me out here?"

Bennie swallowed her nerves. "A friend and I went in to get a reading. My friend did a little magic trick to tease Delancey and then we left. We didn't yell or steal nothing from her."

"Yeah, that's pretty much what I thought." Mark sighed, rubbing the back of his neck. It was clear that he didn't like this, either, but that didn't make Bennie feel better. "Can I get you to follow me to the station real quick?"

Bennie's heart dropped. "What for, Mark?"

"I need you to sign an affidavit. Mostly just saying that we had this little chat and that I found you reliable and all that. She called the office ten times this morning, saying you drove by her house, threatening her."

"Now, that ain't true," Bennie said calmly, hands in fists by her sides. "There ain't no way to avoid passing her place if I'm driving from my home to town. There's barely three roads across the county, and everyone lives on the same damn stretch."

Mark nodded, sympathetic. "I know, and I ain't charging you, or even questioning you. I'm more asking a favor so I can tell Delancey with authority to stop calling us. We got enough problems with responding to the cave-ins and rock-slides that I ain't got patience for her."

Besides Bennie's obvious distrust of authority in general, it would be at least an hour-and-a-half drive there and back, plus whatever time it took to get the paperwork in order. Giles County was huge, and Kiron was at the edge, closer to West Virginia than any other town. This was more than a hassle.

"You sure this can't wait?" Bennie asked, keeping her voice sorry.

"Afraid not, Bennie. We can't keep having her calls tie up the line while we got collapsed mines and sinkholes. She's gonna end up killing someone if we can't get to services."

Mark wasn't exaggerating. Last she asked, it was just him, a second deputy, and the sheriff contracted to serve Giles County and the county just south, a massive span of the land. This entire area was understaffed by design.

"Yeah, all right," Bennie agreed. This wasn't a great time, but Motheater did say it would take hours. Maybe she had a few to spare. Bennie didn't let herself think that maybe she was just finding another excuse to run away from her connection with the witch. "But I'm not staying to chat. If Sheriff Tuppence tries to get me to talk to her about birding one more time, I will cry."

"Please talk to her about birds, Bennie, I can't take it nei-ther." Mark smiled as he walked back to his car. He waved and got in the cruiser, flashing his lights once and pulling out of the gas station, waiting for her. Bennie snatched her wallet off the hood and got into the front seat. She texted Zach that she was going to the station and then followed Mark out of the convenience store lot.

She felt angry and anxious, hating to have to deal with the police over anything, much less something as trivial as a white lady calling the cops on her nonstop for four days. Dealing with it now was better than letting it wait, but the entire thing made her skin crawl.

Bennie hoped that her desire to distance herself from the witch didn't make her too much of a coward.

She followed Mark down the country roads, passing by the turnoff that led to Motheater, Zach, and Jasper, deliberately staring at Mark's bumper.

Their drive to the station was uneventful except for a pair of deer that seemed to have a death wish. The animals didn't move out of the road until Mark nudged the cruiser forward enough to shift up against them. At that, the doe carefully stepped around the cruiser, not running or starting at all. It was strange, but deer were damn eerie creatures anyway, and Bennie knew better than to stare at them as she passed in her truck.

The thought struck her that maybe this was Motheater's doing. Or Kire's? She absolutely, *definitely* didn't look at the deer.

At the precinct, the process went smoothly enough, although Bennie did get sucked into a bird-watching chat when she casually mentioned to Tuppence an overly friendly blue jay had followed her home. Still, it didn't matter much; she read over the statement twice, took a photo, made a copy, and folded up her version for later. The Giles Sheriff Department was more concerned with hunting disputes than anything else, and their typical Monday included Narcan deliveries to small towns, but it didn't hurt to be cautious.

Mark gave her a coffee and an apology as she left. Bennie smiled, nodded, and got out of there as fast as she could without raising eyebrows.

It was only after she had left the sheriff's office and slid into the front seat that she realized her hands were shaking. She took slow, long, deep breaths and pulled out of the driveway, focusing on her hands, the road, the thrum of the engine ahead of her. Bennie put the implications of the encounter in a small box to talk about later, when she had time. Right now, she had been away from Motheater and Zach for nearly four hours.

She might not have wanted to stick around, but even she knew that this wasn't good.

Bennie turned north, back toward Kire. It was the tallest peak in the area, and with the GPS flickering in and out of service, it was often easier to just find a road and go toward the big rock. As she rose up over the Potts ridge, she had a view of Kire Mountain across the valley, Little Mountain to the north, the low Locust Ridge and Hatfield holler. She smiled a little, taking it all in. The whole ridgeline was green and gold, bright, spring-touched, full of promise. The storm she had felt in the holler was just breaking in the north. It was slow, a high-up pressure, and it wouldn't hit for a few hours.

She loved it here, she really did.

Then, the mountain *moved*.

Kire, all of it, the hulk of it, lurched forward. The cataclysmic shift sent trees to the ground, and small clouds of dirt, dust, and sludge billowed across the ridgeline. Bennie gasped and pulled the vehicle over, hauling herself out of the front window and climbing into the bed of the truck.

The sirens were starting and stopping intermittently through the valley, too many signals crowding the system. Rockslide, cave-in, mudslide, collapsed buildings, all the cacophony of a small town living on the edge of a mountain screaming for relief. Her eyes were huge, her hands clutched at her coat's collar.

Kire didn't move again, not for the full fifteen minutes that Bennie stood on the truck bed, one hand on the roof of the cab, the other shadowing her eyes as she tried to make sense of what happened. Out of the woods, a small pack of coyotes darted across the street, heedless of Bennie's truck, moving around it like salmon in a stream, yipping as they fled from the destruction.

Kire Mountain had moved. Not a shudder or a shake, not a slow heave where a tunnel collapsed and the air was forced to the surface in a geyser's rush, but a deliberate move. It was coming. Motheater was right, of course she was right, but it was so much more than just a mountain awake. It was a titan waking up and coming for Kiron.

Bennie was trying to make sense of it, but there weren't enough to make sense of. The mountain had moved. Rolled its shoulders forward as if hunching its back, a turn, a mega-lithic *thing* that was pulling itself out of the bedrock of the Appalachians.

But Motheater could stop it. She had to stop it. She would pull Jasper out of the tree, she would find her memories, she would draw up all her fire, and she would stop it. Bennie re-cited this over and over in her head. *Motheater would stop the mountain. She would save Kiron. Motheater would stop the mountain. She would save Kiron.*

Bennie couldn't breathe. Motheater had to stop the mountain.

After Bennie's senses had come back to her, she slid into the front seat and turned the engine over, resisting the urge to run, to flee. Instead, she pulled onto the road and went into the valley, panic settling over her bones like a rain in the night. She had to stop the mountain.

⌒꙳

The return to the DeWitt property took about an hour. Bennie was driving slowly on one-lane roads as most of the population of Kiron ran away from Kire. That didn't even account for the fact that all the beasts of Appalachia seemed intent on running as well. Birds flew in cacophonous flocks, a set of deer jumped in front of her truck, and she even saw a black bear trundle along the side of the road, a sight that nearly stopped Bennie's heart. It was huge, and it was running.

As Bennie pulled into the driveway that led to Jasper's holler, she saw it had been nearly five hours since she had left on a trip that should have taken no more than forty minutes.

Scrambling for her phone, she tried to reach Zach through the emergency network, but the shift must have knocked out any towers in the area. No new messages, and her last text to Zach was still unread.

Horror sank into her stomach. Bennie grabbed a water bottle, leaving the snacks in the front seat, and jumped out of the truck. She crashed through the brush. It was late, nearly sunset now, and that made the shadows longer, the path strange. She found the holler and slid down the stones and rocks to the low part of it. Trees were down across the property, but the beech were steady, like silver needles raised up from the dark stone. The sycamore's leaves had turned from a dark jade to the color of dried blood.

It took Bennie a few seconds to take in what was happening. Zach was kneeling in front of the sycamore's seam, cradling Jasper's torso, easing him out of the tree. The man was arched over, his face turned into Zach's chest, arm out like a Pieta.

But then Bennie saw Motheater. The witch was still kneeling, unmoved in five hours, hand still clasped on the root. Around Motheater's wrist and arm, something dark had

wrapped itself around her. At first Bennie thought it was another snake, but it was a root.

"What happened!?" Bennie yelled, looking over at Zach.
The young man had his arms around Jasper, eyes glazed over,
entranced. He was sliding his hand down Jasper's leg, pushing the mast and moss away before nudging him out just a
little bit more. Increments, less than inches. Zach didn't even
glance at her.

Bennie nearly fell trying to get closer to Motheater, bile
rising, eyes huge as she saw that the sycamore was starting
to drag Motheater into the ground, that there were branches
and roots across her arms, legs, and chest. Motheater's hand
was swollen and pale from the blood being cut off, and above
Motheater's head, five small fairy crosses floated. This was a
magic like the kind that had uprooted the church, and Bennie
was terrified. Already she could feel the phantom roots
around her own arms, across her own chest, twisting up to
her neck.

She stared up at the crosses, confused. They were a
natural rock form, dark granite-colored and angular, and
they must have come out of the draft, drawn to the work
Motheater was calling up. Or maybe they had been loosed by
Kire, brought to the surface like worms in rain.

Motheater's face was unmoving; she was barely breathing.
Bennie stared at Motheater, at a loss. Slowly, as if being pried
open by a crowbar, Motheater's mouth opened and—nestled
inside her cheek, growing out of her throat and curled on top
of her tongue—was a green and wandering branch of the sycamore tree.

29

Esther

It took an hour of Job, but she finally pulled the sycamore apart, six feet of it, mast and ring exposed to the night air. When she stepped back, her hands were red, splinters in her fingers, blood smeared alongside the pork bone she had ground up to serve the tree's new purpose.

She looked back, and sure enough, Jasper was still behind her, swaying in the near-dawn light.

"I know you don't understand, and you ain't condone this," Esther said, going to Jasper and taking his hand. He tried to resist, and pain lanced through her, sharper than the shards of sycamore digging into her palm. She felt it then, a fear, a regret, an echo of an emotion she had refused time and time again.

"This is for you." She held his hand tighter, for a few seconds. Her grip was a dark usher, a dread lead. Around them the foxes prowled, the lightning bugs creating a forest floor that pulsed, pounded, breathed. "I won't keep you here long, I promise. Just a few months, till I figure a new bargain."

Jasper stepped into the hollow tree, compelled by the witch. Still, he glared at her as she arranged his arms and jaw just so. The needle she had stuck in his chest kept him fast, and Esther felt angry, hurt, desperate. This was her fault. This was all her fault. She would have to regain her bargains with Kire before she could cut Jasper loose, before she could save him. It would take more blood than she had in her own veins, more worship than she could offer at once, and she needed to keep Jasper safe until then. "Can't you see what I'm doing for you?"

Jasper didn't respond, and that might have been for the best. She didn't want to hear what he had to say, didn't want to know what he thought of her now. Maybe he would understand in a few weeks, maybe he would forgive her when she pulled him out, free from Kire's hold. Maybe she was damning him. He would return from the tree and destroy her, he would return and leave, he would return and never, ever look back.

So be it. At least he would return.

She dug in her pack and placed herbs and salt in the tree's wound. She wept as she took the snake and placed it in Jasper's pocket. She didn't wash her hands in the stream nearby, letting her blood and pig fat mix in her palms. When she finished the altar she had made of the sycamore, the sun was breaking behind her, its gasping touch reaching for the old mountains.

"*For there is hope of a tree, if it be cut down, that it will sprout again, and that the tender branch thereof will not cease.*"

The foxes moved in closer, a canid leash drawing nearer and nearer. Esther gripped the sides of the sycamore tree, pulling the bark together with her hands. "*Though the root thereof wax old in the earth, and the stock thereof die in the ground; through the scent of water it will bud, and bring forth boughs like a plant.*"

This was the perfect time. This was the perfect spot. The last of her bargained power flowed into the tree, a rush, all at once, as she asked it a favor deeper than the land could provide. The wind picked up as the sun began to heat the mountain. The small draft near her feet seemed to stop, seemed to halt its move down to the White Rock River. It would protect Jasper, too. It would heed her call. She groaned as she pulled the tree together, breathing hard, sweat on her brow. Caught on the head of the needle was her heat, her strength. It was a deep-seated beacon, and as long as she lived, so would Jasper.

"But man dieth, and wasteth away. Yon, man giveth up the ghost, and where is he?"

Jasper turned to look at her as she reached his hip, half sealed into the tree. He was moving his jaw, flexing, trying to say something, trying to do something, but he couldn't. This was Appalachia, and she was their witch. Even Kire wouldn't be able to unlace Jasper from the sycamore; it was a tree that was wholly itself. The spell burned itself into the trunk, a hot coal, a burning venom, and a part of her was pulled into the mast and root as well. Her fate tied to his, inexorably.

"As the waters fail down from the sea, and the flood decayeth and drieth up," she gasped, pulling back from the tree, chanting, an intonation that flooded the roots. She pulled the bloodied knife out of her bag. *"So man lieth down, and riseth not: till the heavens be no more, they shall not awake, nor be raised out of their sleep."*

Esther spat on the knife, and the blood became slick. She spread it on either side of the seam, sealing DeWitt's bloodline to the land, to this tree. *"O that thou wouldest hide me in the grave, that thou wouldest keep me secret, until thy wrath be past, that thou wouldest appoint me a set time, and remember me!"*

DeWitt's blood would act as an anchor, a fixed point. The whole tilt of the DeWitt line would center around

Jasper as its axis, while Esther found a way to break his deal with Kire. While Esther held Jasper's soul, DeWitt would keep his body.

Around them, the foxes paced. They would declaim to Kire, they would whisper to stag and painter. They would make it known across the spine what she had done.

"*If a man die, shall he live again?*" Esther pulled at the bark, the tree wrapping around Jasper's torso. "*All the days of my appointed time will I wait, till my change come.*"

As long as she was alive, Jasper would live. It was a fast curse, but undone by the most common thing in the world. Wrong, in many ways, but after she made her deal with Kire, her friend would be released. Maybe it was time for her to rest. Maybe progress was its own magic. Kiron had made their choice, hadn't they? She should honor that.

"*Thou shalt call, and I will answer thee.*" Esther gave Jasper all the power she could spare, keeping only the dregs she needed to speak to Kire. Her will rested in him, a part of his heartbeat and heel. She finished the verse. "*For now thou numberest my steps: dost thou not watch over my sin?*"

The foxes watched. Jasper watched. The sun rose; it watched. The mountain slept; it watched also.

Esther reached into the sycamore and brushed her fingertips over Jasper's cheek, barely enough room between the bark's seam to slide her hand close. He shut his eyes, slowly, fighting her, unable to move.

"*My transgression is thus sealed, and thou sewest up mine iniquity.*" Jasper lost; all lost.

It was only for a short time. Just until she could turn away Halberd, just until she could find a way to pull Jasper away from Kire. It wasn't a fair exchange, but life wasn't fair, and neither was Esther. With the next few utterances, she sealed Jasper's soul with a shard of her own until she could come back for them. This would release him when she died.

"And surely the mountains falling cometh to nought, and the rock is removed out of his place." Esther shuddered as she pulled the last of the bark around Jasper's face, as she captured him with blood and love and snakes and bones. *"The waters wear the stones: thou washest away the things which grow out of the dust of the earth; and thou destroyest the hope of man."*

She stepped back, drained, empty, swaying on her feet. She did it for the love of her friend. Selfishly, she had done it. Esther had many sins on her shoulders—what was one more in service to saving a life?

The sycamore had a red scar, a giant rope, from root to about seven feet up. It didn't look like much had been done, and the coppery leaves trembled under the power that had been imbued in them.

Underneath her feet, she felt a shift in the distance, something wide opening wider. Kire knew something. Esther's mouth went dry. She near ran out of the clearing, not looking back at the sycamore as its leaves started to shake in the morning breeze.

༄

Try as she might, there was no opening she could find with Halberd—after they had shown up at the meeting place, they had never left their outpost so abandoned. She had thought that they would get comfortable, but instead they simply closed ranks. It stung, knowing she had been so close to destroying them, but placing Jasper away from Kire had been more important.

It didn't mean she hadn't tried. She was far from welcome in Hatfield, and she didn't much care for the idea of facing down a complement of guns. After a week of prowling around the camp, she gave up on infiltrating. It would take too much spite and power to destroy the machines from afar, and at this point, half-from-whole, she doubted she could do it.

She had told DeWitt that he had to protect the sycamore in order to preserve Jasper's life. He didn't quite understand, but the holler was far enough away from Kire and coal that he had been able to make it a part of his corporate compensation. Esther tried not to be disgusted.

DeWitt hadn't been able to sneak her into the encampment, either. He had been relegated to administrative duties and had barely left the camp.

It didn't matter.

Esther woke up with bark under her nails. She laced her boots tightly and gripped the glory of the morning in her hands. Kiron was heading up to the mines.

She had thought to make dumplings or some kind of caramel with the last of her sap, but decided to come instead without pretense, disguise, or guile. She was their Neighbor. Surely, Kiron would recognize her. Surely, they would see her as she saw them.

As she walked through the woods to the mine shaft, she could feel Kire under her feet. It was still furious, even more so that Esther had left its stone. It boiled without her. It boiled because of her. She had woken Kire when she was a child, and she had paid for it her whole life. This is what happened when witches were made without care.

Esther didn't take the conventional path to the Kiron mining operation, appearing out of the woods like an animal against its prey. There was a hush among the miners. It was still the early parts of the excavation: hollowing out the stone, setting up the beams, carting away the rocks, boring air shafts. The drudge work.

"Morning," Esther said. Her mouth was dry. She felt, suddenly, the heat from the sun at her neck.

The miners glanced at each other, and then, from behind the group, Maisie snorted.

"Ain't no one gonna offer the witch a tour?"

The group stiffened. Esther narrowed her eyes, looking over them. Will Gresham ducked his head; Jack Spencer was suddenly very interested in the hem of his sweater. The bad manners around them had nothing to do with the earliness of the hour. Maisie sighed and pushed through the lot, sending them back to their tasks with a glare.

"Useless," she muttered, looking back to Esther, who was slightly annoyed that Maisie was the one who made the miners jump to rather than her own presence being enough. "Well, come on." Maisie gestured toward the mine. "See what the Halberd folk brought up."

Esther felt something settle in her bones. Loam, dirt, something rough and overwhelming. "After you."

Maisie turned, leading Esther toward the opening. Esther hesitated. She had come here to talk to the miners, but nobody seemed to need her. She stood at the edge of the shaft and saw beams supported by studs, lanterns hanging in precise order, even a layer of packed dirt on the ground, clearly cemented with some kind of glue or fastener.

And there, deeply, a hatred pulsed from the stone. Had she been so hateful? Had she made Kire into this creature of Armageddon? She didn't want Kiron dead, she just wanted power, wanted what Kire had. But it was nothing without Kiron to protect from people like Halberd. It was her will that turned Kire into this raging thing. Guilt clawed at her like a hawk.

She must have paused for too long. Maisie glanced back at her.

"The new kit's nice," Maisie said, looking over the beams that caught Esther's eyes. "After what happened with Gresham, Halberd offered to give us what we needed to build out here at a future fraction."

Already the miners were making deals for the incoming profit from Kire. They used to make deals with her. She resented them for being passed over in the weeks she had been gone. Or did Kire hate it? Was there a difference?

Esther touched the welds that supported the structures. They were good joints, strong. She pulled her hand back, and Maisie stepped forward to catch her palm, holding her fingers tight.

Esther's dark eyes went wide.

"You ain't gonna do nothing to this mine," Maisie said, squeezing Esther's hand. The witch regarded her: tight black hair turned gray with rock dust, her hand rough against Esther's, tall but not stately, with big shoulders, wearing men's clothing and a thick kerchief. "You hear me, Motheater?"

The moniker struck like a knife in the dark. Esther nodded. She didn't hate Kiron after all.

"This is what's gonna protect us." Maisie frowned. "You ain't gotta worry about us."

"You have no idea," Esther muttered, "what toys with you in the dark."

"Same thing I'm holding in my hands, I'd bet."

Esther looked down the shaft. It was much longer, it ran deeper, it appeared safer. This was a true reassurance. No matter how many times Esther placated the mountain when the men crawled on their bellies like snakes to reach the farthest vein, they would be destroyed in limbs and lessons. She didn't try to pull away from Maisie.

"I can't let Halberd in here."

"Halberd's here, Esther." Maisie squeezed her hand again before stepping back, dropping it. "You need to make peace with that."

Esther was still staring down the mine shaft. She had encouraged Kire to hate Halberd in spells and furious whispers in the forest, and it had listened to its witch. But what did Kire know between industry and your average folk? It was without discernment, and now more people were going into the mines.

Esther pulled her hand back, not looking at Maise. "It ain't about Halberd."

"No?" Maisie didn't move, her voice unyielding. "What's it about?"

"All of us." Esther looked at Maisie, golden in the half light, in the dawn and lantern. "And it ain't gonna be over until Kire sees us all dead."

Maisie's breath hitched. She was still, silent as the hammer in her hand. The miners weren't digging into stone. They were digging into death. A death that Esther had culled from a power she could not control. Esther pressed her mouth and turned, heading out of the shaft.

In the morning sunlight, all the miners had come up from Kiron. They were sharpening their tools, arranging the buckets, even preparing the large cauldron where a meal would be in a few hours. Esther held her head up as she walked around the camp, retreating from the miners around the fire.

She was about to disappear into the woods when a man caught her arm.

"Esther—"

"Don't touch me," Esther snapped. Her heart had left. Only Jasper would touch her so casually. And she had put him in a tree, and his soul promised to Kire, and Esther had no idea how to bargain for him. He had given everything. Hacking away parts of herself on Kire's altar would never be enough.

William Gresham looked stricken. "Apologies. I just . . . I wanted to let you know that your father asked to see you."

"He did?" The question came out before she could pull it back. Will smiled.

"Swear it. I'll take you up tomorrow."

Tomorrow was Sunday. Best to come prepared to the Lord's house. She would concoct something this evening. Now, she needed to commune with Kire, ease its soul, speak tenderly. Maybe she could stave off destruction for a few weeks, enough time to solicit Kire for Jasper. Esther nodded. "You'll find me in the wood."

Will nodded and dropped his hand. He was red-faced, his grip was soft. What was wrong with him? Esther gave him an appraising look.

"Aye, at dawn? We can go before service."

Esther nodded, still trying to figure out what Will was blushing over. She took one last look at the mine shaft, at the metal and steel driven into the mountain. What wounds did stone bear? What scars?

None that would heal.

Her breath caught in her throat. How many of Kire's hurts were her fault? How many spells did she cull from Kire's power? How many demands in hatred had she made? Maybe she needed to sow forgiveness among her people if she were to have any chance at bargaining with Kire for more. Getting Kiron to love her seemed easier than trying to bargain with Kire now.

"Walk in tomorrow then," she said, turning from Will and heading into the woods. "We'll go see the preacher."

30
Bennie

Bennie tried to shake Motheater's shoulders, but the witch barely moved, roots and branches wrapped around her, holding her fast. Bennie felt Motheater's pain, a phantom sycamore branch constricting around her arms, too. Bennie eyed the green twig in between Motheater's teeth and turned again to Zach.

"Zach, I need your help!"

He didn't look over at her, his legs pressed against the tree, knees spread as he slowly levered the man's legs out of the trunk. Jasper's back was against Zach's chest, his head lolling along his arm. He was entranced, caught by some strange magic that Bennie hadn't been there to interrupt.

Bennie tried to pull a root off Motheater's ankle, but it didn't budge. The blue jay swooped down and pecked at one of the branches, but the branch turned under his wings, as if it controlled the wind around itself, as if the sycamore was protecting the time that it existed within. The bird reeled back, tumbling beak over tail until it regained its balance and swooped over the Epling Draft.

Bennie cursed and ran over to Zach. He was focused entirely on Jasper, totally lost, held by whatever magic had tied Jasper to this place. Bennie held a hand just under Jasper's mouth and felt breath there. She leaned in, hands framing Jasper's face, her fingers pressing under his temple.

"Jasper, if you're in there, I need you to wake up."

What was it Motheater had said about faith? About knowing deep in your bones what you could do? Motheater was slumped over near the tree, a root winding its way up her arms like a trellis. There was blood pooling at her knees, a dark and viscous sap.

"Jasper Calhoun." Bennie's voice didn't shake. Above her, the sycamore rattled its branches, the draft swelled like a whelping cur, the water soaking into Bennie's sneakers and knees. It felt too warm for the spring storm that threatened to break. Everything was changing. "Motheater needs your help. She's being taken, and you need to wake up. You need to get to her." Bennie dug her nails into Jasper's thick salt-and-pepper hair.

There was a soft thump, and Jasper's leg was finally out; his boot, rotten and soft, fell apart as soon as it hit the stones surrounding the sycamore. Zach still wasn't looking at Bennie, hand wrapped around Jasper's ankle, guiding him away from the trunk. He was free of the trunk, but he wasn't waking up. There was a sound like a groan as the gash in the sycamore widened, shifted. The wood, once pale, was now a dark, stony green.

"Oh, God," Bennie murmured as the jay screamed above her. Motheater, already soaked by the draft, was totally ensnared, turned toward the lost space where Jasper used to be. The fairy crosses were still floating above her head, glowing haint blue and bobbing with the ebb and flow of the draft against her hem. Bennie lurched toward the tree and ignored Zach's hand, jerking Jasper further away from the tree. She helped lay out his legs and then leaned over him again, tapping his cheek.

"Jasper! You need to wake up!"

The man blinked slowly, eyes milky green, a sage that had been blued by a century. He shifted against Zach's chest, taking a deep breath, eyes held on Bennie. Bennie's heart raced and she nodded, keeping her hands against his jaw, tilting his head up.

"Motheater is being eaten by the tree," Bennie said, enunciating carefully, terror washing over her like a calming tide. Focus. The tree groaned threateningly behind her. She didn't have time for men to come to their senses. She needed Jasper now. "*Wake up.*"

Jasper shuddered under her call. His eyes became clearer, a dark hazel, clever and bright. The film was gone; he was awake. Bennie leaned back, and Jasper got a good look at Motheater, unconscious and held up by roots that had slid into her skin and broken into her bones. The branches and roots were slowly pulling the witch into the tree, and she was half up against its bark, one hand already in the mast.

"Old friend," Jasper murmured, leaning up. Zach and Bennie immediately shifted to help him balance. Once it was obvious that he wanted to stand, they eased him up, helping him as got his feet under him. He stood over Motheater, becoming more steady with every breath. He was heavy, far heavier than his slim build would suggest.

"Can you help her?" Bennie asked, her hand digging into Jasper's wrist.

"She's too stubborn to let a tree kill her," Jasper said softly. His voice was gravelly, like a smoker who had been finishing a pack a day for a decade. "Going to be Witch-Father himself that drags her down, mark me."

At Jasper's approach, the small fairy crosses that were floating above Motheater's temples began to circle her head like a broken halo, reflecting the light of the setting sun.

Jasper's eyes were wide. Bennie gripped his side tighter, looking up at his profile, his hair flowing down his back.

"She has to undo her work herself . . ." he said, looking at Bennie. "I need a snake, water from upstream, and some kind of lantern."

"Do you need light or fire?" Bennie asked, knowing that there was a difference to the strange people that had stepped out of the past.

Jasper frowned and nodded. "Fire will do."

"Hold him up, Zach." Bennie stepped away from Jasper, and he leaned more heavily on the miner, Zach's arm tight around his waist. Bennie quickly whistled, heading to the river, picking up the discarded water bottle. She knelt at the edge of the stream and was relieved as the jay swooped in, screaming on a rock near her. She really needed to give the bird a name.

"I need a snake," Bennie said hopefully. "Can you get one for me?"

The blue jay turned, fanned out his tail feathers, and with a screech, darted away. Bennie could only hope that he knew what to do. She pushed the water bottle into the stream, closing her eyes for a second, letting herself feel the fear, the anger, the desperation. It was good to feel these things; it was good to acknowledge that she was terrified as hell that Motheater was about to become a permanent woodland fixture. It would help her process.

"Fuck processing," Bennie growled, running back to Zach and Jasper. She was going to do something about it. She couldn't lose Motheater now. She couldn't give up with Kire rising and all the witch had said coming true. She loved Kiron too much, the whole messy shit of it. Motheater was going to save Kiron, Bennie was counting on it.

"The blue jay is getting the snake," Bennie said, and without asking permission, dug into Zach's pocket for his lighter.

He didn't smoke anymore, but he still always kept his lighter on him. She held it out to Jasper, showing him quickly how to open it, and flipping the flame on. They were lucky it wasn't a cheap thing and could hold the fire without the constant pressure.

She looked up from the lighter and gasped.

Ghostly creatures, mostly made of smoke, had appeared around the edge of the clearing. Their bodies swirled, milky and white, misty heads shaking to and fro as they stepped into the holler. Bennie took a step back, into Jasper's chest, and he put a hand on her shoulder.

"Don't fret none," he murmured, voice low and gravelly. "Just the spine come to witness."

"What?" Bennie's voice wavered.

"My family. They have long kept me company," he said, providing no clarity at all as he took the water from Bennie and stepped in front of Motheater. Zach was still supporting him, and Bennie could see Jasper's legs shaking with the effort of staying upright.

The tree's groaning was soft, a panting, a moaning. It ached. Bennie went to Motheater and sank to her knees, reaching for her wrist. Zach spoke up. "The snake?"

"I hope that damn bird is smart enough to know what I was asking . . ." Bennie caught the look Jasper gave her, something between amusement and confusion. "The blue jay. He's been helping us out."

"Us, or you?" Jasper asked, much more prescient than he had any right to be for spending nearly a century and a half sewn up into a sycamore.

Motheater shuddered, and Bennie clutched her tighter. There was a seedling coming out of Motheater's neck. Bennie touched Motheater's jaw, and to her surprise, the witch slid closer to her, pulling against the bark and wood grown into her.

Bennie shivered, her hands trembling against Motheater's face. She could feel the roots inside Motheater, turning her bones to wood and mast. This was too much, too big, too much magic right in front of her. It wasn't a spell or sound; it was like the weather, something that surrounded you.

Standing just behind Motheater, facing Jasper, was a large, misty stag. She knew she shouldn't, but she stared at it, and she felt it staring back. This was some greater spirit, and she felt her own heart stop in its presence. The other deer were closing in, stood at attention, ears pricked toward Jasper. The big stag was more solid, and Bennie could see lacey, coal-burnt bones through its immaterial legs and neck.

Overhead, the blue jay ducked down, dropping like a stone onto Jasper's shoulder, holding a small, mostly black snake in its beak. Bennie recognized it: a small ring-necked snake, similar to the ones that Motheater had across her body. She shifted to stand and leave some room between herself and the witch, but Jasper shook his head, stepping forward.

"She will need you." He held his hand out, and the stone crosses moved away from Motheater and circled his wrist. He opened the water bottle and poured it over the back of his hand, and the water pooled under his palm, a trickling waterfall that moved down the valleys of his knuckles, to the ground, and then rose up, around his wrist, an infinite cycle of moving water. The crosses followed the water once and then held themselves just in front of Jasper's fingers, turning stars in front of him.

"What are you doing?" Bennie asked, kneeling next to Motheater, trying not to pay attention to the roots under her, the shoots and branches she could feel moving. Her thigh pressed against Motheater's, and she clutched her tight.

"A baptism," he said. "She tied Kire's magic to me. It must be returned."

Above them, the sycamore shook.

He stepped closer, and the water began to pour over Motheater's face, down her shoulders. Bennie gripped Motheater tightly, the water pouring over her head and shoulders as well. She shivered under the levy.

Jasper gestured, and Zach intuitively knew to offer him a light. Jasper held Zach's wrist and lifted it to his mouth. He blew on the flame, and it spread to circle them, dark licks that flickered above each deer's head. Bennie wanted to close her eyes, wanted to turn away, but couldn't. Zach had shifted, averting his gaze. What were they, caught in between these creatures?

Bennie's breath came faster. Her arm tightened around Motheater's waist.

Jasper took the ring-neck from the bird, and it swooped away, flying out of the circle of family deer. With a shaking hand, Jasper placed the snake on Motheater's shoulder, and Bennie flinched.

"Stay steady," Jasper murmured. "She will listen to the low spirit. It was how she first learned to listen."

Bennie, soaking wet by now, shivered next to Motheater. The deer stepped forward, lowering their heads, not bowing, but keeping the world in check, hemming the four in at all sides. The snake slid around Motheater's neck, despite the baptism coming from Jasper's hand, and pushed itself up her jaw, curling over her ear, its head right next to Bennie's.

She turned toward the snake.

Despite the waterfall, the soft shush-hush of family, the draft, the breathing, the beating of her heavy heart in her arms, she could hear something else rising above all that. She didn't have words for it, but there was power in the strangeness, in the left-behind voices. Bennie shuddered, turning to press her face against Motheater's shoulder, and pushed down a sob.

It didn't take long. Bennie felt it, knew it, heard it. The grip around her chest loosed, the chill fell off her like leaves in autumn, the magic in Motheater heating her up from within. Wasn't this a relief?

Motheater was pulled forward. The branches and roots that had taken over her body, forcing themselves along her bones and muscles, disappeared in a jittery collapse. The water receded from around them, going back to the draft's normal banks. Around Motheater and Bennie, the bloody sap that had collected around the witch's knees spread out. The water from Jasper's hand turned it the color of muddy rust, washing it to the draft.

Motheater gasped. She took a big, full-chested breath and stood up faster than Bennie could follow. Bennie scrambled back, cutting her hands on the rocky ground. Jasper quickly pulled Zach out of the way as Motheater spread her arms, shaking off her bark-skin flesh, anger rolling off her in waves that sent the coal-hoofed stag darting for the birch. She bared her pointed teeth, her fingers forming dark claws. She was more creature than girl, more monster than witch.

Bennie might have been in love at that moment.

"I will not be punished." She stepped forward again, and the roots that had pushed up above the ground and stones slid out of her way. The tree shuddered, and the helicopter seeds of the sycamore spun down, turning into ash before they hit the ground, a ripple of flame ignited by Motheater's rage. Bennie could feel it, too, the heat deep within her chest, the anger, the fury, the magic of Motheater unfettered.

It was an echo of the land around them. The corrupted Kire, the same heat, the same anger. Bennie scrambled up and put another arm around Jasper. The three of them tripped over the stones as they backed up, and Bennie was grateful that Zach had the presence of mind to keep them all upright. The deer-shaped creatures had all dispersed, but the milky, bone-lace stag that stood behind Motheater was still waiting. It turned its head toward the three of them, and Bennie got the sense that it was waiting for Jasper, that it had been waiting a long time.

"Jasper?"

"It kannae harm us," he said. "It is an emissary."

Bennie had to admit that she wasn't entirely reassured. Still, he was smirking, something wry tugging at his mouth. Bennie couldn't decipher it, but it looked like satisfaction.

The sycamore began to burn, a coruscated tree that did not crumble, that wore its flame like an autumn coat.

"*As the fire burneth a wood, and as the flame setteth the mountains on fire*," Motheater declaimed, and her hair began to burn as well, a slow-moving singe up her braid. She didn't notice, or didn't care, or was perfectly aware of it and knew exactly what she was doing, Bennie had no idea. She wasn't wearing her sweatshirt anymore, and her arms were exposed. Around Motheater's wrists, the tattoos curled and moved, winding their way up Motheater's arm as she spoke power.

"*So persecute them with thy tempest*." The wind picked up, and the roots of the sycamore creaked, snapping like a taut rope, pushed too far beyond their limit. Motheater was standing, facing the tree, and she raised her hand, putting it into the heartwood, setting the tree on fire from the inside out. "*And make them afraid with thy storm!*"

The sycamore screamed.

There was no other way to describe it, this great tree, which had held a man for years, protected and loved and shielded him, which had done everything Motheater had said, but when it sought additional payment was burned up; it howled. Bennie pressed a hand to her mouth, and Jasper squeezed her shoulder, reassuring her.

The tree bent backward, slowly, surely, moving like a human and not a tree, the entire trunk ripping itself open around Motheater's hand, like a flayed kairn on the side of the road. The leaves of it brushed against the ground, its canopy dipping into the draft. The howling was took up through the entire holler, and the birches swept themselves up in the noise, rattling, bending back from Motheater. The witch bared her teeth and spat another verse as the bark flew off the tree, skinning it, baring its graying flesh to the air.

"*Let them be confounded and troubled forever,*" Motheater said, voice lost amid the howl and the shudder. "*Let them be put to shame, and perish.*"

With that, the sycamore split in two, dark flames of brassy green rising up inside of it. It was consumed with the spirit, possessed by the Greater Power that leant their ear toward Motheater. The leaves became ash, the branches white chalk, the trunk a brand against the oncoming night.

Motheater stepped away as the tree consumed itself, the roots curling back and falling into the fiery pit of the sycamore trunk. The heat was intense, and even though it caused Bennie to turn away, Motheater seemed unaffected. What was that like, Bennie wondered, clutching Jasper, to command the world to burn and have it go up in flames?

The witch turned and took another step back, face-to-face with the great misty stag that had witnessed the display of her power. Bennie started, wanting to go to Motheater, but Jasper's hand fixed her in place. She glanced at him, and he shook his head once. Bennie didn't want to stand still, she didn't want to do nothing, she didn't want Motheater to stand alone against the great creature.

"Steady," Jasper whispered. "She enters alone."

Bennie saw Motheater, full of soot and anger, full of rod and fury, reach out and put her hand on the stag's head.

"I'm sorry," she said, softly. Bennie knew she shouldn't have heard it, but it echoed in her ears, a whisper that she caught like a creature on a hook. "I meant to reason with you."

The stag snorted, lowered its head, pressed it against Motheater's chest.

From across the holler, among the twisting birch, Bennie turned to Jasper. "What's happening?"

"She's bargaining with Kire," Jasper murmured. "The magic she used to put me in that damned tree destroyed it. Now, she returns to her cradle."

Motheater's hair had stopped burning. It was short, just above her shoulders. The tree was gone, only falling ash marking its absence. Bennie couldn't feel the branches, the bark, the fire, the magic. It was still, calm. Motheater's face was tilted upward, and neither she nor the stag had moved, the sycamore ash passing through its lace without impediment, but collecting on Motheater's shoulders.

Jasper shifted again, slumping a little against Zach, who still hadn't said anything, who seemed wholly transfixed. "We will see if her stone father listens."

31
Esther

The next morning, Will Gresham did as Esther in-
structed and walked into the woods in the small hours
of the morning. She could feel it in the ground, in the
mice and mole, and when Esther stepped out of her home to
meet him, he appeared around a bend in the path without
any trouble at all.

"I presume you didn't want to talk in front of the others,"
Esther said, stepping next to Will. He jumped and put a hand
over his heart, pretty cornflower-blue eyes far bigger than
they should be.

"Oh, aye." He shifted on his feet, seeming unsure. "Well,
they're keen on what Halberd's done."

Esther felt a flare of rage. Keen, now! Keen for now when
support and structure was offered, when they didn't demand
a blood price, when they didn't steal wages and time and lives
and health.

"And you?" Her voice was arch, sharp as a pick.

"I am not so sure," William said, looking around, trying to orient himself after the mountain had pulled him so thoroughly off his compass.

"And my father?" Esther pressed. She did not move, made no attempt to orient William, to pull him onto the path, to lead him to church. The breeze picked up around them, and Will finally stopped searching for the way out, his face pale.

"I am even less sure."

Esther nodded. That was good enough. Maybe this was her chance to convince her father to align with her against Halberd, despite the wormwood blood between them.

"Mass is starting soon," Will said, looking around again. "Care to lead us out?"

Esther hummed, dug her fingers into Will's arm, and set out on the path, the moss and loam moving under feet to show her the way. The base mountain was still available to her, requiring no water from her empty well.

Will closed his eyes, letting Esther lead him through the weald. She squeezed his arm again, and he opened his eyes one at a time, like he was afraid of where she would pull him.

"Don't look so scared," Esther teased, leaning in. In only a few minutes, they were standing in front of the church, the area around the whitewashed walls and polished windows covered in the verdure. "He's just a man."

Will looked at her, and Esther couldn't read the look on his face. He pulled his arm away from her grip and walked to the church himself, pushing the doors open, as if announcing her, as if she were a queen. Esther knew better.

Still, better to have Will enter first, better to draw Silas's attention to a man rather than her. From where she was standing, just outside the doors, she could see her father standing by the altar, a tall lean shape against the jutting sharpness of Kire against the church. It smelled of dirt, of dark, rotten, wonderful things. As she stepped forward, almost to the sycamore pews, she noticed that there were more people in the church, more men around her. Jack Spencer and Nathan Benneke stood around. She frowned, looking over them, unsure of this strange congregation.

"You wanted to see me?" She stepped in regardless, head up. There was the rising mist off the cold stone, warmed by the sun, warmed by the fervor of Silas's faith. He stared at her and then nodded once.

Behind her, the doors shut quickly. She turned and saw Ochiltree holding out a broom made of an oak staff and with thorns instead of stalks for a brush. Wrapped around the shaft was raw meat, tied tight with catgut. It was a cunning, not a prayer.

"Where did—"

She stumbled back, away from the fascinator. It was old magic, old hedge, old work, and it would take her magic. She turned to her father, but Will Gresham was at her left, and Jack Spencer at her right.

"Now, Gresham!" Silas called out, running over and grabbing the nape of her dress. The collar caught along her neck, choking her. She scrambled for purchase against the flagstones, but the three men were stronger than her and pulled her bodily through the chapel.

She tried to call out to the snakes, but they didn't come from their cages. The magic around her fizzled, and the meat began to rot on the broom. The heat fled her, her hands turned blue. She couldn't even turn away this hedge. She had nothing left.

"The snakes—" She gasped, turning, looking at the stone altar as they passed.

There they were, all six rattlers and copperheads, laid out headless and bloody. Sacrificial lambs to the dark call that her father was pulling out of Luke's gospel. Didn't Abraham try to slay his son? Wasn't that *foolish* of him? Who would follow God so blindly? Who wouldn't question the unforgivable demands of God? Esther wished she were stronger than her magic, but she was half-unmade and split from Kire.

The snakes' deaths hit her like hard liquor, and as she felt the last dregs of her quicksilver magic rot along the oak shaft, she gasped for air. The venom in their mouths now poisoning her soul, corrupting what was left to degrade. Mountain magic, tuned to the whisper of Silas's words chanted over their bodies. So he did make bargains with Kire over the Lord's altar. So he knew his Christianity was made of stone slabs: like Moses, like fire.

"Hypocrite," Esther hissed, baring her teeth, struggling against her father. Her fingers twitched, and the headless snakes moved on the altar, attempting to heed the last call of the witch of Kire Mountain. "You preach God and worship yourself."

"Quickly!" Silas yelled, shoving her against the stone, his hands around her neck as the men held her fast against the rock. Her eyes were wide, the breath at her neck cold and familiar, the chill of a ballaun-water in winter, the moon in her belly, the haw on her tongue. Her father's face was all she saw, dark and carved from coal, greed making his teeth long.

She bared her own, and as the mountain began to pull her in, she spat shards of her own teeth at her father, marking his face. She felt Jack's grip weakening.

"Who is this that darkeneth—"

"Cover her mouth!" Silas growled, tightening his grip on her neck. He had fully abandoned his veneer of godliness, intent on slaughtering his daughter in the same way she had been made. Esther tried to kick out, but one foot was already trapped in the slate. They had opened the gate into Kire with the snakes, Kire's own children, those closest to him. Now, Kire felt Esther's rage, and it opened itself to her, eager for blood.

Ochiltree reached around and put his soft, large hand over her mouth. With his other hand, he dropped the meat-laden broom and put a communion wafer against her forehead. She felt a panicked laugh in her throat. What did he think the manna of her own father would do?

She glared at him, head tilted back, and bit down, her sharp teeth cutting into his flesh like a wolf. Job continued in her head. She imagined herself the whirlwind.

Still, Kire surrounded her, pulled her in, happy to accept the witch. As her elbows were pulled into the stone, Will and Jack pulled back, leaving parts of their knuckles, shards of flesh against the sharp rock. They pressed her body, hands against her chest, her hips, her thighs, pushing her into the rock. She felt the sacrificed snake heads bite onto her hands, one onto each of her feet, another coiled around her stomach, a sixth attached to her neck. This was her father's Sinai; it would be her Nebo.

"Die, witch," Silas spat. "Darken not my doorstep."

She struggled. She pulled her shoulders forward from the stone, but her hips were pulled back in. The men stepped back quickly, only parts of her showing above the rock that dragged her back. Esther's heart was beating furiously, her eyes bulging. She took one last breath in.

"*Hast thou perceived the breadth of the earth?*" she spat, daring her father. The slate slid around her neck, replacing his hands. All she could taste was blood. "*Declare if thou knowest it all!*"

The last curse, the sneer, his disdain. Her last words would remind Silas that every time he prayed, he would pray over her body.

Her head was pulled back into Kire, and she caught a glimpse of Will Gresham, pale and shaking, as Kire claimed her again, bound up with its dead children, their tie severed and nerves raw.

In the cold stone, she felt the intention and violence in her bones, aching as the mountain pulled her down, pulled her deeper, traveling through a coal vein into the heart of itself. The snake heads traveled with her, a dreadful sacrifice. They were a strong binding, having spent years being handled in a church that echoed with Kire's own power.

She tried to breathe, but Kire was tight around her. It cradled her, it softened itself around her, a womb, a tomb. Esther had no more fire in her, had only a few embers in her chest. She was moved through the mountain and then cradled, nestled in the dark stone. Her anger burned, and as it calcified, it became preserved, an ever-living thing, a furious hammer constantly beating against her chest.

Was this it? There would be no more bargains now. The witches of the ridge were gone; Jasper was gone. Her own mountain held no love for her, surrounding her; all her snakes, now dead. She let the stone into her lungs, dark and ossifying. Would her soul be a moth, too?

Esther closed her eyes and let go. She was the witch of Kire. It stood to rights she would be buried in it.

The cold mountain moved on its foundation, and the spark inside of Esther burned like hell, even as she drifted into the darkness.

32

Motheater

Motheater followed Kire's emissary under the world. When they reached the end of the earth, she rose up, her hand resting gently on the stag's back. They reappeared in the old holler, when the sycamore was still young and green.

The creature walked through the valley, avoiding dark, tar-like pits that Motheater didn't notice until the spirit carefully stepped around them. Surrounding them was the sound of crickets and cicadas, and as the sun set, moths settled around Motheater's shoulders.

They arrived at the top of the hill, and Motheater could see the ridgeline of Kire over the next low valley. The emissary spread his legs, leaning his head down. He dug his nose into the loam and snorted, and Motheater watched as the land was stripped away from the stone. The forest was lifted first, pine needles melting into cotton. Then the dead leaves were brushed away, and the moss, the trees evaporated into clouds, finally the dark dirt of the earth itself, all of it lifting into the air like a swarm of locusts.

Motheater covered her eyes as the dirt flew into her face, through her singed brassy hair and into the sky. When she looked around again, all that was there was the bedrock, the massive shape of Kire, the lurking-ness of it, the way it leaned forward, the way it seemed to almost have shoulders, the ridge of its eastern side like a spine, the peak the curve of its neck.

And then it moved, and Kire looked at her.

There was no dust, no birds to disturb, no roots to snap. She felt the heat of its gaze, the anger that she had left there, and she knew that Kire was doing this because of her. The mountain was waking up *because of her*.

The mountain looked at her, and she knew that to Kire, to the Old Mountain, she was a worm in the dirt. She might have been less than dirt. But she had spoken. And it had listened.

The titan shifted, set stony hands on the ground, on the flesh of its mother, and pushed itself up. The leviathan ripped its mass from the bedrock of the world, the jutting of the valley. Kire shifted and looked along the Appalachian line, at its sisters and brothers that had been beheaded, slumped over. Many of the great titans had passed, hollowed by human hands, leaving rocky, monstrous boulder-skulls.

But there were some, a few siblings down the ridge, in West Virginia, maybe near Charlottesville, that would answer when Kire called, when the mountain howled. There were some that were just sleeping, like Kire had been sleeping. Kire stepped up, out of its cradle, and spread its arms, the many arms, the many hands, the shifting cleavage and planes that made up the old titan of the new world, and stretched.

His joints popped, and the sound was like thunder. Motheater's ears rang with the pressure.

She had never seen him like this, never imagined Kire like this. It was huge, easily three times taller now, six-limbed, with a face carved from stone. It was ursine, an amaranthine beast that appeared like a calamity. Motheater resisted the urge to go to her knees as Kire went down on their front limbs.

Then Kire looked at her again, the little witch, and Motheater knew that if it came down to a match of fury between the mountain and Old Scratch himself, there was no telling who was angrier. The mountain wanted Motheater's revenge, wanted all of them dead, and its power was palpable. It opened its mouth, dark, gaping, a hell-maw, and Motheater couldn't breathe.

There were the pockmarks against cleavage and stratifications, the great, gaping wounds rent into stone. The wounds were dark, oozing black gold sludge from every cut and shaft. Kire had been bled for centuries. Kire saw her, and it moved toward its witch.

And then the emissary moved around Motheater, dragging her back into the modern holler, and Motheater shut her eyes. When she opened them again, she was face-to-face with the bone-lace creature, standing alone in a stream that did not end.

"I will stop this." Motheater's voice cracked. "I can lay Kire to rest." She was responsible for this. And she had to finish it. "I still need Jasper," she whispered. "I still don't know my name. He's still got a part of me."

The admission hurt, but it was true. He had returned the magic she had sent into the tree to connect them, but she was still unmade. There were parts of her she still didn't know, bone shards left in the rock when she was hewn out of Kire. It still claimed her.

The stag sharpened its tines along Motheater's jaw, a warning. The waters began to rise, over her calves, now past her knees. She would drown here, in this in-between space.

"I will never leave these mountains. I will never leave this place. My soul will never bear a moth, my power will extinguish, I repent all holds, even those I only dreamed to claim. I am sorry I took Jasper's choice. He should have it back."

She thought about her cabin, the opossum families she fed. She thought about Bennie, the softness of her bed, the expression on her face when she found something exciting. And Zach, she thought of his family, his doggedness. And then, Bennie again, her fingers spread across a map, her hands on a steering wheel, her hands on Motheater's shoulders.

"I would give it up. I would trade all of it. I will give myself back." She would trade everything she had. A powerful bargain.

Jasper had done the same. He had his own life, his own powers, a town that loved him like a son, and he had given it up to bring Motheater back. The water was at her chest, rising to her neckline. It would be so easy to slip under, to give up, to let herself be washed away. When she exhaled and opened her eyes, she was back in the holler.

The giant bone-lace stag walked over the draft, its hooves disappearing into the water. It took only seconds, and then the spirit passed through some veil and left. Motheater felt a new weight in her chest, another hagstone tied around her neck. Another burden.

Motheater was shaking. The deal was in motion. She pulled the unquilted scraps of herself closer. Glancing over at the grove, she saw Bennie, scrambling to run down into the vale, coming to her. For a few seconds, all Motheater could see was her face. The world slid down to Benethea Mattox and the way she looked as she skipped over the large rocks that led down to where Motheater was.

Bennie's braids had been burned in the fire, some singed almost through. A jolt of guilt struck through Motheater, but before she could say anything, Bennie had pulled her close, wrapping her up in a tight hug.

Motheater's heart might have gone right out of her. She held onto Bennie, closing her eyes, her arms around Bennie's waist. She smelled the sweat, the stale car, the bad gas station stench that still clung to her after a long day in the western Virginia heat with no respite, and felt like maybe Kire didn't matter so much compared to Bennie holding her right now.

"I was so fucking worried," Bennie said, pulling back, putting her hands on Motheater's face. Motheater tilted her head up, smiling just a little.

"Sorry," she said, keeping her hands on Bennie's hips. "I got a little lost."

"Yeah, you think?" Bennie chuckled, then leaned down to press her forehead against Motheater's.

Motheater took a deep breath in, slow like the draft. She felt the connection between her and Bennie had been made stronger for all Motheater's resolve to give her up. When she pulled away, the little fairy crosses had found the two of them, surrounding them like the rings of a planet, five of them turning around them. Motheater held a hand out, and the crosses fell, single file, into her palm.

"Sorry about your hair," Motheater said, tucking the crosses into her pocket as they walked up the holler toward Jasper and Zach.

"It's fine," Bennie said, waving her hand. "It's synthetic. I'll try to fix it tonight."

Motheater blinked. "I don't know what that means."

Bennie laughed. "Of course not."

Motheater smiled and let it lie. When they got to the top of the holler, she went to Jasper, looking him over slowly.

"You look good," she said quietly.

"Mm." Jasper was not smiling. He looked shaken and gaunt, white streaks through his long hair, lines across his face. He wasn't the man Motheater remembered. At least he hadn't aged the full time, only about twenty years. "I suppose

I have to thank you for giving that tree a mind to keep me as alive as it did."

"I didn't mean to do that," Motheater said quietly. "I would never have just left you."

"And yet, there I was, done left."

Motheater clenched her hands. "I was forced away," she said, voice measured.

Jasper was a different man. His cheekbones sharper, eyes more pointed, mouth full and stained slightly red, like the leaves of the sycamore. He had grown even taller, become handsome and bright-eyed, tempered and aged within the tree. He might have been fetching back in time, but now he was devastatingly beautiful, and Motheater marveled at their difference, that she became a hollowed creature, and he had left the sycamore more refined than when she had left him there. He deserved to be alive, he deserved to live, even if it had to be now.

Motheater noticed that Zach hadn't looked away from Jasper once.

"All right." Bennie interrupted the tense moment, taking Motheater's hand again and starting to head toward the path. Motheater followed, happy to get away from Jasper's glare, happy to have Bennie's hand in hers. "Catch us up on the way out of here. It's nearly dark."

Before she and Bennie stepped into the forest, there was a loud creak, and then a snap. Motheater turned as a sheaf of trees slid down Kire. A whole patch of land shifting, dislodging the earth and stone, creating a massive mudslide of trench and branch. Any birds that had refused to leave their new-laid nests swarmed up, a cacophony of despair as their eggs scattered, as their homes fell. The trees moved together, like a running river, turning down the western side away from Kiron.

"What in the hell is going on," Zach said, speaking for the first time in hours, voice cracking. A spell had been undone, again. "What the fuck was that?"

Bennie squeezed Motheater's hand.

The witch looked at Bennie, something unknowable caught in her throat, a different kind of heat in her belly. She only had a short amount of time. They needed to prepare. She looked back to Kire, the shifting mass, the hulk, the leviathan of Appalachia. "The mountain's awake."

33
Bennie

The four of them decided to head to Zach's house. It wasn't like Bennie and Motheater had anything pressing at her apartment, and they needed to regroup. Motheater was pale and shaking in the car, and Jasper kept falling asleep. Bennie and Zach shared looks in the mirror, commiserating and deeply worried. Bennie drove slowly, avoiding the downed wires, the broken branches, the new rocks made out of asphalt that made the road nearly impassable. Kire was a slow hurricane destroying Kiron.

Her knuckles were ashen as she made her way through her old neighborhood. She had been out of Zach's home a month, and she hadn't realized until right now how much she missed it.

This was the whitest, most suburban part of Kiron, and it was still hard to find two houses close enough to see your neighbor. Lawns were mowed around the small orchards, hedges by the road, fences whitewashed. It was cute, comfortable, and the fact that Bennie didn't hate it made her mad.

Bennie pulled into the small brick rancher and parked the car, immediately putting her hands back on the wheel. In the back seat, Zach slid out and then offered his hand to Jasper, helping him out of the truck. They walked in together, Zach's hand hovering protectively over Jasper's shoulder.

"You don't look well," Motheater said, turning toward Bennie.

"I never wanted to come back," Bennie muttered. "While I was here, so much of myself slipped away."

Motheater looked over the house, and Bennie couldn't tell what she was thinking. How did it look to her, someone who had grown up with dirt floors and soft walls? Bennie refused to feel bad about her decision, refused to back down. She steeled herself, but Motheater just reached for her hand. Bennie, like a fool, let her take it.

"Sometimes the places that keep us safe keep us small."

Bennie just stared at the house.

"I need to see to Jasper," Motheater whispered. "If you need to leave, I ain't going to fault you, but . . ." Motheater hesitated, her finger sliding along Bennie's palm, intimate, tender, needy. "I don't want to do this without you."

"You can do anything," Bennie said quickly, ignoring the way her heart lurched.

"Not alone."

Motheater's words hung between them like sparks thrown up from a disturbed fire. Bennie turned to look at her, the strangeness of her, crooked nose and blurred cheekbones and brown eyes. Motheater caught a chill and shivered. She squeezed Bennie's hand, and then dropped her fingers to graze Bennie's knee before stepping out of the truck, heading into the home.

She disappeared into the rancher, and Bennie was by herself.

Inside the truck, without anyone watching her, Bennie let herself tear up. She was frustrated and angry; the sirens had been going on and off all day, and even as they drove into the suburb, she had seen a veritable caravan of respectable folk with places and means to go evacuating Kiron. She knew that if she went over to the Hallside neighborhood, the Black and brown residents there wouldn't be so privileged. Some of them could leave, piling two families into the one working van they shared, but many others would have to wait here, under Kire's shadow, doomed to be crushed under rockslides and power failures. God, it was the same story breaking her heart every time.

Bennie had hoped they would find Jasper's grave, do a séance, get some backstory, and then go home. She thought they had time. They didn't. They only had right now.

Bennie sat in the car for another half hour or so, wasting gas, fighting with herself as lights turned on inside the house, as silhouettes began moving around. Zach would be putting a frozen meal into the oven, Motheater would be collecting moths from the basement that they had been hoping to renovate and never got around to, Jasper might be nursing a strong drink with his thousand-yard stare.

And where would Bennie fit in?

The engine hummed. She *could* leave.

Would she be on the couch, reading a book she had left behind? Organizing Zach's clothes so that the coal dust didn't spread beyond his side of the closet? Doing her hair in the large antique vanity mirror she and Kelly-Anne had thrifted from a Yardville swap and shop?

Everything was tied up in that house. Inadequacy, grief, the loss of her best friend. If she went in, she wouldn't be just doing it for Motheater, or for Kelly-Anne . . . she had to do it for herself, too. They were going to stop what had killed her best friend, what killed nearly thirty men and women in the dark.

She could handle one night. They needed to plan how to put the mountain to rest. Bennie finally turned off the engine and got out of the truck, pushing her hands into her jacket. Motheater had asked her to stay. She would stay.

When she went in, she headed down the hall to the guest bathroom, not looking at the group crowded around the kitchen counter. Nobody stopped her.

In the bathroom, she washed her face and dug through the drawers, finding a pair of scissors and a set of clippers that she had gotten for Zach years ago. Normally, she wouldn't be so aggressive, but she wanted to get her burned hair out and get it over with. She snipped the braids and unwound the synthetic hair as much as she could. God, this would take forever.

She stared at her half-undone hair and sighed, the ache of the past week weighing on her. This was useless. The clippers were next to her right hand. Why shouldn't she just get rid of all this?

Looking in the mirror, Bennie turned her head left and right. She had kept her hair just long enough to put hair extensions in, but she didn't need long hair to fit in, or look pretty, or be passable. She didn't need to make the Greshams like her, or pretend to be a part of the church, or any of that. It was just her in the mirror. Maybe it was time to make some things easier.

Her mama would hate it. Bennie smirked as she turned on the clippers, remembering her mother twisting her hair back into an intricate braid, ironing it straight before church, flattening it down to keep her from being bullied in school.

But Bennie was a grown-ass woman and she wasn't afraid of bullies anymore.

Her dark hair fell to the ground, still half in braids as she began to carefully clip away at the remaining ones. Bennie knew she should have gotten someone to help, but she didn't care. She wanted her hair gone, now. After the braids were gone she took a few minutes to look at the horrorshow on her head. Embarrassing. But she had been taught how to clip a fade back in college and managed to get her hair looking presentable. She'd get it done after and see what the salon could do for her, if she wasn't laughed out of the door.

It took nearly two hours, and she heard a few people walk by, but nobody knocked. After her cut was finished, she realized that she had never seen her hair so short. She felt exposed and resolved, that this was her, this was real. More real than how she felt with braids or rows or flattened hair. Bennie put all the hair on the floor in the trash and then took off her clothes, stepping into the shower.

34
Motheater

Motheater had trusted Zach when he had told her that Bennie was fine, but Bennie had been in the bathroom in back near two hours on and hadn't come out.

While she waited, she had arranged all of them in the living room, Jasper and Zach on the couch, her on the floor, a chair waiting for Bennie. She had laid out Bennie's map carefully, trying to ignore the rumbles, groans, and creaks she heard from the ground, knowing that she was the only one who felt those small shifts, who had a consciousness buried deep in the bedrock, a part of her soul tied to the mountain.

Kire wasn't going to wait much longer. Already it was rearranging its muscles along the strata, finding new ways to move. By sundown tomorrow, the leviathan would be unbound.

Motheater couldn't look away from the little marker Bennie had drawn on for the Church of the Rock. If she had stayed in the stone, Kire might never have had its taste for blood sated. She hoped that maybe she had held it back during her time in the rock. Losing miners in ones and twos seemed a small price to pay considering the kind of revelation Kire threatened now. Maybe Kire would have woken anyway, and it was good luck that she had been pulled out now. Maybe Kiron was waiting for the witch of Samuel to face down Goliath.

It made her nervous. She rubbed at her hands, the tattoos writhing under her skin. After meeting Kire, they had resettled in new places. The snakes lay curled in her palm; a small section slid around her wrist and the back of her hand, where they tilted their heads back, mouths open. There were small dots above the teeth, which Motheater thought resembled flames.

"If I go back there," Motheater said, pointing to the slough where she had been dumped after Zach struck her from Kire. "I might be able to find the source of the pain and ease it."

"It's beyond healing," Jasper said, his hands clutching a hot mug. "Might be beyond you."

Motheater bared her sharp teeth at him. "Nothing is beyond me."

"You're as much a fool now as you were then," Jasper said, not gently. "You have mined suffering like a capitalist and now you dream of freedom."

Motheater searched for a smile, for something charming, but found nothing. It hurt, thinking that he had no more love for her, that he might have had it seeped away like sap out of a maple. What was all this for if she couldn't help those she loved? The light admonition was enough to make her turn away from him, glare at the floor.

"What happens if it wakes up?" Zach asked, looking over the scope of Kire on another map. "What will it do?"

"Not if," Jasper murmured. "When."

"It will rise," Motheater muttered, running her hand through her cropped hair. She had taken a pair of shears to it, cutting a straight line to give herself a bob that she could just barely tie back with a ribbon. Her emissary-given vision echoed in her head, dangerous and huge, difficult to imagine, impossible to articulate. "Kire is unknowable. It was not hewn nor birthed."

But it had been influenced. It had been spoken to. Motheater frowned slightly. Kire was like this because of her. Kire was angry because of her, because of what she said. No other mountain had risen up. No other mountain threatened destruction like Kire. And the only difference between Kire and Huckleberry, or Sarton, or Dameron, or any other mountain gone hollow, was the fact that Kire had a hateful witch nestled inside of it.

Bennie's map must have been taken from the White Rock office because it was marked with little picks, showing the vast range of terror that industry had wrought on the area. Coal mining, man killing, mountain cutting.

"Kire's angry," Motheater said. "There must be other titans that want to rise, but have not a witch encouraging them to sit up and pay attention."

"You can't blame yourself for this." Bennie walked into the living room, and Motheater's eyes went wide as she looked up. Her eyes darted over Bennie's new hairstyle, and she marveled at the way Bennie looked strong and stately, self-assured and lovely. She caught Bennie's glare and flinched. "You can't."

Motheater let go of the maps. A green moth appeared out of nowhere at her shoulder, and then a pink one by her hand, darting into the light from the dark corners of the room.

She was not blameless. She remembered nearly her whole past now, sin to stone, and hadn't she opened Kire's wounds and demanded power? Hadn't she been furious when that power was threatened? She was supposed to be a Neighbor, and instead, she became a mountain haunt. Jasper had been right about her; she'd sacrificed Kiron to serve her own selfish desires. She should have protected Kiron then. And now? It seemed impossible.

Bennie walked around the couch and sat down next to Motheater, kneeling thigh-to-thigh with the witch. Motheater focused on the line of herself that met against Bennie, her heart beating fast.

"So now that we're done feeling sorry for ourselves, what's the plan?"

Motheater pointed to the slough where she had been found. "I need to find my excavation. With what's been happening . . . It might be caved in, or destroyed, or . . . any number of things. But I'll go in and see what I can do to lay the mountain back in its bed."

"Going onto Kire sounds dangerous," Bennie said, pressing her mouth. "Even going near that mountain is a death wish."

Motheater nodded, looking up at Jasper. His face was set. "I could hear something while I was in the sycamore," he said. "A growing wound. Cut skin is most tender before it begins to heal."

"Scared beasts bite hardest," Motheater said, like it was a call-and-response, like they were themselves again. She smiled at Jasper, and when he didn't smile back, she swallowed her upset and turned to the maps again. "I need a few hours. There ain't a thing about this mountain I don't know. I just need to remember it."

༄

Motheater and Jasper sat opposite each other in the backyard. Between them was a small handheld mirror, a glass of whiskey, and a ham bone that Zach had found in the back of the freezer, a remnant of Bennie's cooking that he hadn't even known was there. When Jasper looked confused, Motheater had just sighed and told him that apparently nobody kept hare or chickens anymore.

Jasper made a face that made Motheater laugh.

Outside, they sat close together, with the arrangements of their communion placed in front of her. She and Jasper had been inseparable once, not too long ago by her recall, but the bonds of magic were tied to different things from memories. Around her, moths fluttered, and soft glowing lights appeared like vines from the ground. Jasper eyed them as they rose up and then glared at Motheater.

"Did nobody tend the flock?"

"Don't act accusing at me," Motheater said. "I didn't ask to leave."

Jasper shook his head, and Motheater suddenly laughed.

"What?"

"You look like your father," Motheater said, grinning. "Age suits you."

"Well, you still look like a child," Jasper said, and this time his air of disapproval was too much, and Motheater giggled into her wrist, ducking her head. When she looked up, Jasper was smirking, but trying to hide it. He shook his head, sitting straight again.

"Aye, well, all the better." She tugged her ear, winking at Jasper. "Nobody expects a child to be their end."

"Half a miracle you're alive right now, the kind of soul-needle you stuck in me," Jasper said, almost angry.

"I'm sorry, Jas," Motheater said wearily. "I'm sorry for what I did to you. I'm sorry for what I did to Kiron. To Kire, even."

Jasper sighed, closing his eyes. "You even apologize like a child."

Motheater pressed her mouth, humiliated. He was right. Look at what her pride had done. "Let's get that needle out." Her voice was less than a whisper. "And after that . . ."

"If'n you say something foolish like 'move out of Kiron,' or 'live in your truth,' I will kill you myself," Jasper snapped. "You can't hope to settle Kire without me."

Motheater sucked her lips, nervous. "You don't hate me?"

"God help us all," Jasper sighed. "No, you wicked creature. I love you still. When did you become such an insecure brat?"

"Well, you see, I was in a mountain for some time—"

Jasper groaned, and Motheater laughed again, delighting in teasing her friend again, finding so much of him remained. She reached out and took his hand, and he held her fingers tightly.

"I could never hate you," Jasper said quietly. "I held your soul for all those years."

Motheater shivered, squeezed his hand tighter. She shifted even closer to him, misty and soft in the moonlight, with her friend. "We held each other."

The glowing lights bobbed around them, a swarm of living lightning bugs. Motheater's smile faded. It really was something to see, these restless creatures caught in between phases of the moon. When did the last soul-bound Neighbor leave Appalachia? Had she been the last fool to tamper with powers beyond her hold? Were hedge witches all that remained? Hedge magic was bargains between herb and hand, loving spirit-flights and beeswax protections.

Jasper was quiet, eyes closed, listening to the holler, the soul-ritual forgotten for a moment.

"There's too much blood in this land." Motheater spoke quietly, watching the knockers in the backyard. It was an appetite she had fed.

"There's always blood, Esther."

Motheater blinked. She looked at Jasper, her eyes wide. Her breath started to come faster. Jasper's eyes were closed, and he didn't see the color rise in her cheeks, the heat along her arms. Over her collarbones, the snakes moved, brands searing into her skin, wrapping around her neck like a noose.

There's always blood, Esther.

Motheater was pulled back; she was on Kire, in a small pool she had dug out at the peak, a ballaun filled with shine and tears. She wanted to wait for the right moment, when her blood came at the same time of the full moon. It would make her powerful, visceral, immediate. It would give her deep magic.

She was young—fourteen—but she already had roped muscles across her back and arms, stretched tight from hard living in Appalachia. Her hair was streaked with white, and moths and bats swooped at the peak of the mountain, alighting in her hair, in trees, sending dark, dappled silhouettes across her naked body. She had been raised by the woods, had run amok in the forest, and it had told her secrets beyond hedge and hollow. The snakes themselves, ambassadors of power, had told her of Kire's sleeping heart.

When the moon was at its zenith, she slid into the shinepool, her body pale and small in the moonlight. She shivered and let her monthly bleeding trickle around her thighs. She raised her hands and brought the moon down, into her heart, into her head. Turning, Esther knelt on the bottom of the pool, holding the moon's reflection in her cupped hands.

She murmured words of power, starting with Exodus, her conjure bone held on a twine around her neck.

"*The Lord is a man of war: the Lord is his name.*" Her voice was steady as she recited the verse, the moon full above her and full in front of her and full beneath her. She formed the white thread with the moon, drawing it down into her, feeding the fire in her blood. "*Thy right hand, O Lord, is become glorious in power: thy right hand, O Lord, hath dashed in pieces the enemy.*"

This was her god, angry and merciless, the god that commanded his followers to wander in the desert for forty years after a single night of wavering faith. The god who appeared in a whirlwind of fire, the god who named all the stars in the sky. She knelt, and declaimed, and bled into the water, more than she should have, more than any woman does during their month, and her small pool became a plague of Egypt.

"Who is like unto thee, O Lord, among the gods? who is like thee, glorious in holiness, fearful in praises, doing wonders?" Esther's voice rose, and she felt the blood turn the moon red, felt her fire attach itself to her words, to the world, to the mountain underneath her. She was making magic; she was commanding it. *"Thou stretchedst out thy right hand, the earth swallowed them."*

Under her, Kire broke apart.

She killed the moon in her hands and slid under the blood.

The earth swallowed her. Kire, sick and sad and sluggish, welcomed her with an open maw, drank her blood and consumed her, all of her, and gave her the power she knew she could have. Esther became the agent of the mountain, beloved of it, its protector.

Esther floated in Kire, letting the bedrock hold and caress her, sliding along the striations of the great beast, the dark and lonely titan of the earth. All her veins became coal, all the mountain's full of blood. It had her, all of her, and asked only constant devotion.

Esther woke up in a depression on the peak of Kire Mountain, completely dry, coated in black coal dust, reborn. She had been baptized twice, once in the Church of the Rock, by man and water. Her second baptism was by Kire and blood. She dug her fingers into the stone and stood, naked as the deer, eyes turned up to the black sky. She took a deep breath and howled at the dead moon.

Motheater woke up with Bennie leaning over her, holding her shoulders. She blinked a few times, all the sounds around her muffled, as if she were underwater and missing every other word. Shifting, she tried to sit up, and Bennie moved with her, arm around her gently, supporting her. Bennie's mouth moved, but Motheater couldn't hear her right, and after a few seconds of staring at her face, gave up. Every part of her ached. The witch let herself sink against Bennie, trying to clear her head.

Her name, her name, her name. She hadn't needed to take her soul out of Jasper. He had given it to her. He had given it back, freely, without hate, and she was whole.

Bennie's hand moved against her shoulder, and Motheater leaned into her side. The tide went out, and she slowly picked out words again, but not many. The crushing pressure against her temples was gone, and she opened her eyes, slow and heavy, looking out at the yard where she and Jasper had communed.

The glowing knocker-haints had left, and she could feel their weight against her skull. It was still dark, the moon curved and nudged gentle against the mountains, the tip of a whiskey cup as it left its last liquor on your tongue.

Jasper was standing, arguing with Zach, who was keeping himself in between Jasper and Bennie. Motheater waved her hand a little, getting Jasper's attention, and he seemed to calm down, staring at her. Zach didn't take his hand off Jasper's chest, keeping him back. She took a deep breath, found her fire, and let it ignite her.

She was Kire, too.

The stillness was a blessing. It made room for her to take the embers up in a whirlwind.

"I know how to calm the titan," Motheater muttered, shifting against Bennie, trying to sit up a bit better.

"Do you?" Bennie asked, and although she still sounded faraway and muffled by a wind, Motheater could hear her well enough. She nodded.

If she went back, if she curled up in the mountain, she could hold it steady. Her bargain would keep her in the ridge, and maybe Kire would become a dead mountain instead of a dormant one. She was supposed to protect Kire. Instead, by her own meddling, she had made it vulnerable.

"Where did you go?" Jasper demanded, crouching down in front of her. "You left, and the mountain shifted again. It ain't waiting for you to pull its strings."

Motheater shook her head. "We got a little time. We were both remembering."

She wanted to curse, but blasphemy was a strong invocation, and she'd save damnation for that which deserved it. Instead, she pulled away from Jasper and sat up on her own. Still, she kept close to Bennie.

"It will wait for the low creatures to warm." She attempted to stand and was grateful that Bennie helped her up. "The snakes are its eyes and ears. It's too old for eyes; it relies on the beasts. We can rest for a few more hours and walk up to the mine shaft where you pulled me out at daybreak."

Zach nodded, pale. "White Rock's officially suspended operations indefinitely. Nobody is going near that mountain."

Bennie snorted. "Waited until the last minute, didn't they?"

Motheater stared up at the peaks that dominated the landscape, at Kire that had seemed to rise, that had turned its head out of the earth and toward the sky, toward her. She felt the cold chill of the stone, understood the darkness that was filling her, the sureness of its power, and what it promised.

She glanced to her side, and seeing Bennie stare up at the mountain as well, something big and hurt rose up in Motheater. She reached down to grasp Bennie's hand, squeezing tight, and Bennie looked surprised.

"Your company's turned out," Motheater murmured. "Ain't your fight anymore."

Bennie snorted. "I wanted to keep people safe. It was my job then, it's my job now."

Motheater smiled a little, and then looked up to Kire again, her heart entombed somewhere different than it had been when she had first been thrown into the slough.

"Tomorrow," Motheater said, soft enough to keep secrets, "we'll meet with the last titan."

35

Bennie

ennie kept a hold of Motheater's hand as they walked into the house, leaving Zach and Jasper on the front porch. The two women were silent, the enormity of what they had to do reverberating between them. At dawn, Bennie thought, they would go bargain with Kire.

It was ludicrous, but in the past week she had seen mountains move, churches fly in the air, ghosts walk, a man come out of a tree, and gave her former boss a candle to cure a generational curse. It wasn't so strange, was it, that at the end of this they had to go to Kire and appeal directly.

"We can sleep in here," Bennie said, leading Motheater to the spare bedroom. It was very spare, with a mattress that bowed in the middle and only a nightstand for furniture. She hadn't expected Zach to improve on the room, but it was kind of absurd that he hadn't even turned down the sheets since she left. Bennie was, at this point, very much trying not to think about the fact that she and Motheater were going to be sharing a bed, a real bed, after spending most of the last few hours holding hands.

Motheater had walked around the bed, dragging her hands along the duvet. Bennie turned so she wouldn't have to watch her, wouldn't have to think too hard, and sat on the bed. It was only after she had taken off her jacket and boots that she realized just how tired she was. This whole day had been exhausting, and she ached. The stress, the fear, the anxiety, the magic. All of it weighed on her.

"Bennie?"

She picked her head up out of her hands, not realizing until just then she had been leaning over.

"I'm fine."

She was, mostly. She tried to focus, she tried to sit up, but before she could, she felt the mattress dip behind her and Motheater's arms around her shoulders. They were slim, strong, pulling Bennie back against her chest.

Bennie did not panic, absolutely not, and her face did not flush at all, but she might have made a noise that was not completely ladylike as Motheater held her tight. Her heart was beating faster, her hands spread over her jeans, absolutely not sweating at all. Nope. She was fine, she was totally fine, and she had this completely under control.

"Don't fret," Motheater murmured, sliding closer, her bare thighs bracketing Bennie's hips, her face crushed against Bennie's shoulders. "It'll turn out."

"Will it?" Bennie asked, and she could probably pretend that her voice wasn't higher than normal. She swallowed, ignoring the soft heat of Motheater against her, ignoring her sweaty palms. She focused on the crickets outside, the last creatures who seemed too oblivious to know that the mountain was coming for them.

"Aye." Motheater's voice was soft, feathery against Bennie's neck. "I'll make it so."

Bennie laughed. She shook her head and swatted at Motheater's arms. "Move over."

Motheater shifted back, and Bennie promptly shucked off her jeans and slid under the covers. The witch was down to the same, pulling a long-sleeved tee shirt over her palms, holding onto the fabric. It was dark enough that they couldn't really see each other, but they were close, knees bumping against each other.

They faced each other, and Motheater reached out first, running her hand over Bennie's jaw.

Fuck it. Bennie turned her head and kissed Motheater's palm, relishing the soft exhale she got from the other woman. Her hands found Motheater's hips, and she pulled her close, kissing her hard. They only had tonight.

That got a slightly different reaction, and Bennie chased Motheater's mouth, hands fisted in Motheater's shirt. She smiled as she kissed the witch, as the witch kissed her back, dragging her short nails across the back of her neck. Bennie shuddered and licked into Motheater's mouth. Sharp teeth shouldn't turn her on as much as it did, but there was no accounting for that, was there.

Motheater arched into Bennie, and whatever puritan preconceptions Bennie had of Motheater flew swiftly out the window. Bennie did not mind that at all. Her hands slid up Motheater's shirt, and she felt the witch shiver under her fingers.

"I like this," Bennie sighed, pulling back as Motheater gripped her shoulders tightly. She swallowed and looked at Motheater's too-sharp face, her hazel eyes, her dull, brassy hair and splotchy pink-and-green blush spread across her cheeks. Bennie knew that she had something ethereal in her hands. She knew that it couldn't last.

Motheater nodded, humming. She leaned in to kiss Bennie again, and Bennie let her, want pooling in her stomach. Her hands were on fire, her legs were burning between Motheater's. She wanted this horribly.

With a strength that Bennie wouldn't have guessed Motheater had, Bennie was shoved onto her back, and the witch straddled her hips. Bennie's eyes went wide for a second before Motheater kissed her again, her clever hands sliding under Bennie's shirt.

Oh, shit, *oh shit.*

Bennie turned her head, pushing Motheater away, sliding up the headboard, pressing her head against the wall. She was breathing hard, but so was Motheater, her eyes wide, a little manic.

"I know what I'm doing," Motheater said, leaning in to kiss Bennie again.

"No, I got that." Bennie laughed, actually laughed, something nervous and stupid and full of terror. She grabbed at Motheater's hands and forced them down onto Motheater's thighs, holding them still. Motheater was breathing hard, and Bennie watched the witch's eyes flick over her face. Bennie didn't know why she was hesitating. Why should Bennie wait, when all she wanted to do was kiss Motheater until her lips were bright and swollen?

It might have been the gray-green bruises around Motheater's neck that made her pause. It may have been the bony hips, the way Motheater looked as desperate as Bennie felt. It might have been the way that Motheater seemed to glow, pale and ghostly in the dark room. She wanted this; they both did.

"Oh, goddammit." Bennie groaned, leaning forward and wrapping her arms around Motheater's waist. She pulled her close, and Motheater made a cooing noise, sliding her hands across Bennie's head gently. It was almost like she was calming down a particular cat, but Bennie wasn't minding.

She sighed, and Motheater kissed her temple, cradling her gently, being soft in a way that a witch made of sharp edges shouldn't be.

"Let's just get some sleep," Bennie said finally, an ache pounding at her chest. Motheater raised her eyebrows, a look of hurt flashing across her face. She nodded, shifting to slide off Bennie. Bennie felt wounded, too, and they both slid down to lie flat on the bed.

There was something raging inside Bennie, but fucking Motheater right now would feel desperate and sad. She wanted to feel love. She deserved better than an earnest, fumbling, terrified tumble with a woman she wanted to know so completely.

In the dark, Bennie could just barely see the mottled bruises around Motheater's neck. She reached out and found Motheater's hands, searching for a small comfort. The witch gripped her tight, and they ended up curled into each other, foreheads pressed together, breathing the same air.

Bennie screwed her eyes up to keep from crying in frustration, to keep her just barely apart from Motheater.

"You scared?" Motheater whispered.

Bennie paused, then nodded. "Yeah."

The admission hung between them, fragile and soft. Bennie closed her eyes tightly, and her breath didn't come easy.

"Me too," Motheater said, leaning in to press her face against Bennie's. "But I'm with you."

"What's that got to do with anything?" Bennie's voice did not crack, it did not at all. This, too, was fragile.

"Because you make me brave," Motheater said quietly. Now, something broke inside Bennie. She opened her eyes again, watching Motheater in the off-light of the crescent moon that barely came in through the window. "Because you're brave. I love you," Motheater murmured, her voice like a river. She gripped Bennie's hands tight. "I love you like a mountain."

Bennie laughed, furiously heated, and buried her head in the pillow next to Motheater's head. She felt Motheater tense up next to her and quickly turned her head to kiss her. She didn't know if she believed Motheater, if this was something compelled, if this was real, but they had something strung between them, some common thread, a connection that didn't mean much to time or space. They were queer in Appalachia, and these folks didn't come around quick. It was futile, grasping, and Bennie couldn't help the way her heart pounded through her whole body, even down to the tips of her fingers. "I'm your mountain?"

Motheater nodded, leaning into Bennie. "Aye, my mountain."

Bennie grinned, kissing Motheater quickly a second time. Fuck it. She could kiss the woman a little bit. Who cared? She was just a woman half in love with a witch out of time. This was enough. "You're my mountain."

36

Motheater

In the early morning, before dawn broke, in the sweet pink light that draped across the range just before the sun came up, the four mismatched Appalachians met in Zach's kitchen.

Motheater had taken one of Zach's jumpsuits and rolled up the arms and legs, giving her huge cuffs, exposing her tattoos. She was nervous but ready: prepared. She spread Bennie's map across the table, the most likely routes into Kire's fenced-off land marked in pencil.

"No movement in the night," Jasper reported, leaning against the wall, arms crossed.

"Were a low moon, with snakes too cold, Kire won't be seeing much," Motheater said, mostly to Zach and Bennie, who were awkwardly standing on the other end of the table. "If the snakes are asleep, Kire will be waiting. He needs to make sure his momentum is spent just so."

"You have everything?" Bennie asked, her arms folded. She seemed nervous, and Motheater thought it was a resignation deeper than fear that made Bennie's shoulders tighten like that.

Motheater nodded, checking her pockets for the herbs she had picked an hour before, the small shard of quartz she had found in the house, which Zach had mentioned that he had found while on Kire, and a thatch-broom of thorns she had made from the weeds at the back of the house.

"Enough, I think." It was not enough, Motheater knew, but it would have to be. She would make it enough.

"Do we really need to do this?" Zach asked. Both Motheater and Bennie fixed him with a sharp glare. "I mean it."

"What you mean?" Motheater said softly. She could feel her power surrounding her, whole and without any consignor; the world seemed eager to bend to her. Jasper stepped forward, in front of Zach, a hand out as if to physically block her anger.

Zach, blue eyes wide, swallowed. "Look at all this," he said quietly, gesturing to the map. "White Rock can't go back into Kire with all this movement. Kire's the problem, but if the mountain shifts too much . . . I mean, everyone is leaving—"

"Not everyone's leaving." Bennie's voice was sharp. "The poor families aren't going nowhere. Hallside and all the double-wides aren't leaving."

"They're not *staying*." Zach pushed. "And if most of Kiron isn't even here—"

"Most ain't all," Motheater said quietly. She reined herself in, the echoes of her emotions reverberating, but soft enough that Jasper pulled back.

"This isn't our job," Zach said, exasperated. "None of this—"

A massive shudder swept through the home, sending Motheater to the ground. Bennie fell back onto the couch, and Zach and Jasper slammed into the table, Zach losing his footing and knocking his head against the corner.

"Zach!" Bennie scrambled off the couch, going to the man on the floor. As Motheater stood up, Zach was already draped across Jasper's thigh, and her friend had his hand across Zach's forehead, frowning deeply. Motheater felt her own veins going into Jasper, their connection never severed as he used her to heal Zach. All it took was faith, and Jasper had fixed Zach, who was blinking foolishly up at him.

"Ain't gonna stop," Motheater said, frowning deeply, Jasper holding Zach, Bennie gripping his hand. They weren't being taken from her; they were only helping. "There could be other mountains who will answer Kire's call when he revolts from his cradle."

"She's right," Bennie muttered as she looked between him and Motheater. "It's not gonna stop, and we're the only ones who know how to stop it."

"Do you even know?" Jasper asked. "Any of your witchcraft prepare you for this?"

Motheater's heart leapt near out of her chest, her mouth went dry. "I have to try."

"We have to try." Bennie squeezed Zach's hand and stood up. "Leave if you want, Zach."

Zach groaned, pushing Jasper's hand away to touch his forehead, where blood was still drying on top of healed, pink skin. Motheater knew it would scar. "You get proven right, and you find something else to prove," he complained. "Fine, you win."

"It's not about winning." Bennie reached down, holding her hand out. "It's about helping people, jerkface."

"I plead the Fifth," Zach muttered, taking her hand and helping himself up. Bennie and Zach smiled at each other, sharing some kind of secret joke, and Motheater's stomach clenched.

"Let's get going," she said, turning on her heel and going to the door. "As soon as the sun's up, Kire will know what we're up to."

She was jittery as Bennie ushered everyone into the truck, and she didn't miss the way that Zach stayed close to Jasper, following her old friend like a puppy.

Motheater wondered, briefly, as she climbed into the front seat, if some of the binding enchantment had been passed to Zach Gresham when she unlaced Jasper. Maybe it was loosing DeWitt's curse, maybe it was Kire magic. Maybe it was nothing but Zach infatuated with a man who had the gall to look like that without invitation.

This time, Zach directed Bennie from the back seat as they went up to the White Rock holdings on Kire. It was technically trespassing, but Motheater didn't care much for the law, and Zach had said that most of the power lines on Kire were out anyway. No recordings. Motheater sort of knew what a security camera was, but only vaguely. It wasn't important enough for dead souls to pass on knowledge of security cameras.

As they drove, they passed great sinkholes and felled trees in the road, courtesy of Kire's movements. Motheater moved a large oak with a flick of her hand and a proverb. Her resolve was great, and it made her powerful, steady. They got to the first fence that Motheater likewise shoved open with a Word, and then the second, and then were met with a ridge that hadn't been there last week, that was still moving upward, slowly shifting toward the sky, the breathing god.

They stopped in front of the rock as the fault line moved slowly upward in centimeters and breaths. Scuttling bugs crawled out of now-exposed holes. Across the ridge, great sighs went up from the stone, cool mist evaporating as the shelf lifted itself skyward.

Bennie made a noise. "Well I'll be fucked."

"Jesus shit," Zach said, causing Jasper to snort.

"We're not even close to the part of Kire I need to go to." Motheater glared at the ridge as she got out of the vehicle, going to the sliding ridge and putting a hand on it, just her fingers. "We're still in the White Rock holler," she said, stepping back.

Bennie jogged over. "What do you want to do?"

Motheater took a step back as the shale shook. "I'm going up the mountain."

"We don't even know what part of the mountain is what at this point," Bennie said, frowning. "How are you going to find the cut you were torn from?"

Motheater frowned. Would the mountain reveal itself? Had she been shut out from Kire? Was it going to rise and destroy her regardless?

"I'll find it." She turned back to Bennie and gestured back to the truck. "You all should go. Ain't safe." The sounds from the mountain were clear enough. There was shifting and breaking, a thundering like cannon fire. Kire was moving fast now.

"I didn't sign up for safe," Bennie said quickly, grinning at Motheater and running back to the truck. "I'm coming with you!"

Motheater flushed again as Bennie explained something to Zach. Zach leaned out of the window to yell something, but Bennie made a rude gesture instead of getting in the car. She ran back to Motheater, her blue jay flying out of the trees, screaming behind her. Motheater felt some kind of blessed.

"Let's go." Bennie got serious again as she came back to Motheater, looking up at the moving ridge.

"Wait!" Jasper called out, easing out of the car unsteadily before loping over to Motheater. He pulled at Motheater's shoulder, leaned down, and whispered in her ear.

"You got nothing left," he murmured, his hand tight on her shoulder. Past his arm, Motheater saw Bennie take a few steps away, giving them privacy. The wind was picking up.

"Your soul is Kire's, your body, Kire's. What do you have left?"

Motheater swallowed, eyes wide. "I dunno, Jas."

"Hedge ain't gonna settle the titan."

"Call the souls I dinnae tend," Motheater said, voice shaking. "Head up high, and when I need them most . . ."

Jasper squeezed her shoulder again. "I'll see you in hell, Esther."

She managed a small, wry smile as he stepped back. "Not too soon, I hope."

Motheater took a deep breath, resolved, her features hard as Jasper loped back to the truck.

Bennie glanced between Motheater and Jasper, focusing on the witch as she paced along the ridge, trying to find the best place to scale the rock. "What'd he say?"

"Goodbye," Motheater said, swallowing. Already the truck was out of sight, and the noises of the mountain creaking, shifting, owls crying, squirrels and chipmunks chattering, overwhelmed them. "And you? Where's Zach heading?"

"Told them to keep watch from Wind Rock on Potts. I dunno how helpful it'll be, but I think the fewer people in danger the better, right?"

Motheater nodded. Maybe it would be better for Bennie to go with them, but the truck was out of sight. So this was the army they had brought before Kire. "Aye."

Motheater looked up at the peak, hidden by broken trees and rockslides, and felt the dark pull in her chest, the hollow where Kire was supposed to be. Motheater steeled herself and pulled herself up along the cliff, hearing Bennie scramble after her. They made it up the rising stone to a ledge, and the stone settled. She stood still, and Bennie came over to hold her hand as they waited for the world under their feet to stop turning.

"You good?" Bennie asked, squeezing her hand.

Motheater nodded. "All right."

They walked through the holler, coming to White Rock Creek within half an hour. "We cross this, and we'll be on Kire," Motheater said, stepping into the river without hesitation. It was only a half-foot deep, barely a creek at all.

Bennie followed just behind. As she crossed over, Motheater heard Bennie pause. The witch glanced back, frowning. "Bennie?"

"Why the *fuck* does this river smell like whiskey?" Bennie asked, her perfect mouth opened in a soft bow.

Motheater's eyes widened. She dipped her hand in the creek and brought it to her nose, and then tasted magic there. She whirled and looked up as the smell of heat and copper rose from the draft, strong and clear.

"We may be too late."

Bennie crossed the shinewater and stood next to Motheater. The small rumbles and tears of stone and tree they had been hearing all through their walk came out fast and strong. All around them, roots popped like tendons. Motheater pulled Bennie down, and with a shout of Micah, the uprooted trees landed feet away from them, only a few branches scraping their shoulders. The rocks that were rolling downhill stopped in their tracks. A screech came, tearing metal, falling worlds, and when Motheater and Bennie looked up, in the early dawn of the last day, they saw the full breadth of the titan, standing on six legs, leaning forward among the ruins of the valley, bleeding dark coal from gashes and cuts along its sides.

Motheater stood, eyes fixed on Kire, the beast just under a mile away. Her bones shook as the great old one turned, wounded, betrayed, and stared right back.

༄

"Give me your hand!" Motheater yelled over the booms of ancient, sliding stone. "Bennie!"

A shift under them had made Bennie stumble away, but she quickly stood and ran to Motheater, hand out.

Motheater took her thatch-broom of thorns out of her pocket and drove it into Bennie's hand. She pressed the thorns into their palms, drawing blood. Bennie gasped, tried to yank her hand away, but that only worsened the wound. Her eyes teared up.

"What are you doing?"

"I'm sorry!" Motheater was half sobbing herself. She pulled her hand off the thorns roughly, making Bennie cry out. The motion left dark streaks against the plants she had so carefully wound together. She tossed the thatch to the ground and pressed their bleeding palms together, hard hedge and bargains made. "I wouldn't need to do this if we had more time!"

"*Goddamn that hurts!*" Bennie's voice echoed, even above the clamor, even above the great mountain stretching above them.

And under her shout, the shattered forest held together for a few more seconds.

Time slowed down, Bennie's yelp carrying around the small clearing that her blasphemy had made. She looked down at their clasped, bloody hands, held tight and painful. Around them, the leaves stopped in midair, the blue jay's flight was frozen, wings and tail spread. Behind them, the sounds of the moonshine river stopped, all noise around them turning to silence. This was the last calm moment, held by the first command of a new mountain.

The snake tattooed around Motheater's wrist slid across their fingers, wrapping itself around Bennie's wrist, its tongue out, lapping at the blood trickling down her wrist. Bennie gaped at their hands.

Motheater was grinning like a fool, watching Bennie's face, the spark of realization, the understanding, and like

Motheater's magic turned her hair white and silver, golden freckles appeared at Bennie's temples, winking as the ridge fell apart around them. Motheater felt it. Their thread, the binding magic.

The magic wouldn't have held if Bennie hadn't wanted it, if she had decided Motheater wasn't worth saving, that Kiron wasn't worth saving. But they were aligned: Kiron over Kire, even if it meant Motheater would have to destroy that which she once loved. She couldn't save Kiron without a Neighbor to anchor her.

But Motheater loved Bennie, admired her, wondered at her, thought that if anything in Kiron was worth saving now, it was her. This was the last thing she could give her. Maybe it was the only thing. This was the end Motheater made for herself. This was the grave she dug out of coal.

"You got my title now, Benethea Mattox. You gonna make bargains in love. You gonna break the world." Motheater leaned in and kissed her, hard and half off her mouth, holding their hands in between their chests, blood smearing at the hollow of Motheater's neck.

Time was speeding up around them. Leaves were starting to fall again. One passed by Bennie's shoulder. Motheater saw it in her eyes; Bennie knew a goodbye when it bled on her.

"Motheater—"

"My name is Esther," she said, eyes welling up with moonshine tears. "This is my fight. You're gonna have to find another."

"Esther."

The way Bennie said it, like she was trying it out, like it was something reverential, made Motheater cry, tears floating down like samara fruit. She stepped back, not letting go of Bennie's hand. Kire was behind her, agonizingly slow with the power of Bennie's first True Blaspheme still hanging in the air. Such was the weight of a First Curse, the debut of a new Appalachian witch.

"You need to go back. Jasper and Zach will help you," Motheater said.

"I can't leave you." Bennie's pleading nearly broke her resolve. She could spirit them away, couldn't she? Motheater didn't want this fight, but she had it. It was hers.

"You gotta make off, Bennie." The blue jay turned in the air, wings coming in toward its body. A groaning came from the great amaranthine creature behind her. Motheater squeezed her hand. "And I gotta meet Kire."

The leaf was almost at the ground, the last grain of sand.

"You can't fight a mountain!" Bennie held Motheater's bloody hand with both of hers, begging.

Motheater grinned, kissed her again, and finally pulled her hand away. The leaf touched the ground. Blood dripped on the river stones. Time turned to fire in her belly.

She was thrilled, every nerve of her alight and terrified in the shadow of the leviathan. This, right here, this was what she was made for. She was ready. Bloody and aching, she was a thorn in the paw of a lion.

"I ain't going to fight no mountain," Motheater said, looking up at Kire, who had just taken his first slouching step toward Kiron. She felt her old assurances again, thrumming through her. She was bound to no god but hope, held by no chains but love. "That mountain's gonna be fighting me."

37

Bennie

Bennie was panicked, crashing through the underbrush, heading back to the road. The rendezvous point on Wind Rock was halfway up the next ridge. Screaming at her shoulder was the blue jay, as brave as she was, keeping up with her easily as she pushed through downed trees and new boulders. Bennie's breath came in ragged gasps, and she could feel her pulse in her bloodied hand.

Motheater had told her that there was a witch who traveled in a flock of blue jays.

Bennie's breath stopped in her throat.

Was she a witch now? Was her pain great enough? Motheater said with a bargain and faith, you could be a place of places. Bennie screamed, running up a rock that was still moving out of the ground, and jumped off a new cliff.

In a second, she was a bird. She became an entire party of blue jays, near two dozen of them. She flew—a flock, an upheaval—and with her first familiar at the lead of the scold of them, winged up into the air. She could barely see, all different parts of her giving her too much information, and

Bennie knew, instinctively, that she was too green for this much flight.

She turned toward Potts Mountain, south of Kire, toward the state park's office on the top of the mountain. She could feel them tearing at her, the magic too much for her to hold, but she begged for strength. She held herself together by sheer grief. Ahead of her, the first familiar felt a tenuous terror, and Bennie knew that it was a matter of seconds and not minutes until she lost her hold on the party. She dove, not quite at the office, and when she was near the ground, the jays swirled around and left her human body on hands and knees at the edge of a megalithic lookout.

Bennie coughed, exhausted, shivering in the spring chill. She couldn't bring herself to look up at the bearlike monstrosity that she had fled, and she considered, briefly, that she might puke. She stayed on her hands and knees, breathing hard, until her head stopped spinning. Around her, the thunder from Kire was impossible to escape—it was like being inside a coal mine with a machine on and no protective equipment muffling the noise.

A beak dug into her shoulder. Her familiar winged off, returned, left again. She groaned, found some strength within her, and stood. She followed the blue jay up the rocks to the Park Office at Wind Rock lookout, holding onto trees and boulders as she went on the unblazed path.

She finally got there and saw that Jasper and Zach had made it. The pair were standing on the overlook, watching. Bennie pulled herself out of the brush as the bird screamed for their attention. She didn't realize how hazy she was until the two men rushed to help her walk to the small ridge. Her hands were shaking, and her palm was still bleeding, thorns still embedded in the meat of her palm.

"What happened?" Zach asked.

At the same time, Jasper said, "Where's Esther?"

Bennie shook her head, looking over at the leviathan made of Kire as it continued to slowly make its way through the valley. It was ever-shifting, the slate moving around its form as it walked. It was at least six hundred feet tall, its shoulders rising clear above the nearest peak. The sheer breadth of it made it hard for Bennie to breathe. It had something like the shape of a head, something like a mouth, but it was not a mouth.

Jasper looked at Bennie's bloody hand, which he had pulled over his shoulder. His eyes widened in horror, and he stared at Bennie.

"What did she do?"

Bennie found herself again. "She tied the ridge to me," she said, noticing that along one of Kire's legs, or what looked like a leg, a creeping green, a sheet of tree mass, attempted to hold it fast. "She had to fight the mountain alone."

They all stood still as the ursine Kire turned toward Kiron, a standing, shifting mountain wrenching free of its binds. Bennie was breathing hard as a suburb of Kiron was trampled under the first massive step of the ridge come alive.

Jasper held her wrist tightly, closed his eyes, and took a breath, reciting a prayer. They were magic, and echoed in her head.

"Did everyone get out of there?" she asked softly, tearing up. All those homes, crushed under a righteous indifference. Kire deserved revenge, but Kiron deserved forgiveness. Who decided who died under the mountains?

"No," Zach said, frowning.

There was something heavy beating in her chest, something horrible and full. She closed her eyes and shook her head and tried to breathe, tried to plan her own escape from Kire, tried to imagine how she could help Motheater. This was too big, too much.

Zach made a noise, touching her back. "Bennie."

She opened her eyes. Rising from Kiron, from mountains and rivers, were soft clouds of creatures, swarms of moths. Her eyes went wide, her breath caught. Next to her, Jasper's face was tilted up, watching the moths. Bennie knew that he had called them. Her new binding allowed her to understand, intimately, that he had spent years gathering souls, maybe hoping he would find one that would confirm his witch had died. Or, perhaps, waiting for the moment when he could shepherd them to the Appalachian psychopomp.

And now, that witch was fighting a mountain.

Zach looked awed, his mouth open, stunned.

"All those people—" Bennie said, feeling them flutter in her own chest. She recognized them now. She knew them. They would come to her soon. "All Appalachia rising."

"Aye," Jasper said, as a cloud of beating wings began to rise from behind them, from farther south, from Carolina and Kentucky. "The Witch of the Ridge has sounded the horns of Jericho, and today, we heed her call."

38
Motheater

Motheater had caught up to the gargantuan titan. This was a thing of legend, a rising that Motheater hadn't realized could happen until the bear of Kire shook itself free. But she couldn't hesitate because she was facing something mythic. She had to stop it here.

Bennie's blood was still warm in her hand, and she squeezed her fist tight, drawing up the heat, that bit of bargain that was not hers fueling this magic. She ran forward and slammed her hand against Kire, and with a huge sweeping movement, put a binding on the mountain. It wouldn't last long, and it would likely only hold a single leg fast, but Motheater saw trees, needle and root, turn and wrap around the stone, a snake of nature trying to squeeze the breath from a breathless thing.

"*For we wrestle not against flesh and blood, but against principalities,*" Motheater yelled out, and her hands were coated with a sharpness like a pickaxe, and she began to climb up the leg of the beast. She was grateful that her blood seal had done enough to keep it still for now, but Kire was clearly more powerful than her small cunning. This was all just delaying the inevitable. "*But we wrestle against powers,*" she gasped, her hair flying out of its tie, "*against the rulers of the darkness of this world.*"

If this was inevitable, so be it. She wouldn't be accused of giving up.

She made it up to one of the tunnels that had been opened up in Kire, a dark and eviscerated thing. The leviathan had been curled up, nestled in the cradle of the bedrock that had brought it to the surface, and the exposed tunnels were abrupt, cutting off at strange points on its body. She looked up, spotting above her a shear going right down its chest, across where its heart would be, if it had one. Beneath her, the trees were beginning to quake.

Motheater stared into the tunnel. Hadn't she made shafts into the mountain to rescue lost miners? Wasn't she a dowser? Hadn't she opened a hollow in herself for Kire to make home? Tunnels were made of purpose, and Motheater was a door herself. She finished the verse, turning into the beast.

"*We wrestle against spiritual wickedness in high places.*"

Paul might not have intended wickedness to mean a stone leviathan, but then again, maybe he had written that letter just for her.

Motheater dragged herself into the dark.

Motheater made her way through the labyrinthine mass of tunnels, sometimes climbing straight up, sometimes squeezing through a passage barely wide enough for even her small frame. She wheezed as the coal dust got into her throat and eyes, but it was dark in the mountain, and as stone moved around her, she didn't need to see, she just needed to know.

She heard the crunch of Kiron, the destruction of buildings; she felt the mountain shift on its six legs, heading deeper, closer to Kiron, closer to other people. Beyond Kiron, there were other mountains that Motheater knew still breathed. Was Kire hoping to bring out the other titans?

Motheater fought her way through the shifting creature, trying to find the heart of the beast. Kire seemed to not know that she was inside of him. What bear fears the ant?

She would not falter. She would not. She was squeezed in between two sheets of stone, totally alone, in the dark. She could barely breathe. This was it then. Motheater gasped, tried to find a verse, a word, a proverb, even a hymn, but nothing came from her tongue. She closed her eyes and gasped for air.

Was this it? Was this how she died, crushed inside Kire? It wouldn't hold her anymore. It wouldn't nestle her like it had three times before. It would just kill her, accept her blood, her loss, and kill another. It was right to do so, it was justified, it had reason. Maybe she should let Kire go. Maybe her hatred would finally get the better of her.

Then, suddenly, like rain on a hot day, Motheater felt something move around her. She closed her eyes and bared her teeth and felt the lost souls of Appalachia surround the mountain like a shroud, like a heavy blanket, like the night. They gave her strength, reminded her of what she fought for.

She grasped the stone and heaved herself up, pressing with her back and feet against the strength of an entire mountain. No. No! She would fix her mistakes, she would stop Kire, she would keep Appalachia safe for those who lived in the tor and holler.

Kire might be too far gone, but there were other mountains to preserve, other ranges to protect. And didn't Appalachia just get a new witch?

She gave a shout and pulled herself forward, the stone under her no longer cold. She was getting close to the heart.

39

Bennie

"Can't we do anything?" Bennie asked as the titan moved over Kiron. They weren't high enough to see the next ridge over, but Bennie knew that Lone Pine Peak was over there, and many more beside that had been touched by mining in some way or another. Were they alive, too? Motheater had said there were others; maybe Kire was looking for its kin.

"Like what?" Zach asked, his eyes fixed on Kire. It moved like a many-legged beast, a crawling doom. He seemed to have accepted that Motheater had failed after the moths disappeared, shrugged like dust from the titan's heavy, low shoulders. "Throw sticks at it?"

Jasper squeezed Bennie's arm gently, pulling away from her.

"I never knew much about Esther's magic. Her words made incredible things happen, and that was enough. I had no need for faith, I could see it." He spoke softly, and Bennie turned to him, eyes burning with tears. "But she needs our faith now."

"So what do I do?" Bennie shook her head. "I don't know magic." She couldn't even talk to the mountain, she couldn't feel anything around her but her familiar in the air, the heaving death of the moth swarm. That wasn't her magic.

Jasper smiled, finally, and Bennie started. He was ethereal, beautiful and strange, a creature like Motheater, but shaped into something perfect. No wonder Zach was staring.

"You don't need to know magic," he said, unblinking as Bennie collected her wits. "You *are* magic."

Bennie had never felt so small. She closed her eyes and shook her head, curling over, hands pressed to her chest, her back arched over. She put her forehead near the ground, held her hands over heart, and reached out, trying to find the threads that tied her to Motheater, to her witch, to this place.

She put her hands on the stone outcrop and tried to feel what she had felt on the road to the Church of the Rock: some kind of connection to the earth, to the mountain. Without Motheater . . . without Esther, it felt impossible. Why didn't she get witch lessons or something? A handbook would be nice. Bennie hiccuped and tried again, leaning over, trying to drive her soul, her spirit, her familiar-flock-of-blue jay into the stone.

All she felt was anger, rage, hurt. Kire wanted blood. Kire didn't care—it was corrupted, blackened from the inside out. This was the cost of humans' meddling in the mountain.

But that wasn't right. Bennie was the mountain, too.

Bennie pressed her hands against her sternum. She thought about Motheater, all alone, small and brilliant and brave, and she reached out with all of herself. Around her, she felt warmth.

She sent out love, she sent out strength, she thought of the way Motheater laughed when she surprised Bennie, the way she sounded so resigned when faced with something modern, how she was fierce and angry and burning, the way she tended the flock of moths that descended on her every night. She thought of the way her mouth felt on hers, the way she moved in the night, the way Motheater's blood clung to her hand. This was a mourning love, a last breath, and Bennie knew it. Esther had to undo what she made.

But she wouldn't be alone.

Bennie sent out love. She sent out all the love she had.

40

Motheater

Motheater had made it to the heart of Kire. Bolstered by Jasper's sent-over souls, she carved new tunnels, and once she had to hold still for minutes to make sure the mountain didn't collapse on her, but she was here, at the dark, coal-black, pulsing magic heart of the titan. It was solid, a black, dark thing, without faults or cracks.

The heat was unbearable, and Motheater had to stay a few feet back. None of her magics could help, and her own power had seeped out into the stone; she was just a girl in the rock. Her shoes were covered in the black sludge that beat slowly out of the heart. She couldn't go farther, and she couldn't see either, the darkness all-encompassing, as living as Kire itself. She took deep breaths, tried to calm down, tried to think of the meager work she had put into her pockets.

Suddenly, there was a pull. Something outside the mountain, something great. She tugged on the string and felt Bennie's faith overwhelm her, all her love. It hit her hard and drove her breath straight from her chest. Suddenly, Motheater could see again, glowing in the golden magic of

Bennie's fledgling power. God bless the new witch, God bless the raw power of her. *Let her work never be unmade,* Motheater thought, *let her warp hold fast.*

Motheater grinned, holding up her golden hands. Maybe Paul had written the letter for her.

"Put on the whole armor of God, that ye may be able to stand against the wiles of the devil!"

The golden light became sheets of mail and chains, a uniform, the whole goddamn armor. She laughed, the heat no longer bothering her, shielded as she was by Bennie's love. She found herself holding a spear like a spark.

Motheater had been armed by the love of another, and it made her stronger than she had ever been when she was tied to the mountain she had made hateful. Right now, Bennie's love was the strongest thing in the whole world.

Motheater turned the corner, running toward the shifting, rocky, engine-like heart of Kire. It was oozing sludge and sulfur, great sheets of heat and steam, but Motheater set her hands and charged the soul-spear of herself into Kire's dark soul.

Coal, like magma, pushed out of the heart, swallowing Motheater's legs. She faltered, but from behind her a swarm of souls came, a cacophony of moths, jarflies, and mosquitoes, every buzzing thing, pulled into the mountain itself, as if Motheater were the flame that called all mountaineers to her. Burgeoned by the homeland that she had tried to turn against, she drove the spear home, covered in Appalachian wings.

"O tower of the flock, the strong-hold of the daughter of Kire," she recited, yelling out despite the sulfur, despite the world collapsing around her. She drove the spear deeper and deeper, toward the diamond heart of Kire, the pressure of the whole earth, the whole abuse of humans, all three hundred years of harm coalescing into a pure bright thing, a promise

to do better. "*Unto thee shall it come, even the first dominion; the kingdom shall come to the daughter of Kiron.*"

The tip of the spear touched the diamond heart of Kire Mountain, and the whole earth stood still.

And then, the mountain collapsed.

41

Bennie

The newspapers called it a "freak mining accident," which was the most absurd, whitest fucking thing Bennie had ever read, having seen both mining accidents and a mountain literally stand up on its own legs and march over God's green earth, but it's not like she could write a letter to the editor.

She decided to let it go, which was wise once she found out that poor Vikki Delancey had chosen to go visit her family in Roanoke permanently rather than subject herself to the Giles County Sheriff's Department conducting wellness checks multiple times a week after she refused to rescind her statement about walking stones.

Everyone else seemed to agree that the party line was "freak mining accident." Or, perhaps, as Jasper said, some of her magic had protected the people of Kiron from too much mental trauma, with one notable exception.

Some of Kire returned to its womb, staggering back into the cradle of the bedrock where it had come from, but most of it was spread across the valley. A lot of Kire had shattered across the town of Kiron itself.

They had found no sign of Motheater, and frankly, Bennie was sure by the time that they had cleaned up what was left of Kire—if they ever did—there wouldn't be anything for them to find. She had been inside the great titan when it had collapsed. If she wasn't crushed inside of it, the fall certainly did her in. It was what Motheater—Esther—expected, after all, and Bennie didn't cry much. Maybe a little.

Once the media got a hold of what happened in Kiron, immediately people wanted to help. A few mutual aid networks popped up, alongside some fundraisers and campaigns, and more than a few folks had offered to come in with fancy equipment. That wasn't going to fly; Zach had stepped up and helped assemble a cleanup committee, taking the money from lowland folk and using it as the town saw fit.

Bennie was proud of him. Jasper seemed to be warming up to him, taking over a section of Zach's backyard and erecting a chicken coop and planting discolored jars at the land boundary.

Miles's hardware store was one of the first buildings back open, even if half its back wall was full gone. Normal shifts meant that Bennie had her mornings free, and she had taken to hiking along the Appalachian trail, along the Potts ridge and into West Virginia, along Little Mountain and even up the trails on the Forks peaks. She tried to feel the mountains every time she reached their peak. She was getting better at it, but she suspected that most of these places had passed a long time ago, that these ridges wouldn't be able to protect themselves like Kire did.

White Rock wasn't gone. Coal was never really gone from Appalachia. But they had stopped digging into the nearby ridges, were working to transition to safer practices, and Bennie took some small comfort in that. It wasn't justice for

Kelly-Anne, but when the mountain collapsed, Bennie knew that justice was buried underneath. She would have to settle for grief instead.

It wasn't her fault. She was still learning how to let go of hurt. At least she found her magic came easy—she didn't need Bible verses or hedge (maybe she would take a class at the Foxfire Museum, but that was a ways off yet), all she needed was love. Bennie took to country grammar like meat to salt.

Once, she went back to the hollow where Kire Mountain used to be. There were cameras and fencing, of course, but that didn't mean anything to her anymore. In between her blue jay familiar, a new ash stave, and her golden magic, there wasn't anywhere she couldn't go. *Who cared about cameras,* she thought, pushing through a hole in the fence. She was a fucking witch.

Bennie picked her way down into the new-made holler. It was more or less a rock scramble for nearly ten acres across. There were some impossibly large boulders, but plenty of smaller stones she could carefully slide down.

Other than the stones, there was nothing here. Some uprooted trees, moss occasionally, but this was the base of the mountain, the inside of Kire, and nothing had breathed on this land ever.

Bennie's tattoo began to itch and she paused. She had made her way into the very center of the holler. She knelt down, pulling her pack around. Out of it came Motheater's old dress. Bennie took a deep breath and placed it on the stone in front of her.

It nearly matched the slate in color, and Bennie closed her eyes and said a small prayer, not something out of the King James, but a prayer of passing that her mother had taught her to say as they drove by graveyards. She swallowed her grief, her sadness, her tiredness, and spoke slowly. *"As I am now, so once you were; As you are now, soon I will be."*

She took another deep breath and opened her eyes.

The dress was still there, a little frayed, but unmoved. Nothing had changed. That was fine. She didn't know what she was expecting. Bennie smiled and stood, finding manageable rocks and rolling them on top of the dress, building a small cairn. She would carry this loss, too, but she wouldn't let it eat at her like Kelly-Anne's death. She would be stronger for knowing Esther, for loving her.

It was hot work, and she focused on her hands, feeling the calluses built up there, feeling how it hurt. Esther had come into her life like a hurricane, but had left it bigger, more expansive. Bennie had so much more now.

When she got to one of the last rocks for the makeshift memorial, a movement under the rock startled her, and she yelped, pulling her hand back quickly. But the rock didn't move, and no sound came from the dark space. Carefully, Bennie crouched down to see what it was, holding her hands to her chest.

A small ring-necked snake, young and bright-scaled, slid out of the stone. Bennie's eyes widened, and she reached out her hand to it. The snake, drawn to her heat, immediately went to her palm, curling around her left wrist, a mirror image of the tattoo on her left arm. Bennie grinned as she stood up, looking over the small ring-necked snake.

This was it. The last binding, the great love. Tears welled up as the snake slid over her wrist, as she felt its cool scales slide along her skin. Magic welled up in her, a whole lifetime, a whole town, a whole mountain. This, she would protect. She took a deep breath and smiled, feeling the heat from the rising sun beating down on her, a daughter of Appalachia.

"Hello, Esther."

So ended the first days of the witch, Benethea Mattox.

Historical Notes

All of the mountains named in this book are real. You can hike them, touch them, watch them move. You just need to stick around long enough.

The characters in this book, however, are not real.

Kiron, likewise, has never existed. Kire stands guard at the border.

Pentecostal snake-handling churches rose to prominence (infamy?) in the early 1910s, but there have been folkway recordings of snaking being used in churches as early as the 1880s. The father of snake handling, George Went Hensley, traveled throughout the area of the Appalachians where Kire Mountain lies. Imagine Silas as a horrible godfather of the practice, dead before he could be named in history books, a mean rumor.

Additionally, Wilbur Zeigler and Ben Grosscup traveled extensively in North Carolina and recorded the history of that area of the world in one of the most complete written histories of the area that we currently have. They did not travel into Virgina, but . . . maybe they could have. You can read their anthropological text, *The Heart of the Alleghenies; or, Western North Carolina*, really anywhere. It's in the public domain, and the drawings enclosed are gorgeous. It is full of conversations with locals, a deep curiosity for the folklore of the area, and a respect for the nature of that area of the world that is hard to find, even now.

If you want to learn some incredible old Appalachia phrases, you'll learn them in that book.

I have blurred western Virginia and western North Carolina cultures in this book. They are sisters.

One of the most impressive and moving first-person accounts of contemporary underground mining comes from Gary Bentley's column, In the Black, which published for two years in *The Daily Yonder*. His writing directly inspired this book and characters like Zach and Helen.

Appalachians Against Pipelines have been fighting the Mountain Valley Pipeline since before the inception of this book. While I was writing *Motheater*, a group of tree sitters perched in the area around the fictional setting of Kiron. They were the Yellow Finch Tree Sits, led by a coalition across generations, including elders as well as queer and Indigenous peoples. AAP fights the MVP still. This book owes a debt to the mountain wardens, resistance fighters, and water protectors. Some of the unofficial mottos repeated by Yellow Finch—and AAP—became the lodestones for this novel.

Protect what you love.

Doom to the pipeline.

Acknowledgments

The first draft of this book came together in forty days as I hiked through the Hudson Valley during lockdown. I wrote this book in voice notes and on napkins while walking along the New York section of the Appalachian Trail, through the Catskills, and up Storm King mountain (where I spent hours watching the boats go up and down the river). Over the next four years, a variety of people helped me shape *Motheater* into the book you hold in your hands. (*Motheater* is my debut novel, so this section is going to be sentimental and tedious; feel free to skip this.)

First, to my friends who read early, *early* drafts of this book and somehow knew that it would make it this far. Beth, who was one of the first to read the whole thing. Sara, who still hasn't (but only because she was waiting for the final product). Leland, who wants a sequel to be about a cat and has never gotten tired of the joke. Caroline, who is always ready to organize a friendship event. Chris, for hosting many dance parties. Away from the two-mile radius of my home, I want to thank Mandy and Maggi, two of my oldest friends, for reading and loving this book.

I had many critique partners, but chief among them are Whalley and Ash. Their support means so much, more than I can really say, and I can't wait to write more books alongside them. There are so many writers and friends I've made over the past four years, please know that I can't name you all, but I'm grateful for the community across many Slacks, Discords, and even on Twitter.

My agent, Bridget Smith, went above and beyond for this book. She read it when it was a mess and was kind enough to give me a phone call to talk it over. At least three times. And that was before she was my agent. Thank you to Sarah Guan, who read this book and really, truly got it. I cannot tell you how much I appreciate her vision, which I needed to truly carve this into something decent. Thank you to the team at Erewhon, especially Viengsamai and Marty, one of whom championed the book for months and the other has been a good friend for years, and is championing the book now. I want to acknowledge the work of my sensitivity reader, Stacey Parshall Jensen, who helped ensure this version of *Motheater* was authentic and kind. Last, thank you to Erica Williams, who gave this book a truly gorgeous cover.

A huge, massive, inenarrable thank you to my parents, Robin and Lou. My mom, who has kept all my writing since I was a kid, who knew I was going to the University of Virginia when I was in eighth grade, who took me to the library every week, and who has always been loving and kind, even when I was very, very weird. My dad, who read *The Lord of the Rings* trilogy to me as a bedtime story when I was a kid, at least twice, and instilled a love of reading in me. He also read Edgar Allan Poe's poetry and *Treasure Island* and dozens of other stories. The two of them are to blame for all of this. (Thanks also to my brother, James, for being very nerdy with me throughout my childhood and much more often now.)

Thank you to the Appalachian folks and mountain defenders putting their bodies on the line to stop exploitative industries. Thank you to the Yellow Finch Tree Sits. Thank you to the mountains, and the mountains, and the mountains.

Thank you for reading this title from Erewhon Books, publishing books that embrace the liminal and unclassifiable and championing the unusual, the uncanny, and the hard-to-define.

We are proud of the team behind *Motheater* by Linda H. Codega:

Sarah Guan, Publisher
Diana Pho, Executive Editor
Viengsamai Fetters, Assistant Editor

Martin Cahill, Campaign Manager
Kasie Griffitts, Sales Associate

Cassandra Farrin, Director
Leah Marsh, Production Editor
Kelsy Thompson, Production Editor
Stacey Parshall Jensen, Sensitivity Reader
Sydnee Thompson, Copyeditor
Lakshna Mehta, Proofreader

Seth Lerner, Cover Designer
Erica Williams, Cover Artist

. . . and the whole Kensington Books team!

Learn more about Erewhon Books and our authors at
erewhonbooks.com.

Find us on most social media at
@erewhonbooks.